Can't Stop Thinking About You

Katrina gave a wry smile. If the new doctor had been the woman her mother was hoping for—and that hope still confounded her—then perhaps she could have suggested a house-share arrangement. But there was no way on God's green earth that she was ever suggesting that idea to Dr. Josh Stanton. She could just imagine his reaction.

Thinking about him exploded the memory of his naked chest in her mind. It was hard not to think about it, given it had always been at eye level this afternoon. He was so much taller than she was, so unless she tilted her head all the way back, her gaze had constantly been facing his delineated pectoral muscles with their light dusting of sandy brown hair.

Soaking him in. Wondering what they felt like.

She pulled her suddenly itching hands out of the dishwater, feeling hot and disoriented. Flicking on the faucet, she ran cool water against her wrists and sighed. Thinking about Josh had to stop, because no matter how decadently sexy he was, the antipathy that ran between them was palpable. It had disaster written all over it, and she was not falling back into bad habits. Coming home to Bear Paw was supposed to protect her from that.

D0681820

MONTANA
Actually

——————

Fiona Lowe

B

BERKLEY SENSATION, NEW YORK

THE BERKLEY PUBLISHING GROUP
Published by the Penguin Group
Penguin Group (USA) LLC
375 Hudson Street, New York, New York 10014

USA • Canada • UK • Ireland • Australia • New Zealand • India • South Africa • China

penguin.com

A Penguin Random House Company

MONTANA ACTUALLY

A Berkley Sensation Book / published by arrangement with the author

Berkley Sensation Books are published by The Berkley Publishing Group.
BERKLEY SENSATION® is a registered trademark of Penguin Group (USA) LLC.
The "B" design is a trademark of Penguin Group (USA) LLC.

For information, address: The Berkley Publishing Group,
a division of Penguin Group (USA) LLC,
375 Hudson Street, New York, New York 10014.

ISBN: 978-0-425-27695-2

PUBLISHING HISTORY
Berkley Sensation mass-market edition / January 2015

PRINTED IN THE UNITED STATES OF AMERICA

10 9 8 7 6 5 4 3 2 1

Cover art by Aleta Raftan.
Cover design by George Long.
Interior text design by Kelly Lipovich.

To Doris. For the cherry pies, friendship and support over ten thousand miles.

Acknowledgments

In one way, the writing of a book is a very solitary endeavor, but in another, it's a team effort and my team is made up of many people and all are equally important in their support of me. Thank you to my readers; hearing from you and knowing you have taken precious time out of your busy lives to reach out keeps me writing. Many thanks to my wonderful agent, Helen, for always being in my corner, and to my editor, Wendy, for embracing the town of Bear Paw and its many and varied inhabitants. It's the place to be if you ever need a sexy doctor or hanker to meet a cowboy. Thanks to the team at Berkley; from the art director to the copyeditor, the production people and the distributors, all of whom contributed to *Montana Actually* becoming a reality and in your hands right now.

I owe an enormous debt of gratitude to Kari Lynn Dell, (*Montana For Real*) for all her Montana ranching information, her stories of life on the land, her speedy e-mail responses and for the laughs. I couldn't have written this book as accurately without her help, and any mistakes I have made are mine. How did authors write books before Twitter? To all the doctors and nurses on Twitter who probably wonder why an author is following them, thank you. Your tweets are both hilarious and heartfelt and strangely educational as well as great book fodder. Go #FOAMed.

On the days when writing is tough, my fellow medical romance writing mates, who totally get my obsession with TV medical drama and all things medical, are always on the other end of an e-mail for support. Their photos of sexy men both in and out of scrubs also help.

Last but by no means least, huge thanks go to my family of men who keep the faith when I lose it, tackle domestic chores with true heroic strength and leave encouraging albeit cheeky notes on my computer such as, 'Finish the damn book.' And finally, a special shout-out to Barton, my "Boy Wonder" who designs all my website, Facebook and Twitter banners and cheerfully tackles any artwork suggestions I throw at him. Love ya!

Chapter 1

The thirty cows blocking the road were a good indication
to Dr. Josh Stanton that he was no longer in Chicago.
That and the inordinate number of bloated roadkill with
their legs in the air that he'd passed in the last few hours
along Highway 2 as he traversed the north of Montana.
Sure, Chicago had its fair share of flattened cats on its busy
inner-city streets, but he'd stake his life no one living
between North Halsted and North Wells streets had ever
had to step over a deer.

He watched the cows lurch from decisiveness in their
chosen direction to utter chaos as two border collies raced
at their heels, barking frantically and driving them determinedly toward an open gate on the other side of the road.
Josh's fingers tapped on the top of the steering wheel as
they always did when he was stuck in traffic in Chicago's
clogged streets. What was the collective noun for a group
of cows? Bunch? Herd? He'd once seen a documentary on
ranching in Australia and they'd said "mob" in their flat
accent.

He guessed he'd find out the name soon enough, as he

was close to finishing his 1,458-mile journey across Wisconsin, Minnesota, North Dakota and three-quarters of Montana.

When he'd left home three very long days ago, he'd thought the north woods of Wisconsin were as isolated as things got, but now, as he gazed around him and felt the howling west wind buffeting the car, he knew Menomonie was positively urban in comparison to the endless grass plains that surrounded him. Where the hell were the trees?

An older man on a horse, whose weather-beaten face told of a life lived outdoors, stopped next to Josh's low-slung sports car. Josh wound down the window, his gaze meeting jean-clad legs and horse flesh. He craned his neck.

"Taking a trip?" the cowboy asked conversationally, as if they had all the time in the world to chat.

I wish. "Relocating."

"Yeah?" His gaze took in Josh's Henley shirt and the computer bag on the seat next to him. "You're a bit far north for Seattle. Don't reckon you should risk the mountain roads driving *that* vehicle."

Josh automatically patted the dash as if the car's feelings needed soothing. Granted, his sports car wasn't the latest model this side of five years, but it was in great condition and he loved it. The buzz it gave him when he drove it more than made up for the extra money it had added to his outstanding loans.

"I'm not going over the mountains," he said, his mouth twisting wryly as he checked his TripTik. "I'm going to Medicine River County and a town called Bear Paw."

A town that was wrenching him from his home and staking a claim on his life that went straight through his heart. A town that Ashley had refused point-blank to even consider visiting, let alone living in.

The cowboy called out an instruction to his dogs, who immediately raced behind a recalcitrant calf, and then he lifted his hat and scratched his head. "Bear Paw. Okay."

Josh wasn't certain what to read into the statement. Sure, he'd seen a photo on the Internet of the small hospital, but short of that, he didn't know much else. "My cell's out of range, so I've lost my location on the map, but I think it's about twenty miles away. Do you know it?"

"Oh yeah. I know it. What takes you there?"

Debt half the size of Montana. "Work. I'm the new physician."

The man nodded slowly. "Ah."

Unease skittered through Josh's belly. What did the cowboy know that he didn't? "What the hell does 'ah' mean?"

He laughed. "Relax, son. Your trip's over."

As the last cow finally conceded the grass was indeed greener on the pasture side of the fence and had moved through the gate, Josh looked down the now clear road and saw nothing. Nothing if he discounted some sort of a crop and a hell of a lot of sky. He squinted and just made out what looked like a communications tower. "So where's the town?"

The older man pointed down the dead-straight road. "Three miles gets you to the outskirts and another mile to the traffic signal. Two miles past that, you're done with the town and heading to the mountains."

That distance in Chicago wouldn't even get him from his apartment to his favorite deli. How small was this place? "What if I turn at the traffic signal?"

"Right? Now that will take you straight to Canada, eh." He grinned at his own joke.

The town couldn't possibly be so small. "According to Wikipedia," Josh said, "it's got a population of three thousand people."

The cowboy scratched his head again. "I guess if you include the ranches, it does. It's surely bigger than Bow. Mind, just about everywhere's bigger'n Bow."

Disbelief flooded Josh as he remembered passing a rusty town sign. "That place with the tavern and nothing else?"

"Yup, that'd be Bow." He shoved his hand through the open window. "The name's Kirk McCade. Welcome to Bear Paw, Doctor."

Josh gripped his hand. "Josh Stanton."

Kirk slapped his hand on the roof of the car. "No doubt this baby is a sweet ride, but once you've settled in, best buy yourself an outfit."

"A what?" Surely the cowboy wasn't talking about clothes.

"A truck, a pickup. Winter here's tough on vehicles."

A slither of indignation ran up Josh's spine. He might not be used to wide-open spaces, but he knew weather. "I've just spent two years in Chicago, so I know all about winter."

Kirk laughed so hard Josh worried he'd fall off the horse.

———

KATRINA McCade loved her family dearly, but there were some days she wished they didn't have her cell phone number. Today was one of those days. Every time she got the paint roller primed, raised and in position, ready to paint the living room walls of her cottage, her phone beeped. Over the last hour, almost every member of her family had contacted her.

Her father had been the first—brief and to the point—calling to confirm that she was cooking supper tonight for her mother's birthday. She'd reassured him, and the moment he'd hung up, her mother, who had no clue about the surprise birthday supper, had called. She'd wanted Katrina to check the menu at both Leroy's and the Village Lounge and book the one with the best steak special because her father loved his beef. Even on her birthday, she was thinking of others. Ten minutes after that, her phone had vibrated with the sound of a motorcycle, which meant her younger brother, Dillon, was texting her.

Please buy gift for Mom that looks like I chose it. Also wrap it cos I suck at bows.

The moment that missive had pinged onto her phone, her younger sister called wanting dating advice.

Dating advice? Hah! Katrina gave the roller such a

hard push that it skated across the wall spreading paint in a wide arc instead of the even vertical plane she'd intended. When Megan, her twenty-one-year-old baby sister, had asked her opinion on the best way to hook up with her latest crush, it had taken all of her self-control not to blurt out that *all* men required a police check, marital status verification and blood tests before the first date. Only such a caustic comment would have invited questions she didn't want to answer. Instead, she'd suggested Megan invite a friend to go with her to the Jack-Squat bar.

Her sister had hinted that maybe Katrina might like to come along and meet the guy in question and give her opinion, but the thought of driving an hour and a half south tomorrow night and spending time in a loud and noisy bar with a group of college kids was the last thing Katrina wanted to do. It made her feel old. No way did she need any more reminders that her thirtieth birthday was bearing down on her as fast as the Amtrak that ran through Bear Paw every day at noon. Heck, since coming back to her hometown a few weeks ago after working away for eight years, she'd deflected so many questions about her lack of a boyfriend and her future plans, she could teach a course.

A fine spray of paint dusted her as she found a rhythm, and a sense of satisfaction built on seeing her progress. Her phone buzzed again and she sighed. The only person in her immediate family whom she hadn't spoken to so far this morning was her older brother, Beau. Technically, he was her cousin, but for as long as she could remember, Beau had lived with them and she considered him a brother as much as her parents considered him their son. He preferred to text rather than to talk, but he'd probably just realized the date and wanted her to buy a present for their mother as well. Men!

Wiping her hands on her paint-stained shorts so that she didn't swipe paint onto the phone's touch screen, she hit accept, not recognizing the number. "Hello?"

"Trina." A familiar voice—one that had made her heart flutter for months and now made it cramp in anger and betrayal—came down the line. She could hear the sound of a code being called over a PA in the background.

"Brent." She sighed, closing her eyes and automatically calculating the time zone change. She hated that her mind immediately pictured him coming out of surgery wearing his monogrammed scrubs and distinctive red clogs. She quickly opened her eyes and stared out across the plains toward the Rocky Mountains in the distance, desperately seeking calm. "I thought we'd agreed to no calls."

This time he sighed. "I agreed you needed time and I've given it to you. You've made your point, Trina, I get it, but it doesn't change the fact we still love each other. With some compromise and understanding on your part, we can still make this work."

Still. His arrogance astounded her, although it shouldn't be a surprise. She still whipped herself for having been oblivious to that particular character flaw. His tone said everything was her fault but she was being forgiven.

She pinched the bridge of her nose, welcoming the pain because she had no clue how to even go about explaining that no amount of trying was going to make them work. *Ever.* "Nothing's changed, Brent."

"I miss you."

Her throat tightened as the quietly spoken words caressed her, reminding her of the wonderful times they'd shared. Her resolve wavered.

"Trina, I just want to reassure you that you can get me on this number anytime."

This number. Her brain jolted her back to reality so fast she got whiplash. He'd gotten another phone. Another number just for her. Again. Her knees wobbled and she gripped the doorjamb to hold herself up. Wet paint squelched around her fingers. *Shit.* She pulled her hand away and found her voice. "Good-bye, Brent."

She cut the call, hurled the phone onto the sofa as if it were radioactive and then ran fast and hard on the spot, letting out a scream that came from the center of her being. A deer grazing at the edge of the now weed-choked garden took off at a run. All the feelings she'd spent weeks letting go of surged back, buffeting her like the frigid and biting arctic winds that swooped in from Canada. Anger at Brent. Even more anger at herself and at her own stupidity. Anger period. She hated how it dug in, making her feel so power-less, desperately foolish and immensely sad all at the same time. She bit the inside of her cheek to try and stall the shakes that threatened to send her into the fetal position on the couch.

She never, ever wanted to feel like this again, which was why she'd come home in the first place, effectively putting two thousand miles between her and Brent. Closing the door to temptation and poor judgment.

Her old border collie, Boy, heaved himself off his rug and came over to her, licking her hand. He was deaf and half blind but he always knew when she was upset. She rubbed his ears and buried her face in his coat, thinking about how her life had changed so much. A few weeks ago she'd had a great job and a clear vision of her future firmly set in Philly. When it all came tumbling down, she'd bolted back to Bear Paw, telling herself it was only temporary. A breathing space. She'd even made some calls about doing some health care volunteering in Ecuador, because at least that was a plan of sorts and it reassured her that her time in Bear Paw would be short.

She hadn't told her parents the real reason for her return, because she didn't need to see or hear their disappointment that she'd failed, especially as she'd been heard to say more than once that she preferred living in the city. Instead, she'd skirted the truth and told them she was burned-out from her high-pressure unit manager job and she was tak-ing a break to visit with them and work on the cottage. They'd immediately suggested she work at the Bear Paw hospital like she'd done when she'd graduated, but she was determined to avoid anything to do with doctors and hos-pitals. Instead, she'd gotten a part-time job at the diner and at Leroy's. Although her parents had never been thrilled she'd left Bear Paw and they'd been the ones to urge her two years ago to buy the cottage, they'd silently accepted her decision, but she caught their troubled gazes on her from time to time. She hated that. Hated that her inability to make the right choices in her life had landed her back at home.

Giving Boy a *thank you but I'm fine* rub around the ears, she grabbed the roller with a jerk and quickly made short work of the rest of the walls. By the time she'd finished and was surveying her handiwork, she'd found a modicum of hard-earned calm. The new paint had gotten rid of the nicotine stains left by the stressed-out accountant who'd run from town the moment tax season was over. He'd been a lousy tenant despite Walt, her Realtor, promising her six months ago that he came with great references. After the mess he'd left behind, Katrina was convinced the previous landlord wrote the glowing report just to get rid of him.

The fact that her tenant had broken the lease was timely, because as much as she loved her family, she'd lived alone too long to go back to living in the ranch house. Coming home for short visits was one thing, but there was something about moving into her childhood room that turned back the clock. She ceased being Katrina McCade, independent career woman, and became Katrina—dutiful daughter, sibling mediator and general go-to person. It was all wrapped up with a distinct lack of privacy and it was wearing her out.

The moment the paint fumes had vaporized, she was moving in, and she'd repair the other damage that had been inflicted on the house. She'd even use some of her savings to renovate the kitchen. After that, she might go to Ecuador and be useful or she might head to California or . . . She had no clue. All she knew was that her plans were open-ended.

You've never done fluid. Her mind went straight to the very scheduled life she'd shared with Brent over the past eight months. She immediately hauled it back. She could do fluid. She could try and go with the flow with one exception. Lesson learned—no matter how much she enjoyed being in a relationship, she was not getting involved with another man anytime soon.

She pulled a screwdriver out of the tool belt around her waist and levered open the paint can containing the lavender paint for her bedroom. She suddenly smiled. At least Bear Paw didn't have a surgeon with devastating charm, or for that matter a physician under sixty. She was totally safe on that front, and for that small mercy, she was truly grateful.

———

JOSH drove down a long gravel road seriously doubting the directions the hospital administrator had e-mailed him. Surely, the house that came with the job would be in the town and close by the hospital? Only he'd passed the hospital, two miles back, where he'd be reporting tomorrow morning at eight. Now Main Street, with its mixture of flat-fronted brick and clapboard shops, was well behind him, too. He appeared to be heading for Canada.

He hit a pothole and his front fender scraped the road. *Shit*. He slowed his speed and zigzagged his way around another four potholes before he pulled over to face the intensive stare of a jackrabbit, whose large ears mocked him. This was ludicrous. It was one thing for his student loans to have mortgaged his life, bringing him to a small town in the middle of nowhere, but surely the hospital wouldn't have rented him a house way out here. He must have missed the turn back in town.

At least he now had one bar of service on his phone. He plugged the GPS coordinates of the house into the app. The melon-colored exclamation point magically appeared one-quarter mile away from his current blue location dot. He looked to his left. He needed to turn onto a driveway that had never seen blacktop or gravel.

"You've got to be kidding me," he muttered as he threw the gear stick into first. No wonder the hospital administrator had said the house would be open and not to worry about a key. It was in the middle of damn-well-nowhere.

Five bone-shuddering minutes later, he pulled up outside

a house or a cottage—he wasn't sure which, and he wasn't certain the builder had known, either. It was a mishmash of design and was neither attic cottage nor log cabin. One section was cladding and the other logs, and he thought he glimpsed some exposed house wrap between the two. The eaves extended over a door that was offset, in fact the whole side of the house he was facing looked as if it had been tacked on as an afterthought. A small satellite dish clung precariously to the roof, and Josh was surprised it hadn't been blown away and taken the house with it.

The property screamed first homeowner's dream, renovator's delight or student housing. It had been a very long time since he'd been a student, and the gloss of living in a house that had seen better days had well and truly lost its shine. A few scraggly trees attempted to survive to create a much-needed windbreak, but most looked like they'd given up on the job. Weeds dotted the short path to the house, and a rusted-out truck was parked outside, possibly abandoned. Just fabulous.

The property was wrong on so many levels that it had to be a mistake. Reaching for his phone, he prepared to call the hospital administrator to complain when he remembered he'd gotten a message from him saying he was out of town today. Reluctantly, Josh pushed himself out of the car, locked it behind him and walked directly to the door. He knocked and waited but no one came, so with a firm grip, he turned the handle. Surprise jolted him when it opened smoothly and without a squeak.

He had to duck his head as he walked through the small entrance with its coat hooks and a boot box, before stepping into a pine-clad kitchen. Circa 1970, it came complete with faded lime green counters and a breakfast nook. It was a far cry from the granite countertop kitchen with all its modern stainless steel appliances back in his Chicago apartment.

Her Chicago apartment.

Not wanting thoughts of Ashley to creep into his mind, he decided that even though there was no way in hell he was going to live here, he'd explore the house and list all the reasons why the place was unsuitable. Paint fumes hit him the moment he crossed into the living room, and moving carefully, so as not to get paint on his chinos, he soon found himself facing a small, steep staircase.

Years of experience running between floors of the many different hospitals he'd worked in had him taking the stairs two at a time. His head suddenly slammed into the sloped ceiling. "Jesus."

His vision swam and he rubbed his scalp, already feeling a lump the size of a golf ball rising under his fingers. He mentally added another reason to his mounting list. Not only was the house in the boonies, it was built for dwarfs. Moving decidedly more slowly, he took the rest of the stairs one at a time with his head bent low. He didn't risk straightening up until he was well and truly on the landing.

Raising his head, he realized there was no landing—he was standing in a room. A dormer bedroom. He blinked in surprise. An old dog lay sleeping on a rug, and a short woman stood on a ladder with her back to him and with white earbuds in her ears. She was carefully painting the area where lavender walls met the white ceiling. Her heavy leather work boots gripped the second-top step and thick, bright red socks peeked out over the top. A paint can perched precariously on a board near her knees.

He almost called out but he didn't want to startle her and risk her falling off the ladder and breaking something. Plus, his gaze seemed fixed on her bare legs. They weren't model-long, but the calves were muscular and sculpted as if they worked out often and were strong for the effort. And the skin was tan. A beautiful, golden tan from sunshine, not the orange tint from a bottle like he'd noticed on some patients after the long Illinois winters. Just as his mind and gaze slid upward, hoping to glimpse what he imagined would be the sweet curve of her ass, denim cutoffs rudely broke the view.

Damn. Still, the shorts hinted that the naked view might well be a good one. A bright blue paisley blouse that didn't remotely match the shorts—and reminded him of his grandmother—flowed over the waistband at complete odds with the wide black band of a tool belt. His brain jolted, trying to merge the juxtaposing images of modern meeting old-fashioned. His gaze had just reached short, glossy black hair when she turned and saw him.

Before he could raise his hands to show her that he came in peace, her enormous green eyes—the color of spring—dilated in shock.

The dog barked.

She moved abruptly, her actions jerky, and her knee caught the edge of the board, sending the paint can flying.

Two seconds later, Josh was wearing lavender paint.

Chapter 2

G ood manners almost made Katrina splutter "I'm so sorry," but self-preservation generated on the back of fear stopped her. Her heart was hammering so fast she could hear it whooshing in her ears. *There's a stranger in my house.* A very tall, broad-shouldered man whose height and breadth blocked her only exit. A man with a menacing two-day growth of dark stubble.

Think! Boy was too old to protect her, so she plunged her hand into her tool belt, her fingers gripping the plastic handle of the screwdriver. "Don't move. I've got a gun."

Boy barked with all the menace of an aging biker.

"So why the hell did you incapacitate me with paint?" Incredulity dripped from his words as paint dripped off him onto the floor.

His eyes were scrunched tightly shut, and he frantically tore his shirt off over his head, exposing a chest with well-developed muscles that bunched and rippled with the movement.

It was poetry in motion.

First rule of safety: Don't ogle the house invader.

He pressed the shirt to his eyes. "God damn it. This stings like a son of a bitch."

"Don't do that." The nurse in her overrode her fear that he might have arrived with intent to harm her and she jumped down from the ladder. Grabbing the tail of the shirt, she whipped it out of his hands. "You'll make it worse. Don't move and I'll help you."

"Yeah, like I'm going anywhere when I can't damn well see." His voice rose, edged with pain. "I need water. Get me to water."

"The bathroom's downstairs."

"Of course it is," he muttered as if the bathroom's location was yet another inconvenience on a very long list of many. "Take me there." He shot out his arm.

She stared at his broad hand. A hand that wide should have chunky fingers, but his were long and tapered with neatly cut nails.

"Hello? Miss? I'm going blind here." His voice combined a thread of anxiety with absolute, authoritative control. "Let's go."

"Sorry," she said, snapping to attention. She slid her hand into his and gripped it firmly, reasonably confident he was too distressed to be of any danger to her. His palm wasn't calloused like a cowboy's, but it wasn't soft and smooth, either, and it utterly consumed her smaller hand. "There are ten stairs."

He immediately grimaced. "The fourth's a bastard. We've already met once and it wasn't pretty."

"Did you hit your head?" she said, thinking of the barely legal height clearance, which conveniently wasn't an issue for her but was for most everyone else. "You need to duck."

"You think?" His exasperation rolled into her as he stooped down in preparation.

Ignoring his grumpy rhetorical question, she talked him down the stairs and into the small bathroom where she turned on the water. "It's probably best if you tilt your head under the shower head.

Before she could direct him, he'd kicked off his shoes,

turned toward the running water and stepped into the shower. "Fuck!" A shudder ripped across his body. "It's freezing? Are you trying to kill me as well as blind me?"

"I never told you to get in," she said, her annoyance with him edging out her guilt about the paint. "It takes a few minutes for the hot water to kick in."

"You're a sympathetic woman, aren't you?" he muttered sarcastically.

A retort rose to her lips but she cut it off. *Treat him as a patient.* "Let the water flow over your eyes to rinse out the paint and everything will feel better."

To her surprise, he did exactly as she instructed. Water sluiced over his face, around the dimple in his chin and then ran in lavender rivulets across his chest and down his flat abdomen before sliding in under the waistband of his chinos. Within moments, his pants were soaked and clinging to him like a second skin. The wet cotton outlined perfectly his tight behind, his solid thighs and the substantial package between his legs.

Big hands mean a big—

Shut up! That's a myth. Be professional. Look away. Look away now!

She dragged her gaze to the faded and peeling wallpaper near the vanity that screamed to be replaced, and she focused on the dated geometric design. "I'm Katrina, by the way."

"Josh."

At least she thought he said Josh. It was hard to understand him with water rolling through his mouth. Her eyes strayed to the mirror where she could see him in the shower. "You need to stay under there for twenty minutes, Josh."

He nodded, blinking furiously as the water cleaned his eyes.

"It was water-based paint," she said, trying to reassure him, "so that's a good thing. Much better than oil based."

He grunted and she interpreted it as "if you say so."

She checked her watch. "Is the water a comfortable temperature now?"

He nodded again.

Granted, he had water flooding his face, but he seemed to lurch between stoically silent and issuing curt instructions like a drill sergeant. Her gaze stalled on his tribal band tattoo, which hugged his left upper arm. Its intricate black design seemed to come to life when he flexed his biceps.

Perhaps he was in the forces after all. *No, his hair's too long.* His sable brown curls, which had bounced in shock and then quivered in indignation when the paint had landed on him, now lay flat and black against his head.

A definite zing of sensation buzzed deep down in her belly and she blew out an unhappy breath. *No way. Not cool. Not even safe.* She refused to recognize that the tingle might be attraction because it made no sense. He was a stranger and she knew absolutely nothing about him.

Remember the top tips to keeping safe.

Rule one was trust your instincts. She took another surreptitious glance at Josh. There was something about him that made her feel he wasn't dangerous or a psychopath. Then again, perhaps even psychopaths were rendered powerless by paint in their eyes.

She hauled her gaze away again and tried to be rational. It wasn't as if she'd never seen a good-looking guy before. She'd even had the opportunity to wrap herself around one or two. And then there was work. As a nurse, she'd seen naked men of all ages, shapes and sizes without breaking out in a sweat. Yet, right now she had a definite glow happening, and this guy wasn't even naked.

There's only one small step between wet cotton and nakedness.

Okay. Time out. Go to the kitchen.

I'm fine. I can stay here and—

"I need saline."

His deep voice made her jump. "Excuse me?"

He sighed. "Say. Leen," he enunciated slowly as if she were slow. "Salt water. I've got some in the blue bag on the backseat of my car. Take my keys and bring in the bag."

She concentrated on his request, glad that he couldn't focus yet and see her burning cheeks. If he had saline, he must wear contacts and by now they'd be long washed away. Great. She knew intimately how bad it was to be without backup prescription eyewear and had the physical scars to prove it. She hoped he had a spare set in his bag. "I'll go grab it."

Once outside, she sucked in some calming breaths, glad to be out of the close confines of the hot and steamy bathroom. She hadn't felt this rattled in a long time, but then again, she wasn't used to strangers appearing unannounced in her house. That was *all* this was about; the leftover effects of adrenaline making her skittish and on edge.

She glanced at the yard and blinked. Parked next to Bessie, the old ranch truck, she saw a sports car with Illinois plates. Bessie suddenly looked like a monster truck in comparison to the low-slung vehicle. Given his type of car and the fact that he'd locked it, he had to have just arrived in Bear Paw, because otherwise he'd be the talk of the town. New men were always a *very* popular point of discussion everywhere from book club to the Pioneer Women's association bake sale, and at any other venue where women gathered. So why was Josh here and, more importantly, why had he walked uninvited into her house?

Slinging what looked like a large, multipocketed athletic bag over her shoulder, she stopped off at Bessie and grabbed a blanket out of the cab. She returned to the house, adding a kitchen chair to her haul, and carried it all into the bathroom. Josh was out of the shower, standing half naked and buff with the thin, old towel she kept for hand drying wrapped low around his hips.

A hot flash of lusty appreciation socked her. *No. Please, no.* "I'm back," she said, her voice coming out in a squeak. She forced it down four notches as she offered him the blanket. "What have you got in this bag? Weights?"

Squinting, he accepted the blanket and pressed it to his face. He seemed to stop and breathe in deeply.

"Are you okay?" Worried he might faint, she shot out her hand and gripped his arm. One very solid arm. "You're not feeling dizzy from all the steam and the heat?"

"I'm fine." He shook off her hand, threw the blanket around his shoulders and sat down in the chair.

Well, there was no ambiguity about any of that.

"Open the main section of the bag," he instructed firmly.

She slid the multisectioned bag to the floor, and as her fingers gripped the large silver zipper, she saw the words *Josh Stanton* written in black ink next to the very distinctive logo of a medical supplies company. Surprised, she unzipped the lid all the way and opened it up to see a fully stocked medical bag.

No. Surely not. The universe couldn't be that cruel. "You're a physician?"

"Yep."

The word held resignation in its depths, in stark contrast to her high-pitched astonishment. A multitude of questions immediately fired off in her head, including a warning as loud as an emergency siren. "So why are—"

"Eyes first," he said in an authoritative voice that was becoming familiar.

The *I'm in charge* tone now made complete sense. Doctors owned a sense of entitlement that seemed to be bestowed upon them with the arrival of the letters MD after their names.

"Can you see the squishy bag of fluid?"

She sighed. "I can see an intravenous bag, yes. You can relax, Josh. I'm a nurse and I've irrigated eyes plenty of times." She thought about last month when she'd treated fifty firefighter's eyes during the forest fires.

"I'm not that reassured," he growled softly.

Great. A doctor and one who had little regard for nurses. "Why not?" She plunged the cannula into the bag with more force than necessary before priming the tubing.

"You threw paint at me."

She leaned over him, perversely happy that she was the one in a position of power. "I did *not* throw paint at you. You startled me and I bumped the can. The fact that it landed on you was unintentional."

Cool, gray eyes met her gaze. Granted they were red

rimmed and held a supercilious gleam, but underneath all that was a swirl of emotions that mesmerized her.

His light brown brows rose. "Are you waiting for anything in particular?"

"Just checking you're ready," she said quickly, kicking herself for her lapse of concentration.

Get a grip. He's a grouchy, bossy stranger. Worse than all of that put together, he was a doctor. Doctors were most definitely off her dating list for more reasons than she cared to count.

She'd fix up his eyes and send him on his way. Job done!

Grabbing a disposable towel from the medical kit, she positioned it around his neck to absorb the runoff solution and commenced the irrigation. A moment later, Josh's shoulder's fell slightly.

"It's helping?" she asked hopefully.

"Yeah. They've stopped stinging so thankfully there's no damage."

"Good. Panic's over, then." She let the saline drip at a steady rate until Josh held up his hand, signaling that he wanted her to stop. She shut off the drip and wrapped the tubing around the bag before dumping it in the sink.

He carefully dried his eyes before sitting up. "I guess I should thank you."

Ouch. "Oh, bless your heart," she said, borrowing the favorite expression of her aunt Evelyn from Georgia. One she used when someone was seriously ticking her off.

The corner of Josh's mouth twitched.

"You might want to get that tic looked at." She crossed her arms, intending to give him her best in-charge stare, only she caught an eyeful of bare skin in the mirror. Her bare skin. *Oh God.* Her painting shirt wasn't buttoned up properly and right now her breasts looked set to tumble out of her old bra, which provided no support whatsoever.

She quickly dropped her arms by her side and tugged Nana's old blouse down to cover herself, struck by the irony of its failure to provide modesty. As she looked up, she met

Josh's gaze and instantly knew he'd seen everything. Heat flooded her. "So, Doctor," she said, flustered and sounding terser than she intended, "why are you in my house?"

"Your house?" He shook his head and damp curls spattered her with water before his face filled with something that looked like utter relief. "Thank God. For a while there I was thinking I might have to live here."

She tried hard not to take offense. She knew the cottage needed work and that was the only reason she'd been able to afford to buy it in the first place. "As relieved as you sound, you still haven't answered my question as to why you just walked right on in."

"The door was unlocked. Where I come from, an unlocked door is an invitation to enter whether you're welcome or not."

She'd lived in the city, where everyone locked their doors and shut their windows down tight, so she understood, but Bear Paw wasn't a city and no way was he making this her fault. "No one locks their doors here. It's one of the joys of living in the country, but people usually call out 'hello' before they step inside."

"Hey, I knocked but you didn't hear me." His head tilted slightly and his now-focused eyes zeroed in on her. "You've read the articles about ear damage from loud music delivered by earbuds, right?"

His words triggered the voice of her father and her defenses rose. "My music was not that loud."

He shrugged. "Damage done, then."

His patronizing tone irked her and her temper started to fray. She knew yelling at this guy wouldn't help, so she concentrated really hard on trying to sound quiet and cool. "My level of audio acuity is not under question. Are you going to tell me why you're here or do I need to call the sheriff?"

"The sheriff?" The dimple on his chin seemed to deepen with amusement, making him look sexier than ever. "No need for that. I'm Bear Paw's new physician." His tone inferred that this fact explained everything.

"And that's supposed to reassure me?"

He looked slightly taken aback, as if he'd never experienced this reaction before. "Have you had a bad experience with a medical practitioner?"

Not the way you mean. "Put it this way: I've worked with enough."

All the concern on his face vanished and he nodded slowly. "So you're one of *those* nurses?"

She felt herself frown. "One of what nurses?"

His shoulders rose and fell, the movement catching her gaze as it wove across his chest and around abdominal muscles that were indecently ripped.

"Bitter."

"I'm not bitter," she said hotly, but at the same time mentally checking whether she was or not. The fact that she felt the necessity worried her. "I'm pragmatic."

He snorted. "Call it whatever you need to make yourself feel better." His reddened eyes suddenly narrowed. "Do I have to work with you?"

"God, no." It came out far more emphatically than she'd intended.

He stiffened as if she'd slapped him, and a spot of heat burned on each of his bladed cheeks. "Just as long as we're on the same page."

His arctic tone cooled the hot and steamy room, for which she was thankful. This version of the man she could resist. This version trampled over the unwanted heat her body had so quickly and familiarly given in to. She wrenched the conversation back to where they'd started. "I'm still not clear how you being Bear Paw's new physician is connected to you coming into my house."

He sighed as if she were clearly less intelligent than him. "I get a house as part of the job, and the hospital gave me this address. Obviously there's been some sort of major screwup on their part."

"You get a house . . ." Her voice trailed off as a slow slither of dread crawled across her skin. There was a severe shortage of rental properties in Bear Paw. Surely Walt hadn't rented out the house again without telling her? She tried to recall their last conversation. She was positive she'd told him she was moving in.

She pulled her phone out of her pocket. It had been switched off since she'd cut Brent's call, and she held down the on button. It beeped and vibrated wildly and she stared at the screen. There were six missed calls including two from Walt and a text. *Nooooo.* With a sense of foreboding, she opened it.

Good news, Katrina. Call me. Walt.

A strangled sound came from her throat.

Josh leaned forward. "Everything okay?"

God, I hope so. "I . . . um . . . I . . . I need to make a call."

JOSH watched Katrina rush distractedly from the bathroom, pause and then return.

"Feel free to make yourself some coffee. There's a jar of instant on the bench." She spun on her heel and disappeared from view, her jet-black hair swinging wildly.

Josh shuddered at the thought of instant coffee. He had yet to taste any that didn't make gasoline seem palatable. A coffee connoisseur, he had an Italian coffeemaker sitting in his car waiting to be unpacked in his new house. His colleagues at Mercy Hospital had given it to him as a going-away present, saying he might be going west to the middle of nowhere but at least he'd have decent coffee. The state-of-the-art machine would look ludicrous here. He was sure the kitchen hadn't seen a new device since the invention of the microwave forty years ago.

He heard the echo of footsteps beating a tattoo against the old linoleum floor and the murmur of Katrina's voice. The woman could go from conciliatory to abrasive in a heartbeat, and she definitely lacked the sympathy gene. Still, no matter how much she annoyed the hell out of him, he hoped she hadn't just received bad news. No one deserved that.

He'd been the bearer of bad news too many times, watching people slump as his unwelcome words struck them.

Seeing their heads rise and their eyes fill before they pleaded with him that surely there had to be another outcome. It was the one part of his job that he found the toughest, because he'd gone into medicine to help, not to cause pain. He preferred to deliver good news and have his hand pumped furiously, which he enjoyed more than being enveloped in a bear hug by the emotionally demonstrative patients.

And he'd just received good news. He wasn't going to be living in this half-built, half-tumbling-down house. The blanket around his shoulders rubbed against his skin, and a subtle scent of vanilla, freshly cut grass and sunshine tickled his nostrils. It was unfamiliar but he liked it. Ashley had always worn a bold perfume that frequently scented his clothes. More than one patient had given him an odd look from time to time when they'd caught the heady mix of jasmine and lily of the valley.

He breathed in again and realized he'd smelled the scent once before—when Katrina had taken him by the hand and led him down the stairs. It was *her* perfume. The fact that it was redolent of warm, lazy summer afternoons was an oxymoron.

Nothing about Katrina was warm. The physical package of tight, toned and curvy that was utterly enticing on first glance was still gorgeous, and had that compact body come with a fun and flirty personality, he might have been tempted to enjoy some no-strings good times. As it was, he didn't need the bother of a cold and bitter woman. Given what had gone down with Ashley over the past few months, he wasn't certain he wanted the bother of a woman, period.

He closed his eyes to rest them. The image of sparkling, emerald green eyes that reminded him of moss, shady glades and crystal clear swimming holes scudded across his vision. Eyes he'd stared into for far too long when she was leaning over him.

Nothing cold there.

He wrenched his eyes open against the definite rush of blood to his groin. *Shit.* Why was this happening? He didn't even like her.

Back in college that never stopped you.

College was a long time ago and he'd wised up a lot since then. He'd learned the hard way that *nothing* about women was straightforward. Everything was complicated and came with an emotional overlay he never saw coming.

Used to making quick decisions and acting fast, he stood up. It was time to put on dry clothes, drive back to town and check into a motel for the night. Thankfully, this crazy, paint-filled interlude with Katrina Whoever was over. Tomorrow was another day. Hopefully, it would be one where he wasn't at risk of being injured or insulted.

He strode quickly across the kitchen and outside to his car where he hauled some clothes out of his travel bag. Glancing around and seeing nothing but miles and miles of flat plains and not one single person to offend, he dropped the towel and pulled on jeans and a polo shirt. When he straightened up, he saw what he thought must be a female deer staring at him from across the yard.

After all the dead ones he'd passed on the road, it was great to see one alive. He was surprised at the reddish brown color of its coat, but then again, he'd never given any thought to deer, period, let alone their color. The deer held his gaze for a moment before prancing elegantly away behind the scraggly trees.

The bucolic moment over, Josh picked up the towel and headed back inside to collect his shoes and medical kit. When he had his gear together, he went looking for Katrina to say good-bye. As much as he wanted to avoid another conversation with her, he couldn't in good conscience just leave without telling her.

She was standing in the living room staring out at the mountains in the distance, and her hair stuck up in jagged spikes as if she'd been pulling at it. This time he didn't worry about not startling her. "I'm leaving."

She spun around, her teeth grazing her bottom lip. A very soft and kissable lip. His blood pumped just that bit faster, and he hauled his gaze upward fast, away from the delectable view.

I don't like her. He met her emerald eyes. They sparkled like sunshine on moss like before, but now they held a hint of vulnerability that he didn't want to acknowledge.

Her ebony brows pulled down, giving her a worried look. "Actually, I'm the one who's leaving."

"Excuse me?"

She sighed—a weary, heartfelt sound. "Do you want the good news or the bad news first?"

He knew he should take the bad, but after the paint episode, he figured he deserved the good first. "Good."

Her wan smile barely turned her mouth upward. "This is the house the hospital's rented for you."

His gut rolled over. "If that's the good news, then what the hell is the bad?"

Her face scrunched up in a grimace that under any other circumstance he may have conceded was cute. "Sadly, I'm your landlord."

Right then, he didn't know which one of them was more sorry.

Chapter 3

The long wooden table in the ranch house kitchen was strewn with the remnants of the birthday supper Katrina had cooked for her mother. All that was left of the prime rib, mashed potatoes, green beans and dessert were a few crumbs that had once been part of a vanilla-frosted layer cake.

"Ty Garver's bought the adjoining ranch across the west coulee," her father said when there was finally a break in the conversation.

She gave a silent sigh. Her dad had a large soft spot for Ty, who was the only cowboy she'd ever dated. They'd broken up when she was twenty-two because she'd wanted to leave Montana and experience the East Coast frenzy and have some exciting adventures—live somewhere bigger than Great Falls where she'd gone to college. Ty would have shriveled up and died if he'd left the land, so their parting was inevitable and without rancor. That had been years ago, but the fact that they were both still single seemed to give her father hope.

"I think we should all go visit and welcome him. Katrina,

you can take some of those cinnamon cookies you like to bake."

She opened her mouth to tell her father that he made a better cowboy than a matchmaker but she closed it. Perhaps she should consider her dad's suggestion. After all, choosing her own partners had hardly been a success.

Are you listening to yourself? You're an adult and you make your own life choices.

"Dad, I'm sure Ty's capable of baking his own cookies or he can buy them from the diner. Shannon's baking them fresh every day."

Her father's sky blue eyes met hers, backlit with disapproval. "Have you been in the city so long you've forgotten how to be neighborly?"

Crap. So much for being an adult. "Of course not but—"

"Good. While you're baking cookies for Ty you can also make some for the new doctor who I met today when I was moving cows."

No way in hell. Only this time Katrina wisely kept her thoughts to herself to avoid five sets of eyes zeroing in on her. Eyes filled with what and why; two questions she didn't want to answer.

"Female?" her mother asked as she stood up to clear the table.

"Sit down, Mom, we've got this." Katrina put her hand on her mother's shoulder and gently pressed her back into her chair, wondering why her mother seemed hopeful that the doctor was a woman. To her knowledge, Bear Paw had never had a female doctor.

All evening, her mom had been quiet and she looked tired, which was unusual because Bonnie McCade was always brimming with energy. "Are you okay?"

Her mother looked up at her with a smile. "How could I be anything else with everyone home for my birthday this year? You cooked a beautiful meal, honey. Thank you."

"You're welcome." Reassured all was well, she kissed her mom on the cheek before turning to face her younger siblings. She gave both of them her "big sister" death stare.

"We're cleaning up as part of Mom's birthday treat, right, Dillon, Megan?"

An hour ago, the two of them had rushed into the kitchen asking, "What can we do to help?" Their arrival was perfectly timed to coincide with every task being completed, and the only thing left for them to do was call their parents and sit down to eat the meal. She didn't know how they managed to do this every single time, but they had domestic avoidance down to an art form.

"You forgot Beau," Megan said, sounding fourteen instead of twenty-one. "He never helps with the dishes."

Beau leaned back in his chair and gave his quiet trademark smile. "I butchered the meat," he said slowly and carefully as was his style. "I carved it"—he took in a breath—"and I set the table, so . . . by my reckoning . . . that gets me out of dish detail."

Katrina threw dish towels at Megan and Dillon and turned on the hot water faucet.

"The doctor looks to be in his thirties," her father said as if his conversation hadn't been truncated by squabbling adult children. "I swear they're getting younger."

Bonnie laughed. "I think that means we're getting older, Kirk."

"Never." He leaned across the table and kissed her. "We've got years ahead of us still."

Katrina smiled. She remembered at thirteen being acutely embarrassed when her parents showed any public displays of affection. Now she envied them their deep and abiding love for each other built on a foundation of respect. And she envied their honesty with each other. They were a team in every sense of the word. She'd never gotten close to having that sort of a relationship with another person.

An unexpected ache pressed heavy in her chest, and she had to fist her hand to prevent it from rising to rub it. What on earth was the matter with her tonight? She didn't need a man in her life to be happy, and given her track record, she sure as hell didn't need another one to make her unhappy.

"It's a shame they couldn't hire a female doctor," Bonnie said, sounding disappointed.

Katrina shut off the water and glanced at her mom. "You're never sick, so why the worry?"

"Oh, I was thinking more of the young mothers in the county," she said quickly, waving her hand as if that explained everything. "Sometimes it's easier to talk to a woman."

Kirk and Beau exchanged a look of horror that the conversation was about to stray into the terrifying territory of women's bits and pieces, and Kirk said hurriedly, "And before you ask, I took note. No sign of a wedding ring on his finger and he seems pleasant enough."

Megan, a literature student, elbowed Katrina in the ribs. "A single man in his thirties with good financial prospects. Maybe you should wear a dress to work in the diner tomorrow instead of your jeans."

"I'm not looking," she said more curtly than she'd planned.

Megan looked at her far too intently for comfort. Katrina immediately went into damage control and addressed the room. "Why am I always the one supposedly looking for a man? What about Beau? He's still single and he's older, but no one's hounding him to settle down."

"I don't think Beau's looking for a guy, unless there's something you're not telling us, bro?" Dillon said, flicking him with a dishcloth.

Beau laughed easily and put Dillon in a headlock before dragging him toward the door. "For th-that, you're helping me . . . check fences. While there's still . . . light."

"Hey, you're poaching the help," Katrina protested, but the screen door was already slamming shut behind them.

Her parents headed out to the double rocker on the porch just as Megan's phone rang. She checked the caller ID and her eyes lit up. She immediately dropped the dish towel. "I *have* to take this," she said with all the drama of a just-post-teen.

As she walked out of the kitchen, Katrina heard her say, "Hi. This is unexpected," in the throaty voice she always used when she was talking to a guy she liked.

The old kitchen clock ticked loudly on the mantel as Katrina plunged her hands into the white, frothy suds. She stared out the kitchen window, watching the moths flying toward the light, and she fought the melancholy that she was almost thirty, stuck living with her family who had her placed firmly in the role of eldest daughter, and now she was unable to move into her own place.

She gave a wry smile. If the new doctor had been the woman her mother was hoping for—and that hope still confounded her—then perhaps she could have suggested a house-share arrangement. But there was no way on God's green earth that she was ever suggesting that idea to Dr. Josh Stanton. She could just imagine his reaction.

Thinking about him exploded the memory of his naked chest in her mind. It was hard not to think about it, given it had always been at eye level this afternoon. He was so much taller than she was, so unless she tilted her head all the way back, her gaze had constantly been facing his delineated pectoral muscles with their light dusting of sandy brown hair.

Soaking him in. Wondering what they felt like.

She pulled her suddenly itching hands out of the dishwater, feeling hot and disoriented. Flicking on the faucet, she ran cool water against her wrists and sighed. Thinking about Josh had to stop, because no matter how decadently sexy he was, the antipathy that ran between them was palpable. It had disaster written all over it, and she was *not* falling back into bad habits. Coming home to Bear Paw was supposed to protect her from that.

She plunged the greasy baking dish into the suds, thankful that the day was almost over and that tomorrow was a new day. A perfectly normal day that had absolutely no reason to involve a doctor.

———

JOSH bounced his leg up and down and stared at the pile of hospital forms in front of him, certain his already tender eyes would bleed. Day two in Bear Paw was proving to be similar to day one, but instead of paint and the difficult Katrina with the very kissable lips to frustrate him—lips he was so not thinking about—he had jovial Floyd Coulson, the hospital administrator.

"So complete those forms and then you'll be good to go," Floyd said, handing him a pen. "How's the house?"

Where to start? "It's not in town."

Floyd beamed. "Isn't that great? We thought you'd prefer it out there away from the hustle. You know, get some peace to recharge at the end of each day. We don't want you to burn out on us."

Somehow, Josh managed to cut off a snort of incredulity, but it caught at his throat and turned into a cough. From the little he'd seen of Bear Paw, there was nothing close to hustle, and the only bustle he'd seen was one car stopped at the traffic signal when he crossed. Last night, out at the house, it had been the eerie, howling noise of the coyotes that had kept him awake until all hours. Give him the soothing rumble of the EL anytime.

"The thing is, Floyd," he said, leaning forward, "so I can best meet the needs of the town, it's probably important that I live close by the hospital."

"That's a caring thought, son, but the fact is, Katrina McCade's house is the only rental available at the moment."

He tried not to grind his teeth. "It needs work."

Floyd shrugged. "Looks like a sound house to me, but make a list of what needs doing and give it to Walt or directly to Katrina. She's an obliging young woman and I'm sure she'll organize the repairs."

Obliging? Were they talking about the same person?

The memory of her standing, glaring at him with her arms crossed over her breasts and more than a hint of rounded, smooth flesh peeking out from the top of her blouse slugged him hard. His body instantly reacted with joyful anticipation. *God. Damn. It.*

"If something becomes available in town," he said rather too loudly as he tried to get his body back under control, "I'm moving."

Floyd's friendly smile dimmed slightly at his curt tone. "Noted."

Josh pushed on with his grievances and tapped the paper in front of him. "The job description said board-certified ER physician for the hospital, and that's what I am. Nowhere did it mention a primary care physician."

"Well, son, this is Bear Paw."

Josh was really starting to dislike this expression. Floyd had used it more than once. "And that means exactly . . . ?"

"That Bear Paw needs both types of doctor but can only afford one."

Hell, the whole point of specializing in ER was so that he didn't have to do primary care and deal with a patient or their family for longer than one shift. Not that he wasn't sympathetic—he was. He just did it better in short, sharp bursts. Triage, treat to stabilize and refer on, was his motto. "And if I refuse to work at the clinic?"

Floyd leaned back, pressing his fingers into steeples, looking for the first time like a real administrator. "You'll be breaking your contract, which, as I outlined, comes with some hefty financial penalties."

And coming to Bear Paw wasn't hefty penalty enough? "So basically, I'm screwed."

Floyd shook his head, a fatherly expression on his face. "No, son, you're our new physician and you'll be dividing your time between the clinic and the ER."

"How the hell is that going to work?" he asked, thinking about a waiting room full of patients when he had to dash to the ER.

"It's real close," Floyd said proudly, rising to his feet. "Come on, I'll show you. You just have to walk across the grass, and in winter we keep the path salted and shoveled for you."

Incredulity whipped him so hard his head spun. "I meant the patients. What do the patients do if I'm caught up in the ER?"

"They're used to waiting," Floyd said matter-of-factly, walking out of the office.

Waiting? He leaped out of his chair to follow the man who in essence was his boss. He hated being accountable to a number cruncher who had no clue about the needs of patients. "But that could be hours," he said, catching up as they exited the building.

If Floyd had heard him, he chose not to respond. Instead, he pointed out the ER entrance before crossing a grassed square that had been created by the hospital and two other buildings.

"Pretty, isn't it?" Floyd raised an arm to encompass the scene. "The town raised the money for the picnic tables and bench seats. Makes a nice place for the patients to get some fresh air."

Josh, who was still trying to wrap his head around the fact that he was expected to split himself in half to do the job of two doctors, barely noticed the cheery flower beds. He did, however, see a man in a wheelchair smoking a cigarette. *Fresh air, my ass.*

Just as they reached the door of a squat, flat-roofed building, Floyd's phone started ringing. He checked the screen and with an apologetic smile said, "I'm sorry. I have to take this but you go right on ahead. They're expecting you."

Josh took that to mean his staff, and he pushed open the door, stepping into a waiting room. Two framed and faded prints of the Rocky Mountains hung crookedly facing each other, and the rest of the wall space was taken up with health posters that urged people to quit smoking, lose weight and have their eyes checked. The reception desk had the usual raised counter, and he caught sight of a computer screen but there was no sign of a receptionist. He could, however, see a black hoodie slung over a chair. Kitty-corner to the reception desk was a large basket overflowing with toys, and in the center of the room a small stack of dog-eared magazines sat on a low table.

Matching green upright chairs—all evenly spaced—bordered three sides of the room, making it like most every other waiting room he'd ever seen. The chatter in the room faded as twenty sets of eyes swung straight to him, their expressions a mixture of interest and caution.

With no one available to formally introduce him, Josh took the situation into his own hands. After all, he was the physician they'd been waiting for, and he had experience addressing the media from his time in the ER having treated some of the more infamous gang members for gunshot wounds. Clapping his hands together as a sign that an announcement was about to be made, he said with appropriate gravitas, "Hello. I'm Doctor Stanton from Chicago's Mercy Hospital and I'm in Bear Paw for—"

"Has Randall finally quit to fish?" an elderly lady asked in surprise.

Josh wasn't used to being interrupted. He opened his mouth to reply but another woman got in first. "Lynn didn't mention it when I met her at the grocery store the other day."

The man next to her adjusted his glasses and gave Josh a long, hard stare. "Are you a real doctor or just one of those pretend ones they usually send us?"

"Physician's assistant," someone added in clarification. "He doesn't look old enough to be a doctor."

"Of course I'm a doctor," Josh said incredulously, still trying to come to grips with the way the conversation was flying off on tangents. It was like being on a stage with a cast who'd gone off script. "I'm a qualified ER physician."

"Oh, I used to like that George Clooney," a woman who looked to be in her sixties said with a dreamy smile.

Now he was seriously in the twilight zone. "He's an actor," Josh said firmly, his voice sounding overly loud. "I'm board-certified. A real doctor."

The room went silent and the geriatric inquisition stared at him unhappily. This wasn't going quite like the ticker tape parade he'd imagined.

"I'm quite aware that Mr. Clooney's an actor," the woman said with a sniff. "He made a fine doctor."

The inference was clear—Josh was coming a distant second to a Hollywood actor who'd starred in the role fifteen years ago. What the hell sort of a town had he come to?

"No one can live up to George, Doris," said a new voice behind him.

He turned to see a young woman wearing baggy scrubs, smiling at him.

"That's very true, Millie," Doris replied. "I guess for now we'll have to give Doctor Stanton the benefit of the doubt. Mind you, he's got a look of a younger George with his height and curly hair." Doris sounded slightly mollified.

"I'll do my best," Josh said, uncertain exactly how to proceed. Right now he'd take a patient with a gunshot wound or an off-his-face meth addict rather than face this group of critical seniors. He was used to being judged on his clinical skills, not his ability to look like an actor.

The woman who looked to be in her twenties stuck out her hand. "I'm Millie Switkowski, nurse practitioner, and I'm your go-to person here at the clinic. Welcome to Bear Paw, Doctor Stanton. I'm looking forward to working with you."

He gripped her hand like it was a life preserver in a choppy sea. Finally, he'd met someone who seemed professional and competent. Hell, she was the first person he'd met in Bear Paw who seemed normal.

The memory of dancing green eyes, a sassy mouth and a sweet behind flooded him, and he immediately tried to shut it out. Katrina McCade wasn't normal—she was difficult, bitter, bossy and annoying. *And as sexy as hell.*

Someone coughed—a wet and hacking noise that was the insidious sound of heart failure. It immediately focused him. The town and its population might be as foreign to him as Kazakhstan, and he may not have gotten the welcome he'd anticipated, but this he knew. He swung round briskly. "Whoever owns that cough, I'll see you first."

Chapter 4

Katrina usually worked the breakfast shift at the Big Foot diner and then had the middle of the day to herself before pulling beers at Leroy's for a couple of hours in the early evening. Today was different. She was working until midafternoon because Shannon Bauer, the owner of the diner and her boss, had a meeting at the middle school and she'd asked Katrina to cover.

At times, the diner unofficially doubled as the community center, and today a Mommy-and-Me group had taken over the couches Shannon had in the corner for casual coffee. Between the babies who were practicing walking around the coffee table and the ones asleep in their strollers, it was a bit of an obstacle course as Katrina delivered coffee and freshly baked muffins.

She'd always loved babies and had been more than happy to cuddle them and breathe in their sweet smell of milk. To her, that distinctive scent had always represented hope and joy, but just lately holding a baby filled her with regret. Truth be told, everything about her life at the moment filled her with varying levels of regret.

The bell over the door tinkled and a woman walked in pushing a stroller. She stopped and stared. "Oh my God. Katrina McCade? I thought you'd left town and were never coming back?"

Katrina's stomach sank. Eight years ago when she'd left town in a blaze of *I've outgrown Bear Paw,* she'd said things to Chrissie Stapleton that she wasn't proud of. She and Chrissie had been friends in high school but they'd shared different ambitions. Neither of them had understood the other's position, and hurtful things had been aired.

Plastering a smile on her face with the intention of starting over, she said, "Hi, Chrissie. Mom told me the good news. Congratulations."

Chrissie took a pointed look at Katrina's left hand. "Back in Bear Paw and not even engaged?"

She hated the traitorous and totally irrational feelings of failure that threaded their way through her. Not that she'd ever made it a total life goal to get married and have babies, but then again, she hadn't ruled it out, either.

She thought of Brent and forced the rising bile back down her throat. "Not everyone wants to get married, Chrissie."

The beautician raised her perfectly waxed brows. "That's true. I just didn't think you were one of *those* people."

"Coffee, Chrissie?" she said, straining to sound composed. "You take a seat with the other moms and I'll bring it right over."

As she made the coffee she reminded herself that she was not defined by a lack of a husband, partner or boyfriend. She was a modern, independent woman and she was in charge of her own destiny.

How's that working for you living back at home with your folks?

Shut. Up.

She picked up the coffeepot and did a round of the diner for those patrons who'd bought the bottomless cup. The bell over the door rang again and she turned to greet the patron. "H—"

Her voice failed as a flash of heat raced through her,

taunting her and reminding her exactly how much she missed having sex.

Josh strode quickly through the door, filling the diner with his height, his breadth and his restless energy.

Light gray eyes—eyes that no longer looked like a red trail map—met hers. A flare of surprise burned in them along with something that made her shiver in a very good way. As fast as it had glowed brightly, it faded away, leaving her wondering. In its place was the more familiar and slightly detached gaze.

She swallowed hard, determined to sound cool, calm and collected. "*Doctor* Stanton."

"*Nurse* McCade." He eyed the coffeepot in her hand suspiciously. "I hope you're more in control of hot coffee than paint."

The delicious lust-fest her body was rolling in cooled. *Good*. At least her common sense was finally exerting itself. "Only when you're not in my way," she said sweetly, skirting around him and taking her place safely behind the counter. She'd never been so glad to have a wide piece of laminate between her and another person.

She almost asked him how his first night in the house had gone, but the thought of Josh lying sprawled across a bed wearing nothing but boxers had her tongue glued to the roof of her mouth.

"What can I get you?" she finally managed to blurt, her question coming out a lot throatier than she'd intended.

"An espresso."

"Straight up or American?" *Yes!* The barista was back in control doing coffee talk.

"Straight up. To go." He tilted his head, studying her dispassionately like she was a painting on a wall. "You're an RN but you're making coffee?"

He wasn't the first person to have asked that question in the same curious and bemused tone, but she was still smarting from his crack yesterday about her being bitter. She banged the portafilter hard against the disposal unit to dislodge the used grinds. "Making good coffee is an art form, and as I'm the only barista in town, you can either have bitter-free coffee or a bitter nurse. Take your pick."

"Oh, that's easy," he said, his voice a low, teasing rumble. "Coffee every time." He smiled widely, his face settling into what looked like oft-used lines and his eyes crinkled at the edges, softening his frequently stern look.

A tingle shot through her—one she'd been familiar with since she was fourteen. *Damn it, no. Don't flirt with me!*

"Good choice." She looked away, concentrating on tamping down the freshly ground beans and locking the handle onto the machine. Pressing the button to start the water, she then placed the espresso cup in position ready for the dark and tangy brew. She wished he'd ordered a latte or a cappuccino, because then she could have busied herself with frothing milk, but now she had nothing else to do but wait while the coffee brewed.

She could see him turning his wallet over and over in his hands. The man was never still. When she finally looked up, the flirting charm had gone, replaced with a serious look on his freshly shaved cheeks. In one way, she missed the dark stubble, which had given him a relaxed look, but on the other hand the neat and tidy urban professional thing he had going on made him easier to resist. The stubble had merely been a facade, because nothing about Dr. Josh Stanton was relaxed or laid-back.

"If I upset you yesterday, Katrina, I blame the paint."

His ham-fisted attempt to say sorry both surprised and irked her. "That's an interesting apology."

He sighed. "Do you concede that we both said things we probably shouldn't have?"

Put it this way: I've worked with enough. Her own words echoed accusingly in her head, holding a degree of bite. As much as she didn't want to admit it, he was right. She'd let her caustic feelings for Brent spill over to unfairly taint him. "I can see there's a grain of truth in that."

His eyes darkened, taking on the hue of smoke. "There you go. That wasn't so hard, was it?"

Hard. An image of his naked chest, all solid muscle and

power, took residence in her head, begging the question what else about his body was hard. Her knees wobbled as her blood turned into a river of sweet, hot desire. *No. Bad idea. Don't go there.*

She blinked, trying to block all wayward thoughts. "I'm more than capable of admitting when I'm wrong."

He tilted his head and a curl fell over his forehead, stealing for a moment the formidable doctor look he mostly had going on. "Really?"

He's got you there. She didn't want to smile, but her mouth curved up anyway as she popped a traveler lid on his coffee. She met his all-too-knowing gaze. "Well, I'm as capable as you are."

"So in other words, not that capable at all." He grinned at her, the dimple in his chin deepening and lighting up his face. He handed her some notes and accepted the change. "Thanks for the discount."

She shook her head. "I charged you the full price."

"But that's so cheap," he said, sounding astonished.

"This is Bear Paw."

He rolled his eyes.

"What?"

"That phrase is the default setting for everything around here. At least this time, it's a good thing."

She tried not to sigh. Sure, Bear Paw was small and at first glance it didn't look like much, but it was a bit like Montana gold. You had to dig for it. "Never lived in a small town before, Josh?"

He shook his head. "Not unless you count Boston. I've been living in Chicago these last two years."

"So why did you want to come live and work in Bear Paw?"

She hoped he'd say he wanted to improve access to health services for isolated communities or admit to a passion for working with Native Americans or—

"To reduce my student loans to a manageable level."

And there it was. Disappointment clanged through her. "The Hippocratic oath meets market forces?"

"Something like that." His mouth flattened as he caught her disapproving gaze. "What do you want me to say? That I'm thrilled to be here? I have to tell you, after this morning at the clinic, I'm thinking the feeling might be mutual."

She knew the town could be slow to warm, but she had the gut feeling that he probably hadn't helped things along. "What were you expecting? A ticker tape parade?"

Josh felt the spotlight of Katrina's far-too-perceptive green eyes on him and saw the moment she read him like a book.

Her hand flew to her mouth and then she laughed. "Oh my gosh. You really were."

Her laughter made him feel even more isolated from the town, and a surge of self-righteous indignation swelled in him. "Well, hell, why not? I've given up a lot to come here."

She shrugged her shoulders. "Timing is everything, Josh."

"What the hell is that supposed to mean? I should have come in winter?"

She shook her head, her expression sympathetic. "People have to get to know you."

He threw his arms up in the air as bewilderment battered him. "What's to know? I'm the doctor, they're the patients. End of story."

"This isn't an ER in Chicago."

"You think?"

She shot him a look that inferred he was utterly clueless.

He railed against it. He'd given up so much to come to Bear Paw and he didn't need to be told how to suck eggs. He took a gulp from his coffee. Unlike yesterday, when she'd been wearing a voluminous shirt that had hidden her curves, today she wore jeans and a watermelon-colored blouse, which was tucked in behind a leather belt. With her short stature, it made her breasts seem more voluptuous, and like muscle memory, his gaze automatically sought a glimpse of the generous cleavage he'd seen yesterday.

All he saw were green buttons the exact same color as her eyes. Taunting buttons that said, "We're resting on warm, smooth skin that you can't see." An irrational tug of disappointment pulled at his gut and instantly wrestled with the fact that he didn't want to be attracted to her in any way. Hell, he didn't want to notice anything about her, so he focused on the fact that she annoyed him to the nth degree.

She and her sorry excuse of a house. "Instead of giving me gratuitous advice, you need to make your house habitable starting now."

Her eyes flashed with annoyance. "I'm your landlord, Josh, not an employee you can order about. The house is more than habitable."

Disbelief slugged him as his hand slapped the counter. "It's got no internal doors."

"You're living alone so how is that a problem?"

She had the uncanny ability to make him feel like he was the one making an unreasonable request. Damn it, a house should have internal doors at least on the bathroom. "Of course it's a problem," he ground out, struggling to keep his voice calm. "What if someone's visiting and I want to use the bathroom?"

A soft gasp left her mouth, and her eyes widened to huge pools of rainforest green. It took him straight back to yesterday, straight back to the small and steamy bathroom where she'd leaned in over him. He'd wanted to dive right into their depths and find the source of fire that glowed there.

She shook her head as if trying to shift something and the glow faded. "They're already on order."

His wayward mind, lost in the memory of heat and fathomless eyes, scrambled to find purchase. "What?"

Small lines creased across the bridge of her nose. "The doors. They're on order and will be here in a few days."

Her reasonable reply released the valve on his head of steam and he was left feeling like the rules had just changed on him. Again. "Right. Good. Thanks."

"You're welcome."

"I'm going back to work now."

"Have a good day."

He couldn't tell if she was being sarcastic or not.

BEAU was in town to collect a spare part for the tractor, and normally he avoided the diner at this time of day, but Bonnie had texted him to pick up a cheesecake she'd ordered. Her request had surprised him because she always baked her own and surely she could have asked Katrina to bring it home, but Beau had learned long ago not to question the vagaries of his aunt, his female cousins or women in general. Life was easier that way.

"Beau, you're just in time. We need a man's opinion." Ellen Hanson, the bottle-blond wife of the owner of the town's only car dealership, put her hand on his arm in a predatory fashion as he passed by the booth.

"My opinion," he said carefully, using his breathing to try to avoid a word block, "m-may not suit you." He gave a practiced smile. One that gave the impression of him being at ease when in reality he'd rather be kicked hard by a goosey and snorting horse than be ambushed by members of the Bear Paw book club. Or for that matter, any of the women's groups in town. But today it looked like he was shit out of luck.

"Oh, honey," Ellen cooed, "a cowboy who's good with his hands has exactly the opinion we're after." Her eyes raked his wrangler-clad legs before her gaze settled slightly too long on his groin. "The book we're reading has a machine in it and we just can't quite work out how it works. Come sit and explain it to us."

It was well known that this particular group of six women in their forties had far too much spare time on their hands, and rumors about their antics kept the Bear Paw gossip mill turning. Beau had no interest in being any woman's boy toy. Hell, he couldn't even see himself as someone's boyfriend. He always refused to be drawn into the speculation by his mates that inevitably took place at the tavern after a few beers.

He caught sight of the book—an erotic novel that had taken the world by storm. He immediately knew exactly what sort of a machine he'd be expected to discuss and his chest tightened. *Breathe in, blow out the words.*

"I'd like to . . . explain it, but . . ." He hauled in more air, and as he blew it out, he felt his vocal cords relaxing. "I'm expected back at the ranch."

He disengaged his arm from Ellen's manicured nails. "Ladies." Tipping his hat in acknowledgment of the group, he spun on his heel and strode to the counter, ignoring the sighs of disappointment and the naughty giggles that sounded behind him. As relief slid through him that the encounter was over, he hated that he could feel beads of sweat pooling on the back of his neck. Despite years of having almost total control over his stutter, groups of women always took him back in time to his adolescence and threatened to undo all of his hard work.

A woman with long blond hair that was pulled up on top of her head and held in place with what looked like a bamboo skewer was wiping down the counter in wide, slow swipes. Everything about her body said bone-tired, from the lines around her pretty blue eyes to the weary set of her shoulders.

She paused as he approached, stowing the cloth under the counter and wiping her hands on her apron. "What can I get you?"

"Ah . . ." The stalling sound slipped out as he marshaled his words. "Bonnie McCade ordered . . . a cheesecake."

Her lips, which reminded him of a pink bow on a gift box, curved into a soft smile. "Are you Beau? Katrina's brother?"

Cousin. "Yes, ma'am. I am."

"I'm Shannon. Shannon Bauer." She extended her hand in greeting.

"Shannon." He repeated her name to store it and the sound in his mind as he gave her a quick nod. Being very aware that in the past he'd unintentionally crushed women's hands with his firm grip, he held hers gently. Only her hand didn't feel petite and vulnerable in his at all. In fact he was surprised at the juxtaposition of rough and smooth against his own work-calloused palm.

She slid her hand out of his as if he'd held on to it for too long and said briskly, "I took over the diner a few weeks ago, and your sister's been a lifesaver."

"That sounds . . ."—he concentrated on speaking slowly—". . . like Katrina."

Shannon frowned. "You say that like it's a bad thing."

He shrugged. "It is . . . what it is."

"All I know is I couldn't do what I do without her working the breakfast shift," she said, chatting easily. "I've been focusing on making the diner a place for groups to meet so I have customers between the main meal times. Even so"—her lipstick-free lips tilted wryly—"I wasn't totally prepared for the book club's first meeting here. I'm impressed you got away without even a scratch."

Her hands were deftly assembling a white box, and he found himself watching the sure and confident movements as her fingers snapped the tabs into the slots. He suddenly realized that she'd stopped talking and he was staring. He rapidly lifted his gaze only to meet questioning eyes as big and as blue as the skies he rode under out on the range.

The zap of sensation that hit his body jolted him so hard it made him feel like he'd been asleep for years. "Excuse me?"

Her head tilted almost imperceptibly toward the booth of women. "Cougars usually eat their prey. In fact, they pretty much devoured poor Todd Lexington. He's going to have a tough time tonight explaining to his wife how the fire-engine red lipstick got on his collar."

His brain snagged on the image of red lipstick on her lips and promptly emptied. He swallowed against a throat tight with unfamiliar need, and only years of keeping his emotions and speech under strict control kept him from licking his lips.

Her expression said she expected a quip from him to extend her joke.

Sweat rolled down his spine. "Right. Todd. Yeah."

She looked at him blankly like so many people did—as

if he were missing any semblance of an IQ because he spoke slowly and deliberately. It got to him and he blurted out, "Kn-knowing T-Todd, he'll s-survive." *Fuck.* Twelve years of hard work vanquished in a heartbeat. He wanted to smash something. Throw something. He wanted out of here five minutes ago.

SHANNON was having trouble seeing and breathing at the same time. Beau McCade stood at her counter, the perfect specimen of Montana Man—the one every woman east of the Mississippi expected to see when they vacationed in this fine state. From the dusty tips of his work boots and up along his denim-clad legs, he exuded a no-nonsense strength. His black-and-white rock 'n' roll western shirt stretched across wide shoulders, and he'd rolled the sleeves up to his elbows, exposing forearms with bulging veins. She gripped the pie box hard to prevent her fingers from reaching out and touching him.

He's out of your league and out of bounds. Her track record with men was short but not sweet, and definitely not something she was ready to repeat. For five years, she'd chosen not to involve a man in her and Hunter's life. Right now, her priority was getting Hunter to stay in school so he could have a shot at graduating rather than repeating his mother's mistakes. Right now, that plan was looking decidedly shaky.

Beau's black cowboy hat hid most of his hair, but she glimpsed jet-black strands like Katrina's. Strands that matched the afternoon stubble on his cheeks. His eyes were dark, too—a deep, rich brown like the roasted Puerto Rican coffee beans she used in the store—and their brown depths were hypnotic. She was acutely aware she'd been talking way too much, but between his delectable darkness and his overly short responses to her questions, she'd gotten flustered. Whenever that happened, she gabbed on far too much.

Why had she even mentioned Todd Lexington? When

he'd replied, he sounded like he'd been politely holding back from saying, "It's none of your goddamn business," and as a result he'd tripped over his words. Now his previous bland expression was stony, as if she'd crossed an invisible social line only known to the folk born and raised in this town.

"So. The. Cake?"

His slow yet staccato delivery hit her like shotgun pellets—each word stinging like crazy.

"Of course. Sorry." She slid the golden cheesecake she'd made early morning into the box, closed the lid and slid it across the counter. "That's eleven dollars."

He silently slapped some bills down on the counter, tipped his hat, picked up the box and left the diner.

The book club members sighed as the door closed behind him, and Ellen said, "What do you think, Shannon?"

She picked up her cloth and played dumb. "Of what?"

"Cowboy McCade."

Dream-worthy. "It's hard to know. Our conversation was limited to the price of cheesecake."

Ellen shot her a pitying look. "Honey, it's not his conversational skills or lack of that interests us."

Shannon thought about the dark and fascinating bad boys she'd dated in her twenties. Men who'd been big on sex and small on conversation. "Oh, I don't know. I like a man who can hold up his end of a discussion."

The other women laughed as if she were missing something fundamental.

"Wait until rodeo season," Ellen said. "Once you see Beau McCade in chaps, you'll want to ride him as much as every other woman in town."

And going on the way Beau had expertly disengaged himself from those women, she assumed most of them had.

Chapter 5

Katrina stuck her carpenter's pencil behind her ear before releasing the tape measure. It shot back into its casing, and Boy raised his head at the accompanying thwack. "We're getting there, buddy. Only two doors left."

Boy's tail thumped against the carpet.

She'd been at the cottage since one o'clock, and her aim was to have all the doors fitted, the curls of wood shavings vacuumed, and be long gone before Josh even thought about leaving the clinic or the hospital for the day. That was what a good landlord did; fixed problems while the tenant was out so as not to get in the way of their enjoyment of the property.

Don't kid yourself. You're so avoiding him.

And she was. She'd come to Bear Paw to save herself from making yet another disastrous mistake, and she'd been very confident of holding true to that course right up until Josh had flirted with her at the diner. The flutters of delight that had eddied what had been a still pool of desire since Brent's bombshell really scared her.

Weeks ago she'd vowed to herself she was never getting

involved with a doctor again, and the raw and painful memories of Brent and to a lesser degree of Andrew should have been enough to make Josh totally resistible and absolutely undesirable. When she added in his pragmatism at being in Bear Paw for utterly selfish reasons rather than altruistic ones, *that* should have deadened any sexual reaction to him at all.

It didn't with Brent.

It would have if I'd known.

This time she knew up front, but for some unfathomable reason, she couldn't squash the attraction. It bothered her a lot.

It had taken her almost eight years, but with the culmination of a series of hard-earned lessons capped off with the disaster that was Brent, she'd finally acknowledged that her body had a radar for being aroused by totally inappropriate men. Men who caused her pain and anguish. Men she allowed to draw her into their world only to find that no matter what she did they decided she didn't fit. Men she should have avoided from the get-go.

Call her a slow learner, but she was officially done making any more stupid mistakes. This time, she wasn't giving her body a chance to pump heady, exhilarating and addictive shivers through her that made her tumble into bed first and think second. No, this time she was being mature and sensible, and as a result, she was strategizing. It made perfect sense to her that if she was never alone with Josh then she was safe from doing anything dumb that she'd regret. On top of that plan, and to totally safeguard herself from temptation, she'd buy a whizz-bang vibrator that did double duty. An orgasm was an orgasm, right? Surely regular pleasuring of herself would diminish her reaction to Josh.

Masturbating in your childhood room with only thin walls between you and your family? Yeah, like that's gonna totally work.

The thought curdled her stomach. How had she let her life come to this? It was so far removed from the hopeful vision she'd had at twenty-two when she'd left Bear Paw that it was unrecognizable. As she vigorously gored a rectangle into the wood of the doorjamb with a chisel to create a space for the hinge, she decided that a crash course in meditation might be her best and only option.

Today, she'd swapped her contacts for her glasses because they doubled as eye protection, and she concentrated on preparing the next door for hanging. She quickly found a sort of peace in the rhythm of moving the block plane back and forth while keeping a close eye on her pencil markings.

When she was growing up, she'd spent a lot of time with her dad in his workshop over the long Montana winters, and he'd taught her all sorts of things to do with wood and tools. She'd treasured the one-on-one time with him, not realizing until much later exactly how much useful stuff she'd learned along the way and how self-sufficient it had made her. Back in Philadelphia, she'd rarely had to call the super for anything.

Setting the plane aside, she sanded down the edges before lifting the door off the sawhorse to check it against the doorway. She was about to place it on the wedges when Boy stirred again. A second later, the sound of the front door being slammed shut by the wind made the house tremble. Footsteps immediately followed.

"Yes! Doors." Josh's unmistakably deep voice rolled into the room, filled with delight.

Shit. Her mouth dried as her heart leaped into her throat and she gripped the door tightly. What was he doing here at this time of day? It was barely three o'clock and by rights he should be at the clinic, knee-deep in patients and dealing with the health care needs of Bear Paw.

"Hello?"

She heard him come closer and hoped he was in one of his aloof moods. A standoffish, superior Josh was much easier to resist than the Josh who had a twinkle in those gunmetal eyes and a dancing dimple in his chin. She told herself sternly none of it mattered because they both had their roles to play. She was the landlord, he was the tenant and she had a door to hang. A door that right now made a handy barrier between them but whose weight was making her arms burn.

She glanced down and saw his fashionable black suede shoes complete with a film of Montana dust appear in her line of vision. She adjusted her hands on the door and sucked in a calm breath so when she spoke she wouldn't sound breathy. "Hi, Josh."

"Katrina?" His surprise bounced around the room. "You're fitting the doors? I thought you'd get a handyman to do it."

"Why pay someone when I know how," she said as her now burning arms gave out. She half lowered, half dropped the door onto the wedges. The impact knocked them over and the door followed.

Josh yelped in pain as the wood hit his foot.

"Oh God. Sorry." She hastily adjusted her grip on the door. She was about to lift it when his hands closed over the top of hers, trapping them in place on the door. Traitorous warmth stole through her, turning her legs to molasses.

Suddenly, the door rose, and with it, she was being turned as Josh directed the play. His hands and his strength forced her to just follow. The next minute the door was leaning against the wall and she was caught between the two.

His hands fell away and her legs firmed up. When she ducked out from behind the door, Josh was rubbing his foot against the back of his calf.

She couldn't believe she'd inadvertently hurt him again, and she immediately went into fix-it mode. "Take off your shoe and I'll get you some ice to slow any bruising."

One brow rose sharply. "And risk you causing me more damage? I don't think so."

"The ice will help. You know it will." His grumpy tone steadied all tingles and shimmers, and she walked to the kitchen and pulled open the freezer. As he'd been in town a week and a half, she'd expected it to be full of food, but the only contents were a can of orange juice concentrate, a loaf of bread and, fortunately, a full ice cube container.

She dumped the contents into a cloth and returned to the living room to find Josh sitting on the sofa wriggling his toes. He gave her an accusing look. "Nothing appears to be broken."

"That's good. Here you go." She sat down next to him and handed over the homemade pack.

He grudgingly accepted it from her and rested it on his foot. "What is it with you and inflicting pain?"

Her shoulders rose and fell. "Just lucky, I guess. In my defense, my plan was to be finished and gone way before you got back from work, but you're early."

He gave her a long, penetrating look from those rich, expressive eyes. "Are you saying that my getting hurt is my own fault for taking an afternoon off?"

She grinned. "If you say so."

He blinked as if he hadn't expected the answer. Slowly, the tension in his face faded and then he laughed. A full, loud belly laugh that rocked his body and shifted his weight.

One minute there was a safe and healthy distance between them, and then the old sofa cushions caved inward, rolling her sideways. Her shoulders bumped into his arm and then she fell across him. Suddenly, she found herself sprawled half on his lap.

"Sorry," she spluttered as her body squealed in delight. "This sofa is a disaster." She tried to move but the sucking cushions pinned her against him—a solid wall of muscle radiating heat. Heat that wove through her, taunting her with delicious quivers that danced and swirled before rushing straight to the apex of her thighs.

His laughter moved his body under hers and the hard muscles rubbed against her breasts. Her nipples hardened so fast they ached as they scraped against her bra, seeking to touch him. Wanting to break free of the confines of the fabric and feel him, skin on skin. Sensations hammered her—his heat, the collision of his woodsy cologne mixing with a hint of the freshness of antiseptic, and the wondrous feel of him. Her mind clouded around the edges.

His hand gently cupped the back of her neck, halting her slide across him, and at the same time it made her look up. Up into his handsome face now creased by laughter.

Up into eyes full of comedic joy at the ludicrousness of the situation. He met her gaze and a slow, smoldering burn edged out the laughter, turning his eyes the color of silver.

Her body ignited. She recognized that look—primal attraction. Chemical. Sparked by a rush of endorphins and deliciously addictive. She also knew without a single doubt that her expression matched his.

Her fingers spread, pressing against his chest, feeling his heart thundering against them, full of vitality. Calling to her. *I've missed this.* Her resolve never again to trust primal attraction tumbled backward, falling fast and far, far away from every decision she'd made about her life since leaving Philadelphia. Since leaving Brent.

His face was now so close to hers that his breath was caressing her skin. All she needed to do was tilt her chin a couple of degrees and her lips would brush his. She already knew his touch and his scent. Now she craved to know his taste.

One tiny kiss and she'd know.

Are you completely self-destructive? Stop it. Go now!

The protective scream in her head penetrated the fog that had encased her mind. She moved abruptly, wriggling against him and trying to stand.

"Shit! You're stabbing me with a screwdriver." Josh's hands gripped her and suddenly she was up and on her feet.

Her body wept. Flustered, she stammered out, "I'll get out of your way before I cause any more damage. There are only two doors left to hang and they're all trimmed and ready. You fit them and I'll come by tomorrow when you're at work to pick up my gear."

"I don't fit doors," he said, his voice sounding both curt and strangled all at the same time.

The relaxed, sexy and laughing man whose desire-filled eyes mere moments ago had beamed "I want you as much as you want me" had vanished. In his place was the tense and detached doctor who was used to ordering staff around.

Irritation at his terse tone prickled along her skin, colliding with her own frustrations at her inability to control her loose libido. She crossed her arms over her aching breasts, which were sobbing at the loss of all that delicious contact with him.

"A bit of manual labor above you, Josh?"

His shoulders squared and he looked affronted. "No. But I'm certain that's what you want to think."

His words jabbed at her. Oh God, he was right. She didn't know what was worse—the fact that he was so accurately insightful or how small it made her feel. She was deliberately picking a fight with him so she could call him arrogant. It was so much safer to feel a heap of righteous indignation about him instead of the jitters that too easily tipped into overwhelming attraction.

An attraction that was so very hard to fight.

He tilted his head as if he'd recognized her acknowledgment that his assessment was correct. "You're not in my way, and where I come from if you start a job, you finish it. Plus"—he swung his leg up onto the coffee table—"I can't possibly do it because I have a bruised foot."

He didn't add "which is your fault," but it was clearly implied. A double dose of guilt slugged her. "Fine, I'll hang the last two doors."

The tension left his face. "Great."

As she prepared to fit the door, she could feel his eyes on her. Another flash of heat burst through her, flaming her face and drenching her hands. The screws in her palm slipped to the floor, rolling everywhere. "Crap."

"I wouldn't have picked you for being a klutz, but things are adding up. First the paint, then the door and now this."

I'm only clumsy around you. She ground her teeth. "Perhaps if you didn't watch my every move as if you were expecting me to mess up any moment."

His expression was all innocence and he opened his hands outward as if he were being wrongly accused. "Hey, I'm just sitting here icing my foot like you told me."

She mumbled, "Yeah, right," and collected the screws before starting over. As she turned on the drill, she saw him flinch. Desperate to move the conversation away from her lust-induced lack of coordination she asked, "Does the sound give you goose bumps?"

"I did time in orthopedics."

She recalled her time in the OR. "I was totally fascinated the first time I saw an orthopedic surgical set up." She laughed. "It looked just like my father's workshop with its mallet, screws, saws and bone chisels." She drilled in the next screw. "Did you decide orthopedics wasn't for you?"

"Something like that." He readjusted the ice pack. "Thanks for taking care of the doors so quickly."

Had he just changed the subject? "No problem."

"I've made a list of other things that need attention." He pulled a piece of paper out of his shirt pocket. "The rail in my closet is loose, the light bulbs in the bedroom need replacing and I need hooks put into the walls so I can hang some pictures."

All of it was really minor stuff that tenants usually just fixed themselves. "You don't need my permission to do any of that. Just check for a stud before hanging anything heavy."

"I'm pretty busy, so it would really help me out if you did it."

He gave her a beguiling smile that deepened the dimple in his chin and bracketed his lips in sensual lines. Lips she'd come so close to kissing.

Deep breath in. Deep breath out. Deep breath in . . . She worked at blocking the effects of his unfamiliar but devastating smile by focusing on logic. He was on an afternoon off and, granted, he was nursing a slightly bruised foot that was her fault, but he could hardly call himself busy. And that smile was completely different from the repertoire of smiles he drew on when he was with her. They mostly ranged from tight and tense to irritated.

He used that smile when he flirted with you at the diner. When he wanted coffee.

She smelled a rat. A rat who'd made her feel guilty

about asking him to fit two doors. A rat who wanted something from her.

She slapped a hand onto her hip and pointed an accusing finger at him. "You have no clue how to fix any of those things on your list, do you?"

He had the grace to look sheepish for half a second before his eyes twinkled at her and his full lips twitched upward. "But I'm a hell of a good doctor."

Tingles tangoed in her just like the last time his eyes had done that sparkly thing. She stomped on them hard, wondering how he'd got to thirty-something with a total lack of basic practical skills. "How have you gotten through life without ever hanging a painting?"

He shrugged as if it was no big deal. "I lived in college, then student housing where we could only afford posters. When I graduated, I moved into apartments where I paid to have someone from maintenance come do whatever I needed."

"Didn't you learn stuff when you spent time out in the garage with your father?"

His cheeks tightened for a moment. "My father wasn't that sort of a dad." He leaned forward and smiled again, although it didn't quite reach his eyes. "Can you help me out and do all that stuff for me? I'll pay for your time."

Pay me? Money wasn't the issue. Trying to think, she closed the door, checking it latched properly, and then she opened it again, testing the swing. She really didn't want to be coming out to the cottage to be his Ms. Fixit, because every time she was called out, she'd risk running into him. No, that was so far from being a good idea that she lodged it firmly under the category of disaster.

Think.

An idea hit. *No. So not going there.* But although every part of her tried to reject it outright, no matter how hard she tried to think of other ways around it or to come up with another idea, she kept drawing blanks.

A plan always has a difficult part.

And this was definitely going to be difficult, but it would be worth it in the end. It had to be. Taking in a deep breath, she said, "I can teach you to fish."

———

JOSH stared at Katrina, convinced he must have misheard. Ever since he'd come home and found her in his living room wearing those ragged cutoff shorts and that damn tool belt, his concentration had been all miss and no hit. It had totally disappeared when she'd fallen against him on the couch—all lush and soft, and full of sweet, seductive curves he'd longed to explore. He'd almost kissed her and he despised himself for that. Hell, he prided himself on being a man with self-control. He'd managed to be faithful to Ashley for five years no matter the temptations that had presented themselves. And there'd been more than a few everywhere he worked, especially from the medical and nursing students.

So if he could resist twenty-two-year-olds, surely he could resist Katrina. Still, he gave thanks that the screwdriver handle had jabbed him in the stomach exactly when it had, saving him from making an idiotic mistake and a total fool of himself. Why would he want to kiss a woman he didn't even like? She was difficult, at times self-righteous, and she had a way of looking at him that made him question his actions. He really hated that.

He also hated feeling this out of control. He blamed that tool belt. He had no clue why that piece of leather strung around her waist turned him on so much. And those tortoiseshell glasses she was wearing today. Damn, but they made her look sexy. He'd wanted to take them off her, pull the elastic out of her hair and—

Shit. Just thinking about it kicked his heart rate up again. He was intimate with his sexual triggers and they'd been the same for as long as he could remember—sexy lingerie, tight little black dresses, pencil-straight skirts and fitted jackets. Corporate wear. The clothes Ashley wore.

Katrina didn't wear clothes like that. No one in Bear Paw did, and yet here he was getting hard without a single trigger in sight. *Nothing* in this town was familiar or as he'd expected it to be. In a desperate attempt to make sense of this unwanted attraction, he was putting it down to dislocation madness. Added to that, he thought she'd just said she wanted to teach him to fish.

He rubbed his jaw. "Yeah, look, Katrina, is that some kind of a Montana thing, because really, I'm not interested."

She shook her head. "I mean, I'll teach you how to do the stuff like finding a stud and hanging a painting."

An image of her standing next to him with her scent swirling around him and him in a constant state of being hard and telling his body to heel had him dropping his leg back down onto the floor. He stood up. "That's really not necessary."

Her stance widened. "Oh, it really is. If word gets out you can't unclog a drain, you're not going to get any respect in town."

"I'm not a fricking plumber. I'm a doctor!"

She stood her ground at his raised voice and gave him her *you're clueless* look. "You're a man first, Josh, and in Bear Paw that counts for everything. No self-respecting cowboy is going to come see you if they find out you can't do some basic home maintenance chores."

He ran his hand through his hair. "That's ridiculous."

A slight frown marred her forehead. "Exactly how many men between twenty and fifty came to see you at the clinic this week?"

"I don't keep a mental record."

"Ballpark."

He thought back. He'd seen a lot of seniors who'd told him how Randall had always done things and had then questioned every piece of medical advice he'd given them. He'd seen a couple of reluctant teens who'd been brought in by their mothers. They'd sat silently through his explanations and had avoided all eye contact. The rest had been women and children.

She must have seen the realization on his face. "None, right? It's so hard to get men to see a physician, and out here, guys are toughing it out. Montana has one of the highest suicide rates in the country, so it's your duty as a doctor to be able to relate to these men. If you learn some basic skills, then you can hold your own in a conversation at the big boy's shed."

Talking with Katrina was like being on a slippery slope and not being able to get a foothold. "What the hell is the big boy's shed?"

"The hardware store."

"The hardware store? I don't think so. If patients want to see me, they come to the clinic."

"Yes, but if they don't see you around town and get to know you, they're going to hold off coming to see you."

He hated that her logic made a certain crazy sense, given his less-than-enthusiastic welcome from the townsfolk. "I swear to God, I've come to the twilight zone."

"Just small-town America, which is the heart and soul of this great country of ours." She unclipped her tool belt, revealing her firm, toned thighs that matched her compact body.

Glorious legs.

He hauled his gaze upward and he'd just finished telling himself they were short legs and he much preferred long ones when he caught sight of her narrow waist and generous breasts. The memory of them pressed up against him had heat burning through him, and he moved his gaze again, quickly seeking her face. Aiming for a nonsexual part of her. A safety zone.

Green eyes watched him intently from behind those square glasses—glasses that gave her a sexy gravitas. Hot damn, but there was nowhere safe to look.

"Come on," she said. "There's no time like the present."

He cleared his throat, buying time so when he spoke he wouldn't sound like a horny teen. "For what?"

"To go to Addison's and buy, among other things, a plunger, pliers and a pocket knife. You can drive." She flicked some keys out of her pocket and threw them at him.

He shot his arm out sideways, catching them, and he immediately tossed them back to her. "I have a car."

She threw them straight at him again. "We're aiming for street-cred, Josh. Drive the truck."

Sexy or not, her "I know best" manner irritated the hell out of him and sarcasm broke through. "If I'm impressing cowboys, shouldn't I be riding a horse?"

Her very kissable lips tweaked upward. "That comes later."

Damn it, but he knew her well enough to know she wasn't kidding.

Chapter 6

Overworked physician, tapped out nurse, missing receptionist, grumpy patients. Please bring coffee when you can. Order coming. Millie x

Katrina half smiled and half grimaced at the text on her phone. It sounded like Millie and Josh were having a heck of a morning. She hadn't seen Josh in almost a week. Not since their field trip to the hardware store and their first lesson of basic home maintenance 101. The visit to the store had gone better than she'd expected. In his khakis, oxford shirt and suede shoes, he'd stood out from the flannel-shirted tradesmen and the western-shirted cowboys, but he'd shaken the hand of every guy he'd been introduced to and had accepted their unsolicited advice on tools.

She'd been surprised and impressed. She had brothers and she knew how hard they found it to take advice from anyone. She wasn't at all surprised, however, when he'd bought the most powerful and expensive cordless drill in the store. He might lack tool knowledge but he had the Y chromosome that loved power in all things.

Under her instructions, he'd used it to hang the last door and he'd wanted to use it to insert picture hooks into the wall until she'd removed the drill and handed him a hammer. Part of her wondered how many random holes she was going to find when she next visited. The one good thing about that afternoon was she'd discovered that by focusing on teaching him, she'd put a stop to her body's lust-fest. She'd been able to show him how to do a variety of odd jobs and not once had she dropped anything or caused him any harm. Most importantly, the unwanted desire that her body had indulged in on the sofa hadn't returned. All in all, it had been a win-win afternoon.

So how do you account for the X-rated dreams?

Thankfully, her phone beeped again with the clinic's coffee order, saving her from having to answer her subconscious.

Fifteen minutes later, when her shift ended, Katrina walked into the clinic holding a cardboard drink carrier. Apart from the pale blue paint on the walls, it looked pretty much the same as it had when she'd worked here before she'd run off to explore the world beyond Montana.

Bethany Jacobs, a waiting patient, immediately pointed an accusing elbow crutch at her. "They don't have time to stop for coffee. I've been waiting almost an hour already. Randall would—"

"Have kept you waiting just as long," Katrina said, cutting off the complaint. She knew too well how it only took one emergency to throw a day out completely. She also knew people coped better if they knew what to expect. "I'll take these coffees back and try to find out how much longer the wait will be."

She found the nurse practitioner crouched down in front of the drug refrigerator, muttering to herself.

"I bring coffee."

Millie looked up and put her hand on her heart. "You're a lifesaver."

Katrina laughed. "If only it were that easy."

Josh backed out from behind a curtain talking. "Millie, can you make an appointment for Bailey's cast check and—"

He suddenly paused mid-glove-strip with his foot on the trash can pedal. "Katrina?" His dark gaze flicked over her from top to toe.

Her body gave a collective sigh on the back of a jolt of heat.

The bin lid closed with a clang. "Why are you here? Are you sick?"

His terse words centered her. *He was looking at you diagnostically. Stop being pathetic and get yourself under control.* "Coffee run. Millie sent out a mercy call." She passed him a cup after he'd dried his hands, being careful to avoid any accidental touching of fingers or backs of hands.

He shot Millie an easy smile. "And that's why you're my favorite nurse practitioner."

Millie rolled her eyes and grabbed her coffee. "I'm your *only* nurse practitioner and I want to move to the ER full-time. Sweet-talking me isn't going to work. I'm not doing my job and being receptionist, too."

"Where's Amber?" Katrina asked, thinking about the rumblings in the waiting room.

"We're not totally sure," Millie said, "but there's a rumor she left town last night with the lead guitarist from the band that played at Leroy's. I could understand it if he'd been any good, but he really wasn't."

"And she chose a hell of day to do it," Josh said. "It's not even ten thirty and we've had a broken arm, an episode of chest pain and an asthma attack." He downed his coffee in three big gulps as if he were uncertain he'd get another chance to drink it while it was hot.

Katrina tried not to stare at the way his throat worked as he swallowed. She totally failed.

The reception bell rang and Millie hurried off to answer it.

"It's probably Bethany," Katrina said. "She's pretty angsty and I told her I'd ask you how long before she's seen."

"The swollen ankle?" said Josh with a frown. "The gastric reflux and the rash are before her. I gave everyone a number so they'd know."

Numbers? Katrina sighed at his body-part descriptors. "Josh, these people have names."

He crossed his arms. "Not today they don't. Without a receptionist, it's a triage system."

The ER doctor was doing what he knew best, but it wasn't going to win him any fans among the patients of Bear Paw. Randall had dispensed health care with some TLC and fishing advice thrown in for free, and the town had loved him for it. But she knew that if she told Josh that, he'd just get that tight look around his mouth and say, "I'm not here to be friends with them. I'm here to treat them."

She'd thought that after their visit to the hardware store, he might be starting to understand that unlike Chicago, there was no separation between living and working in Bear Paw. They were one and the same. Obviously, she'd gotten that wrong. Couldn't he see he was making things harder for himself?

Why do you even care what he does?

She railed at the unwanted question. *I don't. I care for Bear Paw. The town deserves a doctor who sees them as people, not a series of body parts.*

If you say so . . .

Millie came back down the corridor, her usually happy face creased in a scowl. "I swear if Bethany points that crutch at me one more time I'm going to break it over her head."

Josh snorted. "Katrina will give you a stern lecture if you do, although you'd probably get brownie points for knowing the patient's name."

Millie looked between them, momentarily confused, before turning to Katrina with a sigh. "But you know what she's like."

And Katrina did. Everyone in town knew. "Bethany's lonely, so she creates drama to be the center of attention. If you let her vent and she feels heard, she'll deflate like a balloon and be very accommodating."

Millie's eyes lit up and she clapped her hands together. "Josh, I've got the perfect solution. Katrina can be receptionist today."

"Excuse me?" Katrina squeaked out in panic as Josh said, "I really don't think—"

"I can't run the prenatal clinic and be the receptionist," Millie said firmly. "We've got a waiting room full of patients running amok, the phone is ringing off the hook and no one is going to get their test results or follow-up appointments today. That's going to make the rest of the week a nightmare." She folded her arms across her chest. "Josh, did you know Katrina is an RN?"

"Yes, but—"

"No buts." Millie was on a roll. "Katrina, you're done for the day at the diner, right?"

"Yes, but—"

"I said no buts. We need your help, don't we, Josh?"

Josh ran his hand across the back of his neck, clearly as uncomfortable as Katrina, but Millie had them both over a barrel. If either of them refused, they'd be considered to be unhelpful and unreasonable.

"Just for today." Their reluctant words rolled over one another's in a mix of high and low melodies.

Millie, oblivious to the fact that neither of them was thrilled about the arrangement, high-fived them both.

———

BY six o'clock, Josh had cleared the backlog of patients that the morning's emergencies had caused. He had to hand it to Katrina—she made a hell of a better receptionist than Amber. He'd been ready to kill Millie when she'd suggested Katrina work with him for the day. Hell, he'd barely survived being in close proximity to Katrina in the house when she'd been showing him how to find a stud. Fortunately, he'd managed not to utter, "I'm right here, baby," thus saving himself not only from making a lame joke but also from looking like a total jerk.

Born and raised in Connecticut, he'd always prided himself on being smooth and sophisticated. Ashley had once told him it was his urbane polish that had seduced her, although on reflection it was probably his father's bank account and the hope Josh's would one day exceed it. Sure, he'd been out of the dating game a few years, but that shouldn't change the way he'd always approached women, and jokes like that had never featured in his repertoire.

Damn it, he didn't even want to date and he certainly didn't want to date Katrina. But there was something about her that took the veneer of style that had been instilled in him at birth and cultivated in him ever since and stripped it back to expose a primeval longing. He totally blamed it on the hicksville effect of Bear Paw. He'd only been here two and a half weeks and it was draining his soul.

Perhaps Ashley had been right in refusing to come.

No way. They'd looked at all the options for both of their careers and together they'd made the decision to go first to Chicago for two years and then go rural for three. She'd been the one to break her side of the deal.

I'm not coming to Montana, Josh. Ask your father for the money so we can stay in Chicago. Ashley's steel-edged voice sounded in his head, and the anger he thought he'd locked down sizzled so strongly he threatened to combust. Sucking in some calming breaths, he forced himself back to examining the test results he'd ordered yesterday and earlier today.

Bethany Jacobs's lab results concerned him. She'd need to come back for another appointment to discuss her rheumatoid arthritis. The woman had a difficult personality and a litany of health issues as long as the elbow crutch she liked to wave around. He smiled, remembering how Katrina had calmed her down—how she'd calmed down all the patients.

At first he'd thought the fact that she'd insisted on introducing each patient to him by name was a direct shot at him for having given people numbers, but he'd quickly worked out she was giving him a heads-up on their major concerns. She'd obviously talked to all of them before they'd come into the exam room, discovering exactly why they'd visited the clinic today. It meant he'd been able to go directly to the most vital problem, and it had saved him having to decode a list of rambling complaints before he got to the source of the problem.

The intercom beeped and Katrina's matter-of-fact voice burst into the room. "Josh, can you please come to the treatment room. We've got a walk-in who probably should be in the ER."

He pushed backed his chair on a buzz of anticipation. ER work was his first love. He was addicted to the unpredictability of it, and it was always way more exciting than the mind-numbing monotony of clinic work. He hated that Bear Paw had lured him with the promise of ER work by glossing over the mandatory clinic hours. Hours that dominated each week.

Striding the short distance to the treatment room, he slipped in behind the curtains. A large man wearing a hospital gown lay on his side on the gurney.

Katrina was pulling up a modesty sheet. "Mr. Dreyfus, if zero is no pain at all—"

"It's twenty," the man gasped, drawing his legs up.

"And ten is Jesus suffering on the cross," Katrina continued dryly without skipping a beat.

"Nine point eight. You've gotta help me."

Josh walked around the gurney so he could face the man. "Hello, I'm Doctor Stanton. Exactly where does it hurt?"

"My ass. It's like a fire poker's stickin' me every time I move."

"Are hemorrhoids a problem?"

The patient shook his head.

Katrina handed Josh the chart, but it only consisted of the baseline observations she'd taken. "No history?"

She shook her head. "Mr. Dreyfus, Larry, is from out of town. He's been staying at the motel and says the food there's upset him, which is a shame, as Nancy is usually a fabulous cook."

He caught the hint that perhaps it wasn't the food that was the problem. "How long since you emptied your bowels, Mr. Dreyfus?"

"This morning."

That ruled out the obvious. "Okay, well, I'll need to examine you and—"

The muffled but distinctly tinny sound of Bach suddenly started playing. Josh knew it wasn't his cell and he glanced at Katrina. "Your phone?"

She shook her head.

"It's my phone," Larry moaned, his entire body tensing.

"Is it in your jacket or pants pocket?" Katrina asked, picking up his clothing.

The cell stopped ringing. "It will have gone to voice mail," said Larry.

Josh placed his stethoscope on the man's lower abdomen, checking for bowel sounds. Larry's stomach gurgled, ruling out a bowel obstruction, and then a buzzing started up, followed by Bach, which deafened him.

He tore his stethoscope out of his ears just as Katrina said, "Are you sure you don't want me to answer your phone, Larry?"

For the first time since coming to Bear Paw, Josh had a case that reminded him of a big-city ER. "That's going to be difficult, Katrina, given that Larry's phone is in his butt."

Her eyes dilated so wide he could have floated in them.

"Oh. I see." She hesitated for a moment and then patted Larry jerkily on the shoulder. "No wonder you've got a pain in your ass."

Josh tried not to burst out laughing. She'd just managed to combine sympathy with total understatement.

Larry's face burned fire-engine red. "I had my cell on the bed and I slipped after the shower and fell on it. Damn motel floors."

Josh tried hard not to roll his eyes. He'd heard this story many times before—how men slipped and fell on an amazing assortment of objects. He'd long given up on questioning them on exactly how phones, cans of drink, axe handles and pool balls ended up inside of them. "We'll X-ray you to locate the exact position and hopefully be able to remove it without transferring you to Great Falls for surgery."

Larry paled. "Surgery? Will my HMO cover it?"

Josh tried not to sigh. Did people really think they could stick things in places where they didn't belong without any risk of damage or HMO scrutiny? "One thing at a time, Mr. Dreyfus. X-ray first."

"I'll arrange it," Katrina said, reaching for the wall phone.

———

"SO Larry's discharged along with his phone, which I put in a ziplock baggie," Katrina said an hour later with a slight shake of her head. It had been a long time since she'd worked in a clinic, and she'd forgotten the wild and wonderful cases that came through the door. "Do you think he'll actually keep using it?"

Josh shrugged. "I suggested he get a smartphone. The shape alone should be enough to discourage him from falling on it."

She laughed. "We can only hope."

He checked his watch as he shut down the computer. "Seven thirty. I think we can call it a day. It's not too shabby a time to finish up, given there were moments when I thought I'd still be here at midnight."

He rubbed his jaw, which was now covered in day-end stubble. "You turned a crappy day around, Katrina. Thanks for helping out."

The crisp and unexpected praise warmed her, but thankfully, not in a sexual way. Just like when she'd been teaching him how to attach a towel rail to a wall, working with him today in a professional and clinical capacity seemed to have established the much-needed boundaries. Boundaries she'd struggled with at other times. "No worries. Besides, Millie wouldn't have spoken to either of us if I'd said no."

He grinned. "For sure." He leaned back in the office chair resting his hands behind his head and gave her a long and contemplative look. "You're good at what you do, so why aren't you working as an RN?"

I'm so not telling you the real story. She wrapped her hands around the edge of the desk she was leaning on, welcoming the discomfort against her palm. It blocked the memory of Brent. The lies. The utter feelings of wretchedness. But Josh had an intransigent look on his face, so she knew she had to give him part of the truth or risk an interrogation.

"I've been unit manager of a large cardiac catheterization lab for the last couple of years."

Surprise lit up his eyes. "That sure as hell wouldn't have been around here, then."

"No. It was at Jefferson back in Philadelphia."

"Impressive." A combination of interest and bemusement played on his cheeks. "And yet, of all the places you could have taken a break in and made coffee—"

"And pull beers."

His brows shot to his hairline. "I did not know that."

She matched his brow rise. "You would have if you'd started socializing and met some people at one of the two bars in town."

The edge of his mouth tightened the way it always did when she commented on his lack of connection with Bear Paw. "As I was saying, of all the places you could come do unskilled work, you chose Bear Paw?"

"Hey, there's skill in pouring beer and making coffee."

He gave her a long look.

She shrugged. "I grew up here, my family's here and I have a house here, although that didn't quite turn out exactly as I'd planned." She gave a wry smile. "Anyway, I was tired and losing enthusiasm for the job, so it seemed like a good idea to come home and visit. You know, family ties and all that," she finished brightly.

He stood up. "No, not really."

She thought about what he'd said the other day about his father. "You're not close to your family?"

"We do the holidays," he said curtly. "So, if I'm at your house, where are you staying?"

"I'm at the ranch house with my family."

"How's that working out?"

She wasn't going to talk about that, either. How she loved

her dad dearly but he drove her crazy treating her like she was barely out of high school. "Fine."

As he stood up, he reached around her to lock the filing cabinet and his arm brushed hers. It took everything she had not to gasp as a wave of sensation raced up her arm, landed in her chest and fanned out from there. Every hair on her arm and every cell in her body stood to attention saying "more please."

He flicked the key and dropped his arm, but his gaze stayed locked with hers, as if he were looking for clues. "Well, I'm glad it's you and not me, then. I couldn't think of anything worse than having to move back in with my parents."

"Oh?" The word came out breathy and flirty despite all her good intentions to sound totally normal. "Not even working in Bear Paw?"

"You've got me there." He grinned down at her through long, thick lashes. "Mind you, Larry made me feel like I was back at Mercy."

He was so close, and just like on the couch, she started to feel her brain shutting down as her body took over. Somehow she managed to stammer out, "Thank goodness for traveling salesmen, then. Making you feel at home."

"Indeed." A curl brushed her cheek as he dropped his head in close and the scent of peppermint rushed her. "And now I know you're really a city girl at heart, things might just be looking up."

The timbre of his voice and the erotic touch of his breath against her ear sent a shock of desire ricocheting through her. Silver spots danced before her eyes and her legs trembled. Despite her knowing it wasn't a good idea, her gaze moved up to meet his like she was a puppet on a string. The fire she'd glimpsed in his eyes once before burned brightly there again, calling up her own need and inviting it to come play.

She raised her hand and cupped his cheek, his day's-end stubble gently grazing her palm.

He groaned and, tantalizingly slowly, traced the outline

of her top lip with the tip of his finger. Like a match to paper, she went up in flames as heat and joyful anticipation rocked her. She opened her mouth under his touch, her tongue licking the tip of his finger before her lips sucked it inside her mouth.

The black pupils of his eyes bled into the silvery gray. "Dear God, you're killing me." As he withdrew his finger, his other hand curved around the back of her neck and he kissed her.

His lips fused with hers with the perfect amount of pressure, and his taste of coffee and almonds flooded her—drenching her with his masculinity and making her crave him even more. His hot and enticing lips gently yet erotically explored her mouth as if it were a delicate flower at risk of being bruised if crushed. His tongue slowly explored her top lip, and then he turned his attention to her bottom one with the same single-minded determination of a man used to being thorough. He licked. He sucked. He nibbled.

Her blood turned into a river of sensation, carrying bliss to every cell of her body, both draining and energizing her all at the same time. The kiss was deliciously restrained and divinely decadent. Honor and lust—a kiss of the ages. A kiss any woman would envy.

A kiss that was driving her wild. She wanted to shake the control and unleash the passion.

Tingling from head to toe and desperate to really taste him, she opened her mouth under his, flicked out her tongue and invited him in. He didn't hesitate. He branded her with his heat and his need for her, both giving and taking, and her knees buckled. She grabbed onto his shirt and he staggered backward, bringing her with him.

A crash of metal made her eyelids fly open. A dressing cart had careened into the wall, scattering gauze, bandages, syringes and tape onto the floor.

The sight chilled her. Memories hammered her.

Not again.

She pulled her lips from his, her chest heaving. "I'm not doing this."

His glazed eyes seemed to struggle to focus. "Doing what?"

"Kissing you at work."

He ran his hand up her spine, gently tugging her back in close to him. "I beg to differ. It seems that you're most definitely kissing me at work."

And it was amazing. She swallowed, pulling together every splintered piece of determination she had into some semblance of a whole. "Well, I'm stopping now."

"That's a damn shame. I never took you for a quitter." He stroked her hair. "Why?"

She pressed her fingers into a steeple and grappled to find a plausible answer that wouldn't betray her past. "Because it's so cliché. So Hollywood. The doctor and the nurse . . ."

He grinned at her. "Actually, a lot of those shows are doctors getting it on with other doctors, so you're good."

"No." She shook her head as temptation swamped her so strongly she threatened to drown. "I'm not good at all."

He dropped his head in close again and whispered against her hair, "That's even better."

Flashes of what it would be like to strip him naked and climb on top of him made her flimsy resolve crumble like short pastry.

Remember, there are consequences. Big, bad ones. It's so not worth it. She spun out of his arms, this time putting cool air and distance firmly between them to shore up her resolve. "Good night, Josh."

Somehow, she forced her legs to carry her away from him and out into the night.

STUNNED, Josh watched Katrina walking out the door through a fog of arousal. Every part of him wanted to catch her by the wrist and spin her back into his arms, but he was so hard, he was locked where he stood. That and the fact that she'd made it very clear the kiss was over. He'd never forced himself on any woman and he didn't intend to start now. What wasn't clear was why she'd stopped the kiss. And hot damn, the girl could kiss.

The woman can kiss.

The intensity of her kiss had been unexpected. Perhaps he'd gotten a hint of possibilities when she'd sucked his finger into her mouth, but the moment she'd deepened his testing-the-waters kiss, he'd experienced a side of her he never would have guessed existed. In so many ways she was the epitome of control—organized, focused and bossy. Hell, she'd been telling him what to do and ticking him off from the moment they'd met.

But nothing about that kiss was controlled—not for either of them. It had scorched him before delving down deep and pulling up a response he hadn't experienced in a long time. It had made him feel hot, human and oh so horny. It had made him feel totally alive in a way he'd forgotten.

And then she'd pulled back.

His heart rate slowed to normal, returning his blood to all of his body parts, not just his dick, and his brain kicked back in, asking questions and demanding answers. Why had he kissed her? Exactly why had she stopped? And if she wouldn't kiss him at work, did that mean she'd kiss him someplace else?

He couldn't answer a single one of them.

Chapter 7

For the third time in six weeks, Shannon waited outside the middle school principal's office. She stared down at the highly polished linoleum floor and then up at the display cases filled with photos of smiling faces. Students holding trophies aloft for wins in sports, music, science fair and other academic achievements.

A sharp pain pierced her heart. It wasn't because Hunter's picture wasn't there and it wasn't because she'd never have a bumper sticker on her car that said *I am the Proud Parent of an Honor Roll Student*. It was because all of the faces looking out at her were happy. Hunter was so far from happy that it was breaking her heart.

The office door opened and the principal, Gary Folger, walked out with his hand on Hunter's shoulder. "So tomorrow's a new day, Hunter, with a chance to make it a great day."

Hunter's head was bowed. "Yes, sir."

"So you write your apology letter to Mrs. Ambrose tonight and bring it with you tomorrow."

"Yes, sir," Hunter mumbled as he tried to edge away from the principal's hand.

"Good man. I'll look forward to reading it." Gary Folger gave Shannon a tired smile. "He can't return to class until he's written the letter."

She nodded. "I understand." She'd spoken with him and with the guidance counselor on the phone earlier. Neither conversation had eased her mind any. Hunter was monosyllabic with every adult he came in contact with and had been for a year, well before she'd bought the diner and moved him here. It wasn't that he'd objected to the move, but then again, he hadn't been enthusiastic, either. His guarded ambivalence to everything worried her the most.

She wanted to offer her hand to Hunter like she'd always done when he'd been in elementary school, but he was fourteen now. If she tried it, he'd give her that look of teenage incredulity that said she'd lost her mind, so she clutched the strap of her purse instead. "Let's go home, buddy."

He grunted and walked down the hall a good six steps in front of her, jamming his baseball cap down hard over his eyes. He didn't say a word until they were in the car and she was reversing out of the lot. "This place totally sucks."

She held back a sigh. "Honey, if you'd called any of your teachers back in Topeka a moron, you'd be on trash collection for a week instead of writing a letter."

"I'd rather do that."

And she knew he would. Writing was a form of torture for Hunter. He had a bright mind, but the messages got crossed somewhere between his head and his hand. "Well, you can put out the trash for me at the diner and write the letter."

"Aww, Mom, that's so not fair."

"It's more than fair," she said, taking a left turn. "I didn't raise you to disrespect your teachers or anyone else for that matter."

Hunter slumped in the seat, his bottom lip pouting and his arms crossed. "I hate this place."

He'd said he hated Topeka. "You like the skate park."

He shot her a disgruntled look. "Yeah, but you hardly ever let me go."

Hardly ever was every weekend and one night during the school week. She pulled into the parking space between the diner and their house and threw the gearshift into park. "If you go write the letter now, do your math and put out the trash, you'll still have time for a quick skate before dark."

"I could go now and do that stuff after."

"Nice try, buddy, but no."

He glowered at her before grabbing his backpack, climbing out of the car and slamming the door behind him.

She watched him stomp into the house, and when the screen door banged shut, she dropped her head on the steering wheel, squeezing her eyes closed. When Hunter was one, she'd thought being a single mom was hard, but this? Watching her once loving and affectionate child vanish behind a wall of irritability and unhappiness made those periods of sleepless nights and teething seem like a cakewalk. When was parenting going to get easier?

One day you'll understand. The words her mother had hurled at her when she was seventeen and pregnant rumbled in her mind. She lifted her head and gazed heavenward. "I guess this is what you meant, Mom. Any tips?"

But all she heard was the drumming sound of a woodpecker, hammering home the fact that she was on her own with this and all things, just as it had always been.

———

BEAU hung up his hat, pulled off his mucky boots and washed his hands at the basin in the back bathroom before entering the kitchen. Being taught how to wash his hands by Bonnie was one of the first things he remembered about arriving at Coulee Creek ranch as a bewildered five-year-old.

Used to a tiny one-bedroom apartment, the scream of sirens and the screams of his mother, the vast space of the ranch and the bellows of the bulls had initially terrified him. Now it was the other way round. Thankfully, he didn't have the need to go to Billings or even Seattle very often, but when he did, the noise, the crowds and the traffic made him want to leave the moment he arrived.

He picked up the basket of chopped wood for the wood-burning stove and walked into the kitchen. It was the heart-beat of the ranch house and his favorite room. It always smelled great, and he automatically breathed in deeply as he'd done for thirty years. He stopped short. Instead of the sweet scents of cakes and cookies or the mouthwatering aromas of roasting beef and crispy potatoes, all he got was a faint tang of ammonia with a lemon chaser.

He couldn't remember the last time he'd come into the kitchen at this time of the afternoon not to find something cooking in or on the wood-burning stove. Bonnie fed the family as well as the seasonal ranch hands who helped out at branding and roundup time. Right now, they were build-ing the corral for the branding weekend, and usually his mother was baking to beat the band because come Satur-day, thirty or more people would be on the ranch to help. His father had sent him to check on her because she'd been expected down at the corral with the midafternoon snack for the workers.

Bonnie was sitting at the large, scrubbed pine table staring out the window at the imposing jagged mountains in the distance, which still had a smattering of snow on their peaks. Even if branding weekend weren't coming up, usually at this time of the day she was busy doing some-thing like tending to her vegetable plot.

He set the basket down. "Mom?"

She turned from the window, her face lined with weari-ness and surprise. "Beau. I didn't hear you come in, honey. Is everything going okay?"

"It's all good. Dad asked me to bring you down more wood for the stove and to collect the cake for coffee break."

Startled, she pressed her hand to her throat. "Oh my gosh. Is that the time?"

"It's gone three."

"I didn't realize it was so late. The slices and the cakes are over there."

Two white boxes clearly marked *Shannon's Home-Style Baking* sat on the counter. The memory of vivid sky blue eyes ringed by chocolate lashes slugged him. He pushed it aside. "Why are you buying food from town?" *Again.*

"I'm not," she said quickly. "Katrina brought the baked goods home because they hadn't sold and, well, there's no point wasting good food."

His mom never wasted anything. Ranch life had taught her to be frugal, and she'd been an expert recycler long before it became mainstream. "I guess it's kinda handy Katrina's working there."

Bonnie grimaced. "Seems a waste of her talents, don't you think?"

Beau never questioned anyone their choices if they were legal. He figured, like him, they had their reasons for doing what they did. "She seems happy enough."

"I don't think she's happy at all," Bonnie said quietly.

Beau swallowed. He really didn't want to get into a discussion about feelings. He reached for the firebox handle on the stove. "Do you want me to s-stoke the fire for supper?"

"Yes, please." She pressed her palms against the table and stood up quickly. Her face immediately drained of color and she pressed her hand to her side.

Concern rippled through him. "You okay, Mom?"

"I'm fine. I just stood up too fast, is all." Pressing her lips together for a moment, she steadied herself and then walked to the counter and pulled on her apron. Waving her hand at him, she said, "Go take that food to the guys. I've got work to do."

His moment of unease retreated as the very capable woman he knew and loved returned. He grinned. "Yes, ma'am."

Scooping up the boxes, and with the scent of brown sugar and chocolate assailing his nostrils, he walked to the door. The aromas took him straight back to the diner—to questioning eyes, pink lips and sun-streaked blond hair. Straight back to the fool he'd made of himself, and his ears burned hot at the memory.

He didn't get it. For years he'd been more than content with the company of his dog, his horses, the cows, the guys he worked with and the family. It was a good life—so much better than it might have been—and there was no reason for any of it to change. Sure, there were moments of loneliness, but that happened to everyone, and now and then, when he felt the need, he had a mutual arrangement with a woman in Kalispell. She didn't want more from him than that, and he didn't have it to give, so it suited both of them.

Despite growing up with two female cousins, women perplexed him and at high school they'd taunted him, which was why there was absolutely no reason to suddenly be associating the scent of chocolate and brown sugar with the new diner owner. Or thinking about the touch of her hand in his. No reason at all.

He stepped out onto the back porch and whistled for his Australian cattle dog. With Scout by his side, he marched straight back to the corral, where he was surrounded by cows with big brown eyes whose gaze never once made him stutter.

———

THE bar was quiet for a Thursday night, and Katrina had washed every glass and wiped every surface. The jukebox was playing a country song about the agony of love, and she desperately wanted to flip it to something loud and with a heavy beat, but the guy with the flowing beard who'd chosen the song had a look in his eye that said *leave well enough alone.*

All the customers had their meals and drinks, and sadly, that left her with time on her hands to think. Thoughts kept pinging in her head, and every single one of them was something she wanted to forget.

Like Brent's totally screwed-up ethics. How had she not known things weren't as they seemed? The fact that she was back in Bear Paw and justifying to herself that working at the diner and the bar was what she wanted, but it had only taken one session working at the clinic to remind her how much she missed nursing. And *that* kiss. More than anything she didn't want to still be thinking about that mind-altering, bone-melting, addictive kiss, but her mind and her body kept reliving it in minute detail when she least expected it. It was as if the kiss had unleashed her sex drive, which she'd locked down tight since leaving Brent. And it so wanted to play.

Why the hell did it have to be Josh who'd kissed her and lit her up like Christmas lights? Why not a cowboy or some guy from out of town? Someone safe. Nothing about Josh was safe. He was arrogant, snarky, lacking in people skills and, worse than all of that put together, a doctor. Given her track record, he was her worst nightmare, so why did attraction flow between them like the snap and crackle of electricity? She didn't want to be one of those women addicted to men who treated her badly, and she was determined not to let herself down again. Bear Paw was supposed to be a refuge for her, not a pit of temptation.

No guy has ever kissed you like that.

Lah-lah-lah. Not listening.

Her phone buzzed, and as it was quiet and she was desperate for distraction, she read the e-mail. It contained the information she'd requested from the charity foundation in Ecuador. It came with a list of necessary vaccinations before travel and a selection of available dates over the next year when she could do a rotation at a children's orphanage.

She became aware of a rumble of voices greeting people and, shoving her phone into the back pocket of her jeans, she looked up into a smiling and familiar face. Happiness filled her. "Ty Garver. How are you?"

He leaned over the bar and gave her a warm and friendly kiss on the cheek. "Better for seeing you. Your dad said you were back in town, although he didn't mention you were working here. Have you met the new doc?"

Her mouth dried as Josh appeared at Ty's side, and somehow she managed to coordinate her jaw and her brain to say, "I have." *In fact the last time I saw him, I had my tongue down his throat.* "Hi, Josh."

He tilted his head in a way that said *I totally remember what we were doing last time we met.* "Katrina."

His deep voice rumbled around her and she locked her

knees against the delicious heat that streamed through her. *Argh*. This was the problem. Ancient biology meant she found this type of guy attractive. As a modern-day life partner, it had disaster written all over it. She had a PhD in that.

Pushing two coasters out toward both men, she said, "So what can I get you?"

"Two beers," Ty said, utterly unaware of the tension that flowed between her and Josh. "I met the doc in the hardware store looking hungry, and I told him he hasn't lived until he's tried one of Leroy's burgers."

Her hand paused on the beer tap and she stared at Josh. "You were in the hardware store?"

He met her gaze, only unlike last week when it had burned so hot and bright, it was now back to its more usual observing yet slightly detached expression. "I was. I'm installing a water filter for my coffee machine."

Ty paid for the beers. "I hear you. I installed one for mine but, word of advice, Josh. With this crowd, it's probably best not to talk about coffee machines in the bar."

Josh raised his glass. "Thanks for the tip."

"I'll get your burgers," Katrina said, walking away pinching herself to check that she really was alive and still in Bear Paw. It was necessary because not only had cowboy Ty Garver developed a taste for real coffee, Josh had just accepted some advice from a local without looking like he was sucking on lemons.

JOSH glanced around at the bar. There were plenty of wooden tables with matching country-style chairs with turned legs that looked like they'd been new about twenty-five years ago. There were some booths along one wall, and closer to the bar was a small stage. Two cowboys were playing pool and being cheered on by two young women who looked to be barely legal drinking age. Beer and hard liquor seemed to be the drinks of choice. He couldn't see a single glass of wine anywhere.

When he'd accepted Ty's invitation, he'd had no clue

this bar was the one where Katrina worked, but he was fast learning that it was easier to avoid the common cold than to avoid Katrina McCade. After the way she'd kissed him, he wasn't certain he wanted to avoid her one little bit.

He'd been in town for three weeks and four days, and although the shock at how small the place was had faded slightly and he was slowly finding a routine at work, he hadn't banked on the loneliness. Soul-sucking, mind-numbing loneliness. Sure, he saw people every day, but most of them were patients. The small staff at the hospital was nice enough, but he missed the rush and pace of a city hospital. He missed having other doctors around to discuss cases with and to chat about wine, vacations in warm places and, hell, in a pinch, even golf.

Every day in Bear Paw seemed to be forty-eight hours long, and to make matters worse, he couldn't sleep. It was too damn quiet. It was light for longer. The moon was brighter than a streetlamp, the crickets were too damn noisy and the howling of the coyotes gave him chills. And last night, thoughts of Katrina—her vanilla and sunshine scent, the silkiness of her hair, the way her breasts had pressed into his chest—had him hard for half the night.

"Josh, do you play sports?"

Ty's question thankfully broke into his reverie just as his heart rate was kicking up. "I run."

Ty grinned. "Run east and it's flat. Run west to climb. You been to Glacier yet?"

Bear Paw was on the road to the national park, and Floyd had told him to expect a lot of tourists calling by the ER during the summer months. "Not yet. I'm pretty much hostage to the town. If I'm not here, there's no doctor."

"We're used to that." Ty sipped his beer thoughtfully. "You should make plans to go. Randall will surely cover you for the occasional weekend, and camping there in the summer is magic. It's the best place in the lower forty-eight to see the northern lights."

Memories of visiting the planetarium as a kid on a field trip prompted his memory. "The aurora borealis? Seriously?"

"Yep. This is God's own country out here."

Katrina arrived with two red baskets, each one containing an enormous burger and a side of fries. "Here you go."

"Thanks, Katrina," Ty said with an easy smile. "Are you helping out on Saturday?"

She nodded. "Sure am. Everyone's helping out on Saturday."

Everyone? Josh had no clue what was happening on Saturday.

"It's been a long time," Ty said with an indulgent look on his face. "You still remember how to rope?"

She punched him playfully on the arm. "I'm Montana born and raised, Ty Garver. That never goes away."

Okay, then. Josh was feeling like a third wheel as well as feeling decidedly out of the loop. "What's happening on Saturday?"

"Branding," Ty said, lifting the bun on his burger and squirting ketchup underneath it. "All the ranching families help one another out. This weekend it's Coulee Creek and next weekend it's at my ranch. It's a fun time and there's usually a barn dance at the end of the day. You should come."

"I doubt you'd enjoy it, Josh," Katrina said quickly.

Interesting. This from the woman who'd been pestering him to interact with the locals from day one. It sounded a lot like she didn't want him at the branding. The thing was, he'd never responded particularly well to being told what to do. "Why do you say I won't enjoy it?"

"It's dusty and mucky work."

"You think I've never gotten down and dirty before?"

Her eyes did that wide-eyed thing again, dilating into pools of sea green warmth. "No, of course not . . . it's just . . ."

Oh yeah. God, she was gorgeous when she was flustered, and she'd just answered a question he'd been asking himself for days. Despite her telling him she wasn't going to kiss him at work, she was clearly still attracted to him. And hell, after nights of reliving that kiss and the husky way she'd said, *I'm not good at all*, he'd accepted the attraction was mutual, no matter how little sense it made to him. Added to that, he couldn't face another weekend of long, empty hours to fill between emergencies. Besides, sparring with Katrina came under the heading of fun.

She pressed her hands to her hips and nailed him with a look that said *don't even think about it.* "You don't have any boots."

He scratched his jaw. "Granted, that's an obstacle. I can't possibly imagine where in a town filled with cowboys I'll be able to buy a pair of boots."

Ty laughed. "He's got you there, Katrina. Besides, it's our duty to show our new doctor the real Montana, right?"

Josh saw the war of emotions on her face. The woman raised with country values versus the experienced city woman who wanted to give him the bird. She slapped the bill for the burgers down next to him. "Bring work gloves. You'll need them to protect your hands."

He watched her return to the bar, her tight behind clad with blue jeans and swinging seductively as she walked. He swung his attention back to Ty and realized the cowboy had also been watching Katrina.

"We dated back in the day and I know that tone," Ty said, looking curiously at Josh over the top of his beer. "Exactly what did you do to tick her off so much?"

"I come from out east and I arrived in town," he quipped, using a local expression and hoping it would stop the conversation right there.

Ty's forehead creased in a slight frown. "Katrina's been living out east for a long time now. Gotta be more than just that."

No way in hell was he admitting to an ex-boyfriend of Katrina's that he'd kissed her senseless and that she'd returned the favor. Especially not to the only guy who'd extended a hand of friendship to him since his arrival in Bear Paw.

He slowly shook his head back and forth and went for the default setting in guy-talk. "Who knows with women, right?"

The cowboy glanced toward the bar where Katrina was pulling beer and then back at him. "Amen to that."

Chapter 8

Katrina wrapped her hands around her coffee mug and gazed out the double-glazed glass doors toward the mountains. The sun was rising, hitting the peaks with pink and gold, and she smiled as anticipation fizzed in her veins. She'd always loved spring on the ranch. It was so fresh and pretty and full of hope. The mountains still had pristine snow on their gray and craggy faces, but the plains were emerald green with lush, new growth—perfect food to grow baby calves.

Exactly how many, she'd find out today. It was years since she'd taken part in a branding, and she was looking forward to getting back in the saddle and keeping busy. Keeping very busy all day roping calves and well away from Josh. As a newbie, he'd be on the ground in a branding crew with the kids. She smiled at the thought of Josh being bossed around by her young teen cousins.

Serves him right. She hoped they rode him hard.

An image of Josh on his back with her hands splayed against his naked chest exploded in her head. *No. No. No.* She was not doing this. She was so not allowing herself to fantasize about having sex with him. Not today when she'd be seeing him.

Not ever because you're being sensible about men now, remember?

Oh, why had she tried to talk him out of coming today when she knew he didn't like being told what to do? What she should have said was, "You must come to a branding and see how a ranch works so you understand your patients." That would have kept him far, far away from the ranch.

"Megan, Dillon, time to go," Kirk called as he reached for his hat. "Beau's already out there and way ahead of you."

"Just as soon as I've finished my flapjacks," Dillon said, his words muffled by a full mouth.

"I'm good to go, Dad." Katrina set her coffee mug down on the table. "I saddled Benji before breakfast."

Her father frowned and glanced at Bonnie. "Actually, we have you down for food today."

No. I need to be up in the saddle and far away from Josh. She looked toward Bonnie. "Mom, do you really need me?"

Her mother, who was stirring a pot on the stove, pressed her hand to her lower back. "Actually, honey, I do."

Disappointment rammed her. Her mom didn't usually ask for help. "What about Megan? We could swap and she could help with the food."

"I want to rope." Megan gulped the last of her coffee and stood up.

"You roped last year and you'll rope next year." She hated how whiney she sounded so she shot for logic. "I may not be here next year, so it makes sense for me to rope today."

"Katrina," her father sighed. "We've got hundreds of calves to brand and I need experienced hands in the saddle."

"I'm experienced. I've got more experience than Megan."

He shook his head. "I'm not sure you have. It's been years since you spent a long day working on a horse. We're feeding a bunch of people today and I want you on the ground helping your mom with the food."

Frustration simmered and she opened her mouth to yell

that she was a grown woman and if she wanted to ride, she'd damn well ride, but her mother spoke first.

"It will be fun, honey. This way you get to talk to everyone, and I know the Ellisons are keen to hear your news."

Fun? A day spent dodging Josh without the advantage of a horse? She mustered a smile. "Great fun."

"Good. It's settled," Kirk said, jamming his hat on his head. "Isn't your boss from the diner coming today?"

"Yes."

"Well, you know better than leaving a guest on their own. She can help you and your mom."

She ground her teeth. Living at home was going to kill her.

———

BEAU had been roping cattle all morning. As the sweet sound of the lunch bell rang out, he pulled his neckerchief away from his face. A whoop of delight went up from the crews in the portable corral, welcoming the break in the branding, vaccinating and ear tagging of the calves.

He rode out of the corral, following the other cowboys toward the line of horse rigs and outfits that declared it was a branding day. Swinging out of the saddle, he tethered his horse in some sweet grass. "Enjoy that, Scotch," he said, patting the horse's neck. "You deserve it."

Ty Garver slapped him on the back as they started walking toward the food line. "Not a bad morning's work, Beau."

"It's going okay."

"I hope it goes as sweet next weekend at my place." He pushed his hat back. "I thought Katrina was roping today."

"Nope. She's on food."

As if on cue, Katrina's voice sang out toward the growing crowd. "Y'all need to use the hand sanitizer before you eat."

"Aw, do we have to?" a group of starving teen boys moaned.

"No. Not at all. If you want diarrhea, then you go right ahead and skip it."

As the teens slouched back down the line, Ty said, "She sounds snaky."

Beau nodded. "She wanted to . . . ride but Dad put . . . her on food because . . . she hasn't roped . . . in so long."

Ty pumped sanitizer into his hand. "Hey, Katrina," he called out before leaving the line and walking over to her. "Can you rope for me next weekend?"

Beau moved along the line, his stomach rumbling in anticipation of the pulled beef that Bonnie always cooked on branding day.

"Hi, Beau. Do you want some bread to go with your beef?" Shannon Bauer, her blond hair scraped back in a ponytail and a smile on her face, was holding out a roll toward him.

His throat tightened, strangling all sound. Why the hell hadn't someone, anyone, in his family mentioned Shannon was coming? That way he'd have had some warning.

He sucked in a breath, squeezing it past a fast-closing throat that was intent on blocking all his words. "Sh-annon." It came out deep and censorious. *Just great.* He sounded like a disapproving minister.

Her eyes sparkled brightly. "I can't believe I'm here on a real ranch. I've always thought that cowboys wearing chaps and roping cows only happened in the movies or on dude ranches for the tourists. You know, like *City Slickers* or *Rawhide*?"

Just like the first time he'd met her, her words rushed out quickly and enthusiastically, in stark contrast to every hard-fought sound he ever made.

Despite phrasing a question, she didn't pause for a reply; in fact, she started to sing softly in a very lyrical voice. "Don't try to understand 'em, just rope, throw and brand 'em." She laughed self-consciously and her cheeks pinked up.

She looked utterly kissable. "Yes, ma'am." *Seriously? That's all you can come up with?*

But anything more and his stutter would take over. Fewer words were safer.

A slight crease marred her forehead and her gaze drifted down from his face, seeming to linger midchest before her chin jerked up. "You boys are mighty fine at what you do, but I guess you've all been riding a horse since you could walk."

He didn't count the years before he came to Coulee Creek. "Pretty much." *Say something else.* "Enjoying . . . the day?" *Geez, McCade, she already told you that.*

"Very much. I just wish my son was, too."

You have a son? The only good thing about having a stutter was there was no chance in hell of ever spontaneously saying something out loud that should have stayed unsaid.

"That's Hunter over there." She inclined her head toward a boy who looked about thirteen or fourteen.

She has a kid who's a teen. The kid's age was even more jaw dropping because Shannon didn't look much older than Katrina.

For whatever reason, the boy was sitting apart from the other half dozen teens his age. He had his head down over his lunch plate and earbuds stuck in his ears. Everything about him said *don't bother me.*

Beau was struck by his suspiciously clean clothes. "Didn't he want . . ."—*breathe in, breathe out*—". . . to be . . . in a crew?"

"I'm certain he did, but I'm his mother and it's my job to ruin his life."

He blinked. "Ex-cuse me?"

Her shoulders rose and fell. "I baked some of the desserts and I needed Hunter's help unloading the pickup. By the time we'd done that, it seemed everyone had a job to do. I suggested he just go join a group, but he said he doesn't know any of the boys. I guess they're ranch kids, so they don't hang out at the skate park after school."

The kid looked both miserable and shitty, and it stirred memories. "I'll find . . . him a crew."

"You'd do that?" Surprise and skepticism collided on her pretty face before a smile broke through. As she served him up a huge plate of meat and potato salad, she said, "Thank you so much."

"No worries." He found himself grinning back at her, feeling as exhilarated as if he'd just torn down the pasture on the back of Scotch and roped a runaway cow. He decided he definitely liked it when she smiled. It made her amazing blue-on-blue eyes glisten like sunshine on water and it lifted the weariness that clung to her.

"Stop hogging the line, Beau," Kirk said suddenly from behind him. "Move along, son. Some of us are starving."

"Hi, Kirk," Shannon said, turning her high-wattage beam onto his uncle. "Do you want some bread to go with your beef?"

That smile wasn't special for you. She smiles at everyone that way.

His rush of elation deflated as fast as it had come, leaving him feeling foolish. The way he always felt around women. He spun abruptly on his heel and headed over to the boy to honor a promise.

———

"DOC, you're way too good at that," Dillon McCade said with admiration as Josh quickly castrated yet another calf. "It makes a guy nervous."

Josh laughed. He'd spent the day vaccinating and castrating calves and he'd lost count how many scrotal sacs he'd sliced open. "Best keep on my good side, then."

"Hell, yeah." Dillon released the final calf of the day and slapped Josh on the shoulder. "Job done and now it's beer o'clock."

Josh glanced around to see all the other crews had packed up and drifted toward a couple of pickups with coolers in the back. Not normally a beer drinker, he was hot, he was sweaty and the idea of a cold beer made total sense. He pulled off his work gloves and started walking. "Sounds good to me."

"You made a pretty good ranch hand today, Doc," said Lyle, one of the cowboys, as he passed him a beer. "You've earned yourself some prairie oysters."

A couple of the guys slapped him on the back and a

cheer went up around the group. They raised their long necks in his direction.

For the first time since arriving in Bear Paw, Josh got a sense of camaraderie, and the idea of oysters made his mouth water. "That's great. I didn't know you cultivated freshwater oysters in the lakes around here."

"You might want to try cowboy caviar, too." Lyle turned and yelled, "Hey, Katrina, the doc loves oysters and wants to taste some of Montana's finest."

The crowd parted and suddenly Katrina was standing in front of him holding a platter of dip and chips. It was the first time he'd been this close to her all day.

Unlike all the other days when he'd seen her, today she looked like a cowgirl. From midcalf, her jeans were inside the most colorful and decoratively stitched cowgirl boots he'd ever seen, and her checked western shirt was tucked in behind a large silver belt buckle at her waist. All of it was neat and tidy and showed off her hourglass figure. The only part of her that wasn't controlled was her hair, the pink flush to her cheeks and her very kissable mouth. The jolt of lust slugged him hard, only this time he didn't fight it.

Her mouth twitched. "You want to try prairie oysters?"

"Sure, why not? Do you broil them or serve them raw?"

A few of the men laughed.

"How do you like them best, Doc?" another cowboy called out.

"I prefer them raw with some lemon juice and salt."

"Doc, we're sure gonna love watching you eat 'em like that," Lyle spluttered as laughter made beer squirt out his nose.

The rest of the men collapsed into gales of laughter. He kept hearing the words *lemon juice* and *raw*, and then the laughter would increase in volume again. He glanced at Katina, who was sucking her lips in as if that would stop her from laughing out loud, too, and her entire body was vibrating.

So much for camaraderie and a sense of belonging—

he'd just been made the butt of an in-joke. He hated the feeling of isolation that came with it, and it rammed home how much he missed his old life, the rush and buzz of a big city hospital and living with people who understood him.

People like Ashley and your father?

Yeah, right. Even his subconscious was punking him today.

Feeling foolish merged with strands of betrayal that Katrina had willingly entered into the joke and effectively put him on the outside. He took the platter out of her hands, put it on the top of a cooler and then placed his hand gently under her elbow. Propelling her away from the group, who were now laughing so hard they were holding on to one another for support, he ground out, "Want to fill me in on the joke? It's obviously very entertaining."

Her restraint finally broke and her musical laughter rained over him, pulling at his core of loneliness and disconnection.

"Prairie oysters are calves' testicles. They're also called cowboy's caviar, Montana tendergroin, swinging beef and calf fries."

"Very sophisticated humor," he said, not able to keep the sarcasm out of his voice.

"Oh, come on, Josh. Cowboy up. It's just a bit of fun. I bet you've pranked first-year interns."

He looked back at the guys who'd returned to drinking their beers and wondered if he'd overreacted. "So they pull that joke on every unsuspecting newbie?"

"They do." Deep smile lines bracketed her oh-so-sexy mouth. "You have to admit, it's pretty funny."

"Hilarious," he said dryly, enjoying the way she needed to tilt her head to look at him. She had a very pretty neck.

She laughed again. "Especially when you said you liked to eat them raw."

His stomach revolted at the thought. "I'd like to see them eat gonads."

"You will tonight."

He scanned her face for more teasing. "You can't be serious?"

She swallowed and then abruptly stepped back from him as if she'd just remembered something. She started walking. "I'm very serious."

He easily matched her pace. "So how do you serve these prairie oysters?"

"We bread them and fry them. I'm not a huge fan but it's something everyone tries once."

"In that case, I guess I better eat some tonight. I don't suppose there's any way you can cook them but serve them so they look raw?"

Surprise lit across her face. "And prank those boys right back? I'll see if I can think of something." They'd reached a gate and she opened it.

He walked through and turned to watch her close it, enjoying the fact she had to lean over to do it. She joined him and he noticed she was definitely working on keeping more than an arm's length distance from him. Every time he moved closer, she adjusted her position so there was definitely no chance of any accidental touching. *Damn it.*

She shoved her hands in her pockets as if she were reading his mind. "So how did you find your first branding day?"

First the physical distance and now neutral conversation. He kinda missed the snarky and distracted Katrina from the bar. "Loud. Who knew cows bellowed louder than the bass at a rock concert."

She laughed again and then seemed to stop herself as if having a good time wasn't an option. "Like all good mothers, the cows don't like it when their babies are taken away from them."

"It's not just the cows. There's the roar of the propane, the squeals of the calves, the neighing of the horses and the general yelling. I always thought country life was quiet, but it's as noisy as a Bears' game."

"I'm glad we're able to surprise you."

She walked into a barn and he followed her. The smell

of hay hit him the moment he stepped inside, and he realized he was actually inside a stable. Six horses raised their heads and gave him a long, curious look. He recognized four of them—they were the horses Katrina's father, brothers and sister had ridden today.

Katrina walked over to a horse he didn't know. It was brown and white with a long white slash down the center of its face, and it immediately nuzzled her neck. He instantly wanted to trade places with the horse.

He crossed his arms to stop himself from reaching out and touching her. "Your horse?"

"Kinda. Like Boy, he belongs to the ranch, but when I'm home, both Boy and Benji are mine again."

"So, why weren't you riding today?"

She sighed as she walked toward a stack of baled hay. "Familial responsibilities and expectations."

He knew all about that. "Why were you avoiding me today?"

"I wasn't avoiding you." But the startled look in her now wide green eyes gave her away. "I was busy and so were you."

"Katrina," he said, shaking his head. "Every time you got within three feet of me you made a ninety-degree turn."

"I did not." She cut the twine on the hay bale.

"Yeah, you did. And we've just walked a half mile with you dodging and weaving to keep a good foot and a half between us."

She snapped the pocketknife closed. "Get over yourself."

He laughed. "There's nothing to get over. All I'm saying is you don't have to turn yourself inside out to avoid me. I don't have a problem with the fact that you kissed me."

She pointed an accusing finger at him. "Let's get this straight, Josh. You kissed me; I was the one who pulled back."

He stepped in close. "Sweetheart, we both know you took my tentative kiss and turned it into every man's fantasy."

She shook her head so fast that her hair flicked his chest. "No. I was the one who stopped it."

"Because we were in the clinic." He brushed her hair behind her ear. "But we're not at the clinic now."

Her eyes shone with so many emotions that they overlapped one another and he couldn't decipher any of them except desire. It dominated and cast the rest in shadow. He waited for her to say or do something to tell him exactly what she wanted, but she stayed silent, so he lowered his mouth to hers.

He tasted salt, beer and restraint. He lightly nipped her lower lip.

She moaned, rose on her toes and opened her mouth under his, taking him in.

Thank you.

The memory of their other kiss fueled this one, and he explored her mouth, revisiting the places that made her kiss him hard in return. For nights he'd fantasized about touching her, and now he could. His hands spanned her waist and he tugged her in against him. Her breasts rose and fell against his chest, and her arms rose and she linked her hands around his neck.

God, she felt amazing. He wanted to feel more.

His hands tugged her blouse out of her jeans, and then he was touching hot, smooth skin. His fingers burned with her heat, and he explored her one vertebra at a time, pressing, kneading, feeling, until his fingers discovered her bra catch. Once he'd prided himself on being able to undo a bra with one flick of his fingers, but it had been a while. Ashley had used sex as a weapon.

He found the hooks and twisted. Nothing.

He hated looking clumsy. He tried a second time, adding a flick.

Thankfully, the bra opened and his hand sought the prize. He cupped round, hot, heavy flesh, loving the weight of it in his palm. Picturing what her breasts might look like, his thumb scraped across her already hard and raised nipple.

She cried out, the sound reverberating in his mouth.

Every ounce of blood in his body headed south. She was

so amazingly responsive, and every part of him wanted her. He wanted to see her naked, touch her and explore every inch of her body. His other hand reached to pop the buttons on her blouse.

She pulled away.

Jesus, not again. He was so hard he could barely see straight, let alone construct a coherent thought, and everything from her bright pink cheeks, her glazed eyes and her heaving breasts said she wanted him as much as he wanted her. "Katrina, you're killing me."

She licked her lips. "Are you married, Josh?"

"No."

She nailed him with a look that could have seared meat. "You sure about that?"

Indignation slugged him. "Of course I'm damn well sure."

"Engaged, then?"

He shook his head. "No. What is this, the Spanish Inquisition?"

"Girlfriend back east?"

"Not anymore." It came out harsher than he'd intended.

Her head tilted and her mussed hair swung sideways. "So you're single?"

A thread of panic ran through him that she was interviewing him as a potential partner. He wasn't looking for anything more than the roll in the hay he was hoping to get, but he wasn't having sex under false pretenses. "Categorically single. More importantly, Katrina, I'm intending to stay that way."

She smiled a wide and unexpected smile. "Excellent."

Stepping back in, she pressed her hands against his chest before rising up on her toes. "You passed." She kissed him hard.

Silver spots danced behind his eyes, and all he wanted to do was kiss her until they both collapsed in the hay. *I passed?* His brain kept snagging on the word and he pulled away. "Excuse me? What did I pass?"

"Everything." Her hands tangled in his hair, her fingers

playing in the curls as she pulled his head back to hers. "Even the fact you're not a surgeon."

The Stantons are surgeons. His father's censorious voice crashed into his head, and he set her back from him, his hands gripping the tops of her arms. "I'm not a surgeon? What the hell is that supposed to mean?"

Chapter 9

*W*hat just happened? Katrina felt as if she'd been side-swiped by a truck as Josh's usually warm gaze turned the dark blue gray of an ice storm. One minute he was ready to undress her, and now he was firing metaphorical daggers into her. Why had she even said *you're not a surgeon*? It wasn't like she wanted memories of her worst mistake right here with them in the barn, especially when they were making out.

You're almost thirty years old and you're making out with a guy in a barn. Surgeon or not, this doesn't come close to being sensible. New start, remember?

"It doesn't mean anything, Josh."

His nostrils flared. "People don't say things that mean nothing, Katrina."

The sound of a horn repeatedly beeping made the horses whinny and snort.

"Josh!" Dillon's voice rang out. "Katrina! You here? We need the doc."

Josh's arms fell away from hers and he strode out of the barn. She hastily rehooked her bra and finger-combed her hair as she ran after him. Dillon was in the yard, and the moment he saw them he called out, "It's okay. No one's bleeding to death."

"What's happened?" Katrina asked at the same time as Josh while they piled into the outfit.

"Some kids were riding the four-wheeler and Sam Duckett fell off the back. Nothing's broken and he was walking around playing after, but now he's just puked."

"That's not good." Again, Josh's words rolled over hers.

"You two have to start saying 'jinx,'" Dillon said as they bounced across the pasture they'd walked over only half an hour ago. He pointed through the windshield. "He's over there resting on the Ducketts' outfit."

"Do you have your emergency kit in your trunk?" Katrina asked Josh as they hopped out of the pickup.

"Yeah. Meet you there." He handed her the keys before jogging over to the Ducketts.

Katrina easily located Josh's sports car in a pasture filled with outfits and grabbed the backpack. She arrived to find Josh kneeling in the back of the pickup shining a flashlight in Sam's eyes.

The kid was lying on his back, his usually round and smiling face pale. "That makes my head hurt worse," he said, squinting at the light.

"Lucky I've finished, then." Josh gently palpated Sam's abdomen. "Does it hurt anywhere else?"

"You better not be playacting, son," Christopher Duckett said sternly. "You were running around just fine ten minutes ago."

"I don't think he's play-acting, sir," Josh said firmly. "I think he may have a concussion."

"Oh, is that all." Chris sounded relieved. "All my kids have had a concussion at least once. It's a rite of passage for boys."

Katrina, who'd wrapped a blood pressure cuff around Sam's arm, announced the reading. "Blood pressure's normal."

"There you go," Chris said, slapping Josh on the back.

"It's all good. We're sorry to have troubled you, Doc. We'll take him home and watch him. We know the drill."

Josh looked up from examining Sam's ears and nose. "Actually, I'd like him to come into the ER."

"Is that really necessary?" Chris asked skeptically. "Like I said, we know to check him every hour. Randall taught us that."

Josh's mouth tightened the way it did whenever he was questioned. "I strongly advise that Sam comes to the ER for observation."

"I feel sick," Sam moaned as he rolled over. He promptly threw up onto Josh's knees.

"Can someone go get his mother?" Katrina called out to the small crowd.

"She's with Bonnie at the ranch house," Chris added anxiously.

"I'm on it," Dillon replied, jumping back into the outfit.

Katrina threw a towel at Josh before helping Sam rinse his mouth. "Do you want to put in an IV?"

Josh nodded. "Two."

"Two?" It seemed like overkill, but when Josh raised his gaze to hers, she read real concern. "Two it is."

"None of my other boys puked, Doc," Chris said, looking worried. "Maybe going to the ER is a good idea."

"That's a good call, Chris," Josh said, rubbing anesthetizing gel onto Sam's arm. "This is so you won't feel the needles, Sam."

The twelve-year-old boy swallowed. "I don't like needles."

"We'll be quick," Josh said. "Katrina and I are going to put a needle in each arm at the same time. Who do you think will win?"

Katrina smiled at his distracting techniques and tightened her tourniquet. "I'd be betting on me, Sam," she said as she slid the needle into the vein. "I used to do this every day."

But Sam didn't answer—his eyes were rolling into the back of his head.

"He's fitting." Josh threw his arms over Sam's spasming

and jerking legs to protect him from further injury. "Save the line. We're going to need it for Dilantin."

Katrina did her best, wrapping her hand around Sam's jerking arm.

"Oh my God. Sam!" Amy Duckett's frantic voice split the early-evening air. "What's happening?"

"He's got a concussion," Chris said, his voice wobbling over the words.

As the boy's limbs relaxed and Katrina taped the IV firmly in place, Josh turned to face the parents. "This is a lot more than a concussion. I'm almost certain that when he fell off the bike, he hit his head and this has caused bleeding between the brain and his skull. Now the blood is pressing on his brain."

"His brain?" Amy gripped Chris's arm. "So he needs to go to the hospital in Billings and see a brain doctor?"

Josh shook his head. "I'm sorry, but there's no time for that. We need to get him to the hospital in Bear Paw and drill a hole in his skull to drain the blood." He turned back to Katrina. "Do you know if the hospital's got a burr hole kit?"

She didn't know, but she'd seen Josh's new drill in his trunk. "Dillon," she yelled out to her brother. "Get Josh's hand drill and a half-inch drill bit from his trunk. Lyle, find a hand brace. Now."

"You can't drill into my son's head," Amy screeched.

"I have to, Mrs. Duckett," Josh said quietly but firmly. "If I don't, he'll die."

"Amy," Katrina said, trying to soften Josh's very true but bald words. "I know it's scary but we don't have time to try to convince you. You're going to have to trust us on this."

"But he's my baby," Amy sobbed.

"Do it," Chris said. "Save our son."

"I'll do my very best," Josh said, administering drugs through the IV. "Katrina, you drive and I'll stay in the back with Sam. Let's go."

Katrina jumped down just as Dillon ran up clutching a yellow drill and a container of bits. "Why do you need this stuff?"

"No time to explain," she said, hauling open the driver's

side door. "Call the hospital and tell them we're coming and we'll be doing burr holes. Then go get Mom and Dad and drive the Ducketts to the hospital, okay?"

"Burr holes." Dillon repeated the unfamiliar words carefully as he closed the door and leaned in. "Sam's going to be okay, isn't he?"

Josh banged on the roof of the cabin. "Drive, Katrina. Now."

For the first time, she heard real fear in his voice, and she pressed down gently on the accelerator. The moment she'd maneuvered the vehicle out of the pasture and onto the road, she called the sheriff and asked for an escort into town. Mitch Hagen met them halfway into Bear Paw, and even with his support, it was the longest drive of her life.

When she pulled up outside the hospital, Millie was waiting with another nurse and a gurney between them. The moment she got out of the car, Josh yelled, "Go sterilize the drill bit and meet us in the OR."

Breaking every rule of an emergency, she ran.

———

JOSH had intubated Sam and marked his temple with a Sharpie. Now he was gowned and gloved and staring at the CT scan, memorizing the exact position of the blood clot. The exact spot where he had to drill.

"He's stable," Millie said as she rhythmically squeezed the airbag, keeping Sam oxygenated. "And both the saline and mannitol IVs are running well."

"I've shaved his temple," the scout nurse said before stepping back out of the way.

Josh wasn't particularly religious, but he sent up a prayer to whichever deity was listening. He lacked an anesthesiologist and he'd wanted a neurosurgeon on the other end of the telephone guiding him, but despite many phone calls, no one had been able to locate one, and now they'd run out of time. So here he was. About to operate.

The last time he'd stood in an OR was the day he'd walked away from surgery. Now he had to drill a hole in a kid's head. The irony wasn't lost on him.

Katrina, fully scrubbed, watched him from behind her surgical mask, her green eyes fixed on him. Unlike the many other times when he'd found it almost impossible to read her, right now he clearly saw worry and faith. Faith in him. It had been a long time since he'd seen that sort of confidence in him in the eyes of a woman. If Ashley had ever had it, it had started to fade the moment he'd given up surgery. It had vanished completely by the time he'd left Chicago.

"We're ready," Katrina said. "You're ready."

He was never going to be ready, but he appreciated the support, given he was embarking on unknown territory and he had no choice about it. "Let's do this."

He sucked in a breath and held out his hand. "Scalpel." Making a quick, clean incision was the easy part, and Katrina controlled the bleeding while he used retractors to locate the white bone of Sam's skull.

Katrina handed him the drill. "It's got a clutch mechanism, Josh, so don't stop halfway or it will reset."

Shit. "Good to know." Plunging a drill bit into Sam's brain wasn't something he wanted to do. "Millie, hold his head perfectly still."

"Doing that now," Millie said calmly, although her eyes held grave concern.

"Here we go." His gloved hand closed around the drill. "One, two, three."

The whirr of the drill screamed loudly, seeming to go on forever. Every part of him yelled at him to stop. Surely, he'd gone in far enough? Panic sang loudly and he desperately wanted to overrule the clutch mechanism. His finger twitched, ready to do it, but the drill suddenly stopped on its own.

He huffed out the breath he hadn't known he was holding and exchanged a look of relief with Katrina. "How do I reverse this sucker?"

She pointed her gloved finger. "That button there."

A moment later he'd removed the drill and was using a blunt hook to carefully remove bone fragments. There was no sign of a clot or blood. Dread gripped him. What if he'd gone in at the wrong place?

Acid burned his gut as he raised his gaze to the scan seeking reassurance before dropping it back to Sam's head. *Come on. Bleed.*

After three excruciating seconds, a tiny trickle of blood finally dripped onto the surgical drape. It quickly increased to a steady flow.

Sheer relief threatened to buckle his knees. "Thank God."

"You did it," Katrina said softly, her eyes filled with empathy.

"I did it." A crazy-sounding laugh burst out of him. "I don't want to ever have to do it again."

"Hopefully, you never will." She passed him the drain tube. "I had no idea there would be so much blood."

"You and me both," he said, meeting her eyes and reading admiration in their depths. "How's he doing, Millie?"

"Vitals are stable, Josh. You did great."

"Excellent."

As he stitched the drain tube in place, the scout nurse said, "The MontMedAir helicopter just touched down with Will."

"Who?"

"Doctor Will Bartlett," Millie qualified overly fast in contrast to her usual laid-back drawl.

"He's part of the MontMedAir team," the scout nurse continued. "Usually they send a nurse and a paramedic, but when it's serious like this, he's on board. Every nurse in the hospital gives thanks when that happens."

"Why's that?" Katrina asked.

The nurse fanned herself. "Because the man looks like he just stepped off a surfboard and onto a Hawaiian beach." She laughed. "I guess that should be an Australian beach. He has the sexiest accent."

"In that case," Katrina said, her eyes dancing, "I'm definitely looking forward to meeting him."

"Can we focus on the job at hand, please," Josh reminded his distracted nursing staff.

The OR phone rang and all conversation stopped while the scrub nurse answered it. "It's the neurosurgeon from Billings."

"Now he calls," Josh said, rolling his eyes as the paradox of the situation hit him. But nothing was going to dent his euphoria that he'd located the clot. Sam wasn't out of the woods yet, but at least he'd soon be in the neurological unit at Billings. Josh knew he wouldn't be able to stop worrying for a few more hours. "Put the good doctor on speakerphone so he can speak with Bear Paw's scratch neurological team."

———

AN hour later, Katrina drove a quiet Josh back to his house. His mouth may have been still but his body sure wasn't. He was wound so tight that he vibrated with constant motion. If he wasn't drumming his fingers on the dash, he was tapping his foot. She wondered if it was the effects of the emergency or if it had something to do with his reaction in the barn when she'd said he wasn't a surgeon. Or both. Either way, she sure as heck wasn't about to ask him about it.

She'd figured Sam's accident had saved her from herself and talking about the kiss was just tempting fate. Besides, unlike this afternoon, there was not one iota of a sexual vibe coming from him at all. She'd inadvertently killed it, which was probably a very good thing.

She turned Bessie into the driveway of the cottage and pulled up behind Josh's car.

"How did that get here?" Josh asked, finally breaking the silence.

"Bear Paw magic."

He rolled his eyes. "Really?"

She shut off the engine. "Totally. That and Dillon had your keys."

He laughed, and for some reason, the deep timbre sound made her think of smooth and velvety red wine. Merlot that warmed from the inside out.

"Thank him for me."

"I can do that."

"But will you?"

This time she rolled her eyes at his pedant tendencies. "Yes, Josh. I will thank him for you."

It had been a huge few hours on the back of a long day, and she'd expected him to open his door and say good night, but instead he stayed seated, staring out into the starry night.

Shafts of moonlight cast shadows on his face, outlining his weariness. "Tough day."

"Very tough day."

"A brown trouser day," he said with a wry smile as he turned his phone over and over in his hand.

Without thinking, she reached out and put her hand over his for a moment, stopping the movement. "Sam's one lucky kid. Incredibly lucky to have you here, and you can probably afford to relax some now."

"Not yet." His leg started tapping again. "Not until I get the call from Billings."

That he was still so worried about Sam bothered her, and she could picture him pacing up and down until his phone rang. "When do you think that will be?"

"Around midnight."

"Do you want company while you wait?" *Can you hear yourself?*

Oh for heaven's sake, I can spend fifteen minutes alone with the guy without anything happening.

Yeah, right.

Surprise mixing in with gratitude lit up his eyes. "Yeah. A debrief would be good."

See? We're having a debrief. Two professionals supporting each other.

She hopped out of Bessie and almost ran into his back when he suddenly stopped and gazed up into the inky night sky.

"God, I never knew there were so many stars."

She smiled because she never got tired of watching them, either. "That's why they call it big sky country."

He crossed the short distance to the house and opened the door for her. "I thought they called it glacier country."

She stepped inside and walked directly to the kitchen. "Well, that, too. And there's Yellowstone, the Indian nations, the Wild West history. It's Montana. It's got everything."

"Everything very spread out." He opened the fridge and passed her a soda. "That really hit me today when I knew I didn't have time to evacuate Sam."

His cell rang and he stared at it for a moment. "This is it." Picking it up, he pressed it to his ear. "Josh Stanton."

She carefully watched his face, looking for signs of good news or bad as he listened intently to the voice on the other end of the line. But no matter how hard she studied him, she couldn't decode anything. The guy had a poker face.

As he listened, he rubbed his free hand through his hair and pulled his earlobe. Finally, he said, "Thanks for the call. I appreciate it," and he slowly placed the phone on the counter.

She leaned forward, anxiety making her chest tight. "So?"

He grabbed her around the waist, spun her around and then kissed her hard and fast. So fast it was all over before she'd realized it had even started. When he set her down, her body sobbed at the loss of contact.

"Sam's awake," he said, his face creased in a huge smile and alive with joy.

She raised her hand and high-fived him. "That's so great."

He nodded so fast his curls bounced. "His vitals are stable, he knows the date and the name of the president and he's told the nurses he's starving hungry."

She laughed. "He really is back to normal."

"It's a hell of a relief." He suddenly looked utterly exhausted and rubbed his face with his palms. "I gotta tell you, I really wasn't expecting to do brain surgery as part of my work here."

"This is Montana. Out here you have to deal with stuff a city doctor would refer on. You should write a paper about this."

He tilted his head as if he were considering the idea.

"Maybe I will. It will help keep my name out there while I'm out here." His picked up his can of soda and his hand trembled on the ring pull.

"Adrenaline overload?"

"Yeah. You know how it is." He leaned back against the counter. "It takes a while to fade."

And she knew what he meant. Her head was buzzing as well. "I keep replaying everything over and over. I was terrified most of the time."

"Yeah." His mouth twisted. "Me too."

His honesty surprised her. "No one knew. You did great."

"Not too shabby." His gaze narrowed slightly as his smile faded. "Especially as I'm not a surgeon."

Warning bells, emergency sirens and flares went off in her head at his emphasis on *surgeon*. It was exactly the same intonation he'd used in the barn—the word coming out through gritted teeth. "No, you're a talented ER physician."

"I am." He pushed off the counter, all coiled energy like a bobcat ready to pounce. "Thing is, the fact I'm not a surgeon seemed to bother you back in the barn."

She shook her head. "It didn't, but it obviously bothered you."

"Don't bullshit me, Katrina. You told me I'd passed except for being a surgeon."

"You misheard me." *You don't need to say anything else.*

Only Josh had the look of a wounded animal deep in his eyes, and something pulled at her to explain. "Truth be told, the fact you're not a surgeon was the deal-maker for me."

He stared at her for a moment, and then his sexy mouth curved up into a wicked grin. Running the tip of his finger gently down her arm, he said softly, "Deal-maker, eh?"

A spark of intense need jolted her so hard she almost fell into his arms, but the questions in her head stopped her. "You made it a deal-breaker. Why?"

His finger continued its journey, leaving her shoulder and tracing a line along her collarbone. "You seriously want to have this conversation now when we could be celebrating a hell of a good save?"

He's got a point. Listen to him. Her body begged her to give in to him as her blood thickened with growing desire. She fought it with everything she had. "Something upset you in the barn, and I'm a woman, Josh. We need to talk before we get intimate."

His eyes darkened into sparkling silver as his finger caressed the hollow at the base of her throat. "You didn't need to talk in the barn." He dropped his mouth to her ear. "In fact, if I remember correctly," he said huskily, "you were incapable of talking."

His voice took her back there and heaven knows, she couldn't deny it. She'd moaned at the touch of his mouth, at the touch of his hands on her hot and pleading skin and at the press of his hard body against hers. She'd been lost in the wonder of it all.

Her cheeks burned at the memory and embarrassment made her cross her arms. "You pulled away, Josh."

He lifted his head. "I guess that leaves us one-for-one, then," he said tightly.

She sighed. "So you're not going to tell me what's going on?"

"There's nothing to tell. I'm an open book."

She snorted. "No one who chooses to move to Bear Paw is an open book. They're usually running from something. The law, relationships, themselves."

He cocked one brow. "Speaking for yourself, are we?"

Damn it. He was too smart by half. "I told you why I'm back home."

"Yeah, you're taking a break." Nothing about his demeanor said he believed her. "Why I'm here is simple math. Bear Paw plus work equals less money owed on student loans, and that means after time served, I can head back east and afford to buy an apartment."

"That doesn't rule out running from something. For a man with a plan you're not exactly happy about it."

He tucked her hair behind her ear and goose bumps of anticipation skimmed across her skin. Smiling down at her, with the dimple in his chin dancing, he said, "If I tell you, can we stop talking and have sex?"

A burst of indignation swelled in her. "You're bargaining with me for sex. What an interesting line in seduction."

He stepped away from her, all of his tension returning fast. "Oh and your midforeplay interrogation in the barn wasn't?"

"So, you think we should have just rolled in the hay, no questions asked?"

"No, but you were all hung up on if I was single or not. Not one of your questions had anything to do with sexual health, which was the logical one I was expecting, given we were minutes from having sex."

A slither of panic scuttled along her veins. "I was *not* going to have sex with you in a barn."

But he hadn't heard her. She saw the moment on his face when he'd put two and two together. "The last guy you were with wasn't single, was he?"

She wanted to hide so badly it hurt, but his gaze had her pinned down with no place to run. "No. He was far from single. Only, it took me a lot of months to realize."

Skepticism crossed his face. "How could you not know?"

And this was the exact reason she never told anyone about Brent, because it left her looking like a fool. "Don't judge me on something you know nothing about."

He frowned. "But there had to be hints, right?"

Virtually none. "Not when you're both working a busy schedule, one of you is trusting and the other is a lying and scheming bastard."

"You've left a good job in a cath lab." He started numbering off on his fingers. "You're in Bear Paw and you told me you wouldn't kiss me at work." Intelligent eyes bored into her, and with terrifying clarity she saw all the pieces fall into place. "This guy was a cardiac surgeon you worked with, right?"

"No." But the word came out too fast, too defiant and way too protesting.

His face softened. "If it helps, they're usually arrogant bastards."

She hated that he knew. That he'd exposed the secret she'd held on to so tightly for so long. She didn't want his sympathy for her stupidity. "And you're not?"

He shrugged. "I might be arrogant from time to time but I'm not a bastard."

Memories of Brent's life-changing lie made her come out hitting. "I don't know you well enough to be sure."

"Ouch. And you once told me you weren't bitter."

He raised his can of soda to her in a mocking salute before draining the can. "Look, I'm on your side."

"Oh, sure you are. You just accused me of being blind and stupid."

"No," he said firmly. "You're doing a good enough job of that all on your own."

His words burned with an accuracy she wanted to deny, and she opened her mouth, but he spoke first.

"All I'm saying is that I know surgeons." He ran his hands through his hair. "Believe me, I know them well. My father's one, as was his father and his father before that."

Something about the way he said it made her recall the other times he'd mentioned his father. It had never been in a positive way. "So you're the renegade of the family?" she quipped, moving toward him, desperate to lighten the mood. Between the two of them, it had plummeted as fast as the thermometer in January. She hated the way memories of Brent left her feeling empty, worthless and angry. She craved to forget it all by kissing Josh.

"That's one way of putting it." He crunched the can in his hand and tossed it neatly into the trash can. "Thanks for the illuminating conversation, Katrina," he said, moving sideways and clearly dismissing her, "but it's been a long day and I'm beat."

Regret rammed her on so many levels it made her dizzy. He was rejecting her. He'd found out her secret—the one she'd held on to for weeks—and now he was asking her to leave.

She picked up her purse. "Fine. I guess I'll see you round."

His mouth firmed into an intransigent line. "No doubt, given there's no damn place to hide in Bear Paw."

Ten minutes ago, he'd wanted to get her naked and into bed. Now his entire body language was neutral—the detached doctor she hadn't seen for a while was firmly back in place. All of the exciting and vibrant post-emergency high that had been bouncing off of him had vanished, and along with it, all of his energy and spark.

She made her way to the door.

"Katrina?"

She turned. "Yes?"

"This"—he waved his forefinger back and forth between them—"is a perfect example of why talking is such a bad idea."

As she closed the door quietly behind her, both her sex-starved body and her sad and aching mind agreed.

Chapter 10

J osh was glad it was Monday. Saturday had been his best-ever day in Bear Paw, but Sunday had totally sucked.

He'd spent it feeling dislocated, lonely and cross. Saving Sam had highlighted how much he loved the buzz of ER work and how mundane he found a lot of the clinic hours. He was still pissed at Floyd for concealing the truth of his contract and at Bear Paw for not being what he'd thought. He was pissed at himself for having let the past he was certain he'd dealt with raise its ugly head and do its usual damage.

But he was even more pissed at Katrina for ruining what could have been an amazing night. A great celebration of their teamwork and success. They'd saved a kid's life. God, it was the ultimate high, a powerful aphrodisiac, but she'd gone and stuffed it up—complicated what should have been simple and amazing.

Shit. What was it about women and talking? He and Ashley had talked for weeks and weeks, and for what? She was still in Chicago, living the life she wanted—the one he'd helped her create—and where was he? West of civilization as he knew it. Granted, Bear Paw was a town with many good people, but he shared nothing in common with any of them.

Be fair. Ty's good company. Katrina's—

No. He didn't want to be fair with any thoughts to do with Katrina. He sure as hell didn't want to think about what that bastard in Philadelphia had done to her.

He checked for traffic—there was none—before stepping off the curb, crossing Main Street. He'd left his car at the garage for an oil change and was walking to the clinic. He passed by the hardware store where a group of men were standing outside in the almost summer sunshine, drinking coffee.

"Hey, Doc," Brody Addison, the owner of the hardware store called out to him, "I sold you that drill for making holes in wood, not skulls."

All the men laughed.

Grinning at the attention, Brody continued, "You need any more tools for the hospital, you let me know. A mighty fine circular saw just arrived in stock."

"Thanks," Josh said, walking over to the group, "but I'm not planning on doing any open heart surgery."

The man paled. "You serious? They use a saw?"

Josh grinned, enjoying the fun. "They sure do. They open the chest with it. It makes a hell of a lot of noise and bone chips fly everywhere."

The guys gulped their coffees and Josh stifled a laugh.

"So how's little Sam doing?" Brody asked a moment later, clearly shifting the subject away from the gory to the more important.

"He's good. He should be back home by the end of the week."

"Oh, that soon?" He slapped Josh on the back. "That's real good to hear."

"You might not be from around here, Doc, but you seem to know your stuff," another of the men added. Everyone nodded their agreement.

Josh reckoned this was probably as demonstrative as it was going to get, but he appreciated the taciturn sentiments.

It was certainly more than he'd gotten in the weeks he'd spent here, and it made a change from the grumbles that he did things differently from Randall.

His phone rang with an unknown number. "Excuse me, fellas, I should take this."

"Sure thing. You have a good day, Doc."

"Thanks." He swiped the touch screen. "Josh Stanton."

"It's Joe Beck from the radio station, Doctor Stanton. I hear you drilled a hole into Sam Duckett's head with your power drill."

Word had obviously spread. "I did emergency burr holes, yes."

"Right. Thing is, I'm getting calls from a lot of other stations in the state wanting an interview from you. Can we do a live telephone interview now?"

He started walking toward the clinic. "Sure. Go right ahead."

"And we're on air in five, four, three, two, one. Doctor Stanton, can you tell us what happened on Saturday night?"

Josh answered a series of questions from Joe about the decisions he'd made and why.

"So, Doctor Stanton, do you have to do these burr holes often?"

"Most doctors go their entire career without needing to do burr holes because there's always a neurosurgeon at the city hospitals, but this is Bear Paw," he said, loving that he could use the expression that had been said to him so many times. "I couldn't have done it alone, and I was so lucky to have help from Millie Switkowski and Katrina McCade."

"Well, they're both Montana born and raised, so you were in good hands. Any advice to the listeners out there?"

He knew it would be ignored but he said it anyway. "Wear helmets on four-wheelers."

"And there you have it, folks. That was Doctor Stanton, Bear Paw's new doctor," Joe said, concluding the interview just as Josh arrived at the clinic.

He pocketed his phone and pushed open the door. As he entered the waiting room, applause greeted him.

"Here he is," Doris said. "We just heard you on the radio, dear. You'll be as famous as George soon."

Millie leaned over the reception desk, her spiral curls springing. "Floyd hasn't found anyone yet to be reception-ist, so I told him to call Katrina and yes, you're welcome."

Bethany raised her crutch and pointed it at him accus-ingly. "You're late. So if you're done being a celebrity, I'd appreciate you starting work. I've got bingo at ten."

His fifteen seconds of appreciation thudded to a halt. Life in Bear Paw was totally back to normal.

———

HAVING let Benji have his head for the last mile, Katrina rode into the home pasture and her father strolled over and caught the reins. She swung out of the saddle. "Thanks, Dad."

"It's good to see you riding."

She grinned. "I forgot how much I loved this place."

He walked alongside her as they made their way to the barn. "Ty said you're roping for him on Saturday."

She gave him a sideways glance, wondering if this was a statement or criticism. "He's prepared to give me a go."

Her father grunted. "Of course he is. He's a single guy and you're a pretty girl."

Exasperation exploded out of her. "Dad, I'm a twenty-nine-year-old woman."

"I know you are, sweet pea. Doesn't change the fact that Ty might be trying to keep on your good side. You could do worse than Ty."

Believe me, Daddy, I already have. "Ty's a great guy, but I've been away a long time."

"And you're back now." He gave her shoulder a quick squeeze. "So what are your plans?"

"Brushing Benji, grabbing a shower and helping with supper."

"I meant what are your future plans? Are you staying in Bear Paw for good?"

An image of gray eyes, brown curly hair and a mouth that kissed like a god shot into her mind. An image of temptation.

It bounced off the paternal matchmaking and general frustrations of living back at home. "I'm going to Ecuador for three months."

Kirk frowned. "When?"

"Any day. I'm just waiting for confirmation of the travel details."

"You know the hospital would have you work there. They're always chasing staff."

She thought of Monday's phone call from Floyd offering her the clinic job, which immediately made her think of Josh. Again. She should have been relieved he'd backed off in the early hours of Sunday morning and that yet again, she'd dodged a bullet. Only thing was, she wanted to take one for the team. So badly. And she knew that was poor judgment on her part and it meant going back on every promise she'd made herself. Which was why she was going to Ecuador.

"I'll talk to Floyd tomorrow," she said to placate her father. It was the truth, only not quite in the way her dad thought. She needed to let Floyd know she wasn't taking the job. "Oh, before I forget, I rode to the west boundary and there's a hole in the fence near Ty's place. Two cows were in the coulee mud, but I managed to drive them out."

"Thanks. I'll get onto it now."

She thought about how back in the day she and her dad used to do a lot together. "I'll come, too. It will be fun."

He took off his cap and rubbed his head. "Actually, if you want to help out, give your mom a hand."

Annoyance prickled yet again and this time she cracked. "Dad, you know I can do any job on the ranch. Why are you always pushing me back toward the house?"

His bright blue eyes dimmed. "Because I'm worried about your mom."

The unexpected answer startled her. "Why?"

He sighed. "She's not been herself lately. Surely you've noticed?"

Katrina thought about the last few weeks. Usually, when she came home her mom fussed and wouldn't let her do anything to help. This time, she was aware of doing a lot more around the house, which she'd put down to the fact she was living back at home and not just visiting for a few days. "Has she said what's wrong?"

He shook his head. "Whenever I ask, she says she's fine. I wouldn't call her depressed, but she's not been herself. She doesn't—" He suddenly looked really uncomfortable. "Maybe it's the change. You're a nurse. Can you talk with her?"

Talk to her mother about menopause? The woman who'd never been sick in her life and considered illness a weakness? Not that menopause was an illness. Still, that would be one fun conversation . . . not. "I guess."

Relief swept across his face. "Thanks, sweetheart. I appreciate it. Are you working tonight?"

"No, Wednesday's my night off."

"How about I brush Benji for you and you go talk to your mom. Then, after supper, you and I take a ride and brush up on your roping."

She grinned. "It's a date."

Leaving her dad at the barn, she found her mom on her knees weeding the vegetable patch. "Hi, Mom."

Bonnie turned, but her welcoming smile immediately twisted to a grimace and she pressed her hand to her stomach.

She extended her hand to help her mom to her feet. "You okay?"

Bonnie ignored her hand and stayed put. "It's just a twinge. I turned too fast."

She thought about what her dad had said and kneeled down next to her and started pulling weeds. "Do you get twinges often?"

Bonnie didn't reply.

She suddenly got a flash of memory from Saturday— her mom standing with her hand pressed to her right side at the branding lunch. "Mom? Do you?"

"Okay, Miss Pushy, I do get them now and then. Usually when I twist or stand up too fast."

"In different places or always in that same spot?"

"Pretty much around here." She kept her hand pressed near her hip. "I'm sure it's nothing to worry about."

Katrina would have thought so, too, except for her dad's comments and the fact that now she thought about it, her mom had seemed less energetic for a few weeks. Come to think of it, her face looked thinner. "Have you been feeling nauseous at all?"

Her mother shrugged. "Little bit."

"Feeling tired?"

Bonnie sighed. "It's horrible. I feel like I'm wading through mud. I used to have so much energy. It's probably the change and there's nothing I can do. I'd feel uncomfortable going to see Doctor Stanton."

"Why?"

"I'm a fifty-five-year-old woman and he's a young man. If it's the change, then . . ." Her voice trailed off.

She sat back on her heels, thinking how she could reassure her. "Mom, it might not be menopause, but either way, it's a good idea to have some tests done. There are a number of things it could be, including a grumbling appendix or irritable bowel syndrome. I really think you should go see Josh and get his opinion."

"You think he's a good doctor?"

Josh Stanton might drive her crazy in many different ways, but there was no arguing that the man was a good clinician. "Mom, after Saturday, everyone in the district knows he's on top of his game."

"That's very true. Perhaps I should go see him."

"Wow, you must be feeling bad," Katrina said with a grin, bumping her mom's shoulders with hers.

Bonnie laughed. "I guess I'll make an appointment."

"Good idea. Sooner rather than later. Either way, you need a checkup."

Her mother pressed the trowel into the rich, fragrant soil and gave her a long, penetrating look. "You can't take the nurse out of you, honey, so why are you trying?"

Because I've made such a mess of my life. "Actually, I'm going to volunteer in Ecuador."

"Good heavens." Her mother visibly startled. "That's a very long way from both Philadelphia and Bear Paw."

And that was the general idea.

————

JOSH stepped out into the chilly morning air because, hell, he'd been up half the night and watching the sunrise seemed to be the only payoff for a crappy night. Plus, it would kill some time until his landlord arrived.

Katrina.

Landlord.

In a fit of frustration, he'd called her half an hour ago when he'd been woken up yet again by one of the many problems with the damn house. It had been eight days since Sam's accident, and during that time, he'd only seen her at the diner surrounded by townsfolk. Their conversation had been excruciatingly polite and hadn't ventured beyond how he wanted his coffee and the damn weather. It was the exact same conversation he had with most people in Bear Paw. The weather and their state of health. God, he missed the flirty banter.

You miss real conversation.

I don't miss being told what to do.

Now he was single, he had a choice. It made no sense to put up with difficult women, and Katrina ticked every single box on the "difficult" spectrum.

You'd have sex with her in a heartbeat.

I was the one who said no. He gave his subconscious the metaphorical bird.

And that was the dumbest thing you've done since you got here.

Not wanting thoughts of Ashley or his father to intrude on his day, he focused on the sun instead, which was just peeking over the horizon and spreading its orange and gold fingers across the sky. The morning star was still visible—it's white light bright and refusing to be dimmed by wisps of cloud.

He automatically turned toward the mountains—their

craggy grandeur always made him look and tempted him to start walking. He really must arrange to get to Glacier National Park now summer was only a week away. What was the point of enduring Bear Paw if he didn't use the one advantage this godforsaken place had over Chicago?

As he stood gazing at the snowcapped peaks, it took him a moment to realize there was no wind. God, he'd forgotten what it was like to stand outside without needing to lean forward, and he found himself grinning.

You used to get excited about the opening of a new restaurant and now you're excited about lack of wind?

Irritated by the thought he might be starting to obsess about the weather like every other damn person in this town, he turned at the rumbling sound of Katrina's pickup, happy to channel all his disgruntled energy onto the person inside.

The old rust bucket pulled to a stop, and to add insult to injury, she jumped out all perky and fresh after a full night's sleep. She grabbed a wire cage out of the truck. "Morning, Josh."

He dispensed with pleasantries. "There are rodents having a rave party in my roof."

"I do believe you mentioned that at five thirty-two," she said, her very kissable mouth twitching at the corners as her foot hit the first porch step. "Alliteration before seven in the morning. Well done."

"I've had hours to think about it," he said grumpily, resisting the sneaking temptation to smile at her teasing. "Be grateful I didn't call you at one oh-five, three twenty-seven or four fifty-six. Do you have any idea how loud the scratching and scurrying is?"

"Haven't had our coffee yet, I see." She handed off the toolbox to him before walking into the house.

"I need sleep, not coffee." He followed her inside, feeling hard done by. "It was bad enough being called into the ER for a tourist who'd decided that despite putting up with the pain of an infected toe for one entire week, she couldn't wait another eight hours to see me at the clinic but had to have it treated at midnight."

A flash of sympathy crossed her face. "I'm sorry you had a lousy night, Josh, but I didn't purposefully release rats, raccoons or opossums in your roof just to piss you off."

He didn't want to be placated. "So you say."

In stark contrast to Ashley, who was always impatient with him when he was overtired, Katrina laughed. A full-on, body-shaking laugh. In the face of that, his chagrin started to fade.

She continued to stand in the kitchen and eyed his coffee machine. "Poor Josh. It's a crappy start to the week. Let's have coffee first."

He shook his head. "No way. All I want is for you to commit mass murder."

"Oh. Okay." She didn't move and all her teasing suddenly vanished.

"Come on. Chop-chop. They're breeding up there by the minute."

Slowly, she pushed off the counter and headed toward the stairs.

Was he imagining it or was she dragging her feet? She usually did everything at top speed. He followed her, not complaining at all about the fact she wasn't bounding up the stairs but walking them very slowly. It gave him more time to enjoy the view of her sweet behind. "So how come you're up so early, anyway?"

She took each step one at a time. "You mean apart from being woken up by you? I've got a lot going on with work and getting ready to go to Ecuador."

"Ecuador?" Unexpected disappointment rolled in his gut. "As in South America Ecuador?"

She threw a grin over her shoulder. "There's more than one?"

"Very funny. Be nice to the guy who got no sleep. Why are you going there?"

"To be useful."

"Can't you be useful here?"

But she didn't reply. She'd cleared the landing and was walking into his bedroom. She stopped in front of the small door that led into the roof space, and putting down the cage, she opened the door and handed him a flashlight and a container. "This is the bait. Put it where you see scats."

He recoiled. "I'm not crawling in there."

"Why not?"

"It's dark, full of cobwebs and God knows what."

Her green eyes lit up with a dare. "Oh, so you called a girl to do it?"

The memory of her lush and curvaceous body pressed up against him sent his blood pounding. "No, I called a very capable woman."

"So you're happy for me to let it slip at the bar that you're scared of a few rodents? You do realize that the men of this town will never drink beer with you again."

"They love me now for saving Sam, so they'll forgive me my weak city ways." He grinned, enjoying the fact that for once, he was ahead in the game. "Besides, there was a case of bubonic plague in Oregon not that long ago and that's a bit too close to Montana for my liking."

"Oh, right, but you'll let me catch it?"

She definitely didn't want to go into the roof space, and hell, he didn't blame her one little bit, but he was having too much fun teasing her to let her know that. "Should you get the plague, I'll be happy to treat you with antibiotics."

"So reassuring," she murmured, looking at the door and chewing on her thumbnail. "Are you sure you're not feeling at all emasculated by letting me go in there?"

He shook his head. "There are many ways to be a man in the modern world, Katrina. Saving lives is my thing, and that's pretty heroic."

"So is going into that roof. What if we flip a coin?"

He laughed at the hope on her face. "There's no deal to make here, Katrina. You're my landlord, so face it: You have to go in there. And you know it because you came wearing your glasses." *Glasses that make you look incredibly sexy.*

Somehow, he stopped himself from reaching up and tucking some stray hair back behind her ear. "By the way, good to see you're being so OSHA compliant because there's likely a lot of dust in there."

Her in-charge demeanor faded and the totally together woman who faced down anything cracked. "But it's dark, and full of cobwebs and things that go bump in the night."

Her sudden vulnerability caught him tight, like a lasso, and he had a crazy need to let her off the hook. "So just call someone. Surely there's a pest control guy in Bear Paw."

Horror streaked across her cheeks. "I can't call Ralph. Only townies use pest control. Ranchers bait and trap and I'd never live it down."

"I swear this town has more crazy rules about who does what than anywhere on the planet." He took in her woebegone expression and, as much as he hated the idea, knew what he had to do. "What if I come in with you? I have no clue how to set up the cage, but if you do that, I'll spread the bait."

Her face filled with gratitude. "You'd really do that?"

"I'm as shocked by it as you are," he said, wanting to see her smile.

"Thank you. You're a good guy, Josh."

"Not that good," he said, putting on his best Mafia-style voice. "This is a favor I can call in at any time."

A scurrying noise made them both look down, and a mouse ran between Katrina's legs. She screamed and jumped onto him, wrapping her arms tightly around his neck and locking her legs around his waist. "Close the door," she squealed. "Close it now."

He staggered at the unexpected weight but managed to keep his balance as he kicked the attic door shut against other wandering rodents.

"Where did it go?" Katrina asked anxiously, lurching sideways to look.

Her abrupt movement, in the exact opposite direction from his, sent him tumbling backward onto the bed, bringing her down with him in a tangle of limbs.

Still clinging to him like he was driftwood in a choppy sea, her huge, green eyes stared at him from behind those sexy librarian glasses. "Sorry," she wailed. "Are you hurt?"

He did a quick mental inventory of pain and drew a blank. "Given our track record, surprisingly, no." He could still feel her heart beating hard and fast in fear against his chest, and he automatically wrapped his arms around her for reassurance. "What was all that screaming like a girl about?"

She bit her lip. "Sorry. I'm fine with mice in the barn or outside even, but inside they freak me out. There was a field mouse plague when I was a kid, and they were everywhere, including in my bed. Ever since then—" She shivered again and her body rubbed his from chest to thigh.

He groaned as delicious sensations thrummed through him.

She stilled. "What's wrong? Did I hurt you?"

"Not how you think," he managed to grind out as he went hard, his erection pressing determinedly against her thigh.

She must have felt him because her eyes darkened to the color of moss.

Weeks of sexual frustration peaked, overruling every logical argument about Katrina that he'd been telling himself.

"Don't look at me like that unless you want me to kiss you, and believe me, I desperately want to kiss you. And when I say kissing, I mean I want to start with kissing and finish with sex. That's sex without questions, no changing of minds halfway through, no talking unless it's 'oh yes, that' or 'do this' or 'don't stop.' Just two adults giving in to this insane attraction that's sparked between us from the start and finally doing what we should have done days ago."

He heaved in a breath. "Or not. The choice is yours and I'll respect it whatever it is, but decide now and decide fast, because right now you're killing me."

Chapter 11

It took Katrina less than a minute to decide. She was lying sprawled on top of Josh with the evidence that he wanted her badly pressing into her thigh. God knows, she wanted him, and she was utterly exhausted by fighting it.

She'd never had sex without the relationship part, but as she wasn't looking for a relationship and neither was Josh and she was leaving for Ecuador, it guaranteed there'd be no postsex awkwardness.

And the mouse had disappeared from the bedroom.

And he'd offered to go into the roof space with her, which was the sexiest thing he'd ever done.

She wound a finger through one of his curls. "Do you have condoms?"

He grinned at her and the next minute she was on her back and gray eyes full of desire stared down at her. "You're not the only person who's OSHA compliant, you know." He reached for her glasses.

She put her hand on his. "I'm totally blind without them."

"You don't need to see me," he said, his voice hoarse with need. "You only need to feel me."

Her entire body liquefied and she pulled his head down to hers and kissed him. His now familiar mouth fitted against hers perfectly and she unexpectedly sighed. Crazy relief-filled sensations streamed through her, devoid of all urgency. She'd thought that with the weeks of sexual tension that had vibrated between them, she'd want him hard and fast, but right now, she didn't want to rush a thing. She could lie here for hours luxuriating in the touch of his mouth romancing hers, and just let him kiss her.

She continued exploring his head, running her hands through his hair and loving the soft way his curls captured her fingers. His peppermint and pine scent circled her, and she breathed in deeply, imagining they were outside in a forest of trees. His lips slipped from her mouth and she tilted her head back to give him plenty of access to her throat.

He pressed a series of featherlight kisses along her jaw and down her neck, making her feel as if she were floating on air. Her hands fell away from his head as if they didn't have the strength to hold themselves up, and it was like being in a pleasure cocoon and she never wanted it to stop. His hair tickled her face as he reached the hollow at the base of her throat. He kissed it gently, reverently, and then he swept it with the tip of his tongue.

Every cell in her body snapped to attention with an electrifying whoosh of need. It vanquished every particle of blissful lethargy and she bucked underneath him.

He laughed and traced an X with his fingertip. "Erogenous zone number one."

"I think it's time I found some on you." She reached for the buttons on his shirt, her fingers trembling as she tried to unbutton them in the small space between their bodies.

He sat up and whipped the shirt off over his head, and she immediately pressed her palms to his chest, loving the solid feel of him against her skin. "Let me see . . ." She walked her fingers from his diaphragm up his sternum and across to his nipples. She flicked them with her thumbs.

He jerked and his eyes darkened to charcoal gray.

She laughed. "Score. Now where else . . ." She skimmed his skin with the tips of her fingers, but when she reached his navel, he gently circled both her wrists and pinned them over her head with his left hand.

"One erogenous zone at a time, Katrina." He pushed up her T-shirt and grinned at her bra. "Now, there's a nice surprise."

"What did you expect?"

He traced the line of lace that sat on the swell of her breast. "With the whole tool belt and work boot thing you have going on, which by the way I find incredibly sexy, I figured it would be plain."

Brent had always insisted she wear lacy bras and thongs. In fact, many of his gifts had been just that, to the point she no longer owned any plain underwear. Most of her had wanted to throw it all away, but the practical country girl in her had settled on replacing each item as it wore out.

She couldn't wrap her head around what Josh had just said. "You find my work clothes and tool belt sexy?"

"Oh yeah." He dropped his head and closed his mouth around her aching breast, sucking her through the red lace.

Her body exploded with a shower of bliss. "Take it off," she panted. "Please."

"In a minute." Still imprisoning her hands, he moved his mouth to her other breast and lazily tormented her a little longer.

She bucked and writhed underneath him and eventually he pulled her forward. In a flurry of hands and fingers, they tugged and pushed and pulled at each other's clothes and shoes until they were both naked. Gloriously naked.

She stared at him, soaking him up from the delineated muscles of his chest across the toned six-pack of his abdomen and down to his impressive erection. Pushing at his shoulders, she sent him backward and flung her legs over his. "If I didn't think it would give you a swelled head, I'd tell you that the reality of you naked, even fuzzily out of focus, far outshines the fantasy."

He grinned at her with dimples dancing. "I aim to please."

"So do I." She closed her hand around him, loving the hot and silken feel of him in her palm.

"Jesus, Katrina," he moaned as his hands reached for her. "Too much of that and I won't be pleasing you for another twenty minutes."

"Where's your self-control?" she teased.

"I lost it the moment I met you."

She didn't know what to say to that, and she didn't want to acknowledge the traitorous quiver in her heart, so she kissed him. Hard. Hot. Deep.

His need for her exploded in her mouth, and all that existed for her was him. His heat. His need. The thrust of his tongue dominating her mouth, the feel of his fingers sliding inside her slick and ready body and the pressure of his thumb doing duty on her throbbing clitoris.

After spending days in a state of constant arousal, her body didn't need much help. Sensation built on sensation and her muscles clenched desperately around his fingers, riding them, forcing them against that special spot sobbing to be rubbed. Pleasure became pain became pleasure, the difference infinitesimal, and she craved it all. Her nipples screamed, her lungs ached, her toes curled and she thought she'd explode with the sheer ecstasy of it all. Pulling her mouth away from his, she threw her head back and heard herself cry out as bliss rained through her. She collapsed in a boneless heap on his chest.

"A definite erogenous zone," he said before kissing her hair. "Although I think there are still a lot more I need to find."

She smiled down at him. "I hate to say it but you're really good at that."

"Yeah. I've still got it."

She thought she heard a thread of antagonism under the joking, but it skated past her orgasm-fogged mind. "I have a few skills myself."

He stroked her face. "Is that so?"

Her hand moved down to touch him again. "So name your poison. Hand or mouth?"

"You." He wrapped his legs around hers and commando-rolled them over. "I want to bury myself inside of you."

She shivered with joyful anticipation as he leaned sideways and grabbed a condom from the bedside table. "I can do that for you."

"Maybe next time."

He quickly rolled it on, but instead of entering her as she'd expected—as she craved—he kissed her thoroughly.

She nudged him. "Josh, I'm good to go."

He ignored her and turned his attention to her breasts. The final vestiges of her postorgasm torpor vaporized. "Josh, seriously, I'm so ready now."

"Katrina, you know better than that." Glittering eyes stared down at her and his forehead wore a fine sheen of sweat. "You know I don't like being told what to do."

"Sorry," she said with faux contrition. "I forgot."

"This might make you remember." He nipped and licked and kissed his way along the length of her belly until she was sobbing and writhing in desperation. Her muscles twitched against empty, desperate to feel him deep inside her, driving her to the point of insanity.

She wrapped her legs around his waist, tilting her hips toward him as her hands pummeled his back. "Dear God, Josh, you're killing me."

"Welcome to my world, sweetheart."

As he leaned down and swiftly kissed her lips, he entered her aching body.

Thank you. She closed around him, taking him in, urging him forward, wanting him so badly.

His control vanished and he thrust deep and hard, panting fast. She met each thrust with one of her own, her legs holding him tightly inside her, and the rhythm drove them both upward, spiraling toward release.

She felt him shatter and a moment later she joined him

as their bodies flung them out of their lives for a moment of magic and wonder.

They fell back to reality in a sweaty, panting heap.

———

JOSH rolled onto his back, his body limp with satiation, and he reached out his hand to find Katrina's. "You good?"

"I'm good. You?"

He rolled over to face her and kissed her on the nose. "Way more than good. Thank you, it's been a while."

"Yeah, me too."

Something about her expression worried him. "You're not going to go all weird on me, are you?"

"Weird? No. Of course not." She swung her legs out of the bed and tugged hard, stealing the top sheet. Wrapping it around her, she started searching quickly for her clothes.

He had an inexplicable feeling of sadness that she'd gotten out of bed so fast. "So this isn't you acting weird and desperate to get out of here because you're regretting we had sex?"

"This is me being late for work at the diner." She threw his boxers at him. "And if you don't want to be running behind all day, you'd be acting weird, too."

He looked at the clock. "Shit. How did it get to be seven thirty?"

"I know, right," she said, pulling on a scrap of lace that barely qualified as underwear. "I'd expected a quickie, but you're not so quick."

He caught her around the waist and pulled her back against him, burying his face in her neck. "But I'm thorough."

She half laughed and half sighed, and her body slackened against his for a fraction of a second before she leaned forward and pulled on a sock. "You are so full of yourself."

"Only with the important things." His phone rang and he had to let her go to answer it. "Josh Stanton."

As the night nurse from the hospital gave him an inpatient report, Katrina finished dressing and plonked the rest of his clothes on the bed. She mouthed the word *bye*.

Before he could say anything, she'd run down the stairs. By the time he'd gotten off the phone, she'd left the property. His phone rang again. It was time to face Monday, and hell, for the first time since arriving in Bear Paw, he was looking forward to it.

———

SHANNON hadn't worked the early-morning breakfast shift at the diner since Katrina had starting working for her, but this morning, she'd been late. So late that Shannon had opened up and started cooking. Katrina had arrived forty minutes later, flushed, flustered and profusely apologetic. Since then, she'd worked solidly and without a break for the next three hours.

Now that the rush was over and the morning coffee seniors had left, Shannon took advantage of the lull and made coffee for them both.

"I'm really sorry," Katrina said for the tenth time. "I know you like to be home in the mornings to see Hunter out the door."

Shannon waved away her apology. "Hunter wolfed down your pancakes and got to school on time, so stop apologizing."

"I'll try." She sipped her latte and sighed. "The last eight days have been crazy."

"I know, right? I feel guilty that Sam Duckett's accident has been the best thing that's ever happened to the diner. I think everyone in the district has bought a coffee and a slice of pie just to talk to you about it and ask questions. You're my star attraction."

"Not anymore. It's a new week and Bethany was all over Twitter this morning with a photo of a bright light she saw in the sky last night, so now the town's on UFO watch." Katrina sipped her coffee. "With working opposite shifts, I haven't really seen you to ask, but did you have a good time at your first branding?"

Embarrassment seeped into every cell, and Shannon worked hard at not burying her face in her hands. Every time she thought about her ditzy behavior that seemed to come out of nowhere whenever she spoke to Beau McCade, she burned with shame. Heaven help her, she'd sung a television theme song.

She had no idea what the heck was wrong with her, but all it took was one glimpse of his serious but handsome face, his wide shoulders and rippling muscles, and she not only developed verbal diarrhea, she sounded like a total blonde. Granted, she was blond, but with everyone else in town she was a sensible woman—a business owner and the responsible mother of a teen. But with Beau, she sounded vacant, and his short responses confirmed he thought so, too. She'd blabbed on so much at the branding lunch that the poor guy had offered to help Hunter out just to get away from her. She'd consoled herself the rest of the afternoon by stealing surreptitious glances of Beau on horseback.

"I sure did enjoy myself. Thank you so much for inviting Hunter and me. It got me thinking, though . . ."

Katrina put her mug down. "How's that?"

"In comparison to branding and to how you and Josh treated Sam, making coffee must seem pretty dull."

"Oh, I don't know . . ." Katrina ran her finger distractedly around the rim of her coffee cup. "Sometimes a girl needs dull."

"Dull's safer, for sure."

Katrina's head jerked up. "That sounds like the voice of experience."

Shannon liked Katrina, and since moving to Bear Paw she'd been working so hard she hadn't had the time to make any friends. Not that she usually self-disclosed much at all, but today it felt right. "Back in the day, I had this thing for bad boys. Let's just say it took me a while, but I finally worked out they don't mix so good with a kid, so I gave them up."

A deep line creased the bridge of Katrina's nose. "But what about good guys?"

"I never met one to give up."

A stunned look crossed her face. "That's so sad."

Shannon didn't want sympathy. "Hunter's my priority right now."

"I get that, but I want you to know, Shannon, that some of the guys you met at the branding are good men."

She thought about every guy she'd been with since she was seventeen and had trouble making connections. "You're telling me they actually exist?"

"Of course they do. My dad's a good guy. Ty Garver is a great guy."

What about Beau? She pulled her mind back fast. Good guy or not, he was only ever excruciatingly polite to her, and even if he'd shown some interest, she had her hands full with Hunter. "What about you? Why do you feel the need to do dull? You're single and there has to be someone in this town you can have sex with?" she said, enjoying the girls' talk. "I suppose there's Josh, if that kind of wound-up, tight-jaw tension is your crack."

Katrina spurted coffee out of her nose.

She laughed and handed her a napkin. "Good point. If you got sick, he'd be your doctor and *that* would be totally awkward."

Before Katrina could respond, Shannon's cell beeped with a text and she instantly recognized the school office's number. Her heart sank. "I'm sorry, Katrina, but can you stay and do coffee for the Mommy-and-Me group? I have to go to the school."

———

BEAU was driving back from the feed store. He had the radio blasting and was singing at the top of his lungs. His dog, Scout, howled in either protest or participation; Beau was never quite certain which. The irony of it all was that despite how bad and off-key Beau's singing was, his stutter vanished whenever he belted out a tune. If he could go through life singing and only talking to animals, he'd never stutter again. Sadly, that would probably land him in the asylum.

Sun glare poured through the glass, showing just how badly the outfit's windshield needed cleaning. He squinted around the greasy residue and in the distance saw what looked like a calf on the side of the road. As he got closer, he realized it was a kid dressed all in black with a baseball cap pulled down low and he was trudging along the edge of the blacktop. The boy turned at the sound of the engine and shoved out his thumb.

Beau slowed, wondering who he was. Town was five miles back, and a local kid would have gotten a ride from someone. He couldn't imagine anyone from Bear Paw not driving a kid to the ranch gate. He applied the brakes and wound down the passenger's window. "You need . . . a ride?"

The kid nodded and then looked up from under his cap.

Beau recognized Shannon's kid immediately. "Hunter." He leaned over and opened the door. "You lost?"

The kid didn't say anything. He glanced around at the flat, grassy plains that stretched for miles as if seeking an answer and then he seemed to slump.

A thought struck Beau and a thread of anxiety wound through him. "D-did your mom's car . . . break down? Are you w-walking . . . for help?"

Hunter stared at the tops of his skate shoes.

Breathe. "Is your mom . . . okay?"

The boy nodded. "Yeah."

Relieved that Shannon wasn't stranded or hurt, he wondered why her son was so far from the diner. He patted the seat. "Get in."

Hunter didn't move.

Beau thought back to when he was fourteen, which in many ways seemed a lifetime ago and in other ways only yesterday. The kid was out here for a reason, and he obviously didn't want to go back to town, but at fourteen, he had no choice. Beau didn't want to force him into the vehicle, but he had to get him in somehow, so he used logic.

Stretching out his arm, he said, "Nothing but cows . . . and ranches that way." He moved his arm forty-five degrees. "Rocky Mountains, bears . . . elk . . . and sh-sheep if you go there." He pointed across his chest. "Canada but . . . they talk f-funnier than I do."

Hunter's head jerked up, his eyes round as if he couldn't believe Beau had just made a joke against himself.

"So, buddy . . . I guess that . . . leaves Bear Paw."

"That blows."

Scout had edged forward and was now trying to get Hunter's attention by sticking her nose under his cap.

Beau was about to say, "Down, Scout," when Hunter laughed. Maybe the dog was the way to get him to come back to town. "She wants you . . . to scratch her . . . under the chin."

"What's her name?"

"Scout."

"Hey, Scout." Hunter rubbed her ears with both hands, and Scout's tail went wild, thumping hard on the seat.

"She's gonna wh-whine if you don't come with us."

Scout barked as if she'd just read his mind.

Hunter looked at Beau and then at Scout and slowly swung his backpack onto the floor and hauled himself up onto the seat. "Do you need any help on the ranch?" he asked, his voice full of hope. "I could do that first before I go back."

He felt for the kid, but it was close to suppertime and surely he was expected home. "I'm guessing . . . your mom doesn't know . . . you're out here?"

Hunter stuck his face in Scout's fur and didn't say another word.

Beau grimaced. A virtually silent teen and a stuttering cowboy. It was gonna be a fun ride back to town.

———

THE burning pain radiating from Shannon's solar plexus was a constant reminder that Hunter was missing. Hours had passed since she'd arrived at the school expecting to collect him from the principal's office for yet another infraction, but when she'd walked in, Hunter wasn't there. Instead, a concerned yet resigned Gary Folger had told her that after lunch, Hunter hadn't returned to class. Then he'd asked her if she knew where he might have gone.

After she'd ruled out home and the skate park, she'd drawn a blank. Despite her encouraging Hunter to bring friends home, he never had, and she wasn't certain which boys he hung out with. If the students in his class knew where he was, they weren't saying. She'd spoken to Mitchell Hagen, the sheriff, but he hadn't been unduly concerned. He'd given her a critical look and asked how things were at home. She'd told him that home wasn't the problem, but school was an issue. He'd said he'd keep an eye out for Hunter but that kids usually turned up around suppertime.

Shannon had wanted to yell at him, "Obviously you're not a father!" but she'd realized there was no point. Plenty of fathers took no interest in their kid's life—Hunter's dad being a perfect example.

She glanced at the clock. Six thirty. Suppertime and still no Hunter. How much longer did she have to wait before the sheriff took her seriously? Hunter didn't know enough people in town to be visiting anyone, and even if he was, surely their parents would be home by now and the boys would have been discovered.

She heard the squeak of the back door and her breath caught. "Hunter?" Rushing into the hallway, she stopped short, surprise and anxiety making her dizzy. Beau McCade stood in the small and narrow space, completely filling it.

He jerkily pulled his hat off his head, looking decidedly uncomfortable. "Ma'am."

It made no sense that he was in her house and hope sprouted. "Is Hunter with you?"

She heard the clatter of nails on wood and then Beau turned and she glimpsed a black dog with tan ears followed by Hunter. "Oh, thank God." She pushed past Beau and wrapped her arms around her rigid son. "Are you okay?"

Hunter tried to shake free of her maternal grasp. "I'm good."

"You're good?" Her voice rose as anger skated in over

relief. "You've been missing for hours, Hunter, and no one knew where you were. You can't just disappear like that."

The dog barked at her loud voice.

"Quiet, Scout," Beau said firmly.

Shannon tried hard to lower her voice. "I've been worried sick."

Hunter shrugged his thin shoulders. "I'm back now. What's for supper?"

Fury at his cavalier attitude exploded inside her. "Supper?" She couldn't keep the shrillness from her voice. "Supper? I haven't cooked any supper. Do you have any idea how desperate I've been? I had no idea where you were. For all I knew you could have been hit by a car and lying in a ditch."

"None of that happened."

It was like talking to a brick wall, and tears pricked the backs of her eyes, threatening to spill over. How could he not see that what he'd done was wrong? She wanted to shake him and make him see how his behavior affected her, but she was worried she'd just end up a blubbering mess. Digging deep, she ground out, "I'm too angry to talk to you right now. Go to your room."

He glared at her before bending down to the dog. "Bye, Scout." He scratched the canine behind the ears before looking up at the cowboy. "Bye, Beau." Ignoring Shannon completely, he walked down the hallway and out of sight.

Her heart, battered and bruised by the afternoon's stress, wobbled in her chest. Where had her dear little boy gone? She heard the sound of someone clearing their throat and suddenly remembered that Beau McCade was still standing in her hall. He'd been a silent witness to her brooding and resentful son and her complete meltdown. She wanted to die on the spot.

Somehow, she managed to pull herself together. "Thank you for bringing him home."

Beau's fingers played around the brim of his hat and he gave her a curt nod. In that small movement, Shannon felt his criticism of her parenting circle her with condemnation.

Throughout the afternoon she'd had the unspoken censure of the school principal and the sheriff—she was the single mom unable to control her increasingly disconnected kid. She surely didn't need disapproval from a childless cowboy who, from the very first time she'd met him, had only ever spoken the bare minimum to her—just to be polite.

Her fingers curled into her palms. "Where did you find him?"

His nostrils flared as he sucked in a deep breath. "Near . . . Pioneer Road."

Shock socked her in the chest. "But that's miles away. How did he get all the way out there and why didn't you call me as soon as you found him?"

A slight frown creased his forehead. "I don't . . . use phones."

His slow and deliberate words mocked her. "What are you? Amish?" Her voice rose again. "So I'm left scared out of my wits for an extra half hour because you don't use phones?"

His cheekbones suddenly seemed stark on his face as tension turned his entire body rigid. "He . . . was . . . safe."

She threw up her hands, not able to believe him. "Yeah, well, my crystal ball didn't tell me that."

His gaze dropped away and he didn't say anything—it was Hunter all over again and she saw red. "You think that by saying nothing, you don't have an opinion, but you do." She pointed an accusing finger at him. "It's in your stance, on your face and in your eyes, so why not say it? Come on, spit it out."

He raised trouble-filled chocolate brown eyes to her face and three beats of silence passed. "He's . . ."

Her jaw was so tight she could barely get the words out. "Just. Say. It."

"He . . . he's not h-happy."

She barely heard him over the deafening thumping of blood in her ears. "You think I don't know that? You think that I want him to run away, that his misery doesn't eat at me and tear me apart? It's fine for you to stand there all superior, thinking you know best, but you don't know anything at all. I want you to leave. You need to leave, now."

A pained expression crossed his face, and his dog came and stood next to him, gazing up at him as if to check whether he was okay. "I . . . kn-kn-kn-" He dragged in a breath as his face turned red. "I . . . kn-kn-kn-" His hand slammed against the wall. "Fuck!"

Shannon jumped at the fury behind the yelled expletive, fright making acid burn the back of her throat.

Then she gagged. *Oh God.* What had she done? Beau McCade wasn't the judgmental asshole of few words that she'd just accused him of being. The reason he spoke slowly and deliberately and used very few words was because he was working hard to conquer a stutter. And she'd just made him lose control.

Spit it out. Her words reverberated in her head so loud and hurtful that she wanted to sink through the floor and hide from them. From him. "Beau, I . . ." But before she could say more, he'd stormed past her, pushed open the door and disappeared outside.

Chapter 12

Beau strode to the outfit, his boots crunching loudly against the gravel, needing to put as much distance between him and Shannon as possible. This was the perfect example of why he avoided women. Not only had he lost all power over his mouth, he'd seen the shock, the revulsion and the accompanying sympathy in her eyes. He never wanted to see any of those emotions again. He didn't want to see her again. He was as mad as hell with her.

He reached the outfit.

"Beau!" Shannon's voice implored, followed by the slamming of a door.

His hand gripped the car door handle as he heard the sound of running feet.

"Wait. Please wait." Her hand closed around his arm. "I'm so sorry. I should never have said what I said. I didn't realize . . . I had no idea . . . shit. I mean, about the phone. I get it now. Why it's hard for you to use the phone. Sorry."

Her eyes sought his, full of remorse and desperation that he please believe her. "I made it all about me and I shouldn't have. You did a wonderful thing. You brought Hunter home and I was such a bitch and you have every right to hate me but I hope you won't because what I said back there was all about me not you." Her words rushed on. "It's hard being a single mom anywhere, let alone in a small town where it's virtually against the law not to be married, and I know the principal blames me for Hunter's behavior. Hell, I blame me and . . ."

She kept talking and talking, and despite the volume of words, her sincerity wrapped around him. Despite himself, he felt his anger ebbing away and he found himself watching her mouth, fascinated by the way her plump lips moved, how the creases that bracketed her lips deepened and smoothed as they easily formed words. Words he'd long stopped hearing because all he wanted to do was kiss that amazingly expressive mouth.

"Shhh." He gently pressed his forefinger to her lips.

Her sky blue eyes darkened to royal blue as her mouth stalled midsentence, leaving her lips slightly parted. It was the most erotic thing he'd ever seen. Throwing years of caution into the Montana wind, he leaned down and pressed his lips to hers.

———

AS Beau's hot lips fused against Shannon's and her surprise faded, all she could think was that he might not be able to speak very easily but he had no problem at all with kissing. His strong arms cradled her gently against him as if she might break if he held her too tightly, and his mouth roved over hers softly. Oh so softly that she thought she might die of bliss. There was no groping, no excessive saliva, no probing or forceful tongue. Just perfect pressure. She'd never been kissed quite like it, as if she were precious. Valuable. Not just as a woman who might put out.

And then, all too soon, he pulled back, leaving only a hint of his masculine taste on her lips and a touch of wind and dust. The kiss was over. Dazed, she opened her mouth to speak, but for once in her life words failed her.

He gave her a quiet smile, silently tipped his hat, swung into the truck and drove away.

She stood rooted to the spot, mouth agape, watching him disappear in a cloud of dust.

———

SO?

Katrina stared at the single-word text on her phone that had come through from Josh thirty hours after they'd had sex and fought down the shadows and voices of the past. Her body was sitting up and panting but her brain was recoiling. With Brent, texting had become the dominant way of communicating when they were apart, and the record of it existed to highlight her naïve stupidity. Josh, on the other hand, based on the codebook of one-night stands, shouldn't even be texting her.

With other men, the sex signaled the start of something. With Josh, the sex was both the beginning and the end all rolled up into one. Like he'd said, they were two adults giving in to the insane attraction, nothing more, and nothing less.

When he'd asked her if she was going all weird on him, he hadn't been too far from the mark. She'd been freaking out ever so slightly. Although she didn't regret the sex one little bit, she'd only done it because she was leaving town. Except, in her lust-fogged mind, she hadn't thought it through very well at all. She really should have waited until the eve of her departure to have sex, instead of a week out. Now she was facing unchartered territory and she had no clue what happened next. Part of her wanted to avoid Josh altogether, because pretending they hadn't had mind-blowing sex and talking to him about the weather was definitely going to be difficult.

Based on what her girlfriends told her, she assumed that pretending it didn't happen was what guys did after casual sex. They certainly didn't text, let alone send such a cryptic message.

So?

What did he mean? So what? So, are you okay? So, are we good? So, are we having sex again?

Yes, please.
Shut-up.

"Hey, Katrina."

She looked around, startled to find Ty standing next to her and leaning in to give her a kiss on the cheek. "Oh, hi, Ty."

"What's got you so distracted?"

"Sorry?"

He smiled. "You've been staring at your phone for as long as it took me to park outside the post office and walk here."

She gave a nervous laugh and shoved the device in her pocket. "Dillon sent me a silly YouTube clip. So," she said, desperate to change the subject, "you turned out your cows yet?"

"Heading out tomorrow, which is why I'm in town grabbing supplies." He shifted his weight back and forth, his boots levering against the pavement. "You had so much fun on Saturday roping with me, I wondered if you wanted to ride out?"

She hadn't ridden out on the range in such a long time or spent a night under the stars, and the offer tempted her like candy. Then she thought about her to-do list before leaving for Ecuador. "Ty, I'd love to but can I let you know? I've got a few things I need to organize first."

"Sure." He shoved his hands in his pockets. "No problem."

"Thanks." She gave him a quick peck on the cheek, appreciating how uncomplicated things were with him. He wasn't the sort of guy to lie to her like Brent or send her cryptic texts like Josh.

As Ty walked toward the grocery store, her phone rang. This time she recognized the number. Brent called her at random times, which was ironic, given he'd never called her when they were together. Her finger hovered between the accept and the decline buttons, leaning slightly toward the green. Part of her wanted to take the call and tell him he hadn't broken her; in fact, she'd just had sex. Great sex.

Most of her didn't want to risk a conversation with him.

Despite her fury at him and everything that had happened, he'd always been able to sweet-talk her, and although she was fairly certain she wouldn't cave, she didn't want to take the risk. Decision made, she punched the red button firmly, cutting the call, and the missed call text came in. She immediately deleted it.

A moment later, her phone buzzed again. She held her breath, wondering if it was another puzzling text from Josh. Irrational disappointment slugged her when she saw it was from Beau asking her if she knew anyone with puppies for sale.

"MA'AM, you have vertigo," Josh said to the hippy-looking tourist who'd come into the clinic complaining of dizzy spells.

"No, I'm a Gemini."

Josh wanted to hit himself over the head with the chart. "Well, that may be, but the dizzy spells you're having are called vertigo and they're not at all connected with your horoscope."

A horrified expression crossed her face. "Everything's connected to the horoscope."

He wrote up a drug order and wondered how many more eccentrics the warm Chinook wind was going to blow in today. "You have a viral infection that has inflamed your inner ear. It should resolve in seven to ten days, but meanwhile, I'm prescribing you something that will ease the nausea. If the symptoms persist, see your own doctor when you get home."

He walked her out and Millie met him in reception looking glum. "Floyd just told me that Katrina said no to the job, which means my transfer to the ER is on hold." She sighed. "Again." She looked at him with hope in her eyes. "Do you think if you asked her nicely, she'd reconsider?"

He thought about yesterday morning—the last time he'd seen Katrina—when she'd been under him, her nails digging into his back as she was crying out his name. As much as he wanted a repeat performance, there was no way on earth he was asking her to stay in Bear Paw, just in case she misread the situation. Mind you, she hadn't replied to his text he'd sent this morning, so perhaps he was misreading the situation. Still, by his reckoning, there was enough time for them to have sex at least once, hopefully twice, before she left town.

"She's set on going to Ecuador to feel useful."

"She could be useful here," Millie whined, "so that I can take the ER job."

"Yeah, well, believe me, we don't always get what we want, Millie. Who's next?"

"Bonnie McCade. She's in exam two waiting for you. I've done her vitals and tested her pee. It's all good."

"Thanks," he said, washing his hands before entering the room. "Hello, Mrs. McCade."

"Call me Bonnie." An older version of Katrina smiled at him. "Sorry to bother you, but my daughter insisted I come see you for a checkup."

He could picture Katrina, a mixture of gentle persuasion and rock-hard determination, suggesting her mom come to the clinic. "She can be insistent."

Bonnie laughed. "You've noticed?"

He gave a wry smile. "I now own the first tool kit of my life as a result." He scanned Bonnie's brief medical history on the computer, which was comprised of three normal childbirths and one episode of pneumonia. Not a lot to go on. Turning back to face her he asked, "So what's brought you in to see me today?"

IT was seven the following evening and the clinic was closed when Josh hovered the computer's mouse over the file that contained Bonnie McCade's test results. He sent up a hope that this time his gut feeling and his diagnostic skills were wrong.

He clicked on the file and read the ultrasound report first, followed by the blood work. *Shit*.

Pushing back his chair, he stood up and leaned against the windowsill, gazing out through the grove of pine trees, which struggled valiantly against the gale-force wind. Beyond them, he could see pasture grass laid flat and the jagged gray, rocky outcrops climbing the sides of a coulee. The landscape was as stark and unforgiving as Bonnie's test results. Results he had to give her.

Results that would change everything for the whole McCade family. *Shit. Shit. Shit.*

He ran his hand through his hair. For his entire medical career he'd had to give bad news, but there'd always been the buffer of the patient being a total stranger. After spending a day with the McCade family on their ranch, none of them were faceless strangers. They were men and women, children, parents and partners. And then there was Katrina. After Monday morning, in one way, she was the antithesis of a stranger.

As if she knew he was thinking of her, his phone beeped with a text from her.

So long. Leaving for Billings in the morning for Ecuador stuff. It was fun. Katrina.

He stared at the bald words, acid burning his gut as patient confidentiality ran smack bang into an emotional minefield. He couldn't imagine Katrina would want to leave Bear Paw if she knew Bonnie's diagnosis, but he didn't know Bonnie well enough to know if she'd share the news with her daughter, especially if she thought it would prevent her from doing something she wanted.

Leave it alone. Don't get involved. It's none of your business. His father's voice droned in his head.

He longed for the anonymity of a big city where this situation wouldn't be a dilemma. Hell, he wouldn't even be thinking twice about it, but now it had lodged in his brain, burying in like a tick and taking hold.

Legally, he wasn't allowed to say anything to Katrina, but for the first time in his career he found himself questioning the ethics. From the few things she'd told him about her family and after watching them in action, the McCades were very different from his own. They were close. They likely cared.

He paced up and down the office, suddenly questioning principles of medicine he'd blindly accepted as sacrosanct. His job was to protect his patient, and every time he settled on that, Katrina's face swam into his head. In Chicago, he'd have sought out a colleague, but here he was on his own. He respected Millie but could she be a true sounding board when she knew the family?

You debriefed with Katrina after Sam's surgery.

The paradox hit him hard in the chest. The one person he felt comfortable talking with about work, he couldn't consult. With the thoughts in his head going around and around in circles, he pulled on his running gear and headed out into the wind.

———

KATRINA had sent her parents out onto the porch rocker while she and Beau cleared up the kitchen after supper. Dillon and Megan had left earlier to go to a bonfire twenty miles away and catch up with old high school friends.

"If you want another dog, why aren't you using the same breeder you got Scout from?" she asked curiously.

"I w-want a mutt."

Farm dogs were working dogs right up until they got old like Boy, and then they got to laze about in their retirement years and be a pampered pet. "But a mutt won't know how to round up cows."

"It's not . . . for me."

Beau lived and breathed the ranch, and his friends were other cowboys, none of whom would want a mutt for a dog. "Who's it for?"

But before he answered they both heard voices on the porch and Kirk was calling out, "Katrina, honey, make a pot of coffee, please. We've got company."

The door opened and her father's voice continued, "Just through there, Doc," indicating the direction of the bathroom.

Josh? She dropped the spoon she was holding as her mouth dried faster than a puddle in the desert. *No. Not here*. He was breaking all the rules. Casual lovers didn't turn up unannounced and meet parents.

Josh being here was wrong on so many levels. Her folks would take his visit as a sign he was interested in her, and although she knew he was, it wasn't in the way her parents would be hoping.

Beau gave her an odd look as he bent down to rescue the spoon, just as Josh stepped into view.

Dressed in a running singlet and shorts, the scant work-out gear didn't hide much at all. He was all gloriously bunched muscles, sweat-slicked skin and heaving chest.

Just like when you saw him last.

Lah lah lah. So not going there, especially not here.

"Hey . . . Josh," Beau said, breaking the silence, his slow words tinged with astonishment. "You *ran* here . . . from the c-cottage?"

"Town," he puffed out, still getting his breathing under control.

"Town?" Katrina heard herself squeak. "But that's miles away."

He nodded. "The wind behind me made it an easy run."

Beau shook his head slowly, partly in awe at the achievement and the rest questioning Josh's sanity. "If you say so . . . Doc, but there's no one . . . around here who runs . . . unless they're being ch-chased by a bull."

"I'll get you a towel," Katrina said hastily, drying her hands and walking fast toward the bathroom, wanting to separate Josh from her family as quickly as possible. She closed the door behind them and the memory of the first time they'd met rolled back in. "Didn't you get my text?"

"I got it." He splashed his face with water.

"So, I was pretty clear. Don't get me wrong, the sex was great, but I'm busy and—"

"Don't panic, Katrina," he said dryly as he accepted the proffered towel. "I'm not here to see you."

"Oh." The disappointment that slugged her was ridiculously out of proportion to the miniscule sliver of relief that followed. Then confusion hit. "If you're not here to see me, then why are you here?"

His gaze slid away from her. "Like I said, I was running past." Having dried his face, he handed back the towel. "Thanks."

"No one runs past, Josh."

He opened the door. "No one from Montana runs past, although I've been told Californians have been known to."

"You do realize the word *Californian* is code for crazy."

He gave a half smile and walked away, leaving her standing in the very familiar bathroom feeling as if she were in a foreign country.

She brewed coffee and took it into the living room where everyone had gathered. Boy had settled himself next to Josh, who was absently fondling the old dog's ears. Her father was chatting to Josh as if his unannounced arrival on foot was a normal, everyday occurrence. Kirk asked him if he'd ever gone fly-fishing. He hadn't. Her mother was unusually quiet.

The conversation quickly reached a lull, driven by the unspoken questions that filled the room. Bonnie finally spoke. "I'm thinking this isn't purely a social call, Doctor . . . Josh?"

He ran his hand through his hair and his already tense face contorted for a moment.

Katrina's building unease heightened and she glanced between Josh and her mother.

Kirk set down his mug. "Bonnie told me that she went to see you yesterday and you ran some tests."

Josh's gray eyes sought Katrina's, his gaze both troubled and resigned. A silent scream rose in her throat. This was why he'd come.

"I did run some tests, and she has an appointment to see me tomorrow morning to discuss the results."

Bonnie kept her gaze fixed on Josh, but she reached out her hand to Kirk. "I'd rather you tell us now. Here, at home."

The loud tick of the old clock and Boy's snoring reverberated loudly in the room, and Katrina thought she'd go crazy. *Say it. Say it now. Say it fast.*

Josh leaned forward, resting his elbows on the armrests and making a steeple with his fingers and thumbs. "I'm afraid it's not good news, Bonnie. The tests show conclusively that you have ovarian cancer."

The silent killer. Katrina closed her eyes as a soundless shriek rocked her with its resounding *No!*

"Cancer?" Bonnie asked with a quiver in her voice.

"Judy Reynard had cancer and look at her now," Kirk said loudly, going straight into denial. "She's as fit as a flea. Cancer's not the death sentence it used to be, right, Doc?"

"Bonnie needs to go to Great Falls and see the oncologist there," Josh said quietly and professionally, neatly avoiding giving Kirk the reassurance he craved. The reassurance Katrina knew he couldn't give. "The cancer will need to be staged to find out how far it's spread, and the treatment will depend on that."

Bonnie paled. "And if it's spread?"

Again Josh glanced at Katrina for a split second. "Then I won't lie to you. The battle will be a very tough one."

Katrina moved to her mother's side and kneeled down, capturing her hands in her own. "I'll be here, Mom. I'm cancelling Ecuador. I'm not going anywhere."

Bonnie put her hand on her head. "I should say no, honey, but I think I'm going to need you."

"D-don't w-worry about the r-ranch," Beau said before kissing Bonnie on the cheek and quickly leaving the room.

Kirk went into organizing mode. "When can she see the onc—the cancer doctor?"

"I'll make the calls first thing in the morning and set up the appointments." Josh rose to his feet. "If you both come see me at eleven, I should have everything ready."

Kirk shook his hand. "Thanks, Josh."

He gave a silent nod, as if being thanked for bad news were an oxymoron, and headed to the door.

Katrina rose to her feet. "I'll drive you back to town."

She grabbed her keys and walked out into the now dark night, her head spinning with a thousand thoughts.

As if reading her mind, Josh said, "Want me to drive?"

"Might be safer." She gave him the keys and swung into the passenger seat.

Cancer. Her vibrant, amazing mother had cancer. And not just any cancer. She had the one stealth cancer that had usually spread far and wide, wreaking damage, before it was even detected. She couldn't wrap her head around it. She didn't want to have to. "You know, I thought it might have been a rumbling appendix or diverticulitis. I never thought . . ."

"Why would you?" Josh turned onto the main road and reached for her hand. "Ovarian cancer's a bastard that way. It mimics so many other less noxious things."

She felt the warmth of his hand in hers, and it suddenly hit her what he'd gone and done. "Do you usually run to patients' houses to give them bad news?"

He slowed to take the turnoff to the cottage and slipped his hand back on the wheel. "Like so many things in Bear Paw, this was a first. I went for a run to clear my head, but my feet literally took me to the ranch. If your mother hadn't asked me straight up, though, and told me it was okay, I wouldn't have said anything."

She thought of the doctor who'd issued patients with numbers in his first week in town, and she struggled to comprehend the change, especially given the fine line he'd walked with confidentiality. "But why? Why not wait until tomorrow's appointment?"

He was quiet for a moment. "You texted me saying you were leaving town in the morning. I thought you'd want to know."

Her heart turned over in her chest—he'd bent the rules for her. A lump formed in her throat and she fought it. "You thought right. Thank you."

"You're welcome." They bumped over the cattle guard and the truck pulled to a stop outside the cottage. The new moon hung tentatively in the sky, one of the few things to defy the wind.

"God, I hope it's not in her liver," she blurted out, voicing her worst fear.

Josh didn't reply, and the silence of the unknown bore down on her, suffocating her with dread. Despite a mammoth effort to hold herself together and not cry, the tears she'd held at bay since hearing the news trickled out quietly, one by one. Soon they were streaming down her cheeks in a river of shock and grief.

Two strong arms went around her, and she buried her face in his shoulder as great, racking sobs shook her. Josh didn't tell her to hush or offer her empty words of hope; he just held her and gently brushed her hair, giving her a place to shelter. And she took the shelter, seeking it like a hiker looking for a warm and dry refuge from a storm.

Her sobs slowly eased and she gulped in some longer breaths, trying to bring her breathing back under control. As her sniffles lessened, she felt his warmth and care seeping into her, and somewhere buried deep down inside her a voice said *This is a place worth staying.*

For the briefest instant she agreed, and then common sense thundered in. Once, she'd believed in the dream of loving a man who truly loved her for who she was and not the person they wanted to make her. But she was wiser now and knew it was just that—a dream. Brent had burned her so badly that she was never going anywhere near that dream again. This was just Josh doing what any decent person would do when someone was sobbing their guts out. Nothing more. Nothing less. Neither of them wanted anything of the other, and now it was time to sit up, wipe her face and cowgirl up.

She moved and suddenly became aware of the sticky dampness of his skin under her cheek from her tears, the taste of salt on her lips and his strong masculine postrun scent. Her body stirred with the familiar tingle of longing, and she remembered how she'd lost herself in him in his bed. How he'd driven her to the point of insanity before flinging her out into the stars, far, far away from everything that tied her to her life.

Her less than perfect life that mirrored her many failings.

For a short time she'd floated in bliss, impervious to all thought and utterly lost in the maelstrom of sensation that had consumed her. She craved to feel like that again. She wanted that temporary sanctuary where everything felt amazingly wonderful. She wanted to forget that her mother faced the biggest battle of her life and that her own was disappointing because of her lack of judgment. She wanted to blast away any lingering temptation to feel sheltered in his arms.

Nothing emotional. Nothing but sex. Sex that made her forget.

She raised her wet face to his and sought his lips. At first touch they were cool, but as her tongue traced the seam of his lips, fire burned her. His arms, which a moment ago had cradled her simply and without agenda, now tightened around her, pulling her in against him.

Her body leaped from despair to desire as he returned her kiss, his mouth fusing with hers and greedily taking everything she offered. She wanted to climb up his body, but the steering wheel was in the way so she leaned back, pulling him with her.

He tensed and broke the kiss. "You don't want to do this in a truck. Also, I'm disgusting after that run."

She was beyond caring where they had sex; she just wanted it. Wanted the escape. "I don't mind."

"I do. Come on." He pulled her up and they ran to the house and he led her to the bathroom. "I've wanted you in the shower with me from the moment I met you."

She shivered as heat pooled between her legs. "Same."

He spun open the faucets, only this time instead of stepping straight in, he kissed her. Then he unbuttoned her blouse. She kissed him back and tugged his running singlet over his head. He reached for the snap on her jeans, but as his fingers fumbled with it, she easily pulled his running shorts and briefs down to his ankles. He stood before her, gloriously naked.

"You have way too many clothes on," he grumbled as he finally got her jeans down over her hips.

She kicked off her shoes, freed herself from the clinging denim and whipped off her bra. "Better?"

He hauled her against him. "Perfect."

Steam now filled the room, and they stepped under the shower, filling the small space. Water sluiced over them and she lathered him with soap, loving the feel of his skin—taut over muscles—under her palms. He groaned and captured her mouth with his, deliciously lashing her with his tongue.

The bar of soap slipped out of her hands and her legs threatened to buckle as need for him streamed through her, setting every cell alight with begging lust. She wasn't sure if she crawled up him or if he lifted her or if it was a bit of both, but suddenly her arms and her legs were wrapped tightly around him and her back was pressed up against the tiles.

All of her quivered with unmet need and her body screamed for him. "Fill me up."

Snowstorm gray eyes gazed into hers, filled with matching need. "Now?"

"Yes, please, right now."

He pushed up. She pressed down and beseeching muscles gripped him tight, so tight it was as if they were scared he might change his mind.

Finally. Feeling him deep inside her, she gave a momentary sigh of blissful relief, savoring the touch she desperately wanted. The touch that would take her away from everything.

"Okay?" His guttural voice broke through her fog of bliss.

"Perfect."

He started moving inside her, and relief was short-lived, exploding into all-consuming need and stripping her of coherent thought. She threw her head back, and with each thrust, a tie to her real life unraveled, freeing her to soar.

Josh's breath came hard and fast. Speech deserted both of them. Her breasts ached, her nipples tingled with pain, every muscle in her body screamed for release but still it wasn't enough. Like fire hungrily consuming every ounce of oxygen in its path, she needed more.

She needed it all.

Panting, she dropped her head to his and kissed him, sucking his heat and energy into her. He gasped, drove up hard and shuddered against her. Color took over. She swam into it, desperate and dizzy, surfing the crest of the wave of utter fulfillment, clinging to it and never wanting it to end.

The wave rolled out, losing momentum, and she whimpered, frantic to hold on to it for as long as possible. Fighting the pull of reality. She lost. It slipped from her limp body and she sobbed as her arms started to shake.

"That was . . ." Josh's stunned gaze sought hers. ". . . intense."

He lowered her down and she slumped against him, the shaking now spreading to every part of her body. She tried to speak but nothing came out.

"Katrina?"

Unease filled his face, but her teeth were chattering so hard she couldn't talk.

Josh quickly turned off the water and wrapped her in a towel, rubbing her dry. "Do you think you can walk up the stairs?"

Her legs felt like jelly and she shook her head. The next minute she was hanging over his shoulder in a fireman's lift.

"Sorry, but I can't get you up the narrow stairs any other way without the both of us hitting the wall or the ceiling and getting hurt." He carefully made his way out of the bathroom, up the stairs, past the bastard turn and into the bedroom.

He gently lowered her down, pulled up the quilts, dried himself and then crawled in next to her, spooning her into him and absorbing her shakes.

As his heat warmed her, the trembling slowly eased and she felt her body starting to still. She rolled over to face him, and his hand smoothed the strands of her damp hair out of her eyes. "Feeling better?"

"I am." She felt self-conscious. "That's never happened to me before."

He grinned. "I've never sent a woman into postorgasmic shock before."

"You want a medal or a chest to pin it on," she teased, rather ineffectually, because as chests go, his was pretty much perfect.

"A framed certificate will do just fine," he quipped before kissing her gently on the nose.

Her fingers traced the outline of his tribal tattoo. "When did you get this?"

He rolled onto his back. "When I was seventeen. We were on vacation in Hawaii and I wanted to piss off my father."

She couldn't picture Josh being that much of a rebel. "Did it work?"

"Hell yeah. He was furious." He tucked his other arm behind his head and stared at the ceiling. "It almost did double duty. I got close to being kicked out of prep school, too, but I wasn't that lucky."

She knew her face would have conveyed her surprise. "You went to a prep school?"

"Connecticut's finest."

Her brain scrabbled to work everything out, but nothing matched up because Josh was in Bear Paw to pay down his student loans. "That's serious money."

A muscle ticked in his cheek. "My father called it an investment, only it didn't pay the returns he wanted."

She thought about their last conversation that had featured his father, and given what had happened, part of her didn't want to ask, but curiosity won out. "But you got into medical school, graduated and have continued to succeed, so how is that not paying returns on his investment in your education?"

Chapter 13

Josh's sigh rumbled through him, eating away at his relaxed postsex torpor. He wound strands of her drying hair around his fingers and for a moment toyed with the idea of not telling her anything about his fractured relationship with his father, but he didn't want to argue with her. Not today when she was gutted by her mother's news. Not when she was lying up against him all snuggly warm with her legs entangled in his. But talking about his father always put him on edge, and he didn't particularly want to lose the languid relaxation that had him feeling mellow and content. There weren't many times in Bear Paw he'd gotten close to content.

"Josh?" she prompted, propping herself up on her elbows and fixing him with an intense and questioning look.

Damn it. He should have made up some bullshit story about the tattoo when she'd asked, but his brain wasn't firing on all cylinders yet after the most amazing sex he'd ever had in his life. Sex he wanted to have again. If he ducked this answer to her question, she'd continue to press him, so he really had no choice.

"I did go to medical school but not to Yale. All the Stantons have gone to Yale and graduated summa cum laude."

Her fingers continued to follow the intricate diamond-shaped design. "More rebellion?"

"No such luck. I fooled around in the first year of college, so I didn't make the cut. I grew up, went to Columbia, worked my ass off and graduated summa cum laude."

She smiled. "And that made your dad happy."

He grimaced at her optimism. "Not much about me makes Phillip Stanton happy. He may have forgiven me for going to the wrong school—"

"There is nothing wrong with graduating from Columbia," she said hotly.

Her indignation on his behalf surprised him, and he didn't quite know what to make of it. "Um, thanks, but no one in Connecticut is going to agree with you, especially my family. On top of Columbia I added insult to injury."

"Because you didn't do surgery?"

She was far too insightful. "That's the one."

"Did you want to do surgery?"

No one had ever asked him that before, either, and he blew out a breath filled with the complicated emotions—the ones that always raised their heads whenever he thought about his father. "When you have a family history like mine and you're the only child, you grow up from the cradle knowing you're going to become a doctor. A surgeon. I resisted it for a while—"

"The tattoo?"

"Yeah, and coasting the first year of college until a professor I really admired called me on it. Then I knuckled down, and once I got accepted into medical school I never questioned that surgery was my future. And it was, right up until the end of my first year as a surgical intern."

"What happened then?" she asked, dropping her head on his chest.

He stroked her back, loving the feel of her skin. "I discovered what I loved best about surgery was the emergencies. The adrenaline charge when I greeted the ambulance as it arrived at the ER, the rush of the unknown as I triaged and the beat-the-clock work to keep the patient alive and stabilized enough to get them to the OR. All of it gave me a buzz that general elective surgery couldn't touch. I started thinking about the years of my working life stretching out before me, and I just couldn't do it. I transferred out of the program."

"That makes sense. Surely your dad understood?"

He couldn't stop the harsh, barking laugh that erupted out of him. "That's like saying there'll be peace in the Middle East one day. My father's very much the surgeon. Everything is cut-and-dried. You cut out a problem and stitch it up, end of story. There's no room for sentiment."

She scrunched up her face. "I think it's important to do what you love."

He opened his mouth to say *And yet you're not doing that*, but then he remembered Bonnie's diagnosis and he closed it.

Katrina continued. "You've accomplished a lot."

He rolled his eyes. "Oh yeah. I'm Bear Paw's finest and going backward fast because I'm doing more primary care here than emergency medicine."

She dug her fingers into his ribs. "Don't do that."

He flinched as her nails pinched. "Do what?"

"Belittle your achievements. You saved Sam Duckett's life. You should be proud of yourself."

Her words punched him as images and voices he thought had faded with time came back loud and clear. His father standing in his library with his palms pressed down on his leather-topped oak desk. *I've put up with your nonsense for years, son, but if you choose this course of action, you're on your own.*

I'm not asking you for anything, Dad. I'm just informing you of my decision.

His mother's silent pleading for Josh to change his mind.

His total confidence that the woman he thought loved him would support his choice just as he'd supported her. *Don't worry, Ashley. I have a plan. It's all going to work out fine.*

Have you lost your mind, Josh? Do you even care about me? About us as a couple? Your student loans will cripple us.

He felt the past tugging at him, sucking him back toward the emotional black pit he'd spent so long fighting his way out of, and there was no way he was going back there. He was in Bear Paw. He didn't want to think about the past or the future. He just wanted now.

He pulled Katrina over him until she was straddling his legs and then he cupped one hand on her breast and the other between her thighs. He hooked her clear and hypnotic gaze. "I'm proud of what I can do for you."

He stroked her.

She whimpered.

The sound made him instantly hard, and he let his hands work their magic. He lost himself in watching her fall apart.

IF Shannon had thought juggling work and keeping Hunter in school was difficult, she hadn't factored in the three long months of summer vacation. It was only day three and already she was tearing out her hair.

"What are you planning on doing today?" she asked him at eleven, after virtually tipping him out of bed. "Skate park? Invite someone over?"

He shrugged indifferently. "I dunno."

She tried not to sigh. For weeks Hunter had whined and moaned about school and had been miserable. Now that it was summer vacation, she'd expected him to be happier. Hoped desperately that he'd be happier. But his air of disinterest in school seemed to have pervaded his out-of-school life.

Well, she wasn't having him sit around doing nothing. "I need your help washing dishes in the diner today because Katrina's gone to Great Falls."

Katrina had told her about Bonnie's diagnosis, and

Shannon was still trying to absorb the unwelcome and distressing news. She wondered how Beau was coping, but she hadn't seen him in the nine days since he'd brought Hunter home and kissed her. The kiss she thought about far too much.

"Will you pay me?" Hunter asked, half belligerent, half hopeful.

"If you smile, work hard and do what I ask, I'll pay you." She stretched out her hand toward his. "Deal?"

"I guess."

"Good. Get dressed, go eat a bowl of cereal and then come straight over. The early lunch crowd will be drifting in by eleven thirty."

As she turned to leave, she heard a loud knocking at the door. "Are you expecting someone?"

Hunter shook his head but ambled to the door just ahead of her and opened it. "Hey, Beau."

Beau. Beau who'd kissed her as if she were dainty and fragile and had then walked away and not contacted her since.

The cowboy stepped inside and once again filled her small entryway, only this time he didn't pull off his hat and his mighty fine chest appeared to be wriggling.

"H-hello, Sh-Shannon."

Before she could reply, a small black nose suddenly poked out from inside Beau's shirt, quickly followed by two huge velvet-soft ears.

"A puppy. Cool!" Hunter exclaimed with uncharacteristic enthusiasm. It reminded Shannon of the boy he'd been before hormones and school had snuffed it out of him.

Hunter shot out his hand, which was devotedly licked by a little pink tongue. "Does it have a name?"

"No."

"Why not?"

"Stray." Beau handed the squirming golden puppy to Hunter before turning his rich, chocolate eyes onto Shannon. "I w-wondered if you . . . and Hunter wanted . . . her."

What? She needed a puppy like she needed a hole in the head.

"Hell yes," Hunter whooped, laughing as the puppy moved her enthusiastic licking to his face.

"Hunter," she rebuked, embarrassed at his mild profanity and annoyed with Beau for not talking to her about the dog before mentioning it to Hunter. He'd gone and put her in a difficult position—she either disappointed Hunter or she took on a dog, which she didn't want to do.

"It's very kind of you to offer her to us, Beau, but there's a lot to consider. Hunter and I need to discuss it first."

"Aww, Mom," Hunter groaned as he shot Beau a tortured look. "That means no."

Again she was going to be cast as the bad parent. "It means, Hunter, that a puppy is a lot of responsibility. It means walks, teaching it to do its business outside and training it not to destroy the house. I'm busy enough with the diner."

"I can help," Beau said very quietly but perfectly clearly.

His unexpected offer confused her. How could he possibly help? "Hunter, take the puppy and go give her a bowl of water."

Hunter recognized her tone of voice and surprisingly complied without complaint. She stifled a sigh. He must really want the dog.

When he'd left the room, she tried to keep her rising frustration out of her voice. "Beau, I appreciate you thinking of us, but I would also have appreciated you discussing this with me first. How exactly are you going to help with a puppy? You live a long way out of town."

He took in a deep breath—one she now recognized as part of his strategy to reduce his stuttering. "W-what if Hunter . . . and the puppy came . . . out to the ranch?"

She blinked at him. "But your mom's sick and the last thing your family needs is the added problem of a grouchy teen."

"Mom's . . ." He breathed in and blew the breath out.

"She's at the . . . hospital. In Great Falls. With Katrina and Dad."

"Still . . ."

His serious gaze was now a warm, burnished brown. "Do you have . . . vacation plans for Hunter?"

Guilt pierced her. Balancing a new business was hard enough during school time. Right now she couldn't afford to take any time off and Hunter had refused to go to day camp. "Just helping me out at the diner, but that's mostly to keep him busy. I don't want him living at the skate park."

"He can do . . . some ranch w-work. I'll teach him . . . to train the dog."

She wasn't used to being offered any help, so she lacked experience in accepting graciously. "Why do you want him to have the puppy so bad?"

Beau whipped his hat off his head and fiddled with the brim the way he'd done nine days ago. "Animals are less . . . c-complicated than people."

She stared at him, words failing her on so many levels. She had no idea how to respond, so she concentrated on her son. Hunter's eagerness about the puppy pulled at her heart. Oh, how she wanted him to be happy but, she wished she knew the experience with the puppy was guaranteed, otherwise she'd be stuck with a dog.

"If the summer ends and the dog doesn't work out . . ." Her voice trailed off under Beau's expression of incredulity. "Okay. Hunter can go to Coulee Creek if he wants to go."

"I want to go," Hunter said, appearing in the doorway with a look of one who'd been eavesdropping on the entire conversation.

Beau turned to him. "You ready to . . . work?"

Hunter jutted his chin. "Will you pay me?"

Beau laughed. "You help me . . . fence and I'll teach . . . you how to . . . train your dog."

Hunter got a squirrely look in his eyes. "What about riding?"

"Hunter!" Shannon was shocked by his cheeky boldness, but Beau just held up his hand.

"One day . . . at a time. G-grab your stuff. Meet me at . . . the outfit."

Hunter ran to his room and Shannon pulled her cell phone out of her pocket. "Do you have a number in case I need to call?"

A muscle in his cheek twitched and again he dropped his voice to a whisper. "He will be fine."

She noticed that when he spoke softly, his stutter seemed to go completely, and she was instantly reminded of the time he'd told her he didn't use phones. "I know he'll be fine; it's just I'm his mom and . . ." She raised her gaze to his. "I'd only text."

His work-battered fingers lifted her phone out of her hand, the roughened tips gently scraping her palm. Her nerve endings went wild and she clamped her mouth shut and her thighs tight, trying to curb the sensations that raced through her.

He plugged some numbers into the cell. "In the coulees . . . it doesn't work . . . so good."

"Are you sure you want to do this?" she asked, a combination of heady lust and anxiety making her feel unsteady and out of her depth. "I mean, better to change your mind now—"

"Sh-Shannon . . . it's all good."

Was it? She wasn't used to other people getting involved in her life, let alone people with troubles of their own. "I'm sorry about your mom," she blurted out, regretting she hadn't said it earlier. "It must be so hard and . . ." *Shut up now!*

Beau's relaxed demeanor had vanished, leaving in its place six feet of rigid tension. "Yeah." He jammed his hat on his head.

As he reached the door she called out to his retreating back, "I can come by and pick up Hunter after I close for the day if that helps."

He spun back, a gentle smile tweaking up his lips and reminding her again of their kiss. The kiss that now seemed a lifetime ago. "Can you bring something sweet?"

She laughed. "I can do that."

"Good." He disappeared out the door to the sound of ecstatic barking.

———

BEAU and Hunter sat in the shade of the outfit, eating a cowboy sandwich—two thick pieces of bread and some leftover steak. They were taking a break from the hot and dusty work of digging fence holes and installing posts. Hunter had done whatever Beau had asked him to do and had been a quick study. He didn't say much, but neither did Beau, so conversation was limited to general instructions. Even so, the kid looked less miserable than the last time Beau had seen him.

Scout sat next to Beau keeping a close eye on the now-sleeping puppy who was curled up against Hunter's thigh. No way was she going to let the newcomer get away with anything on her turf no matter how cute she looked.

Hunter stroked the puppy's sleek, golden body. "Do you think Rastas will be able to learn cool tricks?"

"Maybe. She looks like . . . she's got some Labrador . . . and beagle in her. The Lab will worship you. The beagle will . . . try and escape." He took a slug of water, thinking how little he stuttered with Hunter compared with Shannon. "You're gonna need to . . . run her hard every day. Wear her out. S-so she doesn't dig."

He remembered Shannon's reservations about the dog. He remembered everything about Shannon—the feel of her in his arms, the taste of her on his lips and her slight resistance. The resistance that made him end the kiss earlier than he'd intended. Still, years of working on a ranch had taught him patience. Some things couldn't be rushed, and Shannon was one of those things. Next time he kissed her, he'd know for sure it was exactly what she wanted.

"Your mom will kill me . . . if Rastas digs holes . . . all over the garden."

"We don't have a garden," Hunter said dryly. "Mom says it's safer that way."

Beau thought about the joy his mother got from her garden and didn't quite understand. "How's it safer?"

"The two years we lived in Kansas, Mom managed to kill eight house plants."

"Lucky you're not . . . a plant, then."

Hunter gave him a sideways glance from under his cap, as if he weren't sure if Beau was making a joke or not.

Fighting off the moral dilemma that questioning the boy to get information about his mother wasn't strictly ethical, he said as casually as he could, "Where did you . . . live before Kansas?"

"Missouri."

"Home of the . . . ice cream cone."

"I guess." He gave a disinterested shrug. "I was born there, same as my mom and dad, and my grandparents, too."

He thought how each move had taken them an increasing distance from their home state. "Do you miss them?"

He shrugged and his bottom lip seemed to jut just a little. "Nope."

Experience made him ask, "Not even a bit?"

Hunter gathered the puppy into his arms and set her on his lap, the gesture telling. "We never saw them much."

He thought about the name on his birth certificate—his biological father's name, a man he'd never known, and his mother, who'd been lost to him for years. "Your grandparents or your dad?"

"Both. Dad left when I was two." Hunter's hand paused on the puppy's ears. "I really want to keep this dog."

Beau understood. When life confused the hell out of a guy, a dog was his best friend. "You've got the summer . . . to train her. Do what I say and . . . when school is back . . . she'll be good."

Hunter grimaced. "I hate school."

Beau remembered stuttering out similar words at the same age. "Why?"

"It sucks."

It was typical teen—a broad generalization that told him nothing. "How?"

Hunter stared toward the mountains. "It's pointless. Who cares what some dead guy wrote in a book?"

Beau had always loved learning and he'd enjoyed many books written by dead guys and living ones. In fact, when he was at school, he'd retreated into books to avoid talking. "You read Tom Sawyer?"

Hunter threw him an incredulous look as if he were as clueless as his English teacher. "I don't read books."

Sad at the thought, Beau got an idea. He was never without a book, because alone at night, out on the range, he often read. He pulled out his phone—the one he rarely used as a phone but frequently used as a weather station, an e-book reader and a camera. Opening up the book app, he found what he was looking for. "You know how . . . sometimes I s-stutter . . . right?"

Hunter nodded.

"Well, I have to . . . do exercises. I do them . . . at lunch." He didn't, but Hunter wasn't to know that, and if there was one thing Beau knew, it was that most everyone enjoyed being told a story. "You take a rest . . . while I do them and . . . then we'll go to work. Okay?"

Hunter shrugged and pulled out his headphones.

Beau hadn't reckoned on that, so he started fast, reciting the words he knew by heart. Hunter's fingers paused half way to his ears and he gave Beau a strange look.

Beau kept reading.

Hunter stuck the earbuds into his ears.

Concentrating on Twain's lyrical words, Beau didn't pause. There was no hurry. He had a whole summer.

KATRINA stopped outside her mother's hospital room, watching her parents through the glass. Hospitals had the uncanny knack of making the healthy look sick. Her father, who usually stood so tall and straight, had stooped shoulders, and the artificial light gave him a slightly jaundiced look. He was bending over Bonnie, helping her take a sip of water.

It was just over a week since her mother's diagnosis and three days since her surgery. The news—in relative terms—was both good and bad. Good in that the surgeon hadn't opened her up and immediately closed her again because the cancer had spread so far that nothing could be done, and bad because the cancer had spread beyond the ovaries. Chemotherapy and radiotherapy had been ordered.

As Katrina observed her father tending to his wife, part of her wished she could be more like him—deluded in his hopefulness. She'd always thought knowledge was power, but in this instance it was like a millstone around her neck, dragging her down into the abyss of bleakness. Very few people with stage three ovarian cancer were still alive in two years, and every time her father asked for reassurance, she bit her tongue. How did she balance reality with hope?

Her mother saw her, waved and beckoned her into the room. Pale and looking her age for the first time in her life, she still managed her trademark serene smile. "You just missed Doctor Josh."

Regret appeared out of the blue, slamming into her like a battering ram. The last time she'd seen him was eight days ago and he'd been sated, sexy and fast asleep on his back with one arm flung out across the bed. A smile tugged at her lips at the memory. Men slept after sex, but women's brains went into overdrive, which was exactly what hers had done. Wide awake after two orgasms—one that had physically crippled her along with reducing her to a scary mess of emotions—she'd quietly crept from the room and had driven back home.

Three days later she'd come to Great Falls with her parents. This time, Josh hadn't texted her, and for that she was grateful. She hadn't contacted him. Thankfully, they were both on the same page. She'd used him to forget about her mom for a while, and she was certain he'd used her to escape the loneliness that came with moving to a new town. For him, Bear Paw was more than a new town; it was like landing on an alien planet.

It was what it was—a convenience for both of them,

and she was determined not to think about him except when she was with him. Despite that, there'd been times when he'd crept unbidden into her head, and right now she was finding it hard to throw off the ridiculous feelings of disappointment that she'd missed him.

"Josh?" She tried to sound casual. "Why was he here?" *Why didn't he wait until I got back from the coffee run? Because he wasn't here to see you.*

"He brought some good news for me," Bonnie said, squeezing her hand.

Good news? How was that possible?

"I asked him if he could arrange for me to have the chemotherapy in Bear Paw."

"He's not going to let you do that, Mom. Not when it's not his area of expertise and the oncologist is right here and—"

Bonnie held up her hand. "Josh told me exactly the same thing when I asked him, but after I explained how I want to be as close to home as possible, he gave one of those big sighs of his." She laughed. "Then he said I could try it. He'll be talking to Doctor Lucas every day, and at worst, I'll have to come back here, but it's worth a try, don't you think?"

"I . . ." Katrina couldn't get over the fact that Josh, the self-confessed emergency medicine doctor who struggled with ongoing primary care, had capitulated. Every time she popped him in a box so she could try and understand him, he did something that busted him right out of it. This only added to the jumbled mess that described her feelings for him. "Yes, of course it's worth a try."

"That's what I thought, and Doctor Lucas says I can go home this afternoon as long as I rest." Bonnie glanced at Kirk, her expression pinched. "We all need to go home."

"The fresh air of home will do you good," Kirk said, his face creasing in a slow smile.

"Seeing Beau, Dillon and Megan will do me good."

A knock sounded on the open door. *Josh?* Hope bloomed in Katrina's chest and she immediately attributed it to wanting to see him so she could thank him for acquiescing to her mother's wishes.

You just want to see him.

But even as she turned toward the sound, she knew it wouldn't be Josh. Doctors didn't tend to knock on doors—they generally strolled right on in.

It was Ty who stood in the open doorway with his hat in one hand and a bunch of cheery yellow Buffalo beans in the other. Her disappointment mocked her.

"May I come in?" he asked hesitantly.

"You bet." Kirk walked toward him, his hand outstretched. "It's good to see a bit of home in this place. What are you doing in Great Falls?"

"Livestock auction." He turned to the bed. "How you doing, Bonnie?"

"Not too bad, Ty."

Katrina rescued the wildflowers from the cowboy's strangling grasp. "I'll put those in a vase."

"Thanks." He smiled and produced a chocolate bar from inside his hat. "I saw this and thought of you."

She stared at the Whatchamacallit chocolate bar and was instantly whooshed back in time to a part of her life that now seemed so long ago it might have belonged to a different person. It had been her favorite treat when she'd dated Ty, and she'd eaten a lot of them. Over time, her sweet tooth had waned, but she smiled at his thoughtfulness. "It's been years since I had one of these."

He nodded, his eyes filled with memories that pressed her to remember, too.

Slivery strands of recollections urged her to listen. *He's a good man. A kind and genuine man who won't hurt you.*

Ty and Brent were such totally different breeds of men that comparisons were pointless.

And Josh?

She wasn't going there. Josh was animal attraction, pure and simple.

Only nothing in life was simple.

"So, Ty, did you find a bull at the livestock auction?" Kirk asked, ever the rancher.

As the conversation took the usual turn when two or

more ranchers got together, Katrina arranged the flowers and wondered whether her twenties and all her experiences had occurred just to lead her full circle, back to appreciate where she'd started—dating Ty. The thought neither distressed nor excited her, it just hung there like an offering.

Her phone beeped, breaking into her thoughts, and Josh's name appeared on the screen.

Her body traitorously leaped as her stomach clenched. *Texting men mean heartache.* With Brent, what she'd once thought of as romantic and fun had turned out to be expediency on his behalf. He'd organized her to fit into his life. Was Josh planning the same?

Cautiously, she opened the text and immediately laughed.

Hi. When you're back in town can you call? Have plumbing issue that's wearing out plunger & maxing out my expertise. JS.

Chapter 14

J osh stared at the text message on his phone and swore. What the hell had possessed him to press send? He'd gone a week without giving into temptation and texting Katrina, and now, in five seconds flat, he'd undone seven days of willpower. He blamed fatigue and a long drive.

He'd been up early to drive to Great Falls so he could be back in Bear Paw for afternoon clinic. As it was, during his six-hour absence, he'd taken three calls from Millie and one from the paramedics, talking them through treatment for their patients. He was learning that Bear Paw lurched from quiet to frantic in a heartbeat with no medium ground in between.

Will Bartlett, the Australian emergency physician who'd evacuated Sam Duckett to Billings, was currently based in Great Falls and had invited Josh to tour the MontMedAir facility. After that, he'd called by and visited Bonnie McCade.

Yeah, about that . . . what happened to diagnose, treat and discharge? When have you ever kept in contact with patients after referring them to the care of another physician?

He'd broken yet another one of his rules about practicing medicine—not getting involved with patients. What the hell was Bear Paw doing to him?

You can't blame Bear Paw this time. You wanted to see Katrina because you miss the sex.

No way. Not even close. He thumped the steering wheel with a fist, hating that his denial was so hollow it echoed loudly. If he was brutally honest with himself, his agreement to let Bonnie have treatment in Bear Paw was in some way connected to Katrina. If she was back in town, there was a higher chance she might end up in his bed again. He wasn't proud of himself, but the grateful smile on Bonnie's face had gone partway toward easing his guilt.

He hated that he felt like a hostage to sex. Hell, between work and Ashley's tendency to withhold sex when she wanted something from him or when she was expressing her displeasure at something he'd done, he was used to dry spells. They'd been part of his life for a few years, but sex with Katrina had kick-started his libido in a way it hadn't known since the heady days of college.

He wanted to have more sex with her—a lot more—but he didn't beg. Not anymore, anyway. Ashley had cured him of that. And what sort of an asshole would he be, chasing Katrina when her mother was sick? He was not *that* guy. Would not be that guy. Still, he couldn't get her out of his mind, and that was doing his head in.

And now, under the guise of a home maintenance problem, he'd sent a text asking to see her and it was out there, unable to be recalled.

Sounds like begging to me.

Fuck off.

He got out of his car and stomped toward the diner. Coffee. He needed coffee.

"Hey, Doc." Wes Phelps, the car mechanic, waved him down. "I got a question for you."

Josh paused, hoping that Wes had good news on the part he was waiting on for his car.

"It's about my clinic bill," Wes said conversationally. "Thing is, you haven't actually fixed me."

Josh wanted to hit himself upside the head. "You've got high blood pressure, Wes."

"And I took those free tablets you gave me, but when Millie checked it this morning, she said it was still high."

"Did you get the prescription filled?"

"Nope."

Josh liked Wes, so he swallowed a sigh and tried not to sound terse. "That's the thing about high blood pressure, Wes. As long as you take the medication I prescribe and lose some pounds like we talked about, that's as fixed as it's ever going to get."

Wes rubbed his jaw in contemplation. "So you and Eddie in the drugstore have a good thing going?"

Josh thought about his student loans and the fact Wes really only needed to see him twice a year. "Actually, I think, given the work my car needs, you're the one in front."

Wes grinned. "You're right. She's a beauty but she's getting older. Come winter, you're gonna need an outfit."

He tried not to roll his eyes. "Which, I'm guessing, you're offering to sell me?"

"Gotta pay for my medical bills somehow, Doc." Wes slapped him on the back and continued down the street.

Josh turned to find a small crowd of people gathered on the sidewalk.

"Doctor Stanton." Chrissie lifted her baby out of the stroller and unwrapped the blanket. "Should I be worried about this rash?"

Josh peered at the tiny, red raised bumps. "It looks like a heat rash. Ditch the blanket now the weather's warmer. If it hasn't cleared up in a few days, bring her to the clinic."

"Doctor Stanton." Lucinda Bradbury bustled toward him as Chrissie and the baby retreated. "I've got this funny-looking spot on my arm." She thrust it toward him, pulling her sleeve up. "See?"

He saw. Vicious red tracks ran up her arm—the indelible pathway of infection—which was spreading from what looked like a bite. "That's nasty."

"I know, right? Can you give me something for it?"

"Sure. Come see me at the clinic this afternoon."

Disappointment flashed across her face. "I'm pretty busy. I thought you could just write it up for me here."

You're pretty busy? Somehow, he managed not to say the incredulous words out loud. "I don't actually have a prescription pad in my pocket, Lucinda."

"Oh," she said, her tone sounding like she'd never considered that option. "Well, I suppose I could come by later and collect it if you leave it at reception."

"While you're at it, can you leave one for me, too?" Leonard Ratzenburger asked. "I need more of them heart pills Randall gives me."

Josh opened his mouth to object when a woman he didn't know placed herself directly front of him. "I've got a sore stomach."

In six and a half weeks he'd gone from the doctor Bear Paw was leery of to the doctor they considered they owned. Josh could hear Katrina's voice in his head about living and working in a small community, but surely not even she would consider sidewalk consultations okay. Ever since he'd qualified as a doctor, there'd been the occasional person at a party who'd cadge for free medical advice, but he could see this situation getting out of hand and fast. He had a vivid premonition of what the next few years would be like if he gave in to any more requests—he wouldn't be able to walk ten feet without being called upon to diagnose and treat.

He looked straight at the unknown woman. "Ma'am, take off your dress and lie on the hood of this car."

"Excuse me?"

He battled the urge to smile but managed to keep his expression deadpan. "Take off your dress and lie on the hood of the car so I can examine you."

"But this is Main Street!"

He rubbed his jaw in the contemplative way so many men in town did. "Thing is, I can't work out what's wrong with you without examining you, so . . ."

Her shoulders slumped. "I suppose I better come see you at the clinic."

"Great idea." He looked over her head to encompass the other six people who'd lined up. "I'll see you *all* at the clinic after I've bought my coffee."

He walked away into the diner, buzzing with the delicious taste of a win. The only thing sweeter would have been if Katrina had been there to see it happen.

The urge to call her and tell her had him fingering his phone. He quickly shoved it in his pocket as Shannon asked, "The usual, Doctor Josh?"

———

Hi, Beau, I just found Hunter's hat in his room. Am worried about sunburn. Shannon.

Hats blow off in the wind. We found him a cap & he has sunscreen. He's fine. See? Beau.

Thanks for photo. Should puppy be on a horse? SH.

Puppy safer in Hunter's hoodie than on ground near hooves. Hunter natural on horse. Thanks for the apple pie. B.

Do you like huckleberry pie? SH.

Does Montana have moose? B.

I've heard the rumors but I've never seen one.

Seriously? You can't call yourself a Montanan if you haven't seen a moose.

I'll pass. I hear they can trample you.

Only if you get too close.

Oh, that's reassuring.

I wouldn't let anything happen. Do you camp out?

Define camping?

Sleeping under the stars.

With the bugs?

You can have a net cocoon with insect shield.

Luxury!

Hunter would enjoy it. Think about it.

Maybe. See u at 7?

With pie?

Always.

————

"MOM'S resting and supper's in the oven," Katrina told Megan as she consulted her list. "Dad and Beau are out checking cows, but they said they'd be back by seven and Mom needs her meds half an hour before she eats. You'll remember, right?"

Megan rolled her eyes. "You've told me twice and you've set a timer, which, by the way, I don't need. Despite the fact you see me as your kid sister, I can step up when required." She gave a guilty smile. "It's just you always jump in first, so most times I let you, but outside of home, I do manage to get to class on time and hold down a part-time job."

The mild rebuke held enough of a sting to make Katrina really look at her sister. Irony slapped her hard. "I guess you grew up while I was gone and I forget that. Just like Dad forgets that I'm almost thirty. Sorry."

Megan hugged her. "No worries. Just go already. What are your plans?"

"I'm plunging Josh's toilet."

Megan stared at her as if she were an alien. "You so need to get a life."

She laughed, not prepared to tell her baby sister exactly what her plans were. "I guess I do. Maybe I'll stop by Leroy's. Happy?"

Her sister shrugged. "It's better than nothing, I guess."

Katrina popped her head inside Bonnie's bedroom to say good-bye. Her mom was home now and starting chemotherapy in a few days. Katrina was determined to make sure she got as much rest as possible before that punishing physical ordeal.

"How you doing, Mom?"

Bonnie paused the audio book she was listening to. "All good." She patted the side of the bed. "How are you, honey?"

She sat down. "Fine."

Her mother patted her on the thigh. "I know I shouldn't say this, but your dad and I are so glad you're back home."

"I'm glad I'm able to be here, especially now." She bit her lip not wanting to cry. "I appreciate everything you and Dad have done for me. I love you, Mom. I want to be here."

"I know you do." She seemed to hesitate for a moment. "I'm just worried about what happened out east to bring you back. You know you can tell me if something's bothering you."

Katrina toyed with the idea for a moment, but as much as she loved her mother, the story was sordid and unpalatable. She hadn't planned on dumping her mess of a life and her bitter disappointments onto her mom before, and she certainly wasn't going to now she was sick. Bonnie couldn't change anything and Katrina wasn't a teenager anymore. She made her own messes and she fixed them.

"It's all good, Mom."

"Well, I hope it is. Life's often a winding road filled with blind bends, but keep driving because when you least expect it, a spectacular view opens up that takes your breath away."

Trying not to think of silver gray eyes, tousled brown hair and a chest she could stay cuddled up to for far too long, she kissed her mother and stood up. "I'm leaving Megan in charge and heading into town."

"Can you take the 'thank you' side of beef to Doctor Josh on your way into town?"

"It's on my list."

Bonnie picked up a card from her nightstand. "Here's the card to go with."

She took it from her. "If he's not home, I'll leave it on the kitchen table with a note telling him there's food in the refrigerator."

"Thank you. Oh, and Katrina?"

"Yes?"

"I think Beau said Ty's playing guitar at Leroy's tonight, so why not drop by after the errands?"

"I'll think about it."

"You do that. Go have some fun."

That's the plan. "I'll try my very best, Mom. I promise."

SUMMER heat arrived like the blast of a furnace and the day had been boiling. Josh had planned to spend his Sunday afternoon at the community pool for a swim, but he'd been called into the ER for a couple of cases, including a kid who'd fallen off his bike and sustained the classic injury of a fractured clavicle. The twelve-year-old had been extremely disappointed when Josh had broken the news to him that not only would bike riding be off his list of summer activities, no plaster cast was going to be involved.

"That totally blows."

"Sorry, dude. Maybe your mom could cover the cuff and collar sling with some superhero material."

"Thanks a lot for that suggestion, Doctor Stanton," Loreen Ryder said grumpily. "I'll add that to my already enormous to-do list, shall I?"

He made a mental note to avoid giving helpful suggestions to tired and overwrought mothers at the end of long, hot vacation days.

Half an hour later, after he'd said good-bye to the Ryders and finished completing the paperwork required by their insurance company and the hospital, he finally got away. He dropped the soft top of his car, enjoying the freedom that came when a job was over. As much as he'd been convinced Floyd was so very wrong about him needing to live out of the town, he'd grown to enjoy the drive. The distant Rockies were as enticing as ever, but down on the plains where he lived in the wind, he noticed that the waving native grasses were now dotted with tiny white flowers. Pastures where crops had been sown in the spring now appeared to be growing an inch a day. To his untrained eye it all looked good, but both the farmers and the ranchers had been grumbling about the lack of rain.

At the intersection of the highway and his gravel road, the resident jackrabbit gave him his usual mocking stare, reminding him that even though he might feel slightly less of an outsider than he had when he'd first arrived, he still was one. As he rounded the final bend, he recognized Katrina's ancient truck and smiled—a huge, wide *thank you* smile.

She'd called him the day after Bonnie had been discharged from Great Falls and told him she'd send someone over to fix the toilet. He'd had to bite his tongue to prevent saying, "Please send yourself." It appeared she'd done so anyway.

Having adopted the local culture of not locking his car, he jogged into the house and quickly came to an abrupt halt. His greeting dried on his lips and his blood drained so fast to his groin that he saw silver spots behind his eyeballs.

Katrina was leaning casually against his kitchen counter like she'd done a few times before, with her tool belt obscuring her shorts. Instead of an old shirt or tank top, she wore a one-shouldered, plain black bandeau bikini top. The functional neoprene strapped firmly against her like a wet suit, fitting perfectly to full breasts whose weight and contours he was intimate with.

"Hi." There was no hiding the rasp to his voice.

"Hi." She tilted her head and gave him a tentative smile. A smile that said *last time we were together we were naked and is this going to be awkward?* "I've fixed your toilet."

"Thanks." His brain was lust-infused fudge and barely computed. *Ask about Bonnie.* "How's your mom doing?"

"It's a week tomorrow since the surgery and she's finding it hard doing nothing. Fortunately, if she tries to do too much, her sutures remind her pretty quick." She moved toward the refrigerator. "My folks really appreciate all you've done for them."

He waved the thanks away. "It's my job."

"It is, but there's ways and means of doing that job. They know it was a lot to ask of you to allow Mom to have the chemotherapy here. They've sent over a card, some ranch-grown beef and a six-pack of beer." Swinging open the refrigerator door, she bent over to indicate where she'd put the food.

He almost choked on his tongue. Gone were the cutoff shorts and in their place she wore black high-cut bikini briefs that matched her top. They sat low below her hips, covering only half of her gloriously round buttocks.

Sweat broke out on his forehead. Who fixed plumbing in a bikini?

She tossed him a beer. "You look hot."

So do you. "Yeah." He cracked open the can and took a long, cold slug of the brew to slake his dry throat and to stop himself from pulling her into his arms. He wasn't doing that until he had a better read on her.

He couldn't shake the image of Ashley lying on their bed dressed in a black corset and come-hither high-heeled boots. It was one of many costumes she'd worn now and then, and the memory slashed him like the blade of a shiv. It had all been part of her plan to control him through sex. Get him hard and horny and then metaphysically knee him in the balls until she got what she wanted. He'd given in more than once and he still tasted his bitter regret. When he'd left Chicago, he'd vowed that no woman was going to control him again.

Was Katrina using the fact he'd told her he found her

tool belt sexy? He didn't know her well enough to have worked out her games, but he knew he didn't want to play any. "Exactly why are you wearing your bikini to fix my toilet?"

She glanced down at the bandeau as if she'd forgotten about it. "The house was a hundred and ten degrees when I arrived."

"And that's the only reason?"

She gave him a look that said perhaps he was missing some brain cells before unclipping her tool belt. "Why? Do you have a no-bikini rule inside the house?"

He thought about Ashley. "I have a straight-shooting policy."

She blinked. "Okay, then." She pushed a cooler with her foot. "As I was about to say before you became the bikini police, there's a lovely deep water hole in the bend of the creek, not far from here." She licked her lips nervously. "I wondered if you . . . I thought it might be nice if we took a picnic supper and went for a swim."

Relief slid through him at her hesitant and guileless invitation, quickly banishing old memories. "So that's why you're wearing your bikini."

"It's what I usually wear when I go swimming." A slight frown marred her forehead. "It was just an idea, Josh. It's fine if you don't want to come." She picked up her tool belt. "I'll leave now and let you get on with your evening."

"No," he said way too abruptly, not wanting her to leave. "A swim sounds perfect."

A disbelieving look crossed her face. "Are you sure?"

He set his beer on the counter, crossed the short distance between them and kissed her quickly on the cheek. "Absolutely."

She still wore an air of tentativeness. "So you really do want to go?"

"I really do." This time he gave her a long, deep kiss on the lips to reinforce his words. "I'll go grab my swim shorts."

She wrapped her hand gently around his wrist. "No need."

This time it was his turn to frown. "I thought we were going swimming?"

She glanced at her feet and then brought her gaze back to his face, her cheeks now pink. "Um, the water hole . . . it's on private property and very secluded."

He grinned at her discomposure, enjoying her inexpert style. He put his hands on her waist and pulled her in against him, loving the way her curves fitted into his. "Are you suggesting impropriety to an upstanding member of the Bear Paw community?"

"So you don't want to go skinny-dipping?" She unbuttoned his business shirt, the backs of her fingers skating across his skin, making him want to lift her up and wrap her legs around his waist there and then.

"I didn't say that." Using both hands, he stroked tendrils of hair back behind her ears. "I just want to be sure that you plan to part with that bikini when we get there. After all, a guy doesn't want to feel used."

The teasing look in her emerald eyes suddenly got serious. "I thought that was exactly what this thing between us was all about. Using each other."

Spoken out loud, the words sounded harshly matter-of-fact, which struck him as being in stark contrast to the amazing sex they shared. "I like to think we're enjoying each other's company when we can."

She gave him a long, assessing look and then swung out of his arms and picked up the cooler. "And right now we have a window of opportunity, so are you in?"

Fun streaked through him. "I'm so in."

A seductive smile lit up her face and she ran to the door. "Let's go enjoy each other, then."

JOSH couldn't remember being this relaxed in a very long time. He sat on a large, flat river rock that had been worn smooth by the flowing action of a gazillion gallons of water over billions of years. Icy cold water ran over his feet, the sun warmed his back and Katrina had heated him from the inside out. He'd never had sex outdoors before, but he could now see its allure.

He handed her a soda from the cooler. "This was a great idea, thank you."

Her mouth twitched up at the edges and her eyes crinkled as the smile reached them. "The picnic or the sex?"

"Both." Ravenously hungry, he bit into his third roll of pulled beef and coleslaw. "You know, this tastes as good as any sandwich from Mac's, my favorite deli in Chicago."

"There's no question it's good, but I'm guessing you missed lunch today, so it tastes even sweeter."

"I did, but it was worth it."

"Dare I ask?"

But underneath her teasing, he knew genuine interest lay and he appreciated it. Ashley had never shown much curiosity in his work, only in his future possible earnings. "I got an interesting case of renal colic come through the ER."

She gently bumped his shoulder. "Probably more excruciatingly painful than interesting for the patient."

"True enough, but I was generous with the narcotics." He was struck by a thought. "I hope that doesn't get out."

"This is Bear Paw, Josh. It's hardly the number one destination for junkies. So how's the guy now?"

"He passed a sucker of a stone and he should sleep well tonight but he's going to be sore tomorrow." He suddenly reached for his pants. "That reminds me. I better check my service."

"You don't need to hide behind your service, Josh," she said sharply as her pretty features hardened like concrete. "This is casual and if you want to leave, just go."

"I don't want to leave." Her antagonism had come out of nowhere, perplexing him, and it didn't make a lot of sense. As a nurse, she knew he needed to check in with his service, especially given he'd been deliciously distracted with her for the past hour. "What's going on, Katrina?"

"Nothing." She looked away but her hands were pressed hard against the rock.

He pressed a kiss into her shoulder. "It doesn't feel like nothing."

Silently, she shrugged him away. At a loss as to what the hell was going on and not wanting to play any games, he rang his service. Given that the mention of it seemed to have sparked something, he put his phone on speaker. Everything in Bear Paw's hospital and clinic was under control and he was not required. He cut the call.

She immediately turned to him, her face filled with a mixture of contrition and something else that was less easy to read. "Sorry."

He was so tempted to say *that's okay* and kiss her, but he needed to know what had just happened. "What for?"

She sucked in her lips as if she didn't want to tell him and then blew out a breath. "Flashbacks."

He stared at her, not understanding.

She dropped her gaze. "Brent frequently called his service."

Brent? Her rigid posture and steely tone hinted at one thing only. "The bastard cardiac surgeon?"

"That's him." She lay back on the rock and stared at the cloudless sky. "He was always checking his service. I thought he was the most conscientious doctor I'd ever met right up until I discovered he'd been calling his wife."

Red-hot fury whipped through him at the unknown man. "The wife you didn't know he had?"

She nodded. "That would be the one."

"How did you find out?"

She sat up slowly and her fingers worried a tiny plant that grew in a crack in the rock. "He slipped up. Made a mistake."

"What sort of a mistake?"

She sighed. "I'm really not proud of this period in my life, Josh."

He thought about his own stupidity and blindness with Ashley. "You're not alone there, Katrina. We've all done things we regret."

She gave him an assessing look. "You've got a story that makes you look like a first-class fool?"

"Maybe."

She pulled the small seedling out of the crevice. "Then you'll understand why I haven't told anyone."

One part of him was surprised, given she was so close to her family, but another part of him understood. Back when he'd worked out she'd been in a relationship with a married man, he remembered saying to her, *how could you not know* and her reply of *don't judge me*. Not that he had any interest in psychiatry, but he did know that at some point bad stuff needed to be voiced. Katrina had been sitting on this for a few months.

"You can tell me and I promise to keep it a secret. Even if Bethany gets wind of it and threatens me with her crutch, I'll still be a vault."

She gave him a faint smile. "Okay, but I'm telling it fast."

"Like ripping a Band-Aid off a wound?"

"Pretty much. Here goes." She blew out a breath. "Brent was one of the cardiothoracic surgeons I worked with. He was great at his job, and his patients loved him because not only was he a talented surgeon, he had a special ability of making whoever he was talking to feel they were incredibly special."

Josh hated him already. "And he charmed you?"

"He charmed everyone." She pursed her mouth as if she'd just sucked on a sour lemon. "He'd ask you about your weekend, ask after people's kids and pets, that sort of thing. And he'd remember stuff like birthdays and if your dog was sick. It wasn't until much, much later, after I'd found out about his secret life, that I realized he did all of this to avoid revealing anything about himself. He was an expert at that."

She started shredding the leaves off of the plant. "The lab was often short staffed, and because my family was across the other side of the country and I didn't have any children, I often took the on-call weekend work. Most of the time, I never got called in, but there was this one weekend about six months after Brent joined the staff. It was crazy, maybe it was a full moon, I don't know, but we had back-to-back emergencies. Every time we said good-bye, plugged in the security code and prepared to leave, we'd get another call."

"I know weekends like that."

"Yeah." She got a faraway look in her eyes. "It was like being in a vacuum, totally separate from the rest of the world, and it was fun. Full of shared jokes." She sighed. "Even now, after everything that's gone down and his utter disregard for the moral glue that holds relationships together, there's no denying Brent was great company."

"It's my experience that most sociopaths are," Josh said, his dislike for this guy rising every minute. "And that's what makes them so hard to recognize."

"And I didn't recognize that about him at all. That's what burns so much, because I thought I was a good judge of people." The stripped plant fell out of her hand.

He thought about her reaction when they'd kissed at the clinic. "So things started that weekend at work?"

"They did. In the on-call room, which should have been tacky but somehow it wasn't. We started dating straight-away. Before Brent, I'd dated a practical cowboy, an accountant who lacked imagination and a cash-strapped intern, so when he started sending me expensive gifts, I fell for it.

"He arranged our dates to fit in with our schedules, insisting that my schedule at the lab match his when he was there. It made sense, and if part of me thought it lacked a certain spontaneity, it was silenced by the times Brent stretched the rules, making everything exciting and fun. I guess that was a sign that I missed. Mostly we caught up midweek, but we got away for some weekends, and I went to Hawaii with him for a conference. When he suggested we keep things quiet because management frowned upon staff dating, I agreed for both our sakes."

He could see how a trusting, country-raised woman had no reason to suspect a thing. "How long did all this go on for?"

"Eight months."

"Eight months?" That shocked him. "You were happy for it to be secret all that time?"

She turned her hands over and studied her palms. "I know, in hindsight it's a big clue, but without family to introduce him to, it didn't seem that much of a big deal. Plus, until we were officially engaged, I wasn't keen to let work know in case they made me move departments. I loved that job and I really didn't want to lose it." She shrugged. "Given what happened, that's the ultimate kicker.

"At six months, things were going so well that I asked Brent to come to Bear Paw to meet my folks. We got out our schedules and pored over them, trying to find a time we could both get off work. He said he'd clear July and come to Montana. There was no reason for me not to believe him and I started planning. He started dropping hints about rings."

Josh's general belief that physical violence was never the solution to anything got seriously tested. "Asshole."

She grimaced. "And then one night when I was out with friends at a party, I saw a missed call on my phone. I didn't recognize the number, and as Brent always texted me, I felt sure it wasn't him." She shot him a self-effacing look. "Yes, with the clarity of hindsight, texting was a *huge* red flag, but I had no reason to question him. I just figured we were both busy and texting worked best.

"I called the number and a machine picked up." Her voice started to mimic the recording: "Hi, you've called Brent, Dana, Sophie, Maddison and baby Jayden. Leave a message and we'll call you right back." She closed her hand around her now-empty soda can, the sound of crushing metal echoing viciously around them.

He ached for her. At least he'd had weeks to see the writing on the wall for him and Ashley, even if he'd chosen not to believe it. "And did you leave a message?"

She shook her head. "I was too busy throwing up in the zinnias. When my concerned friends asked, I blamed it on too many mimosas."

"Mimosas are a travesty and the ruin of perfectly good champagne," he joked, trying to make her laugh and banish the memories that had drained all joy from her face. He picked up her hand. "Did you tell his wife?"

She stared off toward the mountains for a long, long time, and when she finally spoke, her voice was soft. "I planned to. I lay awake nights having conversations in my head where I told her that her life was a lie just like mine was and that it was neither of our faults. I imagined us together, sticking needles into an effigy of Brent. I decided to go see her in person and tell her that her charming and loving husband was a selfish prick who walked through life taking what he wanted as if it was his God-given right, no matter who he hurt in the process.

"I drove out to their picture-perfect, leafy green suburb and their impressive two-story home to tell her, but when I saw her putting the kids into the European four-wheel drive, I just couldn't do it because I wasn't sure who I was doing it for. So, I sat in my car, drowning under an overwhelming sense of sadness. Not just for me but for his wife, for his kids and for the facade that is their life." She sighed. "For all Brent's sins, who knows, he might just be a good dad, and I couldn't destroy that, even though on one level I know it's destroyed anyway."

She wrung her hands. "It's so hard to separate out my anger and hurt from all of this. And sure, even though I screamed at him, threw the gifts he'd given me back at him and deflated his car tires, I feel like he's gotten away with all of it. It's left me holding a loaded gun unable to pull the trigger."

He slung his arm around her shoulder and pulled her in close, feeling a vague need to protect her. "But he's out of your life now, right?"

She bit her lip.

A wave of fury hit him and he wasn't sure who he was most mad at. "Katrina?" Her name came out on a low growl.

She shrugged. "He still calls occasionally."

"Get a new number."

"No."

He didn't understand. "Surely, you're not hoping he'll leave his wife and family for you, because he won't."

Her eyes flashed. "Of course I know that. Why the hell do you think I'm back in Bear Paw?"

"To avoid him?"

"Exactly. I know my own weaknesses and I was worried he'd talk me out of it. He's incredibly good at getting what he wants and he still wants me."

He wanted to shake some sense into her. "Then why take the risk? Change your number tomorrow."

Her chin shot up. "Brent controlled my life with lies and deceit for close on a year. He played on my heart's desires and my confided dreams and he set up the expectation that we'd be together forever. Then he turned my world upside down. He didn't just steal the idea of my future, he stole my job, my apartment and my friends.

"I'm almost thirty years old and living with my parents, Josh. How pathetic is that? I am *not* going to let him take away the phone number I've had for years. I know it sounds stupid, but I've lost everything else and this is my line in the sand. The one thing I've got left."

He felt his teeth grinding. "And what if he uses your phone to come find you?"

She shrugged. "He could do that with or without the phone. I thought I loved him and I told him everything about myself. He knows about Coulee Creek, he's seen photos of the ranch and if he wanted to, he could find me in a heartbeat, but he won't come this far. It's the reason I came home."

Josh wasn't quite so certain, but before he could voice that, she jumped up, pulled him to his feet and, still holding on to his hand, leaped into the water.

He tumbled in after her and surfaced spluttering.

"You trying to drown me?"

"Not even close." Laughing, she wrapped herself around him, pressing her body hard against his, snuggling in.

He was hard in a heartbeat, like he was every time she touched him.

Her eyes, with their often-soft gaze, glittered hard, all facets of green, and she lowered her head to his, kissing him with the desperation of someone wanting to forget.

So help him, he let her.

Chapter 15

Through the blowing dust, Shannon could just make out Beau leaning up against the gate with Scout by his side. It had been three weeks since Beau had given Hunter the puppy and invited her son to work on the ranch. They'd fallen into a routine of her driving out to pick up Hunter and Rastas after she'd closed the diner for the day. On Thursdays and Fridays, when she stayed open late for family-style supper, Hunter stayed at the ranch.

She knew she should be happy, because he was less moody and at times seemed almost happy, but part of her ached that it came from a place that was totally separate from her. A place in which she played no part. Not once in his life had she ever told Hunter how hard it was at times being a single mom—she'd made her choices and only she was responsible for them, not him, but sometimes being the only parent to a child wore her down. As much as she was relieved Hunter seemed a bit happier, it was hard to accept it had nothing to do with her. It shouldn't hurt, she didn't want it to hurt, but it did.

When he was younger, he'd loved spending time with

her and they'd done lots of fun stuff together. It had countered the tough times of parenting, but just lately, she felt like she never got to do the fun stuff with him anymore. She was always the mom. The parent. The disciplinarian. The person who battled with him every morning about going to school, who struggled with him against his learning disability so that at least some of his homework got done. She chased after him to do his chores, she fed him, she tried to find ways to connect with him and nurture him, but so often he resisted all her attempts and was just plain miserable.

Except when he was at Coulee Creek.

Now he got out of bed in the mornings without being asked twice. He fed and took the dog outside to do its business before catching a ride out to the ranch with Lanky, one of the ranch hands who lived in town. How could she compete with Dillon, who'd shown him how to shoot a crossbow? Or with Beau, who was teaching him to ride a horse and train Rastas? Or with Lanky, who'd given him a crash course in mending irrigation pipe? Each night, Hunter came home filthy, exhausted, and brimming with stories about the day. It made her heart sing and ache all at the same time.

As she drove through the open gate, she gave Beau a wave and couldn't help but notice how his dusty jeans sat low on his hips and clung to his strong legs. Driving slowly, she watched him through her rearview mirror as he swung the gate closed and then leaned over it to loop the chain. The denim highlighted his tight ass, and her mouth dried. He was, without doubt, delectable cowboy eye candy. Complicated eye candy.

Earlier in the day, like most days, he'd sent her a photo of Hunter doing some sort of a ranch chore and reassured her that everything was fine. She'd come to look forward to this daily communication.

Really?

Okay, she spent the day on tenterhooks, waiting for the texts. She'd even been known to stalk her phone in quiet breaks at the diner. The moment her phone beeped, her heart rate picked up. Once, at seniors' morning coffee, Doris had actually commented that she looked flushed and had asked if she was catching a bug. But it wasn't just the arrival of the text that got her all warm and tingly; it was the banter that usually followed.

Beau was positively chatty on text messages, even cracking the occasional joke. His relaxed air in text-land, however, didn't translate across to their face-to-face encounters, leaving her puzzled about exactly where she stood.

He was nothing like any of the men she'd ever known. They'd always been very obvious in their intentions to get into her pants, and by now, after three weeks of looking after her kid, they would have well and truly made their move. Heck, they would have done it a lot earlier, and if she was honest, she knew that not one single one of them would have taken such an interest in Hunter. She'd have been flabbergasted if they'd even mustered up the effort to talk to him.

Too many experiences with guys who'd ignored her kid were the reasons she'd given up dating. They wanted food and sex but not the bother of a kid. The irony in this situation was that Beau was basically providing Hunter with summer camp and ignoring her.

Except for the texts and the anomaly of that kiss.

The kiss baffled her. It had been amazing and wonderful, but not once had he ever tried to do it again. Granted, they weren't alone very often, and their face-to-face conversations always took place at pickup and were usually focused on Hunter. Beau was always polite, but none of it gave her any clue as to why he was taking so much of an interest in Hunter. And he'd suggested a camping trip? What did he want from her other than fudge brownies and pie? It was slowly driving her out of her mind and she'd had enough. She was going to find a time to ask him straight up.

Beau reached the car and opened her door as he did each evening. "Hi, Sh-Shannon."

She smiled at him and then dragged her gaze away from

those hypnotic eyes as her feet hit the ground. She glanced around for her son, who was usually close by. "Hi. Where's Hunter?"

"Megan's got him p-p-p-peeling p-p-p-potatoes." He tensed and closed her car door harder than usual. "I try to avoid p-p-p-p-s."

"And *K*s," she said in solidarity, as it was the first time he'd drawn attention to his stutter since the night he'd kissed her. "So really, he's cleaning root vegetables?"

A flash of appreciation lit up his melted-chocolate eyes. "Yep. Earning his . . . supper. You're invited. Can you stay?"

The invitation was unexpected. "I . . . Are you sure? I mean your mom and—"

He held up his hand. "Mom's in the . . . hospital tonight after her . . . chemo session. The rest of us . . . have to eat. Stay. Unless you're . . . busy?"

She was used to his short sentences, and unlike when she'd first met him and would have thought the invitation terse and backhanded, she knew it was genuine. And she wanted to stay. "I guess my laundry can wait another day," she said with a nervous laugh, hoping he understood that meant her social calendar was totally empty. "I'd love to stay."

"Good." The quietly spoken word matched the gentle smile on his face.

Tingles and shimmers set up a dance party in her veins before her common sense reminded her that this was her chance to speak with Beau. Find out exactly what his deal was, only she couldn't ask in front of Hunter or his family. "Um, can you show me the calves Hunter's been talking about? The orphans you're raising by hand?"

"Sure." He whistled for Scout, who obediently trotted to his side.

A whining immediately sounded behind them. Rastas stood on the edge of the porch, her golden legs quivering with anticipation and excitement. Shannon couldn't believe it. "I thought she would have just run to join Scout."

"I said I'd help . . . Hunter train her. She's learning."

So am I.

He called to the puppy, "Rastas, come." The dog obeyed, bounding over to him, barking excitedly and bouncing up and down. "Sit."

Rastas sat.

"Walk on."

The only dogs Shannon had any experience with jumped all over people, and she couldn't help but be impressed. The animals bounded ahead of them, racing through the pasture grass, immune to the panoramic view of acres of green grass dotted with huge, yellow, round bales as tall as she was and the craggy mountains off in the distance.

"This is the prettiest view," she said, filling the silence that was sitting between them. "Before I moved to Bear Paw I never gave much thought to how majestic Montana is. I mean, how lucky are we to wake up every day with the mountains right there? And the sky really is big, isn't it, and . . ."

He was smiling at her in his quiet and contemplative way, and she groaned, pressing her hands to her face. "I talk too much, don't I?"

He shook his head, regret clear in his eyes. "I don't talk . . . enough."

"I only do it when I'm nervous." She blurted out the truth, instantly regretting it.

They'd reached a gate and he stopped, bewilderment clear on his handsome face. "I make you n-nervous?"

She nodded as he opened a gate halfway and motioned her to walk through into the pasture where the young calves grazed.

She ducked between him and the gate, his masculine scent overlaid with sunshine and engine grease swirling around her and filling her nostrils. Filling her. A wave of heat swept her from tip to toe, kicking up her pulse, and all she wanted to do was turn into his chest, pull his face down to hers and revisit that amazing kiss.

For a moment, their bodies touched, and she paused, hopeful that he'd reach for her. He didn't. Agitated and totally at a loss as to what was going on between them, or to be more precise, what wasn't going on between them, she cleared the gate.

Weeks of confusion peaked. "I don't get why you're going out of your way with Hunter?" *Is it anything to do with me?*

He swung the gate closed and took a moment to latch it. "He . . . he's a good kid."

It didn't answer her question. "Thank you, but there are lots of good kids in Bear Paw and they're not out here every day. Everyone tells me summer's crazy busy on the ranches and"—she wrung her hands—"on top of everything, you've got the worry of Bonnie."

His shoulders tensed and he kicked a booted foot onto the bottom rail of the fence. "I . . . I can't help . . . Mom."

She understood how helpless he must feel seeing someone he loved fighting cancer, and she touched his arm in sympathy. The solidness of his forearm and the heat of his skin threatened to fry her concentration and she pulled her hand back. The loss of contact made her realize what he hadn't said.

"You think Hunter needs help?" The wind blew his shirt up like a balloon and he looked away, his expression tight. "Beau?"

He grimaced. "Hunter . . . he reminds me . . . "—the words came out slow and deliberate, as if they were fighting to be formed at all—". . . of me."

She tried to align her just-sprouting son with this big, solid man. "You?"

"When . . . when I was a kid."

Of all the things she might have thought he'd say, that wasn't one of them. "How exactly?"

Beau rubbed the back of his neck, every part of him radiating stiffness. "He . . . he's sad. Doesn't know . . . where he fits."

On the back of Hunter's constant talk about Beau, Dillon and Lanky, his words whipped her. "And that's my fault?"

He shook his head, his eyes wide. "Hell no."

The fact that he didn't blame her like so many outsiders often did cleared her head, and his understanding nibbled at her usual reserve. She found herself volunteering information she normally kept to herself. "Hunter has trouble with reading and writing, which makes him miserable at school. I guess you were miserable, too, with your stutter?"

He sighed. "I think . . . it's more . . . than school."

A zap of fear rolled in her gut. "Why? Has Hunter told you something?" *Something bad he hasn't told me?*

An agonized expression crossed his face, as if he wanted to be anywhere else but here, having this conversation.

Panic started to simmer. Had Hunter been bullied? Assaulted? "Tell me, Beau."

"I think . . . maybe . . . it's his dad."

Malcolm? Relief poured through her at how wrong Beau was, and she shook her head so fast that hair whipped her face. "At seventeen, I was young and stupid and I made a hellish mistake. Hunter was the only good thing that came out of those disastrous few years. His father's a total ass, and Hunter's better off without him in his life, breaking promises and constantly letting him down. There's no way that he can miss someone he's never known."

He flinched. "He can miss . . . the idea."

The softly spoken words carried a sting. "You're a cowboy, not a therapist," she said tartly. "I'm his mother and I've protected Hunter from heartache. I know what I'm doing. Hell, I even stopped dating because I didn't want him to get attached to a guy only to have him walk out on us and leave him devastated."

BEAU heard Shannon's hurt before it burned like a fire in his chest. Hurt he'd brought to the surface. Hell, he hadn't meant to. He was still confused at how they'd gotten to this point. What should have been a pleasant stroll in the pasture had turned into his worst nightmare—talking about feelings.

When she'd asked him why he was spending time with Hunter, he should have fallen back on the puppy training, but he'd been busy avoiding saying that part of the reason was so he got to see her. That would have made him sound like he was using Hunter and, hand to God, he wasn't doing that.

He'd thought that telling a mother her son was a good kid would have been enough, but shit no, he'd gotten that wrong. She'd kept pushing at him and now she was upset. He didn't understand women, but for the first time in his life, he wanted to try. But that was going to involve talking about feelings, and he'd rather be thrown by a bull than do that. Talking about feelings—his or anyone else's—made his stutter come back in full force.

As he concentrated on his breathing as well as carefully choosing his words, his head threatened to explode. "I kn-kn-know it doesn't . . . make sense. The s-sadness . . . it . . . it isn't logical. Doesn't mean it . . . doesn't happen."

Her gaze, which matched the wide blue sky above them, found his. "I don't understand. You said Hunter was like you, but you grew up here with your family. With your father."

He gave up on the controlled breathing and took the emergency tactic of whispering just so he could get the words out. "Bonnie and Kirk are my aunt and uncle."

Surprise flared on her face. "I had no idea."

"No reason why . . . you should. They adopted . . . me at five."

She sat down abruptly in the grass and hugged her knees. "I want to ask why, but are you okay with that?"

Not really. He sat down next to her, hoping that by telling her, she might understand Hunter. "It will . . . be slow."

"That's okay." She squeezed his arm as her pretty mouth curved up in a wry smile. "I promise not to interrupt."

He appreciated that more than she'd ever know. All his life, people had taken his slow speech to be a slow mind and had jumped in to finish his sentences for him. "My father died . . . in a trucking accident. My mother . . ." God, he hated this part. "My mother was a . . . junkie. She tried hard . . . not to be but . . ." His throat tightened, so he decided just to skip that bit. "I was five when . . . I got here. Best thing that . . . ever happened to me. Probably saved my life."

"Bonnie and Kirk are good people."

"The best." Which was why it totally sucked and was viciously unfair that Bonnie was now fighting cancer. He hated that he couldn't blast it with his gun or rope it under control. "They are . . . my parents. I owe them everything." He raised his brows. "Didn't see that . . . at fifteen."

She nodded slowly. "Puberty sucks."

He watched her stretch out her legs and momentarily got distracted by the tiny butterfly tattoo on her ankle before he realized she was looking at him expectantly, waiting for him to continue. "Before that I was . . . happy. My only memory . . . of my mother . . . is fear. With Bonnie . . . it's love. One day when I . . . was fifteen . . . I woke up . . . feeling like there was . . . a hole inside of me. I didn't understand. All I kn-kn-knew was I felt bad . . . guilty . . . that I wanted to see my mom . . . but in my head . . . Bonnie was my mom."

She didn't say anything for a moment, seeming lost in her own thoughts. Eventually, she said, "Did you ask to see her?"

"No. No point. By then she . . . was dead."

She flinched. "Would you have asked if she was alive?"

"I dunno."

She drew circles in the dirt with her forefinger. "Has Hunter told you he wants to see his father?"

"No."

"So it probably isn't that."

He shrugged. He guessed she had her reasons for not wanting to believe him.

"So what helped you?"

"Working on . . . the ranch. Riding the horses. Losing myself in . . . books."

She gave him a contemplative look. "Animals are less complicated than people?"

He smiled. "You bet."

Her hand sought his and her empathy flowed into him like a balm. For a moment, he stared at her white fingers that were interlaced with his sun-browned ones—light and dark, small and large, both work-worn. He brought them to his lips and pressed a kiss to her knuckles.

Her other hand immediately crossed his chest and cupped his cheek, turning his head to face her. She leaned in close, her breath skimming across his skin. "I've wanted to do this ever since the night you kissed me." Reaching up, her lips touched his, all soft, warm and wonderful.

His waiting was finally over, and the relief that she wanted him was equal to his need for her. Both rushed him, sending desire into every cell. He opened his mouth under hers, and she took the invitation and dove right in.

She explored his mouth with her tongue, each flick and lick branding him with her taste of toothpaste and sugar, and promising more. So much more.

God, he wanted more. Wanted it all. He wrapped his hand around the back of her neck, tilted her chin back and took over the kiss. He plundered her delicious mouth, imprinting himself all over it and claiming ownership.

She made a whimpering sound in the back of her throat and threw her arms tightly around his neck, clinging to him. The sound echoed down deep, releasing a primitive urge to protect her from everything except him. He wanted to ravage her in a way that would make her scream with pleasure and beg him for more. He kissed a slow path across her chin, down her neck and into the curve of her shoulder. Her skin smelled of brown sugar, cinnamon and huckleberries, and it collided with the musky scent of sex—the juxtaposition of sweet innocence and eroticism. He couldn't get enough of it. "You smell good enough . . . to eat."

She laughed and pressed kisses into his hair as her fingers trailed gently across his face starting at his forehead, sweeping around his eyes, down his cheekbones to his nose, over his lips and along his chin. He'd never known touch quite like it, and something deep down inside him that had held tight for years gave way.

Putting his arms around her, he rolled them over into the grass, needing to feel her body—the one he'd fantasized about for weeks—fitting against him. As if reading his mind, her legs immediately tangled with his, pulling him down against her. Her hands pulled at his shirt and she slid her palms along the skin of his back with a sigh.

His hands, which could control a wild horse and every tool ever invented, shook as he pushed up her T-shirt and camisole. Her breasts—small and beautiful with their dusky nipples erect and calling—lay there just for him. He dropped his head and suckled her, filling his mouth and feasting.

His blood thrummed hot and fast, the sensations building on top of one another. God, he was going to lose control in the middle of the pasture. He pulled back just as Shannon let out a squeal that was more surprise than orgasmic pleasure.

Her hands pushed at his shoulders. "Look."

He glanced around to find eight sets of big brown eyes staring down at them. Six belonged to the calves and two to the dogs who'd wandered over to see what was happening.

Somehow, despite jeans so tight they threatened to castrate him, he rolled away and then pulled Shannon to her feet. "S-s-sorry."

She laughed as she brushed grass off her clothes. "Don't be sorry. We just need to choose a less public place, and preferably inside, next time."

"Good idea." He grinned down at her. "I'm glad . . . there's going to . . . be a next time."

She put her arms around his waist, her face filled with anticipation. "There's definitely going to be a next time. But where? It can't be at my place because of Hunter."

For the first time in his life he regretted living at home. "It can't be . . . anywhere in town. If Bethany gets a hint, it will be . . . on Twitter."

"Oh my God, this shouldn't be this hard. We're adults,

not teens, and I gave up sneaking around years ago. And then there's the when. How are we going to manage it when we both work huge hours and—"

"I'll . . . f-find a place." He felt her wavering and kissed her, but it was the growing reserve in her eyes that made his gut squeeze. "It will work out."

Her fingers squeezed his forearms. "Beau, Hunter can't know."

He understood. This was the mother bear protecting her cub. What he didn't understand was the stab of disappointment that caught him under the ribs.

Chapter 16

Katrina woke with a start only to realize she'd been asleep on the sofa and someone was in the kitchen. Bleary-eyed, she padded the short distance to find Beau drinking a glass of water. "What time is it?"

"Three. You're up late."

She automatically plugged in the electric kettle for hot chocolate. "Mom was puking her heart out until almost midnight. When she finally fell asleep, I sat down to watch the end of *The Tonight Show*. I guess I must have fallen asleep."

"Should you call . . . Josh?"

"I will when it's light. I want her to sleep as long as possible."

"Good." He set the glass in the sink and sighed. "Is it going . . . to be worth it?"

It was the first time in the seven weeks since Bonnie's diagnosis that Beau had spoken to her about their mother's condition. Up until now, he'd coped by throwing himself into running the ranch and helping Shannon's morose son with his dog. "The chemo? We have to hope it is. Best-case scenario, she goes into remission. Worst-case, it buys us all precious time."

"The chemo's worse this time." He slammed his fist into his palm. "I h-hate s-seeing her like this. So frail."

"Me too." She hugged him tightly, totally understanding his grief because it perfectly matched hers.

He was a tall man and her head didn't even come close to his shoulder, and as her cheek hit his shirt, a familiar scent tickled her nostrils. A scent that had nothing to do with horses, dogs, tractors, cows, sweat or laundry powder, all of which were the aromas she associated with her older brother. This scent was one hundred percent female. Interesting. Since the end of June, Beau had been coming and going at odd hours, but she'd been too distracted with caring for her mom and sneaking times with Josh to really notice.

She stepped back and busied herself making the hot chocolate before passing him a mug. "So, you and Ty were out late, given you're cutting hay in four hours."

"Yeah." He sipped his drink.

"Since when has Ty worn cinnamon cologne?"

He stared at her and she couldn't quite decide if he looked sheepish or hellishly proud of himself. "You'd kn-know more than me."

She laughed. "Good try, Beau, but it's been a very long time since I was intimate with Ty's cologne."

"Ty's not . . . my type."

"Ha-ha, very funny." She knew the scent but she couldn't instantly place from where and it was driving her nuts. "Who's the lucky lady?"

He shook his head slowly.

"Oh, come on, Beau, I need some good news."

"I want to . . . tell you. I want to . . . tell everyone, but she . . . wants to . . . keep it quiet."

Katrina thought about her and Josh and begrudgingly understood. "Does she make you happy?"

"Very."

She kissed him on the cheek. "I'm glad."

Beau headed off to bed and she switched off the lights, intending to go to her own, but the conversation had woken her up. She stepped out onto the porch and Scout and Rastas raised their heads but Boy slumbered on. "Go back to sleep, doggies," she said quietly as she sat on the bottom step and gazed up at the stars.

There was something special and calming about being under a clear summer night sky. She located Cygnus in the middle of the Milky Way and immediately thought of Josh. He'd been the one to point it out to her. He'd bought a stargazing app for his phone, and two nights ago, after they'd made love, they'd snatched some precious time lying together on their backs in the cottage garden, locating constellations.

Making love? It's called "having sex," remember?

Josh and *love* didn't belong in the same sentence. He was as insistent as she was that he didn't want a relationship. Why, exactly, was less clear. Although he knew her sordid story, she didn't know much about his life before Bear Paw, other than he had a difficult relationship with his father.

But that didn't preclude relationships with women. She'd worked in a big hospital, so she wasn't naïve enough not to know that he'd probably enjoyed and accepted the attentions of numerous nurses and interns. A guy who could reduce her to a quivering mess with a few dexterous flicks of his fingers had plenty of experience.

Just thinking about those fingers made the muscles between her legs twitch, and tingling sensations darted deep. Just like that, she wanted to see him. Unlike with Brent, this thing she had with Josh had no structure or organization as to when they saw each other. It was exactly how she liked it. She got away from the ranch when she could and he never asked for more. He accepted her unannounced arrivals and departures in his bed with a bone-melting kiss that kept her coming back.

Not that she'd ever arrived at 3:30 A.M. before, but there

was a first time for everything. She had a key to let herself in, and while she was there she could ask him to stop by to see her mom before he started his clinic day.

Decision made, she stood up and walked to the pickup. He'd either be in bed, sleep rumpled and gorgeous, or he'd be at the hospital. She hoped it was the former because she didn't have much time. She needed to be back by six to start the day. Hardworking ranchers needed feeding before they started out on a long day of haymaking, and her mom would need her to help with showering.

Josh, please be there. Don't let there have been a medical emergency.

The eerie hoot of an owl agreed.

———

"YOU should have called me," Josh said to an exhausted Bonnie, who lay against a bank of snowy white pillows, her complexion a contrasting sickly yellow. He was doing a home visit to the ranch on his way to work because Katrina was worried that Bonnie's lethargy was more than just post-chemotherapy nausea.

Katrina had slid into his bed a couple of hours after he'd fallen into it. There'd been an almost fatal car crash between an RV and a compact on the road to Glacier. He, Millie and Will Bartlett had spent a fraught hour trying to stabilize the driver and passenger of the compact to give them the best chance of surviving the airlift to Seattle. It was so touch and go, Millie had flown out with Will as an extra pair of hands. The moment Millie had texted to say their patients had stayed alive and were in the OR, he'd fallen into a fitful sleep.

A sleep filled with 3-D dreams that lurched crazily between his family's vacation cottage, where Ashley stood in the sea dressed in her business suit, and every ER where he'd ever worked, where she suddenly appeared to stand next to him. She constantly blocked his access to all his patients, telling him they were going to die because he wouldn't operate. With rising anger, he'd been running up and down stairs, desperate to find a way around her when suddenly all his agitation had dissipated and the hospital had faded away.

Languid warmth had seeped into him and he was back at the water hole, lying in dappled sunlight. Katrina was snuggled into him, her breasts pressed into his back and her hands on him, stroking him, rubbing him, and he was coming fast.

He woke just as his orgasm hit to find Katrina in his bed. It was the best start to a day he'd ever known.

Bonnie coughed and the sound centered him, bringing his concentration back to what was important.

"It was a bad night, is all."

"Katrina said you've had a few of those."

Bonnie pursed her lips as if Katrina had spoken out of turn. "I think I waited too long before I got the injection for the nausea. Once it started working, I slept until six when one of those damn hot flashes woke me up." She gave him a look of utter indignation. "Instant menopause is the worst."

He shoved his stethoscope into his bag. "Bonnie, I think it's more than just nausea. Your blood pressure's low, you're not eating and I'm not convinced those hot flashes are due to the fact the surgery removed your ovaries. I want you back in the hospital so I can run some tests."

"I'm fine," she said, her fingers picking at lint on the summer cotton throw.

"You're far from fine," he said quietly.

Ignoring him, she shifted her gaze out the window, looking far into the distance, off toward the green and yellow tractor that was moving up and down the pasture.

"You know, Kirk and I couldn't afford our own tractor when we started. We shared an old one with our neighbors and Kirk and Roy kept it running with copper wire and a lot of swearing."

This was why he'd preferred ER work. In the ER, no one ignored your instructions and told you stories. Or at least he never gave them the chance. He'd just order the tests and walk away, leaving the nurses to deal with everything else. But now, after twelve weeks in Bear Paw, there were fewer opportunities to walk away. Fewer opportunities to see patients just as a malfunctioning body part. More opportunities to see them as people interconnected with their community and family, which was increasingly hard to ignore even when he wanted to. Bonnie obviously had something on her mind and he needed to give her the chance to say it.

He sat down on the bed. "And now tractors are fully computerized, but I bet a lot of swearing still goes on."

"Some things don't change." She dragged her penetrating gaze away from the window and locked it onto Josh's. "Life's going on as normal all around me, only nothing's normal anymore, is it, Josh? I'm getting worse."

He wanted to reassure her. "I know it feels that way, but until the final round of chemotherapy is finished and the scans are in, we won't know if we're winning. Remember, chemotherapy's not without its side effects, and one of those is a drop in your infection-fighting white blood cells. If I were a betting man, I'd say that's the most likely culprit, not the cancer. Once we get on top of the infection, you'll feel a lot better."

Her head rolled on the pillow and her mouth kicked up on one side. "We?"

He knew that ironic tone—Katrina had used it on him in the early days. "Yes, we. You, your oncologist, me, the family." He shot for a reassuring smile. "It's a team thing, Bonnie."

"Well I'm sure as heck taking one for the team, Josh. I feel like someone picked me up by the hair and threw me hard against the wall."

He opened his mouth to say *you'll feel better soon*—it had always been his exit line whether he believed it or not, but he found he couldn't say it. Not this time. "Come into the hospital, I'll start an IV, run the tests and we'll take it from there, okay?"

"Can I come home tomorrow?"

"I'm not making promises I might not be able to keep, Bonnie."

She nodded thoughtfully. "That's both good and bad to know."

"Yeah." He shoved his hands in his pockets, not knowing what to say and hating the feeling.

"I can smell pancakes. Katrina's are not quite as good as mine but they're close," she said, rescuing him from an uncomfortable conversation. "Go have some." Her eyes fluttered closed. "Can you tell the others about the hospital?"

That he could do. "Consider it done."

He entered the kitchen to find the rest of the family, with the exception of Beau, sitting down to a huge breakfast of bacon, eggs, sausage links, hash browns and pancakes. The clink and scrape of silverware on china suddenly stopped and everyone looked at him, their faces filled with apprehension and questions. He wished he had better news for them.

Kirk rose to his feet, dropping his napkin on the table. "How is she?"

"I'm admitting her to the hospital."

He nodded as if that was the news he'd expected. "How long for?"

"As long as it takes."

He sighed. "I'll go pack her things."

"I can do that, Dad," Katrina offered.

"I know, and you'd probably do a better job, but I want to do this."

Megan pushed back from the table. "We'll tell Beau you're at the hospital, Dad."

Dillon stood, grabbing a last piece of toast. "Don't worry, Dad. We'll get the west pastures cut and raked. You stay with Mom."

"If she lets me," Kirk said with a grimace. "It's just as likely she'll insist I come back and cut hay." He put his hand on Josh's shoulder. "It was good of you to come so early, son. Appreciate it."

"No worries. I was awake so it made sense." He glanced at Katrina and couldn't stop himself from grinning widely.

Katrina, who was mid-sip of coffee, suddenly started coughing violently and hers eyes widened so far they threatened to leak color.

Josh immediately thumped her on the back as everyone left the room. "You okay?"

"No." She sucked in a restorative breath. "You're grinning at me in front of my father like you just got laid."

"I did." He bent down and kissed the side of her neck. "And it was amazing."

Her hand touched the back of his neck and her fingers caressed his hair for a moment before falling away. "Not here, Josh. Please."

"Sure." He understood, but as he straightened up an odd, empty feeling slithered through him. He immediately shrugged the sensation away.

"Have some breakfast," Katrina said, pouring him a coffee. "There's plenty."

"Thanks. It looks great." He picked up a plate and loaded it with food. He'd just taken his first mouthful of the light-as-air pancakes when a woman's voice floated through the screen door.

"Hello? It's Rhonda." The door opened and the Bear Paw courier stepped inside holding a couple of boxes. "Got that e-reader for your mom, Katrina."

"Great, thanks, Rhonda." Katrina took the packages and set them on the table.

"Oh, hey, Doctor Stanton," Rhonda said, catching sight of Josh as Katrina signed. "I'm glad you're here. I've got a delivery for you that needs signing for. Can I bring it in now?"

He wasn't expecting anything. "Are you sure it's not something for the clinic or the hospital?"

She shook her head. "Nope. It's got your home address on it. I'll go get it."

Used to interruptions and never getting to finish meals,

he turned his attention back to his breakfast and shoveled in a few more mouthfuls of the crispy bacon and runny egg before Rhonda returned with a large box. As he signed for it, she tapped the label. "It's from out east. Chicago. You have a good day."

When Rhonda left, Katrina passed him some scissors. "Is it your birthday and you didn't tell us?"

"No, that's in November. Maybe the guys from Mercy have sent me my favorite coffee blend."

She rolled her eyes. "Yeah, like you can't buy coffee here. Give me their address and I'll ship them some."

He laughed. "You getting all parochial now you've been home for a while?"

She shrugged. "I miss some stuff about Philly, but I don't miss the traffic or the noise."

Sliding the blade along the brown tape, he pulled open the cardboard top and removed the crumpled newspaper that had been used as filler. An eclectic collection of things lay underneath: some CDs, an old copy of *Gray's Anatomy* he'd always used as a doorstop in college, a bunch of paperback novels, his tuxedo still in its protective bag, a baseball mitt signed by the New York Yankees and some mail bundled together with a rubber band, the top one a slightly yellowed letter from the Mount Sinai Medical Center.

Ashley had done a comprehensive clean sweep of the apartment and sent him all his stuff. He noted with some cynicism that her engagement ring and the expensive silverware his family had given them were not there. The inclusion of his letter of offer from Mount Sinai was a particularly vicious touch.

Fuck you, Ashley. With a burst of delayed fury, he picked up the letter and ripped it into pieces.

———

STUNNED by Josh's outburst, Katrina watched the pieces of paper flutter to the ground. "It seems dumb to ask if something's wrong when obviously it is. Want to talk about it?"

His gray eyes, which recently had glowed warm and

soft whenever he looked at her, had taken on the color of flint. "Not particularly."

"If a patient had just done something like that in front of you, would you leave it alone?"

He grunted. "It's nothing. Just ancient history."

"History has a way of coming back to bite you."

He ran his hands through his hair and then rubbed his freshly shaved cheeks. "Tell me about it."

She picked up the scattered papers and made out the words *Mount Sinai.* "Prestigious hospital."

"Oh yeah. One of the best in the country."

"And?"

He kicked the box. "And I had the opportunity to work there."

And he was in Bear Paw. She poured more coffee for both of them. He looked like he needed something stronger than caffeine, but at seven in the morning, it was the only option. "Did you work there?"

"No. I took the job at Mercy instead."

"Having a choice is fantastic. So why are you upset?"

His brows pulled down in a sharp V. "You're going to keep at me until I tell you, aren't you?"

She nodded. "I think that I am."

"Why?"

Because you look like you've been sucker punched. "Friends tell each other things."

He tilted his head, his eyes far too incisive and intelligent. "We're friends now, are we?" His gaze made her shiver. "I thought you said we were just using each other for sex?"

He'd turned her words back onto her and the effect was unsettling. "I . . ." She rolled her palms outward and then laced her fingers. "Can't we do both? You're obviously upset and talking might help."

"Oh, but that's where you're wrong," he said quietly, his voice edged with steel. "Talking doesn't help at all. Ashley and I talked for months. We went around and around and it didn't resolve a fucking thing."

He'd talked about his father but he'd never mentioned anyone else. "Ashley?"

He ran his hand through his hair. "Yeah." He walked outside and she followed him, sliding her hand into his as he leaned up against the porch rail and looked out toward the mountains.

They stood there silently for a long minute before Josh walked to the porch rocker, taking her with him. "Ashley and I dated for two years, before we rented an apartment together. A year after that we got engaged. We were together five years."

Shock dropped her mouth open and she had to work really hard not to stare at him. For some reason she'd never once imagined Josh in a long-term relationship, let alone one headed toward marriage. "That's . . . that's a long time. When did you break up?"

"Officially? The day the moving truck arrived to pack all of our stuff for the move to Bear Paw."

Unofficially? Memories of the prickly, aloof and angry guy who'd arrived in town three months ago came to mind. She'd never quite been able to reconcile why, if Josh had chosen to come work in Bear Paw, he'd been so detached and irritable instead of enthusiastic in his early weeks. Now she might have stumbled onto the answer. "Ashley didn't want to come?"

He gave a harsh laugh. "That would be the understatement of the year. She said it would be professional suicide."

She thought about how Bear Paw was always chasing all types of medical and support staff. "I'm guessing she didn't work in health care?"

"No. She was in corporate marketing."

"Oh." Maybe Ashley had a point.

"Oh?"

His stony expression made her feel as if she were letting him down in some way. "What I meant was that there's not a big call for that type of work in Bear Paw."

He grimaced. "There isn't, but her company understood and totally supported her telecommuting from Bear Paw three weeks out of every four. They knew it wasn't forever and were bending over backward to help. We were coming out here to knock down my student loans fast so we could do the time, get the hell out of Dodge and start a family."

A family? Her gut thudded to her feet. First he'd been engaged and now he was admitting to wanting to be a dad? None of this matched up with the Josh she thought she knew.

"And . . . um, that's what Ashley wanted? Um, what she agreed to?" She fought to sound coherent while her thoughts splattered across her mind like they'd been whizzed in a blender.

"She'd agreed to way more than that." His thigh was so rigid against hers she could have bounced a ball off of it. "When I left the surgical program, I got offered my dream job in the ER at Mount Sinai. At the exact same time, Ashley got offered a position in the Chicago office of her firm. It was a big promotion for her. She sided with my father about my change in career direction and had been upset with me, but when I discussed my ideas with her on how to reduce my student loans fast, much faster than staying out east, we agreed on a plan. I supported her by moving to Chicago so she could take her dream job, and when the time came, she'd support me and we'd move somewhere rural out west for three years. Somewhere we both agreed on. We struck a deal for our future and got engaged. You know, the give-and-take of a mature relationship." He snorted.

"I'm not sure I've ever had one of those," she confessed with a wry smile.

"Yeah, well, they don't exist," he said bitterly. "I doubt Ashley ever had any intention of keeping her side of the bargain, but she happily let me give up Mount Sinai to get what she wanted."

He'd given up his dream job for this woman, and Katrina clearly saw Ashley's betrayal in the lines on his face, around his mouth and at the edges of his eyes. She thought about her total blindness with Brent. "Hindsight's a bitch."

"She's a bitch."

She squeezed his hand.

A hint of gratefulness lit up his eyes. "When the time came for me to apply for rural positions, I presented her with a list of ten places I'd researched and thought would be good places to work. She chose Bear Paw and I started all the paperwork."

She shifted to face him straight on. "So, wait, I don't get it. If she chose Bear Paw, why did she then refuse to come?"

"Apparently she never thought I'd go through with taking a rural job or expect her to actually uphold her part of the deal." Every muscle in his body clenched. "As we stood on the curb with movers waiting to get into the apartment, she told me that if I'd stayed in the surgical program, none of this would have happened."

"How did she figure that?"

He sighed. "Surgeons don't work in towns this small. Surgery meant we could have continued living in a big city, which was the only place she was prepared to live, and I could have paid off my loans without it impacting her life."

She struggled to understand Ashley's logic. "But you weren't happy doing surgery. Surely as your fiancée she wanted you to be happy?"

His mouth pulled down on one side. "Her solution was for me to go beg my father and ask him for the money to pay off my loans and we stay in Chicago."

An intense dislike for the woman crawled through her veins. "How could she ask you to do that? She must have known how much that would cost you?"

———

JOSH saw Katrina's jutted chin and the spark of indignation in her eyes and heard the pique in her voice. It took him a moment to realize that her reaction was for him and not against him. He wasn't used to the feeling of support from anyone outside of his colleagues, and as it slowly dripped into him, he had to work at not questioning the reasons behind it.

"Ashley believed it was something I should do for both of us. A sign that I was putting our relationship first. She didn't understand why I wasn't prepared to go into financial debt to my father. I knew if I asked, he'd levy a heavy emotional debt on us. He'd likely want my firstborn child and a commitment that, no matter what, the kid becomes a doctor. No way in hell was I committing to that when I'd already broken away. The emotional cost at Thanksgiving and Christmas is more than enough."

"So don't go this year," she said, her very kissable lips thinning fast. "Invite your parents to Bear Paw instead. Show them you're not only responsible for your choices, you're fine with them."

The absurdity of his parents coming out here made him laugh. "Maybe I can even get the town to throw me a ticker tape parade."

"They'd probably do it now." She grinned and giggled. "Wait. I have a better idea."

His fingers toyed with her hair. "What's that?"

"We introduce your father to Bethany. She'd pin him to the wall with that crutch and set him straight."

A rush of something he didn't want to name filled him and he leaned in to kiss her.

She kissed him fast and then pressed her hands to his chest. "You have to go to work and I have to go check Dad's packed everything Mom needs."

He rose, his mind running through his work schedule. "I'll let admissions know your mom's coming in right away and I'll talk to her oncologist."

Her green eyes, which could light up a room, dimmed. "She's not strong, Josh."

He knew that, too. "We'll set up isolation procedures to keep her safe from any hospital bugs, and I'll call you the moment I've got the test results. We'll hit it with everything we've got."

"I can't ask for more than that. I just hope it's enough."

"So do I."

She was standing right next to him, so close and yet so

far away. He wanted to reach out, grab her wrist, spin her back into his arms and kiss her the way he always did just before she left the cottage. He wanted to say, *When will I see you? Next time, come stay the whole night with me. Let's make plans to go watch the aurora borealis.*

But timing was everything, and sadly, this was so not the time.

Chapter 17

Beau McCade, 12:37 p.m. Day 2 of cutting hay. Hunter & Rastas driving the tractor. Don't worry, it drives itself ;-)

Shannon Bauer, 12:40 P.M. He looks happy ☺ S x

Beau McCade, 5:04 p.m. Radar showing chance of rain. Hunter will be at gate at six. Sorry, I can't stop to stutter or steal kiss at pickup. Will miss your smiling face. B x

Shannon Bauer, 5:55 P.M. I left pie at the house for everyone, especially you. I notice you don't stutter when we're having sex. S x

Beau McCade, 6:30 P.M. Thanks for pie. Speech therapist never suggested that particular exercise for stutter. I should practice more.

Shannon Bauer, 6:31 P.M. ☺ S xx

Beau McCade, 11:42 p.m. Long day. Just finishing with hay now.

Shannon Bauer, 11:43 P.M. Are you hot and sweaty?

Beau McCade, 11:44 p.m. Yes.

Shannon Bauer So am I. It's a hot night.

Beau McCade Too hot for covers.

Shannon Bauer Too hot for pajamas.

Beau McCade Take them off. Enjoy the breeze.

Shannon Bauer It's like your breath against my skin. If you were here, I'd like you to . . .

Beau McCade Spray you with a mist of cool water and lick you dry.

Shannon Bauer God, I wish you were here.

Beau McCade I can make you feel like I am.

Shannon Bauer Yes please.

———

SHANNON was cleaning out the diner's fridges when she heard heavy footsteps and the clack of dog's nails on the floorboards.

"Hunter?" She automatically glanced at the clock to check if she'd lost track of the time and was late picking him up. She pushed up off her knees and to her feet just as he appeared. "You're home early. Is everything okay?"

He shrugged. "Beau came into town to visit his mom, so he brought me home."

"That was kind of him." There were so many kind and thoughtful things about Beau McCade that she kept pinching herself to be sure that he was real and not some imaginary guy she'd dreamed up to keep her company at night.

And oh boy, in one way or another, he kept her company at night. The few times they'd managed to meet up at Ty's house when he was out on the range, she got to be cradled in Beau's strong arms and lie against his work-toned body. Those times, she knew he was real. But between his long hours on the ranch and her long hours at the diner and both of their family commitments, those stolen moments in the middle of the night were too few and far between. As much as she enjoyed the sexting, it wasn't the same as being with him.

Rastas padded over to her and sat at her feet, her eyes big and brown, ever hopeful of a treat. "You think if you look cute, I'll give in and feed you."

Rastas licked her hand and she patted her head. "She really is cute. You're doing a great job with her, Hunter."

"I've taught her some really dope tricks. Do you wanna see?"

"I'd love to." She pulled off her gloves and followed Hunter out into the yard.

He pulled some dog treats out of his pocket and Rastas raced around his feet, barking. "Sit." Rastas sat. "Good dog." He gave her a treat. "Stay." Hunter turned and walked a couple of yards before stopping and facing the pup. "Back up, Rastas."

The dog looked at him and thumped her tail on the ground.

Hunter took two steps toward her. "Back up." Rastas rose and took two steps backward. "Now sit." She sat and Hunter rewarded her with "good dog" and a treat.

Shannon clapped. "That's so awesome."

Hunter's smile was wide and proud. "She can do more."

Over the next five minutes he had Rastas stand, take a bow, shake a paw and spin and beg.

"That must have taken you hours."

He shrugged. "I do it at lunch when Beau's practicing his talking."

She stared at him, clueless as to what he meant. "His talking?"

"Yeah. He reads out loud. I thought it was pretty weird at first but I got used to it."

"What does he read?"

"Stuff."

She laughed. "Obviously, but what sort of stuff? Ranching stuff?"

He shook his head. "Nah. He read a book about some kid who built a raft."

Surprise shot through her. "*Huckleberry Finn*?"

"Yeah, like those pies you make."

Hunter wasn't a reader, so she was interested to hear what he thought of the classic story. "Did you enjoy it?"

"It was okay. It was pretty cool how Huck didn't have to go to school."

Trust her boy to think that. "Has Beau read anything else?"

"A crazy book about a pig and a spider."

"*Charlotte's Web*." She smiled at the memories that story evoked. "That was a favorite book of mine when I was in middle school."

"The animals in it were funny, and I liked the rat best." He ruffled Rastas's ears. "It was sad at the end when the spider died."

"I always cried at the end. So what's he reading now?" She expected Beau was revisiting another classic like *The Old Man and the Sea* or *The Chronicles of Narnia*.

"This one's about a boy who's a wizard."

Hunter had seen all the movies about the world's most famous boy wizard, but he hadn't read the books. The fact Beau was reading them was unexpected. "Beau's reading *Harry Potter*?"

"No. This one's about a boy who lives in a place where the only way to practice magic is to write down the spells. He can't do that and then he realizes he's been cursed by some evil magic that's taking over the world. He has to stay alive long enough to work out how to break the curse, write the magic and save the world. It's good but Beau's been too busy cutting hay to read the last couple of days."

Shannon's throat tightened with shock, making it hard to speak. Hunter appeared oblivious to the fact he'd just described his own learning problem. Beau wasn't practicing speaking by reading out loud; he was reading to her son. Showing him that words on a page could be enjoyed by listening—free of the struggle to assemble the letters and compute them in his mind.

Her guarded heart that held everyone except Hunter at bay opened. She was fast falling in love with Beau McCade.

———

BEAU hated hospitals. Truth be told, he feared them, but his father had told him that Bonnie wanted to see him. She wanted to see each one of his siblings on their own. That alone scared the hell out of him. He'd scrubbed his boots clean and showered and changed into fresh clothes before coming to visit, but right now, sitting in a chair next to Bonnie and wearing a paper gown, a mask and gloves, he was petrified it wasn't enough to keep her safe.

Germs from the ranch, from the hospital, from the air were like incendiary bombs to her. Josh had explained to everyone how chemotherapy couldn't tell the difference between the good cells and the cancer cells and just nuked them all. Right now, Bonnie had no resistance to infection. Everyday bugs that healthy people took for granted could kill her, and right now they were doing a good job trying.

The beep of a monitor displaying her heartbeat and a heap of other numbers he didn't understand glowed green, and two IV lines pumped fluid and antibiotics into her. The elastic of an oxygen mask broke the line of her pale and jaundiced cheek.

If Beau had thought she'd looked sick when she was at home three days ago, it was nothing compared to now. "Mom?"

She opened her eyes and reached out her hand.

"I don't th . . . th . . . th . . ." God he hated this mask on his face, suffocating his speech. He hauled in a breath. "I don't think . . . I should touch you."

She pulled the oxygen mask down. "Of course you should."

He wrapped his gloved hand around her now unfamiliarly thin hand, dwarfing it in his broader one. He remembered back across twenty-seven years to the night he'd arrived at Coulee Creek. How she'd kneeled down on the kitchen floor and hugged him tight and stroked his hair with her very capable and caring hands. It was the first time in his life he remembered feeling safe. He didn't feel safe now. He felt terrified he was going to lose her. "Are you feeling any better?"

She squeezed his hand, her fingers lacking strength. "I want to say yes."

His fear coalesced in his belly. She'd always been the one who reassured him. She'd always believed in him and seen his intelligence behind his slow and lumbering speech. She'd insisted that he was the one in charge of his stutter, not the other way around, and she'd been the one to drive the hundreds of miles over the years, taking him to speech therapy. She'd introduced him to the magic of books, encouraged him to go to college and had always been his champion, often knowing what he needed before he did.

"How's Shannon?"

The question caught him off guard. He'd been expecting the usual inquiry about the ranch. "Um . . . she's . . . um . . . good . . . I guess."

Bonnie gave him a mother's knowing look. "I know the two of you are seeing each other."

They'd been so careful. "How do you know?"

"I'm your mother. I might be sick, honey, but I'm not blind or deaf. Trucks that arrive and depart in the middle of the night are noisy."

He wanted to say *Katrina's part of that noise, too*, but

the two of them had an unspoken pact about their comings and goings when they met in the kitchen at odd hours of the night.

"You think you're being secretive, but really, you're not."

Stunned, he stared at her over the top of the mask, not knowing what to say.

Bonnie laughed, but it quickly turned into a racking cough.

Half gut instinct, half pure anxiety, he carefully wrapped his arms around her and lifted her forward so she could catch her breath. When she'd recovered, she patted his hand.

"Does Shannon make you happy?"

How could he tell her that in one way he was the happiest he'd ever been when she was lying here fighting off death as it clawed into her and held fast?

As if reading his mind, she said, "Beau, it's okay. All I've ever wanted is for my children to be happy. If you've finally met the woman I've been hoping you'd meet for years, the timing doesn't matter. I don't want any nonsense about bad timing. If you love her, tell her. If I beat this, I'll welcome her with open arms at Coulee Creek. If I don't, promise me you'll bring her anyway."

Tears burned the backs of his eyes, and his throat was so thick he could hardly speak. "You'll be there . . . w-w-when I bring . . . her home. You have . . . to be."

Bonnie patted his hand as her eyes fluttered closed.

———

THE radio was blasting out eighties rock in Shannon's kitchen as she and Hunter sang loudly and out of tune. She couldn't stop smiling. It was well over a year since he'd joined her in dishwashing karaoke, and tonight, he'd been the one to suggest it. If she'd been given a gift of a diamond necklace, its sparkling facets would have paled in comparison to the joy she was experiencing right now. First he'd shown her the tricks he'd taught Rastas and now this. It gave her hope that he was coming back to her.

"Mom?"

She hefted the lasagna dish out of the suds and onto the dish rack. "Yes."

"Can I go to the skate park?"

"I guess so."

"Cool. I want to show the guys Rastas."

She glanced at the clock. It would be light out until well past ten, but that was way too late for him to be coming home. She braced herself for the whining. "Be back by nine fifteen."

"Okay."

Okay? "Okay."

He dropped the dishcloth and called Rastas. Boy and dog raced out the door together equally excited.

Was this a turning point? Was this period of him being disconnected over? God, she hoped so, because when Hunter was miserable, she was, too. The last two hours had been the most fun they'd had together in a long, long time.

Enjoyable time with Hunter. You've had a lot of enjoyable times with Beau.

And she had. Hopefully, there'd be many more. She wiped down the counters, and when everything was neat and clean, just the way she liked it, she picked up her phone with the plan of texting Beau to thank him for reading to Hunter.

That's the sort of thing you need to say in person.

There was a knock on the kitchen window and she spun around with a start to catch a glimpse of Beau's hat, and then he was through the back door and standing in her kitchen.

He was dressed as if for a night on the town—clean jeans, silver belt buckle, a turquoise, black and white western shirt and boots that gleamed. He'd just come from the hospital and sadness radiated off of him. "Hey."

She walked over to him. "Hey yourself. How's your mom doing?"

He shook his head. "Not good. She's tired. Too . . . tired . . . to . . . fight."

She heard his battle to force every word past his grief,

and she wrapped her arms around him, pressing her head against his chest, wishing she could do something to change Bonnie's condition. "Oh, Beau, I'm so sorry."

"Yeah." He glanced around. "Where's Hunter?"

"He's taken Rastas to the skate park and he won't be back until nine fifteen."

His arms immediately tightened around her, crushing her to him, and he swooped on her mouth like she was vital oxygen required to fill his empty tank. He'd never kissed her quite like it—the rawness of need and the hardness of desperation mixed in with the gentleness of appreciation. It lit her up brighter than the fireworks they'd watched on the fourth of July.

Just as she was about to push him toward her bedroom, he lifted his head, picked her up and sat her on the counter. A shiver of anticipation shot through her.

His glorious brown eyes with their thick, dark lashes hooked onto hers. She'd expected them to be glazed with the same heady desire she knew fogged hers, but although she saw red-hot need, there was something else. Something serious.

Something akin to pain caught her under her ribs.

"Beau? We don't have to do this if it feels wrong because of your mom . . ."

"Mom wants us . . . to be happy." His big hands gently stroked her hair and he sucked in a breath. "Sh-Shannon. I . . . love . . . you. I need you."

She swayed and he immediately steadied her. She'd been expecting sex on the counter, not a declaration of love. She had no experience with this. "You love me?"

His mouth kicked up in a lopsided smile. "Don't sound . . . surprised. You're amazing. I want us . . . to be . . . a family."

A family? She couldn't believe this was happening and her heart beat so fast it could have gone into competition with a hummingbird's. "You, me and Hunter?"

"Yes." His eyes sparkled. "Along with a couple of dogs . . . some horses and . . . a hell of a lot of cows."

He loves me. He really loves me. She could hardly believe it. Beau McCade loved her. She wanted to squeal in delight, but instead, she wrapped her legs tightly around him and pulled him in close. Sliding her fingers through his hair, she brought his head down to her lips and kissed him deeply, using her tongue to claim him as hers.

Her everyday world receded and only Beau existed— his rock-hard ass against her calves, his solid chest against her aching breasts, his gentle hands on her back and his taste exploding through her, diving deep and driving her wild. He loved her. He was hers and she wanted him. Her hands fell to his belt, wanting to free him and feel him.

"Mom?"

Hunter's horrified voice sent shock ricocheting through her, drenching her arousal like a blast of icy water. Her legs dropped away from Beau as her hands shoved him in the chest.

As he took steps backward, she slid off the counter, straightening her blouse and trying to find her voice. Hunter was staring at them both, his face filled with a myriad of emotions, but disgust and embarrassment outshone them all.

"Hi, honey," she rasped out against a tight throat. "Beau was just leaving." She tried to push him toward the door. "Aren't you, Beau?"

All six feet of cowboy stayed firmly where he was, his expression sober and his eyes puzzled. "No."

"Why were you kissing him?" Hunter asked, his voice rising accusingly with each word.

Panic filled her. This was why she'd never involved men in her life. "Like I said, I was just saying good-bye."

"Sh-Shannon."

She heard the critical tone in Beau's voice but she didn't care. Her son was looking at her as if she were slime, and she had to fix this. But dread bounced around her brain like a small rubber ball rebounding against a totally blank wall, and the only thing she could think of doing was to act as if nothing had happened. "You're back from the skate park early. Did you forget something?"

An incredulous look crossed her son's face.

Shit.

"Hunter," Beau said softly. "It's okay. I love . . . your mom. She loves me.".

The boy's nostrils flared as he nailed her with a look of loathing. "Is that true?"

In all the months that he'd been miserable and sad, he'd never once looked at her like this. Desperation filled her. "Hunter, I can explain."

Fury reddened his face. "Beau's my friend. Mine. Not yours." He threw the words at her and they hit, burning and sizzling like acid. "I hate you. I hate both of you." He picked up the quivering puppy and, hugging her close, stormed down the hall.

She rushed after him. "Hunter, wait. Please."

"Go away." He slammed the door in her face, the vibrations rattling the windows. The click of the lock echoed loud and defiant, shutting her out.

Noooo. This couldn't be happening. Not when tonight had been so special. She raised her hand to knock on his door.

———

BEAU caught Shannon's arm before her hand made contact with the wood, wanting to stall her so he could talk to her before she tried talking with Hunter. "No," he said quietly, as he inclined his head back toward the kitchen.

She wheeled around to face him, her face pale but her eyes wild. "No?"

He put his fingers to his lips and gently propelled her along the hall to the living room, wanting to get her away from Hunter's room so he could talk to her without the boy overhearing.

The moment they reached it she pulled out of his grasp.

"What do you mean *no*?" she said shrilly. "I have to fix this."

"And we will," he said as calmly as he could. "Just give . . . him a moment." He wrapped his arms around her tense body, pulling her close, and smiled down at her. "Look at the . . . bright side. We're lucky . . . he didn't come home . . . five minutes later. That would have . . . been worse."

"Worse?" Her usually warm eyes chilled to arctic blue and she threw off his hands. "This isn't a joke, Beau. This is serious. It's a perfect example of why I didn't want him to know we were seeing each other."

He'd never been happy about that decision, because secrets always caused problems. "He knows now."

"Oh God, why did this have to happen? Why now?" She tugged frantically at her hair. "Tonight Hunter and I had the best night together we've had in over a year, and I've just gone and wrecked that new and fragile thing because I let you distract me."

He reached for her, wanting to comfort her, but she ducked him. "He got a . . . surprise, Sh-Shannon. Give him time . . . to get used . . . to us—"

"No." She shook her head. "You heard him. He hates us." Her voice cracked. "He hates me."

He remembered similar outbursts from Megan and Dillon when they were the same age as Hunter. "He doesn't . . . hate you."

She seared him with her gaze. "I know my son and he's never looked at me like that before. We've damaged him."

He rolled his eyes, unable to help himself. "Now, you're being . . . as dramatic . . . as Hunter."

Her lips clamped into a thin, hard line. "You're not a parent, so you can't possibly understand."

He tried to deflect the hurtful words and not allow them to land. "I want to be. I love you. I love Hunter . . . like a son."

She wrung her hands. "We're not going to work."

Anxiety threaded through him that she truly believed that. "If . . . we talk to him . . . together—"

"No." The word exploded out of her, harsh and cutting. "The only person who's going to explain anything to Hunter is me."

His heart lurched. He loved her. He had to make her understand that this situation was their problem, not hers alone. He suddenly remembered something Shannon had told him. *I'm his mother and I've protected Hunter from heartache.* "You've done a . . . great job p-p-p-protecting Hunter, giving him . . . stability but he . . . needs men in his . . . life."

"Plenty of great men were raised by women."

Yes, but you've got me to share this with you. Why couldn't she see that locking him out was the wrong thing to do? She looked so scared and fearful, and he couldn't work out why. And then it hit him. "This isn't all . . . about Hunter . . . is it? Some of it . . . is about you. I'm not like . . . Hunter's father. I won't leave you. I want to . . . be with you."

She flinched. "You had no right telling him you loved me."

He threw up his hands. "I was . . . trying to . . . help. To explain."

"He's *my* son," she said with icy calm. "I don't need your help."

Her words hit worse than a horse's hoof to the chest. Air whooshed out of his lungs and rafts of agonizing, stinging pain radiated to every part of him. "Family . . . help . . . each . . . other."

She shook her head traitorously slowly. "We're not family, Beau."

Ten minutes ago when he'd told her that he loved her and that he wanted them to be a family, she'd kissed him like he was the love of her life. "I thought . . . we were."

"It was just a silly fantasy," she said, her voice trembling. "God knows, I should have known better. I have to put Hunter's happiness first."

Her skewed logic stunned him. "Do you think . . . p-p-p-p- Fuck." He hauled in a breath trying to keep everything together despite the overwhelming feeling it was all falling apart. "Maybe some . . . of his happiness . . . is connected . . . to me."

She folded her arms across her chest and faced him down. "I appreciate everything you've done for Hunter, but it's over. I need you to leave so I can talk to my son. Alone."

Her words shredded his heart and destroyed his dreams. She was dismissing him, her ears now deaf to any of his stuttering entreaties. He'd tried and lost, fighting phantoms he didn't even know existed. Grabbing his hat, he strode from the house without looking back.

Chapter 18

The night sky was as black as the dread that hovered permanently over Katrina. As she gazed out of her mother's hospital room window, she wished the cloud would clear so she could see some stars. Stars always filled her with hope, and boy she needed some of that now. Bonnie wasn't improving the way everyone had hoped, and Josh, in consultation with her oncologist, had changed the antibiotics. Now they waited.

She kissed her sleeping mother. *Come on, Mom. We need you. Dad needs you. I need you.*

Kirk snored gently in the chair, and she threw a cotton blanket over him. His eyes opened. "What time is it?"

"Almost dawn."

He scrubbed his whiskered face with his palms and immediately glanced at his sleeping wife. "Your mom loves the dawn. She always says—"

"It's a fresh day to do great things." Katrina smiled as she squatted down in front of him so she could speak quietly and not wake Bonnie. "I probably should be more enthusiastic about the dawn, but it always comes so darn early."

He chuckled softly. "You get that from me. I might have been ranching all my life but I've always preferred to watch a sunset."

His face suddenly sobered, and he swallowed as if he were fighting for control. "For thirty years, no matter the weather or the worries about stock or feed prices, or what you kids were doing or not doing, I've gotten up because of her. I've wanted to do great things because of her."

Katrina's heart trembled. What would it be like to love like that and be loved back? "You're a great team."

He nodded slowly. "We've had our moments. Every couple does, but we've always respected each other. Tried to put each other first."

She thought about her own relationships and how no guy had ever put her first.

Ty got close. And he had, but she'd been too young to settle down then and she'd left Bear Paw.

Josh? No. It's not that sort of relationship. If she was honest, it was no longer just about the sex—they'd shared too much about each other for that. She respected him as a doctor and she liked him as man. He made her laugh, he constantly surprised her and she was so very grateful to him for the way he was caring for her mother. Caring for the family by explaining everything that was happening in words her father and siblings could understand.

Kirk's hand came to rest gently on her shoulder. "I know you went east for some excitement, Katrina, but that can burn out fast. What your mother and I have is commitment. I know you roll your eyes every time I mention it, but you should give Ty a chance. You might be surprised."

She thought about Ty and his generosity to the family. To her. How he was helping out Beau on the ranch while her father was spending every minute with Bonnie. He was a great guy—a dear friend, and life with him would be steady and predictable. Safe.

And there was the problem. A smile from Ty made her feel momentarily warm like sunshine breaking through clouds on a dull day. A smile from Josh blazed through her like wildfire in the mountains during a hot and endless summer. Both reactions scared her.

"Kirk?" Bonnie stirred. "Can I have some water, please?"

"Sure thing, sweetheart." He shot to his feet, and with one large hand he supported her head and with the other he angled the straw to her lips.

He was a no-nonsense man of the land—big, broad and strong, but gentleness, caring and love emanated from every pore.

Tears stung Katrina's eyes, and an enormous hollow space opened up inside of her. She immediately backed out of the room, feeling like she was suddenly intruding on something intensely personal and private. Something she'd never known.

She blew her nose and marched toward the vending machine. She was sleep deprived and overreacting and she needed sugar and cocoa and she needed it fast. She had a perfectly fine life. Granted, it was on hiatus at the moment caring for her mom, but she wouldn't have it any other way.

Her phone rang and she fully expected it to be Megan telling her what time she was coming in to relieve her and sit with Bonnie so she could go home and grab breakfast and a shower. She pulled the sleek white device out of her pocket and immediately saw Josh's name. Her heart gave a ridiculous lurch.

"Hi." She could hear talking in the background.

"I'm sorry to ask, but all hell's broken loose and I'm desperate. If you're still in the hospital and someone's with your mom, are you able to help out in the ER for an hour? I promise it won't be any longer."

She needed some distraction from all her worries about her mom and she knew he'd only have asked her if he had no other choice. So help her, she was a sucker for a plea that she was needed. "I can do that."

"Thank you." His relief was palpable, rolling down the line and wrapping around her. "You're the best, but you know that, right?"

His flirting made her smile. "And I bet you say that to all the nurses who help you out."

"No." His voice dropped, the delicious bass notes suddenly serious. "Just to you."

This time her heart turned over. *I love him.* Panic followed. *No, I can't love him.* But she couldn't hide from it. She loved him, even though falling in love with Josh was up there with every other dumb thing she'd ever done in her life. He'd been up front about not wanting anything more than sex from the very start, and she'd insisted on it, too, so why, oh, why had she fallen in love with another unsuitable man?

Not able to answer the question and hating herself for even having to ask it, she shoved all her feelings about Josh down deep to join the pool of anxiety about her mother and the lack of direction that was her life. Taking the shortcut to the ER, she pulled on some scrubs and five minutes later she was thankfully way too busy to think about anything except how to keep two out-of-town brothers from murdering each other.

"You stupid bastard," Glen, the older of the two yelled as he tried to grab his brother's shirt. "You were supposed to shoot the fuckin' antelope, not me."

"It was an accident," Lenny groaned as he shrank into the wheelchair, trying to avoid his brother's hand. "If it makes you feel any better, when you grabbed my ankle, I tripped. I might have broken it."

"I should have killed you," Glen roared, heaving himself up on the sides of the gurney before collapsing as pain flattened him.

Katrina took the opportunity to pull Lenny's wheelchair a long way from the gurney. "Gentlemen," she said, using the term loosely, "this is a hospital. Inside voices, please, and no swearing."

"He's not usually like this," Lenny offered up in defense of his brother. "He's been through a lot lately what with April leaving him and the business hemorrhaging cash. This trip was supposed to be some R & R, you know, to kick back, but he's not very good at relaxing."

"You fuckin' shot me," Glen screamed, his face going the familiar puce of someone with hypertension.

She didn't need the guy stroking out on her as well as having a load of buckshot in his ass. "Lenny, time for you to go have that ankle X-rayed."

"I don't want to leave Glen on his own."

Lenny seemed impervious to the fact he was the source of Glen's current rage. "I promise you, I'll be here with him."

His worried brow cleared. "As long as you're sure. Thanks. I won't be long, Glen."

"Argh!" Glen banged the side of the gurney with a closed fist.

The moment Joe, the hospital transporter, took Lenny away, she said, "Glen, I'm going to start removing the shot, but before I do that I'll give you some pain relief."

"I'm gonna kill him."

And a sedative. "Are you allergic to anything?"

"Lenny."

———

JOSH heard the ping, ping, ping of buckshot hitting the mono-metal of a bowl as he slipped in behind the curtain of one of the ER cubicles. Katrina, dressed in identical scrubs to his, looked up, and although a mask hid the curve of her lips, he saw the smile in her eyes. A smile he'd come to think of as his smile—the one she reserved for him.

"Doctor Stanton, as always, your timing is perfect."

He grinned at her. "Just removed the last piece of shot?"

She dropped the forceps into the kidney dish. "Exactly."

"She's got the softest touch," Glen mumbled in sharp contrast to when Josh had seen him last, at which point he'd been roaring. "The kindest hands . . ."

He raised his brows. "Lortabs talk?"

"Right again." She applied a large dressing to Glen's very red and sore butt cheek. "You rest here, Glen, and someone will be along soon with some breakfast for you."

As they left the cubicle and she washed her hands, she

said, "Breakfast he's going to be eating on his stomach. And talking food and stomachs, I could do with some breakfast myself."

"Good idea. I'm buying." Josh ushered her out of the ER and straight into the staff lounge, kicking the door shut behind him before pulling Katrina into his arms. He kissed her, then buried his face in her neck and started caressing it with his tongue.

For a moment she trembled against him before cupping his cheeks and lifting his head. "Hey, you promised me breakfast. You didn't say I was breakfast."

"I wish you were. I can, however, offer you cereal and coffee."

"And here I was fantasizing about one of Shannon's big breakfasts."

"I'm sorry but I've only got ten minutes before I have to start rounds."

"Don't be sorry. I'll take a rain check, and cereal's fine."

"You sure?" He smoothed down her hair, which had been ruffled by the ties of the mask, looking for signs of her being pouty the way Ashley would have been.

Her brow creased. "You do rounds at seven thirty most mornings, and as that includes checking in on my mom, of course it's fine. Why wouldn't it be?"

Her honesty both reassured and discombobulated him all at the same time. "Just checking."

As she moved away from him and pulled out bowls and poured cereal, he turned on the coffee machine. "Thanks again for helping out this morning. I felt bad asking."

She shrugged. "I would have said no if I didn't want to or couldn't do it."

There it was again—reasonableness and a distinct lack of game playing. He could get used to this.

She brought everything over to the table. "So you've had an exciting early morning."

An irrational jolt of disappointment zapped him that the hospital grapevine had stolen his news. "Who told you?"

"No one, but there were some clues. The first one was

that you gave up the opportunity to remove shot out of some guy's butt." She spooned the crunchy cereal into her mouth.

He grinned. "True, that's always tempting. And?"

"Your eyes."

"My eyes?" He had no clue what she was talking about.

She nodded. "When you're excited, they sparkle like sunshine on water. It's how they look right after we've had sex." She winked at him. "So as I know it wasn't that, I'm guessing you've just had one of those magic work moments."

Stunned that she read him so well, it took him a moment to respond. "I delivered a baby."

She dropped her spoon. "Get out of here!"

He knew he was grinning like a loon. "I know, right? It was pretty special."

"So, I want details."

Memories of Ashley looking at her watch or glancing at her phone when he was talking about work burned in the back of his brain. "You're really interested?"

She huffed out an exasperated breath. "Of course I'm interested. This is huge."

He loved that she got how big a deal it really was. "I got called in around four because Kimberly Buffa had gone into labor at thirty-two weeks."

"Preterm labor. Scary stuff."

"Yeah, and I haven't delivered a baby since I was a med student, and Bear Paw hospital is hardly a NICU. I tried nifedipine to stop the labor and gave her corticosteroids for the baby's lungs just in case."

Her eyes were riveted to his face as she took in every word. "And?"

"And despite everything, nothing was going to stop this kid. I called the MontMedAir team, hoping they'd arrive with all their neonatal equipment before she delivered, but just as Will Bartlett touched down, Jacinta Jane slipped into my hands. She looked up at me with huge, dark eyes as if to say *hello, have we met before?*"

"So magic and scary." Her voice was almost reverent as

she slid her hands into his and her wonder flowed through him. "I wish I'd been there."

The emotions of the moment rushed back to him so clearly it was like he was still standing in the delivery room. "It was totally amazing. Well, in a heart-stopping, gut-clenching kind of a way that I don't want to repeat anytime soon."

She laughed, her expression skeptical. "I doubt that. You thrive on this sort of thing."

And he did. "I know, but this time it was different."

"How?"

"Kimberly's my personal banker, and her husband Jett, whom I wave to every morning, is the contractor working on the clinic upgrade. They were looking at me with such faith and trust, as if I knew what I was doing. It was terrifying."

"Missing your anonymity?" Perspicacity filled her smile. "But you did it and you'll do it again."

"Millie and I did it. Thank God she's got some NICU experience."

She squeezed his hands. "I'm so proud of you."

Her words sent cozy warmth spreading through him, which unsettled him. Hell, he wasn't a kid receiving a student of the week certificate. Memories rolled in. The time he'd come home from elementary school so proud of his participation certificate and his father quizzing him about exactly what he'd done to deserve it. The feeling he'd gotten when he couldn't give a specific reason. "I was just doing my job."

She rolled her eyes. "Oh please. You're still using that line? It's okay to be proud of what you've done. Jacinta Jane is your first Bear Paw baby and you rocked it. Enjoy the moment. Celebrate. Life's too sh—" Her face dropped and she bit her lip, pulling her hands abruptly away from his.

Her pain and distress circled him, and he wished he could make things better. "Bonnie hasn't gotten any worse in the last twenty-four hours."

"And she hasn't gotten any better, either." She stood up

abruptly. "So, did Millie go to Great Falls with the Buffas?" she said, changing the subject.

He loaded the coffee mugs in the dishwasher. "No. Will Bartlett had a neonatal nurse on board with him."

"Didn't she fly with that doctor before?"

"Yeah, a few times this summer."

"You know she wants a permanent job in the ER, don't you?"

"Don't we all," he said flippantly, although he had to concede that his primary care load was slowly starting to grow on him.

Maybe you should talk to Floyd, or Will Bartlett might just tempt her away. All he has to do is flash that smile of his and crook his little finger and every nurse in the hospital would put down the bedpans and follow him anywhere." She gave a dreamy smile. "He really is centerfold material."

"I haven't noticed," he said dryly, irritated that he was feeling jealous of a guy he really liked.

She wrapped her arms around his neck and gazed up at him. "Neither have I."

"Good." It came out overly emphatic.

Her eyes danced with teasing. "Well, not too much anyway." Laughing, she rose up on her toes and kissed him. When she pulled back, her expression sobered. "But seriously, Josh, the town needs good health care providers and we can't afford to lose Millie to Great Falls. Talk to Floyd about her working full time in the ER.

He stared down at her as an idea germinated in his mind. "Good idea. I think I will."

———

SHANNON had barely slept. She'd spent half the night scared that Hunter would run away and the other half berating herself for being so stupid. Hadn't she learned after Malcolm and a string of other guys that she and men never worked? That when she tried to have a relationship, Hunter always suffered? Damn it, yes, she knew that. Knew it so damn well that she'd made a lifestyle choice a long time ago and held fast to it until Beau.

And now with that one stupid kiss, Hunter was hurting worse than she'd ever seen him hurt before.

Her heart beat painfully, as if it had been bloodied and bruised with a baseball bat. It was a mother's lot to hurt when her kid hurt.

It's more than that.

She refused to listen to that traitorous voice. It had led her to this miserable place and she'd never trust it again. No matter how good of a guy Beau was, Hunter always came first.

She spun around from the stove at the sound of Rastas's nails tapping on the floorboards. The next moment Hunter was standing in the kitchen, his backpack on his shoulder, his cap pulled down low and his earbuds in his ears.

"Where are you going?" The question shot out of her lips driven by panic.

His head dropped, his gaze fixed on the high tops of his shoes. "Out."

She tried to keep her voice calm. "Out where, Hunter?"

He shrugged. "Just out."

"Have breakfast first."

"No."

Try another angle. "If you're going out, I need to know where you're going."

"Why? You don't care about me."

It was as if something sucked all the air from her lungs. She moved toward him. "Hunter, I love you to pieces. You know I do."

His head shot up, his chin jutted and his eyes shone with hurt and betrayal. "If you love me, why were you kissing Beau?"

And there it was. "I'm so sorry you saw that. I really am." She pulled his rigid body into a hug, wanting to reassure him that she loved him more than life itself. "I regret it so much, but you have to know that you always come first with me." She kissed his hat. "Don't worry. It's over. I won't be seeing Beau again."

He wriggled out of her grasp. "Will I?"

"No, of course not." She pulled her hair back hard behind her ears, welcoming the tug of pain. "I wouldn't ask you to do that. I'll find a camp for the rest of vacation."

"No!" His body vibrated with fury. "I don't want to go to camp. I hate you."

She scooped up the barking Rastas, hoping that Hunter wouldn't storm out of the house without his puppy, and she sat down before her shaking legs gave way underneath her. "Hunter, I don't understand what you want. You need to tell me."

His bottom lip stuck out. "I wanna see Beau."

The puppy wriggled in her arms, desperate to reach her distraught master.

"No." She shook her head, thinking how it would just cause more heartache for both of them. "That's not a good idea."

His face flamed red. "He's *my* friend and you've wrecked everything by kissing him."

He's my friend. Hunter saw Beau as a friend? A friend of his that she'd appropriated. A desperate sinking feeling filled her. Had she gotten everything the wrong way around? "Do you think that me kissing Beau means he isn't your friend anymore?"

He scuffed his foot and mumbled, "He said he loved you."

"Yes." Her heart rolled over in fresh pain. "Why do you think that means he isn't your friend?"

He wouldn't look at her.

"Hunter?"

"If he loves you," he said, mumbling softly, "then he can't love me."

Oh, Hunter. Her heart squeezed so tightly it dripped blood, and she set the puppy down before standing and wrapping her arms around her child. Her half man, half boy. "Love doesn't work that way, sweetheart. You can love more than one person at a time."

He looked at her, his face full of confusion. "You don't love anyone but me."

Oh, but I do. "I loved my mom and dad, but you don't remember them."

He dropped his head into her shoulder, and a moment later she heard the muffled words, "So why doesn't Dad love me?"

The visceral pain that rocked her was like the stab of a knife straight through her solar plexus.

I think . . . maybe . . . it's his dad. Beau's caring voice echoed in her head. She'd been so convinced he was wrong because Hunter had never known Malcolm and had never even talked about him. Yet, his absence in his life, which she took as being an absolute positive, Hunter was interpreting as rejection. And it was in oh so many ways. Ways she couldn't change even if they'd lived in the same town.

She patted his back. "Your dad loves you in his own way."

He sniffled against her shoulder. "What do you mean?"

She closed her eyes for a moment and took in a deep, steadying breath. "It means he thinks about you and hopes you're happy but he doesn't pick up the phone or come visit."

"Is that why you won't let me see him?"

The question shocked her. She'd never deliberately stopped Hunter from seeing Malcolm; it was just that Malcolm was so bad at keeping in touch. "I didn't know you wanted to see him. Do you?"

He lifted his head, his eyes filled with a mixture of bullishness and fear. "I might."

An internal battle raged deep down inside her. The fact that she should encourage and support Hunter to contact Malcolm if that's what he really wanted to do versus the knowledge that Malcolm would inevitably let Hunter down and hurt him. Every maternal instinct wanted to protect Hunter at all costs.

You've done a . . . great job p-p-p-protecting Hunter, giving him . . . stability, but he . . . needs men in his . . . life.

Except there was no guarantee Malcolm would be remotely reliable at being in his life. But Beau had a point she'd totally missed. She tried to push away the anxiety that was rising up to choke her and offer Hunter what he needed. "We can call Grandma and Pa. Your dad moves a lot, but they should know where he is and we can get a message to him that way. Do you want to do that?"

He shrugged. "Maybe."

Maybe? His reply surprised her, because she'd felt sure after all this turmoil his answer would be a resounding *yes.* Perhaps he'd just needed to know it was okay to make contact with Malcolm. "How about you tell me when you're ready."

"Could I just call Grandpa?"

Malcolm's dad was a good man, but since she'd left Missouri, she'd let the contact slip other than at Christmas and birthdays. "Sure. And maybe seeing as we have the spare room, we could even invite him and Grandma to come stay a couple of days."

"I'd like that." He fondled Rastas's ears. "Mom?"

"Yes."

"If Beau loves you . . ."

Loved me. Would he still want them in his life after what she'd said to him last night?

". . . does that mean he can love me, too?"

The desperate hope in Hunter's eyes made her ache to her core. How could she have been so misguided to think that her love alone was enough for him? He needed an entire family of love.

"He already loves you, Hunter."

Incredulity crossed his face. "He told you that?"

She laced her hands, trying to stop them from trembling. "He did. He told me last night just before you got home, which was why I was kissing him."

Hunter's face pinked. "It was gross. You had your legs around his butt."

She laughed and heard the hysterical edge to it. "After what I said to him last night, I don't think he'll want to be kissing me again, so your delicate eyes will be spared."

Hunter frowned. "Do you love me, Mom?"

She hated that he was so insecure. "Of course I do. I tell you every day. I show you every day by everything I do for you. The notes in your lunch box, letting you have Rastas, even the stuff like getting you to clean up your room. All of it is my love for you, and I need you to believe it."

He gave her a long, quiet stare. "Then Beau still loves you."

Just hearing his name made her want to cry, and she fiddled with the edge of a place mat. "How do you figure that?"

"Because I said I hated you but you still love me. What you said to Beau couldn't be worse than that."

The logic of an immature fourteen-year-old boy was very tempting to follow.

I won't leave you. I want to . . . be with you.

Hunter kissed her on the cheek. "I'm sorry, Mom. I don't hate you."

She tousled his hair. "I know you don't, buddy. I know you said it because you were confused, but next time, can you please try and talk to me about it?"

He grimaced. "Talking's hard."

Oh yeah. "Sometimes it is."

"Can I go see Beau?"

She bit her lip. "I have to talk to him on my own first."

He stood up and grabbed her keys, holding them out toward her. "Do it now?"

Chapter 19

Shannon left Hunter washing dishes in the diner with a promise she'd call him as soon as she'd spoken with Beau. She'd texted Beau but she hadn't heard back, and she didn't know if that was because he was out of range due to the bad reception in the coulees or if he was ignoring her. Either way, with anxiety bubbling in her veins, she'd driven out to find him. It was the longest drive of her life. Now she stood on the ranch house veranda holding a peacemaking pie.

Kirk opened the door a second before she knocked. "Shannon?" A surprised look crossed his tired face. "I didn't know you were there. I was just leaving for the hospital."

A different ache pained her. "How's Bonnie?"

"She's . . ." He rubbed the back of his neck. "Thank you for all those pies and casseroles you've been sending over. Much appreciated."

She hated that her well-intentioned inquiry was causing him distress. "It's my pleasure." *Change the subject. Change the subject.* "I was wondering if Beau was here?"

He shook his head. "I'm not sure where he is. Have you

tried his cell? Mind you, if he's out on the eastern boundary, he won't have bars."

She nodded. "I'll keep trying."

"Everyone's either at the hospital or chasing cows, but you can wait here if you don't mind your own company."

"Thank you. I'd like to wait."

Kirk suddenly squinted into the midmorning light. "No need. Here's your man now. If you'll excuse me, I need to get back to the hospital."

"Oh, of course. Absolutely. Please send Bonnie my best wishes."

He nodded quietly as he jammed his hat on his head and walked to his outfit, pausing to exchange a few words with Beau on the way.

Shannon couldn't hear them, but she felt the love flow between the two men in the slaps on the back that they gave each other. Would she one day be able to see a similar exchange between Hunter and Beau? See a manbrace or a full-on hug?

God, she hoped so.

Dread dumped all over her at the thought she might not.

She took in a deep breath and gripped the pie box. This was it. This was where she ate humble pie. She saw the moment Kirk must have told Beau she was waiting. Saw the rise of his head and the shock in his eyes, which was immediately replaced with an unfamiliar hardness. Her throat tightened.

He strode toward her and, ever the gentleman, removed his cap. "Sh-Shannon."

She suddenly realized how much warmth he'd always infused into her name, because today it was absent. "Hi, Beau."

"Come inside." He pulled open the door for her, and after she'd entered the house and had stopped just inside, uncertain of where to proceed, he strode straight past her. A few feet away he turned back to face her. "Wh-what do . . . you want?"

"I . . ." Oh. God. She'd rehearsed what she was going to say, but now that she was facing him and his implacable wide stance and uncompromising grim expression, for the first time in his presence instead of gabbling on, words failed her. "I . . . I'm sorry."

His mouth, already stern, seemed to flatten even more. "For what?"

His words punched her even though she knew he was deliberately choosing short replies to keep his speech under control. All of this was her fault and she had to fix it. For that to happen she had to tell him the truth.

"I'm sorry for panicking last night. For shutting you out. For getting everything so incredibly wrong with Hunter and with you."

———

BEAU heard her and desperately wanted to believe that what she was saying was true. Her pale face and red eyes backed up her claims, but her distinctly harsh words from last night still rang loud in his ears. *He's my son. I don't need your help.*

He blew out a breath. "You did. You got it . . . all wrong."

"I know."

"How . . . how do . . . you know?"

She sighed, exhaustion rising off her. "Hunter and I talked this morning. Not that he wanted to. He really didn't want to have anything to do with me." Her contrition-filled eyes found his. "I was right about Hunter being upset that he'd seen us kissing, but I was so wrong, so way off base about why it upset him so much."

All night he'd replayed the conversations between the three of them in the kitchen, trying to work out how something so wonderful had become something so traumatizing. "Tell me?"

"He thought . . ."—her voice cracked—". . . someone could only love one person at a time."

Sadness for Hunter rocked into him. "He was . . . worried you wouldn't . . . love him?"

She shook her head slowly. "He was upset that if you loved me, you wouldn't be able to love him."

The jumble of emotions that broadsided him physically hurt. Pain for Hunter, pain for Shannon. He gripped the edge of the table. "You told him . . . how wrong that was . . . right?"

She nodded. "And then he asked about his dad, and you were right." She swallowed as the lines around her eyes deepened. "I had no idea he was grieving for something he's never known but feels like he should have had. And I've been so hell-bent on keeping him safe from heartache that I've cut him off from all his extended family to the point he believes he can only be loved by one person at a time."

She sank into a chair, dropping her head into her hands. "I can't believe I couldn't see what I was doing. I'm a terrible mother."

He wanted to haul her up against him and hold her tight but he couldn't. Not yet. They didn't have a future together unless she could let him in to be part of her team. "Not terrible. Never that. Misguided, maybe."

She gave a strangled sort of a laugh. "As I listened to Hunter, I kept hearing your voice telling me that he needed men in his life. The thing is, Beau, I never met any good men until I met you, and by then I was so used to protecting Hunter I had no clue how to let you in to help."

"And . . . protecting yourself."

Lines of strain appeared on her face. "Maybe."

"Definitely."

She opened her hands and gave him a sad smile. "Are you always going to be right?"

A smile broke through his hurt. "Sometimes."

"I love you, Beau." Her voice trembled. "I love you so much it hurts."

She loves me. They were almost all of the words he needed to hear, and it was so hard not to reach out and touch her. "Do you . . . trust me?"

"Not to leave me? Yes. Absolutely, yes."

He watched her face carefully. "Do you trust me with your son?"

She pushed up from the chair and walked toward him until she was standing as close to him as was possible without actually touching him. Her eyes, shimmering with unshed tears, looked into his. "I trust you implicitly with *our* son and with any other children I hope we might have."

Our son. Children. Joy filled him to overflowing and he could hardly speak. "W-w-we're a team, Sh-Shannon."

She wrapped her arms around his neck. "Yes, please. More than anything, I want to be on Team McCade."

He grinned down at her. "Funny. I thought I . . . was on Team Bauer."

"The name's not important."

And it wasn't. He pulled her up against him and lowered his head, capturing her lips with his and searing her with his love and commitment. Her love for him flowed back and he deepened the kiss, losing himself in her taste and her touch.

A loud wolf whistle split the air, and he jerked his head back. Shannon buried her face in his shirt.

"Bro, get a room," Dillon said, respect in his voice and a huge grin on his face.

He dropped his arm onto Shannon's waist and grinned down at her. "We need to . . . get our own . . . place."

She laughed. "We do. But first we have to go tell Hunter."

He immediately sobered, his wondrous joy momentarily attenuated. "And then we go to the hospital and tell Mom."

———

KATRINA slid her arms into Megan's and Dillon's and led them from their mother's hospital room. "Let's give Shannon and Beau some time alone with Mom and Dad."

"It's so exciting that they're going to get married," Megan said. "This is just the sort of news that Mom needs to boost her white blood cell count."

Katrina hoped so, too. Although there was no scientific evidence to support such a claim, she was at the point of grasping at straws. Her mom's fever wasn't abating, and she was sleeping an awful lot. Despite the fact Bonnie had pushed herself up off the pillows to kiss Beau and Shannon, she'd quickly fallen back exhausted. Katrina knew all her energy was being expended just by breathing.

She noticed Cassidy, the nurse on duty, pushing open the door to Bonnie's room to do the two o'clock observations. Since her quick breakfast with Josh this morning, he'd requested hourly nursing checks. He'd also visited Bonnie twice before lunch after her mom and dad had refused his recommendation that she be transferred to Great Falls. Josh checking in on a patient between round times wasn't a good sign. It meant he was extremely worried, and that scared her to pieces.

"Let's take Hunter for ice cream," Dillon said.

"Good idea." Megan laughed. "We can practice doing what aunts and uncles do. You coming, Katrina?"

"You know, I think I'll pass if that's okay. I want to talk to Cassidy, but you two go."

Dillon frowned. "We'll stay if you think we should."

"No, go. I think it's a great idea. Important, even, especially as we need to make Hunter feel welcome, and right now with Mom . . ."

Dillon hugged her. "We get it. We won't be gone longer than a half hour."

"Bring me back some peanut butter chocolate chip."

"It's a hundred degrees out," Megan said, shaking her head. "We'll bring you back a milkshake."

She walked with them to the front of the hospital, feeling a blast of heat as the automatic doors opened. When they closed again, she turned and walked back. As she passed the vending machine, she noticed a side door open up ahead and then Josh appeared, running.

Doctors never ran.

Her heart clogged her throat.

Breathe. It might be someone else. She knew that elderly Mr. Miller in the room next to Bonnie's had heart problems. He was ninety and forgetful, and she'd helped him back to his room more than once when he'd wandered off and gotten lost.

Please be Mr. Miller.

Josh disappeared inside her mother's room.

A scream sounded in her head.

She ran.

———

AS Katrina waited in what was officially called the relatives' room but what every member of the medical staff called the grieving room, she noticed that the paint in the corner was peeling. She'd seen it because she didn't dare look at the shocked expressions on her siblings' faces or the devastated emptiness on her father's. If she did, she'd lose the tenuous grip on her control and fall sobbing to the ground.

"Bonnie's gone into what we call septic shock," Josh said, his face haggard. "This means that her blood pressure is extremely low, her kidneys are failing and her heart's struggling."

"But you can fix it, right?" Dillon asked, clutching Megan's hand tightly.

No, he can't. Katrina kept her gaze fixed on the peeling paint.

Josh ran his hand through his hair. "The infection has taken over her entire body. If we evacuate her to the ICU in Billings and put her on a respirator, that might offer her some time."

"Surely we should do that, Daddy?" Megan said, reaching for Kirk's hand.

He shook his head violently. "No, honey."

"Why not?" Megan's voice rose, full of bewildered despair.

"Because it means your mom will be in a coma with a tube in her throat and a machine breathing for her," Kirk said, shooting Josh a glance to check he'd understood correctly.

Josh nodded. "That's right."

Kirk visibly trembled. "Your mom and I talked about this very thing when she first got sick, and even though we expected to have a few more months together, she was adamant she didn't want her life extended with tubes and machines. She sure as heck doesn't want to die in Billings."

Megan started to cry softly, and Dillon hugged her as much for her comfort as his own.

"H-h-how much t-time does she have?" Beau stood with Shannon beside him, his arm around her waist, clutching her like a lifeline.

"She's in heart failure. It could be a couple of days, a few hours." Josh's throat worked up and down as if he were fighting for control. "I can't say exactly, but it's not very long. If there's anything you want to say to her that you haven't said already, now is the time."

"But she's unconscious," Dillon said, struggling to understand.

"She might still hear you. Hearing is one of the last . . ." His voice trailed off at the anguished look on Dillon's face. "Like I said, if there's something you really want to say to her, I think you should go say it."

"I just got to know her and I'm losing her," Shannon said so quietly that Katrina barely heard her.

She hated knowing exactly what was going to happen. How death was going to slowly and insidiously steal her mother from her, breath by devastating, gurgling breath. Her chest tightened so much it hurt to force air in and out of her lungs, and she reached out her hand, gripping Josh's arm, her fingers digging into his flesh.

"Promise me you'll keep her pain-free," she implored, looking into his shadow-filled eyes. "She can't suffer. She's such a good mom, a great person, and I love her so much. You have to promise me . . ." Rising sobs stole her words and then stole her breath.

Josh made a guttural sound and pulled her in close, wrapping his arms around her and holding her tight. He didn't say a word but he kissed her hair, he stroked her back and he let her cry. She wanted to hide in his arms forever.

———

JOSH hadn't slept in over a day and he was running on adrenaline, caffeine and sadness. His day had started out euphorically with a birth, and now, twenty-four hours later, it was ending with a death. He'd have preferred it to be the other way around, but years of working in medicine had taught him that the circle of life never gave you those sorts of choices.

He was alone with Bonnie, having asked the family to step out for just a few minutes to spare them while he examined her. He checked the drainage from her chest tube and increased her pain relief. She'd held on longer than he'd expected, but with a family like hers, surrounding her in love and willing her to stay, he wasn't surprised. Sometimes people needed permission to pass.

Death was part of his job, and as his emotionally moribund father had always said, if you got upset every time you lost a patient, you'd never get up in the morning. *Cut it out, stitch it up and move on.*

In emergency medicine, Josh rarely had the time to get to know the patient, which made it easier to keep a professional distance, although he liked to think he'd always been sympathetic to the relatives. But like Katrina had said at breakfast when he'd told her about Jacinta Jane, in Bear Paw, he was part of the community now, whether he wanted to be or not. He'd lost his anonymity.

Hell, he'd lost more than that.

He'd been a guest in Bonnie's home and eaten food she'd prepared. *You're sleeping with her eldest daughter.* A slither of guilt pierced him.

Did she know? Would she have approved? Did it even matter? For a reason he couldn't fathom, it did.

Despite being certain she was now deeply unconscious and not able to hear, he started talking. "Bonnie, you did an amazing job with your family," he said, thinking of his dysfunctional one. "Your legacy's going to live on through them in Katrina's lovely smile, Dillon's sense of fun, Beau's persistence and Megan's . . ."—he really didn't know Megan—". . . enthusiasm."

He glanced up at the monitors and suddenly felt self-conscious that he was having a one-way conversation with a dying woman, but the words kept coming and he couldn't stop them. "Thanks for the gifts of food. You didn't have to do that but I appreciated it." He squeezed her hand. "But you didn't just give me food. You taught me that being a good doctor is as much listening as clinical skills."

He made a huffing sound. "I can't believe I just said that. Truth is, Bonnie, if I'd had my way, you'd be in the hospital at Billings or Great Falls, but you were right. You needed to be here. Half of Bear Paw's come to the hospital tonight. There's a candlelight vigil at the church, and I know the ranch house will be filled with casseroles and cakes in the coming weeks. They'll look after everyone."

Bonnie gave a rasping, rattling breath.

He closed his eyes for a moment. "I promised Katrina you wouldn't be in pain, and I hope to God I've managed that."

Placing her hand carefully on the neatly folded bedspread, he walked to the door, pausing for a moment before he opened it. He sucked in a deep and fortifying breath, because facing the McCades' grief was like being sandblasted. He needed every ounce of professionalism to stay in control.

He opened the door. "You can all come in now."

Katrina's pale and tear-streaked face searched his. "Soon?"

He nodded, wishing he could do something to change this situation, but they were all powerless to do a thing. As the others filed into the room he said quietly to Katrina, "I'll step out for a moment so it's just Bonnie and the family."

"Thank you." She brushed his cheek with her lips before closing the door.

With a steadying sigh, he spun on his heel and pulled

out his phone and pressed a name in his contact list. "Dad. It's Josh."

"So the phones work in Montana, then?" His father's supercilious voice rolled down the line.

Josh fought the urge not to grind his teeth. This call was supposed to be about connecting, and he refused to take the antagonistic bait. "How are things?"

"Busy. I've been invited to be keynote speaker at the American Surgical Association's annual conference. You?"

My patient's dying and her daughter's grieving and I hate that I'm powerless to change a damn thing. But there was no point saying any of that because he knew what the answer would be.

There also was no point trying to compete with his father on a professional level, either—talking to the Bear Paw seniors about medication compliance was hardly up there with the ASA conference. "I'm learning about small-town life. There are deer in my garden."

His father sighed and the familiar disappointment Josh always felt came with it. "I was asking about work. I saw a reference in the *American Medical Journal* to an article about emergency burr holes in remote communities. Good work."

The praise was pleasantly unexpected. "Thanks, Dad."

"Of course, if you'd done surgery—"

And we're back. "Dad, don't even go there, okay. It is what it is, and besides, I just called to talk."

Silence echoed down the line, and he had the over-whelming urge to slam his head into the wall. *Talk?* Why had he said that? His father had no clue how to shoot the breeze. He lived and breathed work.

"Google Maps," his father said, "shows you're near Glacier National Park. You've got a chance of seeing the aurora borealis from there."

Josh was tempted to hit himself upside the head to clear his ears out. His father had actually looked up where he was living? "Yes, I'm hoping to see it."

Katrina's words floated in his head, and he opened his

mouth before thinking. "Would you and Mom be interested in coming out at Thanksgiving?"

"I don't think so."

Well now, that was expected.

His father continued, "Next summer, though, on my way to Seattle if the dates work, I might swing by. See the borealis."

This was unexpected, but he knew from experience it was unlikely to happen. "If it works out, that would be good." His pager vibrated in his pocket. "Sorry, Dad, I just got paged. I have to go."

"Understood."

Before he had a chance to say *give my love to Mom*, his father had disconnected the call.

He stared at the phone momentarily confounded. As sad as that conversation was, in so many ways it had been the most positive exchange he'd shared with his father in a very long time.

The pink rays of dawn hit the windows, coloring the white walls of the hall yellow and orange and a warm red. He made his way back to Bonnie's room, opening the door to unfamiliar and now deathly silence.

To a tableau of grief.

Kirk held Bonnie's hand, his head resting on the bed next to hers. Shannon's hands cradled Beau's head on her shoulder, and Dillon and Megan hugged each other.

Katrina stood alone, her hand resting on the monitor switch, having turned off the sound. She raised her gaze to his, her green eyes full of misery and despair. "She's . . ." Her voice cracked. "She's left us."

He walked straight to her, wrapped himself around her and tried hard not to cry.

————

BONNIE'S funeral was a community event, a celebration of a vibrant and sharing life cut short far too early. The church had filled well before the service began, and people had brought outdoor chairs and sat on the lawn. Kirk had insisted that the reception be held at the ranch, and people brought food. So much food, it was as if they hoped that it would fill the empty space inside of everyone now that Bonnie was gone. No matter what Katrina put in her mouth it tasted the same—bland and sad.

Josh had sat next to her at the funeral, and there had been times when she'd needed his quiet, stoic presence next to her. At the reception, he'd offered around food, had poured drinks and had even steered Bethany away from her dad when she'd started telling him all the horror stories she knew about people who'd died from "that terrible chemotherapy."

When the last of the mourners left Coulee Creek and each member of her family had drifted away, seeking some much-needed solitude, she'd pulled on her yoga pants and a soft T-shirt and started washing dishes. She still expected her mom to come in from the garden with her arms full of vegetables and ask her about her day. How long would it take before that feeling faded?

She raised a sudsy glass out of the sink, holding it aloft. "You always liked a nice, clean kitchen, Mom. This one's for you."

The screen door banged shut and she jumped before glancing over her shoulder. Surprise thudded through her as Josh walked in. "I thought you were treating a tourist with a bad burn?"

He walked up to her, his body pressing against hers as he wrapped his arms around her and rested his chin on her shoulder. "All done and Randall's offered to be on call until noon tomorrow."

His heat flowed into her, and her hands stilled on the dishes as tendrils of desire started to dive deep but were suddenly swamped by the overwhelming feelings of being cared for. "It's trout season. How did you convince him to do that?"

"I told him you needed a change of scene and he agreed." He kissed her hair. "I've checked the conditions, and according to the Glacier National Park website, there's a good chance we might see the aurora borealis at Logan Pass. I figured we could take a drive up Going-to-the-Sun Road, stake out a good viewing spot and grill dinner."

She put a plate on the drainer. "It doesn't even get dark until around eleven."

"I've got it covered. I've also packed chairs, sleeping bags, hot chocolate and snacks. I figure we cuddle up and watch the lights and then head home around five in the morning. I'll buy you the big breakfast I owe you from any restaurant between the park and home. Then we crawl into bed together and sleep until noon. After that, we face the real world again."

She turned in his arms, dripping water on him, and tried to speak against a wave of emotion that threatened to reduce her to tears. Very different emotions to the ones that had made her cry over the last week. "You've thought of everything, city boy."

"You betcha," he said, winking at her as he tried using Montana slang. "We're going sluffing."

She laughed. "I hope not."

He looked gorgeously crestfallen. "Bethany told me that meant skipping school."

"Oh, it does, but it's also means a rockslide, and as we're going on a steep road, that's not what we want."

"No," he said his face serious. "That might make my car cadywompus."

"Stop now," she said, her laughter gaining momentum. A tiny spot of happiness flared in the midst of darkness.

"But I have forty Montana expressions I've memorized off the Net that I need to use in a sentence."

She kissed him to shut him up.

Chapter 20

"Tourist season is killing me, Floyd," Josh said emphatically as he met with the hospital administrator.

"Only a few more weeks, son," Floyd said sagely. "Be happy. Tourist season saves our budget every year. In fact, this year it's been so busy the extra funds are going toward buying that new crash cart for the ER you've been yammerin' about."

I don't yammer. Talking with Floyd was a combination of diplomacy and keeping him on task. "That's good," he said, appealing to Floyd's love of the financial bottom line, "but I'm *one* physician and I can't be spread this thin. A month ago, I had to call Katrina in to deal with an ER case because Millie and I were delivering a baby. We don't have enough expert staff. Next summer you're going to have to employ either another physician, a physician's assistant or a nurse practitioner."

Floyd nodded as he often did, but after four months of dealing with him, Josh knew it didn't mean he agreed with him, just that he was acknowledging the words. "I see your point, son, but the problem lies with getting staff to come to Bear Paw." He picked up a folder from his desk. "I've been putting off telling you this, but Millie handed in her notice today."

"What? No." His hand tore through his hair. He did not want to believe the news. "We can't afford to lose her."

Floyd shrugged. "She wants exclusively ER work."

He threw his hands up in the air. "So give it to her. We're busy enough."

"Only in July and August." He dropped the file back on his desk. "Helen and Mason have it covered the rest of the year."

Josh hadn't met Mason, although the hospital staff mentioned his name often. "If this guy Mason's got it covered, why the hell isn't he on the schedule?"

Floyd took a postcard off his corkboard. "Right now he's in Tahiti, but he's coming back."

Incredulity drenched him. "You gave him time off during our busiest time?"

Floyd looked uneasy. "Not exactly. He had to quit to do this travel, but he's coming back."

He glared at him. "When?"

"He's an excellent physician's assistant, and believe me, we don't want to lose him."

He tried to keep a leash on his fast-fraying temper. "So you're keeping a job open for a guy who's not here but you're letting Millie leave?"

Floyd's mouth settled into an intransigent line. "We need a nurse practitioner in the clinic all year."

Josh immediately thought about Katrina. His idea of asking her to work full-time at the clinic had stalled in the face of Bonnie's death. Could he ask her now? Was a month since her mother's death long enough? He didn't know.

She'd started back as the diner's breakfast barista a week after the funeral, and she'd been working with her father at Coulee Creek. She still came and went at the cottage when it suited her, and he missed her when she wasn't there. By her own admission she was "doing okay," but he'd been leery of asking anything of her just yet. With grief, it was a balancing act and timing was everything. Ask too early and get a no. Ask too late and discover she was going elsewhere to work.

He wanted her to take this job because it meant she'd stay in Bear Paw, and the idea of her leaving wasn't something he wanted to think about. "If I can find a nurse practitioner for the clinic, will you give Millie the ER job?"

Floyd looked skeptical. "Good luck with finding someone, Doc."

KATRINA set down her book and walked over to Josh, who was sitting on the couch, quietly swearing at his computer. "Problems?"

She'd invited herself over to the cottage and cooked supper for them both, because apart from the animals, Coulee Creek was empty tonight. Her dad had left on horseback this morning with Beau, Dillon, Hunter and Lanky to check the cows in the far north pastures, close to the Canadian border. They were sleeping out before returning tomorrow, and Megan had gone to Bozeman for a few days to visit friends. The idea of being alone in the ranch house had sent her and Boy over to the cottage.

To Josh.

She hated that since Bonnie's death, her own company wasn't enough. And she worried she was leaning on Josh more than she should. Although superficially nothing had really changed between them—they still had an informal arrangement about getting together—underneath the surface everything had changed. Over the last few weeks, he'd been there for her in her darkest hours, soothing her with his caring and thoughtfulness.

The arrogant guy she'd accused him of being so many weeks ago was totally absent with her. He was considerate to the nth degree, and in so many small and everyday ways he brought light into the darkness of her soul. She was struggling to imagine her life without him in it, and loving him was as hard as she'd expected it to be, especially as he'd not shown any indication that he wanted anything between them to change. For her, however, everything had changed.

He tilted his head back from the screen and looked up at her. "I'm trying to send Dad the video we took at Logan Pass, but the connection keeps cutting out."

Vivid pink, blue and green lights danced across the screen, hinting at the phenomenal natural light show they'd been awed by on the night of her mother's funeral. She'd watched it thinking it was her mother's way of telling her everything was fine in heaven.

"Your dad?" She couldn't hide the surprise from her voice.

"I called him to catch up just before . . ."

She recognized his horrified expression. "Mom died." She squeezed his shoulders. "You can talk about her without me falling apart, Josh. In fact, I want to hear her name and hear people talk about her, otherwise it's like she didn't exist, and that's worse."

"Sorry." He put his hand on hers and pulled her around so she was sitting next to him. "By the way, I took your suggestion of inviting him and Mom here for Thanksgiving, but as I expected he said no."

Sadness for him flittered through her. His family was so very different from hers. Not that hers was perfect, but despite their disagreements, they usually pulled together on the big things. "But you're sending him that video?"

"Yeah."

"Why?"

An ironic look wound its way across his cheeks and kicked his mouth up on one side. "Because although we can't talk about anything to do with medicine without Dad turning it into a competition or a rant about how I should be doing surgery, it seems we apparently share an interest in the night sky."

Astonishment made her voice squeak. "You never knew?"

He shook his head. "Did not have a clue. I know we're never going to be close, but he did ask to see a video of the northern lights if I saw them. Now the crappy Bear Paw Internet is letting me down."

It was the first time in quite a while that Josh had shown his frustration about Bear Paw's lack of amenities. "So mail him a flash drive."

"Good idea. I never thought of that. Thanks. I'll try and get to the post office tomorrow."

"If it helps, you can give it to me and I'll take it after I've finished at the diner."

"That would be great." His eyes lit up. "Can you pick up my shirts from Pressed to Impress?"

The request surprised her. "I guess."

"Great." He kissed her on the cheek. "There's also an order of my favorite cheese at the grocery store and I haven't been able to get there, so if you can do that, too, that'd be awesome."

A vague irritation rippled through her. "I did have some plans for my day, Josh," she said, striving not to sound prickly.

"It's just three errands in the same block." His tone was practical. "The time it will take will be faster than what it took me to drive to my deli in Chicago."

He had a point and she tried to shrug off the feeling of being used, but Brent's voice penetrated her thoughts.

Trina, your schedule is easier to change than mine.

You book the hotel. I'm caught up, babe, you buy the theater tickets.

"Except, Josh, you haven't factored in the fact that there's no dash-in, dash-out component in Bear Paw. Each place involves at least a ten-minute conversation about how I'm doing, how Dad's doing, how Mom is greatly missed and so it goes on." She stood up, needing to move and shake off these unwelcome feelings of being used. "I'll go make us some tea."

He caught her hand and pulled her back down to the couch, his face contrite. "Hey, don't worry about the shirts and the cheese. I'll arrange to have them dropped off at the clinic."

His reasonableness made her feel foolish. "No, it's fine. I'm sorry." She hated that she'd let memories of Brent intrude in this way. "I guess I feel because I'm not out there saving lives, you think my time is less important."

"Not at all, but it sounds like you're thinking that." He turned to face her. "I've been thinking it's time you came back to nursing. I want you to work full-time as the clinic nurse."

Stunned, she blinked at him. "What about Millie?"

"She'll move to the ER."

The idea had some appeal, but at the same time flutters of apprehension stirred her stomach. "Do you think it's wise?" His blank expression made her clarify. "I mean, you and me working together when we're . . ." And that was the problem. She no longer knew what they were exactly.

"Sleeping together?" He cupped her cheeks in his hands and traced the line of her cheekbones, the touch soft but electric. "Actually, I wanted to talk to you about that as well."

Her heart kicked up at his touch and the affectionate smile in his eyes—a smile that said *you're special*. After the amazing way he'd cared for her recently, she'd had moments when she'd wondered if he loved her, too, but for her own well-being, she'd put a restraint on hope. Now hope knocked loudly and encouragingly, and she tried not to squeal in anticipation.

She licked her lips and tried to sound composed. "Oh?"

He nodded as if he knew exactly what she was thinking. "I'd like you to move in with me."

The bald words sounded in her head as loud and deafening as the clang of a cathedral bell. Hope teetered, fast needing reassurance. She cleared her throat. "Move in with you?"

"Yes." Grinning, he leaned in, the dimple in his chin deep and appealing, and then he kissed her.

Everything inside her deliciously loosened, and she felt herself sliding toward that wonderful place he always took her. *Not yet.* With a huge effort, she pulled her body and mind back from the addictive and intoxicating promise of the kiss. "So I move in and what, exactly?"

His brows pulled down in confusion. "We live together. Share a house. Be a couple."

Be a couple. There was no ambiguity there—an offer of commitment or marriage wasn't on the table. Something soft inside her turned to stone. "A mutually exclusive couple?"

This time shock lit up his eyes. "Shit, Katrina. I'm nothing like that prick, Brent. Of course we're mutually exclusive."

"I guess that's something," she muttered. Her heart hammered so hard she felt light-headed, but she pushed on, needing answers—needing to know his plans. Perhaps she had misunderstood. "Exactly how long are we going to live together for?"

"For as long as it works."

Her breath caught in her throat as any remaining hope crashed and splattered like a melon hitting pavement. "That's a positive approach."

He stiffened. "Given what we've both been through recently, it's the sensible thing to do."

"Sensible?" She knew she was sounding like a parrot, repeating everything he said, but his attitude both stunned and devastated her. "How is this sensible? You've given up on us before we've even started."

"No." He shook his head hard. "I'm taking things slowly."

"If we'd taken things slowly," she said, her voice rising, "we wouldn't have been having sex for the past three months."

He reached for her. "I want us to be together."

Relief softened the stone in her gut. "I want us to be together, too."

Reassurance rippled through his eyes and he visibly relaxed. "Good, because for a moment there I thought we had a problem."

Brent's smooth voice oozed back into her mind. *Trina, with some compromise and understanding* on your part, *we can still make this work.*

Her breath turned solid in her lungs and every part of her cramped. Oh God, it was happening again. Despite Josh's convictions, he was more like Brent than he knew.

How hard was it for any man to compromise and put her first?

She stood up, putting distance between them, because whenever Josh touched her, she couldn't think straight. Right now she needed absolute clarity. "We do have a problem."

He tilted his head, contemplation making two lines on the bridge of his nose appear. "You don't think it's a good idea to live and work together?"

She wanted to cry at his total lack of comprehension. "That's the least of it, Josh. You want us to *live* together."

He frowned. "Is this a religious problem?"

"No!" She wanted to shake him. "It's a commitment problem."

He looked genuinely confused. "I am committing. I'm committing to the next level of our relationship."

"The next level? What are we? A computer game?" She started pacing, unable to believe what she was hearing. "You've been engaged before, Josh, so you obviously know how to visualize a future and make a pledge to someone."

A stony expression crossed his face. "And you know how well that worked out."

His words hailed down on her like ice—jagged and sharp. "So what you're really saying is that you're not prepared to make a commitment to me?" Her heart staggered as pain gripped it. *No one commits to me.*

"I'm not saying that at all. I'm offering us a chance."

"A chance? So now we're relationship gambling? We spin the roulette wheel and see where it lands?"

His nostrils flared as tension squared his shoulders. "If the word *chance* offends you so much," he said, with an edge of arrogance to his voice, "what about *opportunity*?"

Fury at him raged through her. "It's only an opportunity for *you*, Josh. You'll have someone to come home to after a long day, decent food on the table, someone to collect your shirts and your stinking cheese—"

"That's not fair, Katrina. I—"

But she refused to listen. "I'll tell you what's not fair, Josh. It's me living with you and never knowing if we're going to reach"—she made air quotes—" 'the next level'. And speaking of levels, what are they, exactly? Do we ever get to skip a level if we've collected enough gems or zombies? Do we start by sharing my house, then if I keep it tidy we might start sharing a bank account and oh, and then what, a child?"

"Are you done?" His mouth was tight, and the detached air he'd worn so often when he'd first arrived in town—an air that had faded to nothing over the weeks—was now firmly back in place. "I have a three-year contract in Bear Paw, Katrina. Making plans beyond that is pointless."

The noise in her head muted and her anger dissolved as understanding dawned. She walked over to him, lacing her fingers in between his. "I'm not Ashley, Josh, and I've moved away from Bear Paw before. I could do it again."

His eyes glinted at her, a hard and blinding silver. "So you'll follow me anywhere a job takes me?"

She thought about her hopes and dreams of having a child and she automatically ruled out Africa. "When your contract's up, we can discuss all the options."

"No." He pulled his hands away. "I've heard that before and it's code for I'm not moving."

Her anger flooded back. "So we've drilled right down to the truth now, haven't we? There is no next level after 'let's move in together.' It comes with a predetermined end date in three years' time."

"I'm not saying that."

"No?" Her sarcasm dripped from the word. "You're not offering me a future, either. You're hedging your bets and asking me to put my life on hold for you. You're calling all the shots and I'm making all the concessions."

Like every other man. The future she hadn't allowed herself to think about now lay smoldering in a pile of blackened, twisted dreams. She sucked in a breath in an attempt to steady her breaking heart. If she'd thought Brent had hurt her, she'd been wrong. His lies and betrayal were nothing compared with this anguish and pain that pulsed through her. Brent was a self-serving bastard. Josh was not, and it made everything ten times worse.

He wanted her but he didn't love her. Three months ago that had been enough. Now it didn't come close. She deserved more but he couldn't give it, and past experience told her that wasn't going to alter. Even though they'd reached the end of a very short road and she knew nothing would change his mind, she needed to tell him exactly how she felt. No matter how hard it was going to be or how much it would cost her, it was the only way forward. The only way that gave her some hope of finding a sort of peace in the future.

She wrapped her arms around herself to try and stop her body shaking. "I'm almost thirty, Josh, and I don't have time to wait or waste. I want a relationship where I'm not on tenterhooks wondering if it's going to end tomorrow or really start. I want a marriage and I want a baby. I'm done with men using me to make their life more exciting or comfortable, fitting me in around their lives and their wives, at their convenience. If you can't love me and commit to me now, there's no point continuing with this conversation."

———

KATRINA'S quiet words slammed into Josh, bringing fear and stirring up resentment. He hated ultimatums—Ashley had specialized in them, hurling them at him at every turn, whether it was a dispute over towels left lying on the bathroom floor or full-blown arguments about their future. He'd thought Katrina was different.

"Suddenly you want me to marry you?" The calm he'd been trying to hold on to vaporized and he shot to his feet. "What the hell happened to 'just using each other for sex'?"

Her head fell forward and she stared at her feet. Slowly, she raised her gaze to his, her face filled with self-loathing. "I fell in love with you."

Poleaxed, he struggled to speak. "I . . . I had no idea."

Her beautiful mouth grimaced. "Believe me, I tried my very best not to."

The quiet and heartfelt words filled with pain made him

ache. He didn't want to hurt her, but that had already happened. "I'm sorry."

Her eyes closed for a brief moment, and when she opened them, he saw her love for him—raw and wounded. "Not as sorry as I am."

Her pain hit him at a visceral level, and he flinched, hating himself and angry with her. She wasn't supposed to have fallen in love with him. Hadn't he been up front from the very start about what he did and didn't want? This wasn't his fault.

Don't say that. Say something that helps. "I really like you, Katrina. I value our friendship—"

"Stop." She held up her hand, grinding out the words. "Do. Not. Say. Another. Word." She crossed the room and picked up her purse before opening the door. "Come on, Boy."

The old dog stood, his tail wagging, and walked over to her.

He rounded the sofa to reach her, torn that she was leaving but knowing he couldn't give her what she wanted. He'd given Ashley everything and that had ended in disaster, and he wouldn't be held to ransom. But he despaired at the thought of them not being friends. "Katrina, please don't leave like this."

She threw him an incredulous look of such blazing intensity that it halted him in his tracks. "Good-bye, Josh."

The crashing sound of the door slamming shut stayed with him long after she'd gone.

———

"YOU did what?" Josh yelled at Millie, not able to believe his ears. "Are you hell-bent on making my life difficult?"

Like every other woman in this town.

Let's be way more specific here. Like Katrina.

One very long week had passed since Katrina had dropped her bombshell on him. A week filled with what Floyd called manna from health insurance heaven and what Josh called vacation-brain stupidity—tourists injuring themselves in a cornucopia of dumb ways. As a result, he'd been called out every night this week.

Not to be outdone by the tourists, most of the residents of the county had caught the summer flu. He'd put out a general advice session on the breakfast radio show targeting the usually healthy to stay home, sleep, drink plenty of fluids and take some Tylenol. The hope had been that the information would ease the strain on the clinic and leave time for him to see the young, the elderly and those with a chronic illness who truly needed his expertise.

It hadn't worked. Everyone was coming in.

He was so sleep deprived he could barely see straight. Usually, he was the king of the power nap and able to fall asleep the moment he fell into bed, but not this week. Every time he dozed off, he woke with a start either by hearing the echo of Katrina slamming his door shut or by the coolness of the sheets when he reached for her. He missed her and he missed their conversations—the cottage was quiet and empty without her. Around four in the morning each day as he stared at the ceiling, and ignored the occasional scratching of rodents and sound of the howling wind trying to blow the cottage off its foundations, he reached for his phone to call her. His fingers never made contact with the device. There was no point. She wanted something he couldn't offer. They were at an impossible impasse. End of story.

She wasn't supposed to have fallen in love with him and then demand things of him. Things he couldn't give.

Knowing all of that didn't make it any easier, though, and fatigue made every nerve jangle, every muscle ache, and he craved some peace and quiet from work and from his thoughts. Now, on top of everything else, the temporary receptionist who'd replaced Amber had up and left.

Millie closed the exam room door and faced him, her curls bouncing and her face stern. "Don't take your shitty mood out on me, Josh Stanton. I'm the one trying to make your life easier. We both have more than a full patient load and granted, it's a stopgap solution, but I bet you can't come up with a better one."

He ran his hand across the back of his neck. "Does she even know what confidentiality is?"

"Oddly enough, she does. Back in the day, when her rheumatoid arthritis was better controlled and before the problems with her hips, she worked as a medical clerk. It will be okay."

"Jesus, I must have crossed over from exhausted to delusional if I can be convinced that Bethany is the solution to our problems."

Millie laughed. "It's just for a few days. It will be over before you know it."

He grunted, clicking the mouse on the next patient file. "Promises, promises."

She paused with her hand on the door handle. "Josh, I've just been accepted into medical school, and when I'm a physician, I'm never going to yell or be grumpy at my staff."

"I'll remind you of that when you've been up thirty-six hours straight," he muttered before her words fully sank in. He shot to his feet. "You're going to medical school? That's fantastic." Letting workplace propriety fall to the wayside, he engulfed her in a hug. "Why didn't you tell me you were applying?"

She shrugged. "If I didn't get in, I didn't want anyone to know I'd applied and failed, but—" She grinned widely as she gave him a double thumbs-up and wiggled her hips. "I start at WWAMI in September."

"WAM where now?"

"WWAMI. It's a program run by the University of Washington and it stands for Washington, Wyoming, Alaska, Montana and Idaho. I do my first year in Montana and then I move to Seattle for three years."

"Come work here in the college summers. Please."

She got a mulish look on her face. "Think Floyd will let me?"

"I've got nine months to work on him, and I think he'll

see things my way, especially if we dangle the carrot of a potential new doctor for Bear Paw if he plays nice."

"Sounds good to me."

She was going to make a wonderful doctor, and he was genuinely thrilled for her. "We should have a party for you to celebrate. I'll send out an e-mail and invite all the hospital staff and call Leroy's to arrange food. Does Friday work?"

She stared at him, utterly silent.

"What?" Had he unwittingly done something to offend her? Never in his life would he understand women.

She laughed. "Josh Stanton, you've gone all squishy and community spirited."

A prickle of sensation gave him goose bumps. "Jeez, it's just some buffalo wings and beer."

"Exactly. No wine or cheese or haute cuisine. Bear Paw's gotten to you."

Her teasing unsettled him. "I didn't say I was going to come."

"Yeah, right. I'll see you there, Friday at seven, you big softy."

The intercom sounded behind them and Bethany's strident voice made him jump. "I've got sick people backing up here and coughing all over me. Quit drinking that fancy coffee and get back to work."

Chapter 21

Katrina galloped across the grassy plains, wishing she could outrun her thoughts and all of her feelings. The intense grief of her mother's death had collided with her anguish over Josh. Over the last few days, all of it had pressed down on her so hard and heavy that there'd been moments when she wondered how it hadn't physically pushed her into the ground.

She missed her mother desperately and she missed Josh. She was furious with both of them—with her mother for leaving her too early and with Josh for not being able to give what she needed of him. For the thousandth time she wondered if she'd asked too much of him, but like the other nine hundred ninety-nine times, her answer was a resounding no. She deserved better—not because she was some amazing person but because she'd finally learned that an equal partnership was the foundation of a successful relationship. Without it, they were doomed before they started.

A loud, whooping whistle sounded behind her, startling her, and she wheeled Benji around. Ty was galloping toward her on his beautiful chestnut quarter horse, a plume of dust rising from her hooves.

"Whoa, Perfect." Ty pulled on the reins and brought the horse to a stop before tugging his neckerchief down from his dusty face. "Hey, Katrina. Great day for a ride."

She patted Benji's neck and rolled her eyes. "Apart from the dust and the wind."

He laughed. "Like I said, great day for a ride in northern Montana. You checking fences?"

Benji threw his head and she reined him in. "Not specifically. More like riding one length of the boundary, soaking it in. I'm going to miss this."

The bright blue of his eyes dimmed. "You leaving again?"

She wriggled her nose, her thoughts on the subject not entirely clear. "I'm thinking I'll go to Ecuador like I'd planned before Mom got sick."

Perfect tried to bite Benji and Ty kicked her into a walk. "Come check the fences with me, Kat."

Ty hadn't called her that in years. "Okay."

"So what does your dad think of Ecuador?"

"I'm gearing myself up to tell him."

"Do you have to go now? Why not stay awhile longer."

And see Josh every day when he comes into the diner to buy coffee? I don't think so. "It's complicated."

He raised his brows. "Maybe you're making it complicated. It doesn't have to be." He kicked his horse into a trot and moved away to study a section of fence that looked to have a definite sag.

She urged Benji forward, and as she closed the gap between them she forced herself to ask, "What do you mean it doesn't have to be complicated?"

"Exactly that." He swung off the horse and looped the reins over the fence post. "You either want to live here or you don't."

I want to live where I'm loved. "Life isn't that cut-and-dried, Ty."

The cowboy who lived according to the cycle of the seasons gave her a long, assessing look. "I don't know what you're looking for, Katrina. I'm not even sure you do. You left here eight years ago for something you couldn't name, and you arrived back here looking as pale as winter's snow. Since spring you've come back to life."

He tethered her horse and helped her down. "I know your mama's death has hit you hard, but what do you think Ecuador will offer you that this place can't?" Holding on to one of her hands, he swung his other arm out to encompass the vista of tall, yellow, waving grass and the distant majestic mountains before turning back, his expression serious. "Stay. Stay for your dad. He needs you for a while longer."

He caught her other hand and gently squeezed them both. "Stay for me."

Stay for me. Tears stung the backs of her eyes and she tried to speak, but nothing came out.

"Give me time, Kat, to show you I can make you happy."

He put his arm around her and gently brought her head to rest on his shoulder. The constant battering of her emotions over the last few weeks, exacerbated by what had happened with Josh, had left her as limp and as exhausted as a rag. Ty smelled of soap and sunshine. His heart beat rhythmically against her chest, and he felt solid, safe and blissfully devoid of any dangers to her own heart.

His kindness seeped into her, promising safe harbor and a life lived by the order of the changing seasons—working together as a team, on the ranch like her parents. All of it called to her like the sirens called to the sailors, tempting her to accept her fate—the one she'd fled all those years ago—and be with him.

She heard her father's voice saying *Give Ty a chance. You might be surprised*, and her mother urging her to spend time with him.

I can make you happy.

The irony of life smashed into her with devastating clarity. She had a man in front of her willing to put her first and treasure her, but she knew that if she accepted his love, he'd be the one to suffer. She loved Ty like a brother, not a lover, and she couldn't return his love to him the way he would want. She knew exactly what that was like and she couldn't do it to him.

Lifting her head, she stepped back, glimpsing the moment in his eyes that he knew; the moment they filled with the same pain Josh had put in hers. "Ty, I want to say yes . . ."

He winced, his face tight. "But you can't."

She bit her lip, not wishing to hurt him but knowing she already had. "I'm sorry." *Throw him a bone.* "I can tell you why if that helps any."

He turned away and pulled a blanket out of his saddle-bag and a bottle of champagne. "Seems a pity to let it get hot," he said with a grimacing smile.

Her heart wobbled at the romantic gesture that she'd gone and spoiled. "You're such a good man."

With a vicious twist, he loosened the cork and then using his thumbs shot it out of the bottle, straight up into the blue, blue sky. He took a long swig before wiping the top with his shirt and passing it to her. "Believe me, Kat, I'm not good at all. This guy, the one who's making you miserable, I want to kill him."

She sat down on the rug and he joined her. They passed the bottle back and forth. "The guy I love . . . it's Josh."

He stared at a square on the rug. "Fuck."

"Yeah." She drank some more champagne, welcoming the fizz on her tongue and hoping the bubbles would take the alcohol into her veins fast.

"We have a problem." A long sigh shuddered out of Ty. "I really like Josh."

"I love him." She took another drink and passed the bottle back. "You love me and I love Josh. It's a total mess."

He gave her a hangdog look. "We don't always have a lot of control over who we love."

She barked out a laugh. "Tell me about it. If you feel as crappy as I do, I'm so very, very sorry. I never meant to hurt you."

"I know," he said grimly before taking another long drink. "You love me as a friend."

The way he'd said the word *friend* made her shudder. "If it's any consolation, I think I might have some idea how you feel."

His taut face said she didn't, and panic built inside her. "We've been friends for a long time, Ty. We go way back. Your Beau's best man and the two ranches share so much. Do things between us have to change?"

"So you and Josh? There's no chance the two of you will work it out?"

He'd neatly avoided her question, and a piece of her heart quivered. She didn't want to lose Ty as a friend, but perhaps she didn't have a choice in that. After all, she'd rejected Josh's offer of friendship as too hard and a poor substitute for what she wanted. "I don't think so."

"And living in Bear Paw with him here is too hard?"

"It's not easy."

For the briefest moment, a spark of bitterness flared in his eyes. "Tell me about it."

She sucked in her lips and wished things could be different. "I'm sorry, Ty, but you'd only end up resenting me. Eventually, you'd want the love and adoration you give me to be reciprocated. Better I hurt you now than later."

He didn't reply so she pushed on. "I think you're right about me not running from Bear Paw. Dad would never ask me to stay, but he needs me around a little longer yet. I guess if you can live here seeing me often, and I know how hard that is for you, then I have to stop being a princess and suck it up, too."

He gave a wry smile. "And not get sick."

"Yeah." She bumped his shoulder. "There is that."

He raised the bottle. "To broken hearts."

Tears splashed her cheeks. "Oh, Ty, I'm so sorry."

He tilted the bottle to his mouth and drank until there was nothing left.

———

JOSH had just finished a virtual consultation—an Internet video call—with a woman living out on a ranch forty miles away. She had a husband and three sick kids, and she wasn't looking too well herself. Fortunately, he'd been able to rule out meningitis and ease her mind that it was the flu and save her an eighty-mile round trip.

The intercom buzzed. "Doctor, there's a guy waiting and I want to go home so get your keister out here."

He ground his teeth. From an administration perspective, Bethany had actually managed to run the clinic over the last two days relatively smoothly. She'd successfully uploaded all the test results where he could find them, and the follow-up appointments had all been booked. But she had the personality of sandpaper—abrasive and scratchy.

I want to go home, too. Except, if he was honest, he didn't. Not really. Katrina's scent still lingered in unexpected places, reminding him of her, and he hated how empty that made him feel. But she'd made her position very clear, and as much as he missed her, he wouldn't be held to ransom.

He clicked his mouse on the screen to bring up the next patient file, but there was none. This surprised him because Bethany had been on top of that from the start. With a sigh, he pushed back from the desk and walked down the hall to the reception office. "Bethany, I need the patient's file."

She raised her crutch and pointed into the almost empty waiting room. A tall man in a tailored suit stood with his back to them.

"Drug company rep?"

"Dunno," Bethany said, opening a drawer to retrieve her purse. "He was asking to see Katrina and when I said she wasn't here, he tried to sweet-talk me to tell him where she was." She crossed her arms and gave off the impression of being a military tank. "Hah! As if I'd fall for that one. He got a bit pissy and asked to speak to my supervisor"—she rolled her eyes as if to say *no one supervises me*—"and as Millie finished half an hour ago, that leaves you."

A man who wanted to see Katrina? "What's his name?"

"Wouldn't say."

It suddenly occurred to him that this was Bear Paw and

if Bethany didn't know the man, then no one in town would. The guy turned and Josh took in the tailored suit, his salon-cut hair, the silk tie and Italian leather shoes and the massive bouquet of flowers in his hand, the cost of which would have spared no change from a hundred dollars. Surely he wasn't Brent?

He won't come this far. It's the reason I came home. Katrina's statement hadn't reassured him when she'd said it at the rock pool and it didn't reassure him now. He took a quick glance out the window and saw a red Porsche parked by the curb looking incongruously out of place amid the dusty pickups. Flashy. Arrogant. A surgeon's car.

His gut tightened as instinct told him this was the married bastard come to Bear Paw. Katrina had underestimated him.

White anger flared at what Brent had done to her, and he wanted to punch him in his very chiseled jaw. Only, he couldn't do that or he'd lose his medical license, but the need to protect Katrina burned so hot and strong that a trickle of sweat beaded on his forehead. No way in hell was he allowing Brent anywhere near her.

Walking across the waiting room, he extended his hand. "Doctor Josh Stanton. Can I help you?"

"I hope so. I'm a friend of Katrina McCade," he said with just the right amount of sociability to establish a rapport. "We worked together in Philadelphia and I only just heard the sad news that her mother had passed." He inclined his head slightly toward the flowers. "As you'll understand, I wanted to pass on my condolences in person, but I'm having some difficulty getting directions to the ranch."

"Hah!" A snorting noise came from behind the partition that separated the receptionist from the waiting room. It was followed by the sound of a crutch hitting the metal of a filing cabinet.

This guy was smooth, Josh would give him that, and then he remembered what Katrina had told him. *He's incredibly good at getting what he wants and he still wants me.*

Well, he wasn't getting her. There was no way in hell

he'd allow Brent to use Katrina's grief over the loss of her well-respected mother to ingratiate himself back into the life of the woman he loved.

His heart flipped as his mouth dried. He loved her.

He truly loved her.

That mass of confused feelings that he'd held for her—feelings that lurched between friendship and frustration, lust and appreciation—was love. He'd loved her for weeks without knowing.

He was a class A idiot. How could he have not recognized that he was head-over-heels in love?

With gut-dropping clarity he knew why, but right now, he didn't have time to deal with any more revelations. He had to stop Brent from getting to Katrina. "I'm sorry, I didn't catch your name?"

"Everyone calls me Brent." Charm oozed out of every pore, his good ol' boy act neatly concealing his surname.

"Well, Brent," he ground out, using everything he had to keep his temper under control and his fists firmly by his sides, "as a doctor yourself, I'm sure you'll appreciate that I have to protect my patients' confidentiality."

The tic in Brent's cheek was the only sign he showed that he understood Josh knew exactly who he was. "Surely, Katrina's a member of staff, not a patient?"

"She doesn't work here."

He smiled a snake oil salesman smile. "Then you're not breaking any moral code if you tell me where Coulee Creek is."

Josh took a step forward into Brent's personal space, matching him in height if not quite in breadth. "Listen, Brent," he spat out the word. "Katrina's told me all about you, so I suggest you get back in that very fast car of yours and head back east to your wife and kids."

Brent cocked an ebony brow. "Just as well I came when I did," he said; his voice dripping in condescension, "if she's been reduced to slumming it with a country physician."

Josh actually growled. "You need to leave. Now."

Brent's eyes took in the mishmash of health promotion

posters tacked up on the walls between the faded paintings and then glared at Bethany before returning his gaze to Josh. "You're right. There's nothing worth anything here."

"You won't find her," Josh said far more confidently than he felt. "Bear Paw looks after its own."

Brent paused with his hand on the door. "In that case, I'm sure when I explain to anyone outside of this podunk medical clinic that I wish to pay my condolences to a valued county family after their tragic loss, they'll have no qualms in showing me the way." The door closed behind him.

Josh frantically pulled his cell phone from his pocket and called Katrina's number. Pacing up and down he muttered, "Pick up, pick up, pick up."

The call went directly to voice mail. "Shit."

He tapped out a text, and as he hit send he remembered some of the last words he'd said to her. *Suddenly you want me to marry you?*

He cringed. There was no way she'd read the text once she saw it was from him. "Bethany, do you have any idea where Katrina is?"

The huge woman shook her head. "None. There's nothing on her Twitter account and she hasn't been in town all week."

I know and that's my fault. "I need to reach her before he does."

"Don't worry, Doc, that asshole won't get to Coulee Creek."

He fished his car's key fob out of his pocket. "How can you be so sure?"

She held up her phone. "I just sent out a tweet. Nobody in Bear Paw's gonna help him."

Gratitude rushed through him and he kissed her on the cheek.

She batted him away with her hand. "Stop sexually harassing me." But the tone in her voice said she wasn't upset. "You need to get out to Coulee Creek."

"If I go, Brent is likely to follow me."

"I think he might be tied up with Mitch checking his

license and registration. You know, just to make sure that that fancy-schmancy car isn't stolen."

Not for the first time since moving to Bear Paw, Josh was starting to see some advantages. "Small-town policing at work?"

"That'd be the one." Bethany pointed her crutch at the door. "Now move it."

———

JOSH covered the distance to Coulee Creek in record-breaking time, not even slowing his baby for the ruts on the long gravel road to the ranch house. Katrina hadn't responded to his text or his call, and neither had Beau or Kirk. Either Katrina had told them what had gone down between them and they were rightfully siding with her and ignoring him, or the damn buttes and coulee cell phone black holes were working overtime.

He needed to find her. He needed to talk to her before Brent got to her. Above all, he needed to tell her that he loved her.

He had no clue if she was even on the ranch, but it made sense in his head that he'd find her here. But if she wasn't and if Bethany's Twitter idea failed them, then at least he'd be here when Brent arrived. If he had anything to do with it, that slimy prick wasn't getting anywhere near her. He bumped over the cattle guards into the yard and let go of a breath he hadn't been aware he was holding. No red Porsche. He'd gotten here first. Then it hit him—there were no ranch vehicles, either.

He got out of the car and checked the house, but although it was open, no one was home. He checked his phone again. Nothing. He walked across the yard to the barn, memories of kissing Katrina on the day of the branding flooding him. Instead of weeks, it seemed like a lifetime ago. Today, the bright afternoon light streamed through gaps in the wooden slats and dust motes danced in the shafts. The horses nick-ered and he recognized Katrina's Benji.

"Hey, boy." He gingerly rubbed the horse's nose. "Where's your mistress?"

"What are you doing here, Josh?"

He spun around at Katrina's voice and saw her standing in the tack room doorway. Backlit by the light, she looked vulnerable despite her hostile voice.

Vulnerability he'd put there. Guilt doused him. "Thank God you're here."

Panic flared in her eyes as her face paled and her hands gripped the doorjamb. "Why? Who's hurt?"

"No one." Straw clung to his Oxford shoes as he reached her and touched her shoulders. "I'm sorry, I didn't mean to scare you."

She shook away his touch and crossed her arms against him as if defending herself. "If no one's hurt, why are you here?"

He smiled at her, knowing the very easy answer to her question. *I love you.* "I needed to talk to you."

Her emerald eyes hardened. "You could have called."

He'd always loved her eyes—how the facets of green seemed to glow with warm light—but now they were an icy arctic green. A slither of unease wound through him. He didn't want to just blurt out I *love you*, but he had to do something fast to show he'd come in peace.

"I did call and I texted but I wasn't sure you got the message. Brent's in town looking for you."

She hauled herself up, her small stature rigidly straight. "So you came out here to save me from myself? How very gallant of you."

That's exactly what he'd done, but her tone and expression said she didn't need him or want him. In fact, she looked as if she'd rather eat poison than have him here. "I didn't want you to have to face him on your own."

"I'm a big girl, Josh. You can leave now."

And she meant it—he could tell by the way her mouth had turned down at the edges. "I just thought . . ." He ran his hands through his hair, trying to find the best thing to say. "You once told me you were worried he'd talk you round."

"I was a different person back then. The last few weeks have hardened me."

Her anger rolled off her, buffeting him, and he knew he deserved every bit of it but he desperately sought to find a chink in it, some evidence that the love she'd professed for him still existed. Something to latch onto with his love for her.

She suddenly jerked as if she'd been Tasered and narrowed her eyes at him. "Given what you told me last week, why would you care what decision I make about Brent?"

This was his moment. "Because I love you, Katrina."

He was hoping for squeals of delight or tears of joy or both. He got brickbats.

"And you worked this out when, exactly?"

She asked the question so quietly that he had to strain to hear above the barn noise. "When I spoke with Brent."

Incredulity widened her eyes. "You didn't love me nine days ago but you suddenly realize you do when a possible threat walks into your territory?" Her snort of derision made the horses neigh. "Your primate ancestors would be so proud. Now I really need you to leave."

Devastating fear lanced him. Had he lost her no matter what he said or did? *Do something.* For the first time in his life, he put his heart on the line. "I know my timing sucks, Katrina, and I'd do anything to change it but I can't. All I can do is stand here before you and tell you that I love you. I really do love you and I'm ashamed it took me this long to work it out. I'm so desperately sorry I hurt you."

KATRINA heard Josh's earnest and heartfelt words. Part of her feared them and wanted to shut them out. The other part of her craved to hear them. The two halves together added up to the new Katrina. She was not the same person she'd been when she'd arrived back in Bear Paw or when she'd met him. Her mother's death and her love for Josh, the pain that love had caused her and by default the pain it was causing Ty, all of it had changed her. Made her wary. She couldn't just blindly accept his love and walk straight back into his arms.

He stood in front of her in a cool, open-neck madras-style shirt rolled up to his elbows, chinos and leather shoes designed for pavement, not the packed earth floor of a mucky barn. Out of place and with every part of him begging her to listen and more importantly hear him. She really didn't want to have another gut-wrenching conversation with him, but then again, she needed some answers.

"Why didn't you understand that what you felt for me was love?"

The tips of his ears pinked. "I'd been viewing all my feelings for you individually, not realizing that collectively they are love." His hand plowed his hair. "It turns out I've been in love with you for weeks."

It didn't make a lot of sense and it didn't mollify her, given that nine days ago he was adamant he couldn't love her. "It isn't like you haven't been in love before. Surely you know what love is, what it feels like?"

He swallowed and his pleading eyes sought hers. "I thought I'd been in love before. I thought what I shared with Ashley was love, and based on that, I committed to her. When she left after months of arguing and breaking her word, I never wanted to make that sort of commitment again."

She saw the turmoil in his face. *I'm taking things slowly.* "Are you saying that if you don't commit, you can't get hurt?"

He shrugged. "Probably. I didn't analyze it, but when I compare what I felt for Ashley to what I feel for you, I know that all I had with her was a toxic mess."

Cautious hope leaped. "What am I to you?"

A smile unlike any she'd ever seen touched his lips. "You're my best friend and my lover. You're my sounding board and my confidant. You're my critic and my staunch supporter, and the idea of living without you by my side is too awful to contemplate." He held out his hands toward hers, stopping just short of touching her. "I truly love you."

Her heart trembled. He *loved her. He truly loved her.* Tears of joy threatened to fall, but then her wounded soul kicked her hard and she kept her hands by her sides. She'd been here once before and it had all turned pear shaped. "So exactly what does this mean, Josh?"

His hands dropped to his sides. "That I love you and I live in fear of losing you."

Her heart spasmed and the protective guards she'd put in place fell away. Yes, he'd been slow to realize he loved her, and yes, she'd been badly hurt by his lack of commitment to her, but now she saw the source of all their heartache. Part of him was convinced a day would come when she'd leave him. "You just told me I'm your staunch supporter."

"You are," he said, his voice slightly disconcerted. "I've never known anyone to believe in me quite the way you do."

"That's because there's so much to believe in." She stepped in close. "I love you, Josh, but I'm not sure you believe me, so let me tell you that you're my lover and my dearest friend. You've been my unbelievable rock since Mom died, and my solace when I thought I'd never be able to smile again.

"That said, there are times when you frustrate and annoy me. Also, you're a hopeless cook and before you say anything, grilling isn't cooking, plus you're a disastrous handyman." She raised her hands to his cheeks with a smile. "Doesn't mean I'm going to leave you. All of those things are far outweighed by the caring, generous man that you are. I love you, Josh, but is knowing that going to be enough for you?"

His brow furrowed in deep ridges and anxiety hung in his eyes. "And if I get an offer at a big hospital out east, will you come?"

"I'll follow you almost anywhere."

"What do you mean by almost?"

"I want to have children, Josh. Do you?"

He gripped her forearms. "Hell yes."

Thank you. "Well, I don't want to raise them in a slum

or near a war zone, but that said, I think we should do some charity work in third-world countries. I've never run from experiences; it's why I left Bear Paw and I'll happily go places for a few weeks with you." Her fingers stroked his forearms. "This is our life, Josh, and we have to create a partnership. I promise you that if I give you my word on something, I won't have made the decision lightly and I won't break it."

He visibly relaxed. "And what if I decided to stay in Bear Paw? How would you feel about that?"

"I want to live where I'm loved, Josh. That means where you are."

He made a strangled sound in his throat and wrapped his arms tightly around her. "Marry me?"

She didn't have to think twice. "In a heartbeat."

"Thank God." He kissed her long and deep, his love flowing into her on the back of sheer relief—relief that matched her own.

They tumbled backward onto fresh straw with hands tugging at clothes and caressing skin, but mouths never parting. When he rolled her under him and gazed down at her, his gray eyes filled with love, she started to cry from joy. She was home. They made love slowly, almost reverently, knowing there was no rush. They had a lifetime together.

———

LATER, as Josh lay with Katrina snuggled up against him, he gave thanks for this amazing woman who'd come into his life and shown him what it was to be truly loved. He plucked straw from her hair. "Sex in a barn isn't quite what it's cracked up to be, is it?"

She laughed, passing him his pants. "Mostly it's just itchy and scratchy."

He pulled his shirt back on over his head, his mind running fast into the future. "Do you know where your dad is?"

"He said he'd be home for supper, why?"

"I need to ask him a question."

Her smile faded as she read his mind. "He might say no."

He stared at her, suddenly apprehensive. "Do you think we should wait a bit longer?"

She kissed him on the nose and tickled him under the ribs. "Just kidding. Dad will be happy if I'm happy."

He thought about Kirk, whom he admired very much. The man had been through a great deal recently, but he knew Katrina spoke the truth. "Yeah, he's remarkable that way."

She pulled him to his feet, reading him down to his soul. "You and your dad have the night sky to bond over, remember?"

He kissed her. "We do. Although once my mom hears I'm engaged she might actually apply some pressure on the old man to come meet you."

"Should I be worried?"

He shook his head. "Not at all. This is our life, our marriage and the Stanton legacy stops with Dad. It isn't going to interfere with us."

Her dancing green eyes gazed up at him. "And if we have a throwback kid who wants to be a surgeon?"

"Then I hope it's our daughter."

As they left the barn, he scanned the yard.

"You looking for something?"

He almost said no, but they were a partnership now. "I was looking for a red Porsche."

"Brent texted me this afternoon asking for directions."

Despite trying not to tense, he did anyway. "And?"

"I wrote him back saying he wasn't welcome and he was to cease contact immediately or I would take out a restraining order."

Unease still lingered. "He was pretty insistent he was coming out here."

She stopped walking and pulled her phone out of her pocket and brought up the Twitter app. "According to Bethany, the sheriff gave a red Porsche an escort out of town." She laughed.

"What?"

"It's got its own hashtag and people have been tracking

the car along the highway. It was last seen at the car rental at Great Falls airport."

"Good." He kissed her. "Because you're mine."

She raised one questioning brow.

He laughed. "Hey, just like I'm yours."

"You better believe it." She wrapped her arms around his neck, her eyes alight with her love for him. "I'm yours to keep forever."

He could hardly believe he was this lucky. "Forever and wherever, always close to my heart."

"Always."

She rose up on her toes as he dropped his head to hers and their lips met in a pledging kiss.

Boy barked as if to say, "Enough already." Laughing, they walked hand in hand back toward the house, their future dazzling both of them with the endless possibilities that grow from love.

Watch for Millie's story in the next
Medicine River romance

TRULY MADLY MONTANA

Coming July 2015 from Berkley Sensation!
Turn the page for a sneak preview . . .

As Millie Switkowski drove into Bear Paw for the first time in months, it seemed both ironic and fitting that her continuous glucose monitor started beeping wildly. It was like a mocking welcome-home message—*you're back where it all started, baby.*

"Okay, Dex," she said to the machine with which she shared a love-hate relationship. "Simmer down. I'm pulling over."

She'd been late leaving Bozeman because last night instead of packing, she'd panicked and done last-minute cramming for her microbiology final. As it turned out, the extra study time hadn't been necessary and she would have been far better off spending the time loading the car, which had been her original plan. Her life was a series of well-thought-out plans, and she knew she really needed to trust them more. If she'd had more faith in her study program, today's road trip would have been divided up into ordered and necessary scheduled breaks rather than her rushing to get here by six and risking a sugar crash.

Parking next to the enormous concrete penguin, which

declared that Bear Paw was the coldest spot in the nation, she smiled at the incongruity of it. She'd always wondered how the brains behind the black-and-white statue had cheerfully disregarded both Alaska and the fact that penguins weren't found in the northern hemisphere. Geography was obviously not their strongest subject. She rummaged through her enormous tote bag until she found a juice box and some fruit snacks.

The last thing she needed was to arrive at Dr. Josh Stanton's bachelor party with plummeting blood sugar. She didn't need the drama of feeling like crap. She surely didn't need the drama of people hovering, or worse still, some well-meaning person telling her parents she'd arrived back in town looking pale and shaky. No, she was striding into Leroy's and the party like any normal twenty-six-year-old woman just back from grad school. Truth be told, most normal twenty-six-year-old women probably weren't invited to their former boss's buck's night, but Josh, like everyone else in town, never seemed to notice she was a woman. She was just Millie. Practical, sensible, dependable Millie—one of the guys. Someone who could shoot pool and throw darts with the best of them.

She checked her appearance in the rearview mirror. Pale face, crazy curls springing everywhere and some freckles on her cheeks left over from spring break in Florida. Without the time or the inclination to spend an hour with a hair straightener, her hair was beyond help, and in a few minutes the sugar would hit and pink up her cheeks. She glanced down at her Montana State sweatshirt and gave thanks it didn't have a ketchup stain on it from the hot dog she'd grabbed when she'd filled up on gas in Great Falls. She gave herself points for clean jeans, kinda clean boots and a clean, baggy tee—the perfect attire for a buck's night at Leroy's.

Millie, honey, there's nothing wrong with wearing a dress from time to time.

She quickly swiped on some lip gloss as if that show of femininity was enough to silence the memory of her mom's often sad and critical voice. Her mom had wanted a girlie-girl daughter to share her love of clothes. Instead, she'd gotten a son who loved fashion and football with equal fervor and a daughter who couldn't tell the difference between a Gucci and a Gabbana. Millie was far more last-season Old Navy and on sale, and she felt way more at home in jeans and T-shirts. Her brother, Evan, did his best to make up for Millie's fashion shortcomings and took their mom shopping whenever she visited him in California. Of course, he also took their dad to football games, so really, he was the perfect adult child. Millie, on the other hand, knew her overriding contribution to the family was a constant source of parental worry.

She drained the juice box with a slurp and sent a text to her mom and dad, who were out of town.

Arrived home safely. Tell Uncle Ken happy birthday from me. Millie x

With the job of reassuring the parents done, she checked her blood sugar. Eighty-six and rising. Awesome. And real food was coming. As Josh's best man, she'd ordered up big on the hors d'oeuvres—BBQ meatballs, layered Mexican dip, stuffed mushrooms, bacon-wrapped Jalapeño poppers and buffalo wings. If they weren't serving food when she arrived, she'd ask them to start.

The good and the bad thing about Bear Paw was that most of the older residents and anyone she'd gone to school with knew she was diabetic. They didn't comment if she ate at a different time from them, although they often had an opinion about what she ate. As a result, in her life outside of Bear Paw as a medical student, she only shared her lack of a functioning pancreas with people on a strictly need-to-know basis. She made sure that need didn't arise very often at all because she had a doctorate in horrified and pitying looks or—worse than those—over-intrusive interest from people who saw her as a training specimen. She just wanted to be known for being Millie—although she wasn't exactly certain who that was. But tonight wasn't the time to tackle that particular chestnut.

Throwing the car into drive, she shoulder-checked, pulled out onto the road and drove the last mile to Leroy's. The parking lot was almost full and some smart-ass cowboy had fashioned a rope noose and hung it over the door next to a banner that said, "Another good man all tied up." Ducking to miss it, she pushed open the door, and a wall of noise and the malty scent of beer wafted out to greet her.

"Millie!"

"Millie's here!"

A welcoming roar went up from the cowboys and assorted businessmen who were gathered around the bar, and they turned and raised their drinks to her.

She grinned and tipped her imaginary hat. She knew all of them, having either treated them at the clinic when she'd worked as a nurse or having bested them here at pool and darts. "Hey, guys. It's good to be back."

"Hey, Millie." Josh greeted her with a warm hug and a perfunctory kiss on the cheek—in sharp contrast to the buttoned-up city doctor who'd arrived in Bear Paw just over a year ago. "It's great to see you."

She hugged him back. "And you. Getting nervous?"

"About the wedding?" He shook his head. "Not at all. About my parents spending a week in Bear Paw, yes. Katrina's dad offered to host them out at Coulee Creek, which probably means I owe him our first-born child."

She punched him lightly on the arm. "They can't be worse than when you first arrived in town with your fancy coffee and stinky French cheeses."

He gave a good-natured smile. "Your parents always greet me with open arms when I place my monthly gourmet food order."

"I can't argue that then, especially as by default you're likely contributing to my generous birthday and Christmas allowance." She raised her hand toward the bar and gave the barman a wave. He'd started at Leroy's not long before she'd left for medical school. "Sparkling water, please, Shane."

"It's a buck's night, Millie. Moose Drool is mandatory,"

Shane said, filling a glass with the amber beer. "You can worry about your weight tomorrow."

And you're home. Her gut tightened. Half of her was grateful he didn't know about her diabetes while the other half of her hated that she'd just taken a hit about her weight. She wasn't obese but, then again, she was hardly willow-thin, either. She knew this was how guys talked to one another and she'd never expected them to treat her any differently before. Tonight wasn't the night to go all girly on them.

"A beer and buffalo wings sound good, Shane," she said brightly. As for the alcohol, she'd have to bolus insulin for the carbs and make that one beer last the entire night. Turning back to Josh, she asked, "How's Katrina?"

"She says hi and told me to tell you that you're not to party too hard tonight because she wants you in good shape at her bachelorette party tomorrow."

"Is that code for me to stay sober so I can keep an eye on you?"

He grinned. "Maybe, although I don't think I've ever seen you even a little bit buzzed."

And you won't. She'd been there and done that years before he'd come to town, and it just wasn't worth the risk. "As the best man, it's my job to make sure you don't get injured when you inevitably fall off the mechanical bull, that I make sure no cowboy takes you outside and sits you backward on a horse, and as the designated driver, I get you home in one piece by midnight."

He slung his arm around her shoulder, the touch easy and friendly. "And that's why I chose you to be my best man."

"That and the fact you couldn't ask Ty Garver no matter how much you want him standing next to you," she said, thinking about the cowboy who'd fallen in love with Katrina years ago.

"Well, yeah, there is that." Josh sighed. "And Will Bartlett's not available. He couldn't get anyone to cover him at MontMedAir for the weekend."

And there is a God. Not that she didn't like Will; she

did. In fact, last year she'd liked the MontMedAir doctor just a little too much. Heat burned her cheeks at the thought. Having a crush at sixteen was normal, crushing on a work colleague at twenty-five probably got a listing in DSM-5. The memory of last spring and summer was still excruciatingly embarrassing, given he'd barely noticed her other than as one of many people he came into contact with through work.

Will was laid-back, easygoing and he had a way of making people feel appreciated and part of a team. That had been her undoing—being appreciated was powerful stuff, and Floyd Coulson, Bear Paw's hospital administrator, could learn a lot from him. So she'd read way too much into Will's generous praise and his oft-said, "You're the best, Millie," when she'd accompanied him on MontMedAir retrievals.

Following him on Twitter and pretending it was because of his #FOAMed tweets—free open access meducation— was borderline stalker behavior, although totally educational. What the guy didn't know about emergency airway management wasn't worth knowing. At least she'd come to her senses before clicking on *add friend* on his Facebook account and for that, she was both proud and grateful. Sadly, she'd undone that bit of clear thinking after a traumatic medical evacuation last August. It was the fifth time she'd been the accompanying nurse out of Bear Paw, and they were airlifting two badly injured tourists who'd been involved in a motor vehicle accident. They flew out between two storm fronts, and the pilot had given her the all-clear to check the patients' vitals. She was out of her seat when the plane had hit an air pocket and she'd been thrown sideways, landing face-first in Will's lap. She still got a hot and cold flash whenever she thought about it.

He'd gripped her arms, lifted her up and checked she was okay before hitting her with his devastatingly gorgeous smile—the one that radiated from his full lips, creased his tan cheeks and crinkled the edges of his unusual dark blue eyes. He'd quipped something about things moving fast for a first date, which had disarmed her all-consuming embarrassment and made her crush-filled brain totally misunderstand what he meant. When they'd landed and had handed over their patients to the Seattle hospital staff, she'd suggested they restart the date with a drink.

"Great idea, Mils," he'd said with his sexy Australian diphthong, sounding as if he truly believed the words. Her heart had soared, flipped and high-fived all at once only to plummet to her feet when he'd continued with, "but I'll have to take a rain check."

Of course he did.

A rain check that made her puce with embarrassment whenever she thought about it. A rain check that never came.

With his surfer-dude good looks, he was likely very used to nurses—heck, probably all women with a pulse— throwing themselves at him. Only she wasn't usually one of those nurses or women because she knew he was so far out of her league it wasn't even worth playing the game. She still blamed the fog caused by low blood sugar and the addition of a post-emergency adrenaline rush for her out-of-character invitation, because she'd stopped asking lesser guys out a long time ago.

As a woman of the twenty-first century, she knew she had the right to ask a guy out, but after a series of flat-out *no*'s, a few disastrous dates and two truly awful one-night stands, she'd learned from her mistakes. She didn't ask guys out, period. As a result, her dating average was zip.

"It's too bad Will can't make it," she said, trying to sound sincere rather than totally relieved. "But I'm pumped to be your best man and I promise to get you to the church on time."

"You're a good friend," Josh said sincerely.

That's me. Everyone's good buddy. "Hey, it's way too early to be getting all D & M on me," she said, climbing onto a chair as much to start the party as to run from her thoughts. Sticking her fingers in her mouth, she blew hard and the piercing whistle silenced the bar.

"Aw, Millie," a voice from down near the pool table, called out, "you're not gonna make a speech, are you?"

"Hey, Doc, I told you not to choose a chick to be your best man," Trent Dattner sighed.

"Millie's not a girl," Dane Aiken heckled and then gave Trent a high five.

"Hah, hah." Millie rolled her eyes, surprised by the dull ache that spread through her. "And yet Comedy Central hasn't signed you up. For that smartass comment, Dane, the bull gets set on high for you."

The cowboys in the room cheered, knowing full well the pizza maker wouldn't last three seconds in the saddle.

She raised her glass. "We've got food, we've got beer and we've got a bull. Let's give Josh a Bear Paw buck's night to remember."

———

DR. WILL BARTLETT was on a mission. He was used to missions—he'd flown a lot of miles doing emergency medical air retrieval in both Australia and Montana, but this particular mission was very different. It was also proving to be a hell of a lot harder than intubating a critical patient at twenty-thousand feet.

"Brandon, mate, we're talking twenty-four hours."

The physician tapped a medication order into the tablet computer in his hand. "You know better than anyone that a lot can happen in twenty-four hours."

A lot could happen in twenty-four seconds—hell, his life had been irreversibly changed in less time than that. Convincing Brandon to swap shifts was his last hope, as everyone else who could have possibly covered his schedule had ironclad commitments. The key, though, was making it look like he was doing Brandon McBain a favor, not the other way around, because if people sensed weakness, they zeroed in on it.

"Only last week you were whinging—" Will immediately translated the Australian word at Brandon's blank look—"whining to me that you were sick of treating the flu and prescription drug addicts trying to get meds. You said you wanted more of a challenge and this is it." He tapped his chest twice with his fist. "I'm offering you the chance of heart-pumping, adrenaline-racing trauma . . . the crack cocaine of all emergency physicians."

"It's tempting."

Yes!

". . . but I just got a date for tonight with that pretty brunette from Orthopedics."

Will knew the intern—he'd enjoyed flirting with her at a party, but she had the look in her eyes of a woman who was seeking commitment. That was his red card, so he hadn't pursued it any further. "Jenna will understand. That's the whole point of dating inside the medical community. They get that work interferes. Promise her a rain check."

Brandon snorted and then shot Will a scowl. "That's your line, not mine. I actually like her and I want to date her. Unlike you, with your weird accent that seems to make every woman in this hospital think you're Jesse Spencer and Hugh Jackman rolled into one, I had to work damn hard to get her to say yes." He walked toward the nurses' station. "Anyway, I thought you didn't like weddings."

Will easily matched the shorter man's stride. "I haven't got anything against them per se, as long as I'm not the groom. Josh Stanton's a good bloke and I'd like to be there. How about I work your next two weekends? That's more than fair. Whad'ya say?"

"I dunno." Brandon plugged the tablet into the charger. "What if Jenna sees changing the date as a chance to cancel?"

Will tried not to sigh. Brandon was a good doctor, but he was hopeless with women, and his dating strikeout rate in the hospital was legendary. Maybe he could get his swap by sweetening the deal and helping a bro out. "You know, if you tell Jenna that you're delaying your date to help me attend a wedding, you'll automatically be more attractive to her."

Brandon finally gave Will his full attention. "How do you figure that?"

"All women love weddings, so by helping me get there you're doing your bit for love. Plus, I'll pay for the flowers you're going to send her as an apology for changing the date and I'll get you a table at Annie's. I know the maître d'."

"Oh, that's good." Brandon's eyes lit up with a calculating light. "If you throw in dating tips so I get a second date with Jenna, I'll swap."

"Jeez, McBain. I've already given you more than you deserve."

Brandon casually opened a candy bar. "Exactly how much do you want to be the best man at this wedding?"

The thought of discussing dating's dos and don'ts with Brandon was up there with sitting in the dentist's chair with the sound of the drill buzzing in his ears. Was getting to this wedding really worth it?

You know it is. Josh Stanton was a good mate—one of the few people he'd really connected with this last year in Montana. Even though Josh was a Yank, he totally related to Will's feelings of discombobulation when he'd arrived from Australia to work in Montana. He'd told Will that for a guy from New York and Chicago, small-town Montana was as strange and different for him as if he'd been the one to move countries. Plus they shared a passion for emergency medicine, and with Bear Paw's proximity to Glacier National Park and accident-prone tourists, they'd worked together a lot. Being at the wedding was an act of friendship that he wanted to make.

Knowing he may live to regret it because McBain would likely continue to seek him out for dating advice long after the favor was done, he clapped his hand on the clueless doctor's shoulder. "Brandon, the first rule of dating is making it all about her and leaving your neediness at the door."

"But I can tell her how grateful I am that she came on the date, right?"

"Yeah . . . no." He shook his head and swallowed a sigh, already tasting regret. "Your job is to ask questions and listen. Be attentive."

Brandon pulled out his phone. "What sort of questions?"

Shoot me now. The MontMedAir pager thankfully chose

that moment to beep loudly, and he pressed it into Brandon's hands. "This is your call, McBain. If I leave now, I'll just make it to Bear Paw for the wedding."

"You're driving on no sleep?"

It wasn't ideal. He started walking toward the exit. "I'll drive with the windows down and the music blasting."

"Text me the questions," Brandon called after him.

"Later." As much as Will respected Josh as a friend, he hoped one of Katrina's bridesmaids was going to make his weekend worth the frustrations of being McBain's date doctor.

———

MILLIE took the short but familiar walk toward the main house. What had once been her parents' guesthouse was now considered her apartment whenever she was living in Bear Paw. She appreciated her parents' generosity, especially now that she was studying to become a doctor and was required by her scholarship to spend her summers working in Bear Paw.

She could see her parents chatting in the kitchen, dressed and ready for the wedding. As she opened the back door she clicked her fingers before executing a soft-shoe shuffle across the kitchen floor, ending in a twirl in front of her folks. "Ta-dah." She'd spent more time than usual getting ready and she thought she looked pretty sharp.

Her mother, dressed in a gray silk shift dress gathered in at the waist with a matching cummerbund and secured with a diamante brooch, stared at her, horrified. "Why are you wearing a tuxedo?"

Millie smiled, already prepared for the question. "Because, Mom, I'm the best man."

"You're the best person," Susie said tightly, "and in my experience, women who stand up with their guy friends always wear a dress."

Stay calm. "I'm sorry you're upset, but I did tell you I was wearing a suit."

"And I assumed you meant something classic, like Chanel."

She laughed, hearing the tightness in the sound and wishing it wasn't there. "A Chanel suit is way out of my price range and besides, it wouldn't have all these awesome pockets for my stuff."

"That's what a purse is for."

Millie looked at her mother's tiny clutch purse, which perfectly matched her shoes and frock. It was barely big enough to hold a phone let alone her blood glucose monitoring meter. "You know I need more room than that."

Conflicting emotions warred on her mother's face, and she let out a long sigh. "Yes, but if you'd let me take you shopping, I'm certain we could have found the perfect dress and purse."

And I would have hated it. "Mom—"

"You look terrific, Millsy," her father said, finally stepping into the conversation as he always did, just as it was getting uncomfortable. "You'll put all the others guys in the shade."

"Thanks, Dad." She kissed him on the cheek. "I better get going or Josh will beat me to the church. I'll see you guys there."

"At least wear some color," Susie said, pressing a pretty wine-stained lipstick into her hand. "You look pale. Are you sure you're feeling okay?"

As a redhead she was frequently pale, but that wasn't what her mother meant. "I'm fine, Mom. The numbers are my friend today. I promise I'll put on the lipstick just before I go into the church, I'll spritz on some perfume and I'll pinch my cheeks. But seriously, all eyes will rightly be on Katrina and Josh, not me."

Thank goodness. As her fingers closed around the door handle, her father asked, "You've got everything, right?"

For the briefest moment, she rested her forehead on the doorjamb and then she patted her pockets. *Dex, keys, tester kit, snack.* "Yep. Bye."

It wasn't until ten minutes later when she was parking next to Josh's sports car, which positively gleamed, that she realized she'd left her phone back at the guesthouse, sitting on the charger. Oh well, she was at the church now and if Josh needed anything he could tell her in person. Feeling naked without her heavy purse on her shoulder, she hurried over. Stepping out of the bright afternoon sunshine into the dimness of the changing room, her eyes were slow to adjust and she fuzzily made out the shape of a guy with his back to her.

"Hey, Josh," she said moving in for a big hello hug. "Fifteen minutes 'til show time." As her arms went firmly around his shoulders, she caught the flash of blond hair, the sharp zip of citrus cologne and the glint of amused dark-blue eyes.

Josh had brown hair, wore woodsy cologne and his eyes were silvery gray. And as tall as Josh was, her cheek was usually closer to his shoulder than this and he didn't feel quite so broad. Who exactly was she body-hugging?

She was about to step back when she heard, "Hey, Millie." Josh's voice was filled with gentle amusement. "On my wedding day, you're supposed to be making a fuss of me, not Will."

Will?

Her brain melted at the exact same moment as her body. *No way! Not possible.* He wasn't even coming to the wedding. But as she glanced up into familiar dancing eyes—eyes she'd spent way too much time daydreaming about last year—she knew. Dear Lord, she had her arms wrapped tightly around Will Bartlett.

Shock dried her mouth and embarrassment made her arms drop away fast from his wide shoulders. She stumbled backward, wishing desperately that she could teleport anywhere as long as it was far, far away from here and Will Bartlett. *Be cool. Be calm. Be disinterestedly detached.* "H-Hi—hello, Will."

Oh yeah, so cool.

"G'day, Millie." A cheeky, lopsided grin lit up his perfectly symmetrical face, and she saw the precise moment he recalled exactly their last meeting—the time she'd fallen into his lap. "We have to stop meeting like this."